For Mark and Kathy Novitsky

CHAPTER ONE

Holding a new book and six-pack of imported Belgian beer, the conventionally-dressed, 45-year-old priest, rang the rectory doorbell. Waiting for someone to answer, he closed his eyes and felt the San Diego sun caress his face.

Just as he was exiting his brief trance and preparing to ring the doorbell again, the rectory door slowly opened and an elderly housekeeper, dressed in a hunter green house dress and white apron, appeared.

"Hi, Honey," the silver-haired woman said with a thick Irish brogue. "Welcome to Saint Declan's Roman Catholic Church. Heaven help us."

"Good afternoon," the priest replied with a smile. "I'm Father Paul Thielemans."

"Please to meet you, I'm sure," the housekeeper answered with a twinkle in her eye. "I'm Mother Murray. My baptismal name is Margaret, but everyone calls me, 'Mother,' because I raised seven children of my own and just as many orphans. I've been running things around here since the saints were choirboys. So, give me what you've got in your hands and follow me to my kitchen."

The obliging prelate transferred the book and six-pack to Mother's outstretched hands, picked up an expensive suitcase and matching attaché, and followed the slow-moving housekeeper into the rectory.

"We weren't expecting you until 5 o'clock" Mother revealed, placing the book and beer on the kitchen table. "I just started supper. I hope you like pot roast."

1

"I love pot roast," Father Thielemans said. "I know I'm two hours early, but I arrived in San Diego sooner than expected. If I'm in the way here, I can take a drive and return in a few hours."

"Nonsense," Mother exclaimed. "Just take a load off, and I'll let the pastor know you're here."

As Thielemans took a seat at the kitchen table and ran a hand through his well-groomed, black hair, the housekeeper walked toward the intercom.

"Father Kittrick," Mother shouted into the intercom, as she leaned against the kitchen wall with the left side of her body and depressed the intercom call button with an arthritic right index finger. "Hello, Father Gordon Kittrick."

The housekeeper waited for a reply and glanced at the wall clock. Growing impatient, she pounded the intercom with her right fist.

"Earth to Father Kittrick," she screamed into the intercom, as her tremulous index finger continued to depress the call button.

"What is it?" Father Kittrick yelled over the intercom.

"The Father is here," Mother answered.

"Who?" Kittrick howled.

"The Father," the housekeeper repeated. "You know, the guest we're expecting for dinner."

"I thought he wasn't coming until 5 o'clock," Kittrick argued. "Entertain him until I take a quick shower."

"Okie Dokie," Mother replied in a patronizing tone. "Over and out, and Roger Wilco."

Adjusting her apron and fluffing her recent perm with both hands, the unperturbed housekeeper walked toward her guest and smiled.

"Well, there you have it, straight from the horse's mouth," she said sarcastically, looking into the priest's dark eyes. "His Highness is busy at the moment, and I'm supposed to entertain you until he honors us with his presence in another hour or so."

Mother took a deep breath and winked at Thielemans.

"Father is down in the cellar with one of the altar boys, and heaven only knows how long they'll be down there," she continued. "He has a gym downstairs, and he coaches boys who plan to try out for the junior high wrestling team. The pastor wrestled in college, you know, and he still enjoys working out with the youngsters."

"Mother, it really wouldn't be a problem if I came back later," Thielemans reiterated. "Just tell me what time you'd like me back for dinner."

"I'd prefer if you just parked your carcass right there for a spell," Mother insisted, as she inspected the six-pack of beer. "What in heaven's name is Saint Bavo Witbier?"

"It's unfiltered wheat beer that is brewed in Belgium," Thielemans replied. "The beer is named in honor of Saint Bavo of Ghent. Saint Bavo lived during the 7th century, and the beer that honors him has been brewed in Ghent by a single family of brewmasters for many generations."

"Oh, my goodness," the housekeeper exclaimed.

"My father was the Belgian exporter who first introduced the United States to Saint Bavo Witbier decades ago," Thielemans proudly added. "He also introduced America to other Belgian beers, wines, and chocolates. I always bring a six-pack of Saint Bavo whenever I'm visiting someone. Not every beer distributor carries Saint Bavo, but I can usually have it shipped ahead of time to a distributor in a city I plan to visit."

"Do you travel a lot?" Mother asked, as she shifted her attention to the book on the table.

"I do," Thielemans replied. "I'm a theologian and author, and I'm usually traveling from one city to another to give a lecture, attend a meeting, or do a book signing. If there is a Catholic college or university in the city, chances are I've already been there or will be going there in the future. During those periods when I'm writing a new book, I lecture at the Catholic University of America in Washington, D.C."

"*Catholicism Astray*," the housekeeper announced, as she picked up Thielemans' latest book. "Did you write this book? Well, of course, you did. There's your photograph on the back cover. My, you take a handsome picture, and you're a fine example of a man in real life as well. You're tall and good looking, and there's probably not an ounce of fat on your entire body."

"There's more than just an ounce, Mother, but thank you for the nice compliment," Thielemans answered.

"So, tell me what your book's about," the housekeeper requested.

"*Catholicism Astray* is an analysis of how a number of the most important changes in Catholicism in the past half-century have impacted Church membership, practices, and attitudes," the author responded.

"And what kind of changes would you be referring to in your book?" Mother questioned.

"The major changes I've analyzed in my book include the Church's change from the Latin Mass to Mass in the vernacular of the individual countries, attendance at Vigil Masses as a means to satisfy Sunday or Holy Day obligations, and the elimination of Friday abstinence from meat," the theologian stated authoritatively. "My book also analyzes several other changes of minor significance."

"Well, I don't know what you have to say about things in your book, but I surely miss the way things used to be in the Catholic Church," Mother sighed. "I dearly loved hearing the Mass said in Latin and listening to the choir singing Gregorian Chant. I also loved how Sundays used to be special when everyone in the family got dressed in their finest clothes and attended Mass together. I didn't even mind abstaining from meat one day a week. We didn't know about things like cholesterol back in the old days, but not eating meat one day a week always seemed to be a healthy thing to do, and it was a welcome relief on the pocketbook as well."

"I couldn't have said it better myself," the author acknowledged.

"Don't you get lonely traveling by yourself?" Mother asked, as she opened the oven and checked the pot roast.

"Before this weekend, I never traveled by myself," the priest revealed. "My sister served as my secretary and traveled everywhere with me."

"Where is your sister now?" the housekeeper inquired.

"She's in Belgium," Thielemans explained. "She was born in Belgium and spent most of her life there. Her husband died unexpectedly a few years ago, and because her children were all grown, she agreed to travel with me as my secretary. She was forced to return home last week because her son was seriously injured in Belgium's suicide bombings in 2016. He's been in rehab hospitals since that time, but was finally discharged last week. Because he lives alone and can't completely take care of himself, my sister decided to return home to help him recuperate."

"Heaven help us," Mother exclaimed. "I remember watching the stories about those bombings on the television when they took place. I can't believe what's happening to this world. It's already April 2018, and you'd swear we were living in the 1940s again. Heaven help us."

Thielemans nodded his head in agreement.

"So, how long will your sister be staying in Belgium?" the housekeeper asked.

"It looks like I may be traveling by myself for the next year or so," Thielemans revealed.

"You said your sister was Belgian," Mother recalled. "Are you also Belgian?"

"I was born in the United States when my parents moved here for business purposes," Thielemans explained. "So, I have dual citizenship. I've spent most of my life here, although I was ordained in Belgium and spent two years there teaching at the American College of the Immaculate Conception in Leuven. Before that, I graduated from Harvard University with a double major in international studies and theology, and studied for the priesthood at the North American Pontifical College in Rome."

"So, with which order or diocese are you affiliated?" Mother inquired.

"I answer to the Archdiocese of Mechelen-Brussels in Belgium," Thielemans said. "However, I have been granted a leave of absence to write, teach, and lecture in the United States. My writing has been well received throughout the Catholic Church, and I donate a lot of the profits from my book sales to the Church in Belgium. So, the archdiocese allows me to work independently."

"I've never met a priest who traveled to so many different countries or had such impressive credentials," the

6

housekeeper stated with a smile. "How many different languages do you speak?"

"English, French, German, Dutch, Italian, Spanish, Russian, and Polish," the theologian modestly replied.

"Me too," Mother quipped. "I speak all those languages except the ones you mentioned after English."

Thielemans looked at Mother and laughed.

"Do you find it difficult traveling by yourself?" Mother asked.

"I do," the priest confessed. "My sister did everything for me. She scheduled my lectures, meetings, and book signings. She reviewed and edited my books and speeches. She handled all my finances. She made sure my clothes and shoes were cleaned and repaired. She scheduled my car maintenance. She made my hotel and dinner reservations. She even booked the cruise I'm going on tomorrow."

"You're going on a cruise tomorrow?" Mother exclaimed.

"Yes, I am," Thielemans replied. "That's why I'm in town. I'm leaving tomorrow on an 18-day, round-trip cruise from San Diego to the Hawaiian Islands. My sister was supposed to accompany me, but her return to Belgium changed all that."

"Will your cruise be for business or pleasure?" the housekeeper questioned.

"Both," the priest answered. "I was already scheduled to deliver the keynote address at the Catholic bishops' conference in Honolulu, and I originally planned to fly there. However, my sister thought I needed a vacation, and was able to find a cruise ship that was scheduled to be in Honolulu the same day I was scheduled to speak. So, she rearranged my schedule and booked the cruise."

"My, you have depended a lot on your sister," Mother observed. "Bless her heart."

"Mother, I honestly don't know how I'm going to manage things without her," the clergyman humbly admitted. "I feel helpless now that she's not with me."

"So, what brings you to Saint Declan's?" Mother asked.

"I met Bishop Joseph Grannick while I was speaking at the University of Notre Dame several weeks ago," Thielemans explained. "When I mentioned I was planning to be in San Diego, he asked me if I would be interested in saying Mass while I was in town. He told me he would be speaking at a conference in San Francisco this weekend, and several local priests, including Father Kittrick, were invited to attend the conference if they could arrange Mass coverage for their parishes. When Bishop Grannick asked me to fill in for a day, I told him I would be glad to help."

"You'll be saying two Masses tomorrow," the housekeeper revealed, as she started preparing coleslaw. "A retired priest usually says Mass when the pastor goes away, but he's saying tonight's Vigil Mass at the request of his own family. The Mass is being offered for the repose of the soul of his parents. A few brothers and sisters have come to town to attend the Mass and go out to dinner afterward. The family does this every year on the date of their parents' wedding anniversary. It gives them a chance to have a nice family reunion."

"That's wonderful," the priest exclaimed.

"The pastor isn't the only one going away this weekend," Mother continued. "I'm going away as well. My son will be picking me up tomorrow morning and driving me to Mexico to do some shopping. I'll loan you the rectory key. You can leave it on the kitchen table when you're leaving tomorrow. Just remember to lock the door behind you on your way out. By the way, did Bishop Grannick tell you he is Father Kittrick's uncle?"

"Why, no," the surprised guest answered.

"Didn't you wonder why a bishop was going out of his way to arrange Mass coverage for a parish priest?" Mother asked, as she seasoned the cabbage and blended in mayonnaise.

"I never thought about it," Thielemans replied.

"Live and learn, Honey," Mother chuckled. "Father Kittrick is Bishop Grannick's only nephew, and the bishop goes out of his way to take very good care of him. They spend a lot of time together and are as thick as thieves."

"I had no idea," Thielemans admitted.

"There's probably a lot you don't know about Bishop Grannick," the talkative housekeeper surmised. "When he first became a bishop, he worked for the archdiocese for less than a year before returning to Rome to study canon law. A few years later, he finished his studies and returned home. He likes to make people think he's some important dignitary who serves on ecclesiastical tribunals and the like, but the only thing he does is oversee annulments for the archdiocese. Because of his position and political connections, he's been able to influence the pastor's many assignments and even arrange for him to have more than his fair share of sabbatical leaves. Why, I could tell you stories. Heaven help us."

"I've only met the bishop once," Thielemans revealed. "He told me he worked in your archdiocese as a canon lawyer, but never got into the specifics of what he did."

Looking at the clock, Mother walked over to the refrigerator and removed a peach pie.

"Take a look at this, why don't you," she said, holding the pie close to his face. "I made it ahead of time and waited to see if I liked you enough to bake it for dinner."

As both Thielemans and Mother started laughing, Father Kittrick, a short, muscular 49-year-old with dark, oily hair, poor complexion, and thick eyeglasses, entered the kitchen.

"What's so funny?" Kittrick asked, as Mother opened the oven door and carefully added the pie.

"Oh, nothing," the housekeeper replied. "I just told the Father only special guests get served both my pot roast and peach pie for dinner."

"Maybe, someday I'll become special enough to get some of your royal treatment," Kittrick quipped, as he adjusted his Roman collar and scratched his beet-red face.

"Now, Father, you know how special you are to me," Mother swooned with a straight face. "It's just that we have a famous guest with us this evening, and I knew you'd want him to feel extra special."

"Paul Thielemans," the clergyman announced, rising to his feet and offering his hand to Kittrick.

"Gordon Kittrick," the nervous priest responded, shaking Thielemans' hand.

"I brought you some Belgian beer," Thielemans indicated. "I thought we could have a taste before dinner."

"Some other time, maybe," Kittrick blurted, as he accepted the six-pack from his guest and quickly placed it on the kitchen table.

"Very well," Thielemans acquiesced. "I also brought you a copy of my new book."

Kittrick accepted the book, glanced at the cover, and quickly handed it to Mother.

"I think I'll let Mother read it first," Kittrick said with a smirk. "If she approves it and puts her Imprimatur on it, I'll pick up the *Cliff Notes* version and have a look-see."

Without saying a word, Thielemans stared at Kittrick. As the room grew silent, a skinny, blonde 13-year-old walked into the kitchen.

"Father, this is Bobby Kucera," Kittrick announced, putting his hand on the anxious boy's shoulder. "He's one of our finest altar boys, and he hopes to become a priest someday. I've been trying to teach him how to wrestle."

"Hello, Bobby," Thielemans said, offering his hand to the disheveled youngster who was wearing a wrinkled, long-sleeve shirt, stained khaki slacks, and tattered sneakers. "I'm Father Thielemans."

"Hi," Bobby answered quietly, shaking the priest's hand and quickly looking at Kittrick.

"Father Thielemans here is a famous author," Kittrick revealed. "He wrote the book Mother is holding."

The youngster looked at the book, the book's author, and then again, at Kittrick.

"May I use the lavatory?" Bobby asked, appearing uncomfortable.

"You just used the bathroom downstairs," Kittrick reminded the youngster.

"I have to go again," the youngster insisted.

"Mother, help us out here," Kittrick requested.

As Mother walked the young boy to a nearby bathroom, Kittrick started sweating profusely.

"Are you okay?" Thielemans inquired. "You seem shaky, and your face looks like it's on fire."

"Don't worry about me," Kittrick shot back. "My face gets red when I work out - end of story."

"If you say so," Thielemans acquiesced.

"Look, I've got to grab my bags and take the boy home," Kittrick explained. "So, I won't have time to eat with you tonight. I still have to get to the airport and catch a 9 o'clock flight to San Francisco. Mother will make sure you're fed and show you to your room."

"Fine," the visiting priest replied.

"You have two Masses tomorrow," Kittrick continued. "The first is at 9 o'clock and the second is at 11 o'clock. There shouldn't be many people at either Mass. At any rate, you'll get the chance to see how all us simple folk in the Church still earn a living."

Confused by Kittrick's hostile behavior, Thielemans just stared at his rude host. As he did, Mother brought Bobby back into the kitchen.

"Here we are, none the worse for wear," the housekeeper said, ruffling the youngster's blonde hair. "I think Bobby could use some ginger ale. The poor lad is probably dehydrated from the heat and physical exertion."

As Bobby sat down at the table and Mother retrieved a can of soda from the refrigerator, Kittrick looked outside the kitchen window.

"Is that your car in the driveway?" he asked, as he admired Thielemans' 2018 ebony Cadillac CT6 sedan.

"Yes," Thielemans answered. "Is there somewhere else you'd like me to park it?"

"You can leave it there," Kittrick advised. "If you don't mind me asking, what does it cost to rent a car like that?"

"I honestly don't know," Thielemans admitted. "I bought the car several months ago."

"You bought that car?" Kittrick exclaimed. "You must have sold a lot of books to pay for it."

"Not really," the author responded.

"Well, then, what is it?" Kittrick asked inquisitively. "Are you independently wealthy or something?"

"Or something," Thielemans acknowledged with a deliberate smile.

Staring at Thielemans, Kittrick approached the table.

"Finish your soda pop," he said to Bobby. "I'll get my bags and drive you home."

"Will you be back for supper?" Mother inquired.

"I've changed my plans," the pastor replied. "I'll be driving directly to the airport after I take the boy home. I'm sure you and Father Thielemans will manage to enjoy dinner without me."

As Kittrick left the kitchen, Mother looked directly at Thielemans and shook her head.

"Don't mind the pastor," she advised. "He's just in one of his moods. I still don't understand why he can't come back for supper. His plane doesn't leave until 11 o'clock, and the airport is only fifteen minutes away."

"I'm sure there's a reason," Thielemans surmised.

After several minutes, Kittrick returned to the kitchen with luggage in hand.

"All right, Boy, it's time for you and me to get this show on the road," he announced.

Hearing Kittrick, the youngster got up from the table.

"Why, Honey, you haven't even tasted your ginger ale," Mother observed, picking up the can from the table. "The soda can is still full. Would you like to take it with you?"

"That's all right," the youngster mumbled, turning away from the table and staring at Kittrick.

"Time to go," Kittrick barked, shaking hands with his guest. "Enjoy being a priest again tomorrow."

Without saying a word, Thielemans watched Kittrick guide Bobby out the door and walk him to his 2017 black Chrysler 200 sedan. As he watched, he noticed how Bobby seemed to be walking with some difficulty.

"Mother, tell me about Bobby," Thielemans said.

"Oh, he's such a sad story," the housekeeper replied. "His father died last year in a tragic automobile accident, and the poor lad's been lost ever since. He lives with his mother and two older sisters. So, he doesn't have the male influence he needs. He's been spending quite a lot of time with the pastor lately, but he seems like he's regressing rather than improving."

"Why do you say that?" Thielemans asked.

"Well, Bobby used to be such a happy boy before his father died," Mother answered. "He took much better care of himself. He was always clean, well-dressed, and full of life. Lately, he's been acting depressed. I think he's even lost some weight."

Mother put her hand on her chest and sighed.

"I tell you, Father, Bobby just doesn't seem to be motivated anymore, and it seems like he's become easily distracted, especially when he's serving Mass," she continued. "He used to be a very good student, but I understand he's no longer on the honor roll. Bless his heart. I pray for him and his family every day."

"Then, so will I," Thielemans offered.

Mother put the six-pack of beer into the refrigerator and directed Thielemans to his room. An hour later, the priest returned to the kitchen, dressed in a green golf shirt and khakis, and carrying two beer glasses.

"Well, it looks like it's just you and me, Honey," Mother announced, as her guest took his place at the kitchen table. "I've fixed a nice pot roast with some tasty vegetables, coleslaw, and my award-winning peach pie for dessert. From the looks of things, I'd say you've already planned the beverages."

"Do you enjoy taking a drink every now and then?" Thielemans asked with a mischievous smile.

"I do, indeed," the housekeeper answered. "And if you're not watching closely, I'll drink you under the table."

"Mother, you're my kind of woman," the priest joked, as he removed two bottles of beer from the refrigerator.

After he removed its cellophane wrap, Thielemans handed Mother an ornately-etched beer glass which featured the inscription, "Saint Bavo Witbier," as well as a multicolored crest and likeness of the saint.

"It's important to drink good beer from the right glass," the beer connoisseur stated authoritatively. "There's a different glass for every Belgian beer, and each has a unique size, shape, and design. This special glass is my gift to you. I have one just like it."

"What's all the extra writing that's inscribed on your glass?" the perceptive housekeeper inquired.

"This is my personal beer glass," the priest proudly revealed. "It was a gift from my father. The glass is the same as yours, but there's an inscription on the back. It reads: 'Paul, I drink to your health and happiness - always! Your Loving Father.'"

"Oh, how touching," Mother swooned.

"Allow me to teach you something about unfiltered Belgian beer," Thielemans offered, opening her bottle of Saint Bavo Witbier. "I'd like you to pour beer into your glass, but make sure to leave a few inches of beer in the bottle. Once you've poured the beer, have a taste."

Mother carefully poured the beer into her glass, studied the beverage's cloudy character, and with a firm grip on the glass, took a hearty swig.

"Saints be praised," she exclaimed. "This is surely nectar from heaven. This is the finest beer I've ever tasted, Father Darling. Two more of these, and I may have to go to confession in the morning."

Thielemans looked at the housekeeper and laughed.

"Now, I'd like you to swirl the beer that's left in your bottle and free up the filtrate you see on the bottom," he instructed. "After you've done that, pour the entire contents of the bottle into your glass and take another sip."

The housekeeper followed Thielemans' instructions, and upon taking another swig of beer, just stared at the priest and smiled.

"Heaven help us," she said. "The second sip was even more delicious than the first."

"That's because the filtrate at the bottom of the bottle is filled with flavorful spices," the beer expert revealed. "Most people just pour the beer into their glass without adding the filtrate and never get to experience how delicious unfiltered beer tastes. So, you can see why I always bring a six-pack of Saint Bavo to everyone I visit. The experience we've just shared proves anyone can learn something new, even when they think they know it all."

Mother smiled at Thielemans and lifted her glass in the air. As soon as the priest poured his glass of beer, the two clinked glasses, and the housekeeper proposed a toast:

"May the good Lord take a liking to you – but not too soon!"

After the two took a hearty swig of beer, Thielemans smiled and proposed a toast of his own:

"May God grant you many years to live, for sure He must be knowing, the earth has angels all too few, and heaven is overflowing!"

Hearing Thielemans' beautiful Irish toast, Mother sighed. As the two enjoyed their beer, she carefully studied the beautiful construction of her beer glass.

"Do you give away many of these glasses?" she asked.

"I do," the generous priest admitted. "They're glasses that are handcrafted in Belgium. I order them periodically and have them shipped directly to my townhouse in Alexandria, Virginia. I get back to Virginia every month or so, and when I do, I put a few cases of these glasses in the trunk of my car. If I start running low on glasses while I'm still on the road, I have glasses shipped to a beer distributor that's close to the venue where I'll be lecturing."

"Now, tell me true, how it is such a priest as yourself can afford a Cadillac, a townhouse, and the lifestyle to which you have become accustomed," Mother requested.

"I wish I could honestly tell you I earned all the money I have through hard work," Thielemans replied. "To be truthful, though, I have earned some pocket change with my teaching, lecturing, and book sales, but I inherited most of my money when my mother and father died. My sister and I inherited a small fortune from our parents."

Thielemans raised his glass toward heaven and quietly took a sip of beer.

"Even before my parents died, I lived like a student prince," he continued. "My father paid my entire tuition at Harvard and the seminary. This was extremely important because it allowed me to do what I'm currently doing rather than being obligated to work as a diocesan priest. Because of my father's many business, political, and religious connections, I was able to study for the priesthood in Rome, become ordained in Belgium, and return to the United States to write, travel, and lecture. Not many priests have such freedom and independence."

"I knew you were different from the moment I laid my eyes on you," the housekeeper revealed, as she smiled, winked, and started bringing supper to the table.

Mother served her guest a sumptuous meal, and following dinner, the two retired to the living room for peach pie, more beer, and a television double feature, featuring Bing Crosby in *Going My Way* and *The Bells of Saint Mary's*. As they watched the first movie, Thielemans and Mother Murray managed to trade anecdotes about Bing Crosby, Irish whiskey, and classic movies, and contribute some nifty two-part harmony when *Swinging on A Star* and *Too-Ra-Loo-Ra-Loo-Ral* were performed on screen.

Hours later, the beer was gone, the movies were over, and Mother Murray was the only one still awake. Her exhausted guest had fallen asleep midway through the second movie.

Appearing so comfortable in his leather recliner, the thoughtful housekeeper decided to put an alarm clock next to her guest's chair, cover him with a blanket, and let him sleep.

"Heaven help us," she whispered, as she took note of the late hour, blew a kiss toward the sleeping priest, and slowly walked through the dark rectory toward her bedroom.

CHAPTER TWO

After a good night's sleep, Thielemans awoke to a clamoring alarm clock and empty rectory. Trying to remember where he was and why he spent the night in a recliner, the well-rested priest followed the smell of freshly brewed coffee and hot cinnamon buns into the kitchen.

Reading the note Mother Murray left on the kitchen table, Thielemans chuckled and helped himself to a quick breakfast. After a soothing shower, he left the rectory and walked to the church's sacristy.

Following a well-attended 9 o'clock Mass, Thielemans returned to the rectory. After another cup of coffee, he locked the rectory door, carried his luggage to his car, and returned to the sacristy to prepare for the 11 o'clock Mass.

As Mass was about to begin, Thielemans was joined in the sacristy by two altar boys. The older of the two, a plump, freckle-faced boy pushed back the long, brown hair covering his eyes and offered his hand to the visiting priest.

"Welcome to Saint Declan's, Father," the youngster said, as he shook the priest's hand. "I'm Frankie Graham, and this is Bobby Kucera. We'll be serving Mass for you."

"Thank you, Frankie," Thielemans replied.

Shifting his attention to the younger altar boy, the priest patted him on the shoulder.

"Bobby and I have already met," the priest revealed. "Father Kittrick introduced us yesterday in the rectory."

"Hi," the boy mumbled, quickly losing his weak smile and looking away from the visiting priest.

Glancing at the wall clock, Thielemans waved to a young female lector to signal the beginning of Mass. As soon as she stepped up to the lectern and announced the entrance hymn, Thielemans followed the two altar boys on a short procession from the sacristy to the altar.

When members of the congregation were told a famous theologian would be saying Mass at Saint Declan's, word quickly spread through the parish. A full house on a Sunday morning was a rarity at the small church, but many parishioners who were anxious to hear Thielemans made attending one of his Masses a priority.

From the very first words of his homily, Thielemans owned his entire audience and convincingly demonstrated why prestigious universities competed for open dates on his lecture schedule. Throughout his sermon, the gifted speaker held the parishioners of Saint Declan's spellbound, and not even the distraction of a seemingly dazed Bobby Kucera leaving the altar could divert the parishioners' attention away from the priest's inspirational words.

In response to the priest's homily, many parishioners blessed themselves while others applauded. As Thielemans left the lectern and returned to the altar, he immediately realized he had won an audience but lost an altar boy.

Concerned about Bobby's well-being, the priest motioned for Frankie to come closer.

"Go into the sacristy and see how Bobby is doing," he quietly requested.

The altar boy joined his hands, bowed in front of Thielemans, and left the altar. Several minutes later, he returned from the sacristy and approached the priest.

"He's not in the sacristy," Frankie reported. "He must have gone home."

Nodding his head, Thielemans continued the liturgy.

Immediately following Mass, a group of parishioners entered the sacristy to thank the visiting priest for his inspiring religious service. Realizing he only had a few hours left to board his cruise ship, Thielemans skillfully juggled cordiality with time constraints and was finally able to end his meeting with the faithful of Saint Declan's.

As he prepared to leave the sacristy, the priest started thinking about Bobby and wondering if the boy left the church because of an illness. The more he thought about the youngster's strange behavior and departure from the altar, the more concerned he became.

With little alternative, Thielemans decided to search the entire church and adjacent grounds for Bobby. Unable to locate him, Thielemans tried to think of some way to find the youngster.

The usually calm and resourceful priest felt helpless when he remembered he locked the rectory door and left the key on the kitchen table. Unable to gain access to any emergency telephone numbers, Thielemans grew even more frustrated when he realized he couldn't remember Bobby's last name which made locating the youngster's family through the telephone directory impossible.

Just as the unnerved clergyman couldn't remember Bobby's last name, he couldn't remember the last name of the other altar boy. Running out of options to locate Bobby and time to board his ship, Thielemans said a silent prayer, got into his car, and drove away.

Distracted by many different thoughts, the anxious priest tried to negotiate the back streets that would ultimately lead to Interstate-5 and a straight shot to the San Diego waterfront. As his attention continued to shift from glimpses of the interstate highway to the monitor of his Cadillac's navigation system, Thielemans approached an intersection and noticed a traffic sign in the distance.

With his eyes shifting from the traffic sign to low-flying jet airliners that were landing at the nearby San Diego International Airport, the clergyman entered the intersection, unaware a pickup truck that was traveling at high speed and carrying three intoxicated teenagers was about to run the stop sign. As Thielemans continued driving, he suddenly heard the sustained sounds of a truck horn, screeching brakes, and screaming teenage boys.

Before the priest could react to the menacing cacophony, the swerving pickup truck crashed into the passenger's side of Thielemans' car. As the forceful impact of the crash jostled the unsuspecting priest, the inebriated driver of the stalled pickup truck restarted his vehicle and quickly left the scene of the accident.

Stunned by the crash, Thielemans slowly exited his car and staggered toward the sidewalk. Not seeing anyone who could render assistance, he removed the cell phone from his belt and dialed 9-1-1.

Waiting for what seemed like an eternity, Thielemans walked around his car and surveyed the damage. After making a few inspections, a police car finally arrived.

"Father, are you hurt?" San Diego Police Officer Jeff Sommers inquired, as he approached the accident victim.

"No," Thielemans replied. "I'm just a little shaken."

"What happened?" the young policeman asked.

"I was driving through the intersection and got blindsided by a pickup truck," the priest explained. "I never saw it coming. The driver of the truck crashed into my car and drove away without stopping. When I was finally able to unfasten my seat belt and get out of the car, I saw the truck turning the corner at the next block."

"Could you describe the truck?" the officer requested.

"It was an old gray pickup truck," Thielemans recalled. "I don't know the make, and I didn't see its license plate."

"I see you're from Virginia," the lanky, redheaded policeman observed, as he noticed the priest's license plate.

"My home is in Virginia, but I don't spend a lot of time there," Thielemans answered. "I lecture at a lot of different universities. So, I'm on the road more than I'm home."

"Are you currently lecturing in California?" Sommers questioned, as he started performing a license plate check on his cell phone.

"I'm on my way to your cruise terminal," Thielemans said. "I'm supposed to be leaving on a cruise at 4 o'clock."

"What ship are you going on?" the policeman inquired.

"I'm going on the Eurodam," Thielemans replied.

"Father, may I see your driver's license, registration, and proof of automobile insurance?" the policeman courteously requested.

Thielemans quickly retrieved the requested documents.

"Officer, what do I have to do now?" the clergyman asked, as he glanced at his wristwatch and started imagining his cruise ship leaving without him. "I've been on a tight schedule all day, and this accident complicates things."

"I already called for a tow truck, and it should be here any minute," Sommers answered, as he returned the priest's documents. "The driver will tow your car wherever you want and let you ride along. There should be an emergency telephone number on the back of your insurance card. Call the insurance company right now and find out where you can take your car for repairs."

"Thank you," Thielemans said. "I'll do that."

"If it were my car, I'd have it towed to the local Cadillac dealership," Sommers suggested. "They're close, they do nice body repairs, and they'll be able to work with your insurance appraiser without you being present. They're closed on Sunday, but they have a dropbox in which you can leave your keys and repair instructions. Make sure to include all your insurance information. Arranging the repairs should only take a few minutes, and if you offer the tow truck driver a few bucks, he'll drive you to the cruise terminal. When you get back from your cruise, your car will look like new and be ready to drive away."

Just as the police officer finished talking, a tow truck arrived, and a burly, middle-aged Mexican climbed out of the cab. As he walked slowly around the car and carefully surveyed the car's damage, Thielemans phoned his insurance company and received authorization to have his car towed to the local Cadillac dealership.

Watching the truck driver starting to attach tow chains and fasteners to Thielemans' car, Officer Sommers approached the clergyman.

"My final accident report will be available within the next twenty-four hours," Sommers stated. "We'll try to search the immediate area for the pickup truck that damaged your car, but I doubt we'll find it."

"Thank you for all your help," the grateful priest said, as he shook the policeman's hand. "God bless you."

"Thank you, Father," the police officer answered. "Is there anything else I can do for you before I leave?"

"Officer, there is one thing," Thielemans realized. "I'm worried about a young boy, named Bobby, who served Mass for me this morning at Saint Declan's. He left the altar during Mass, and I couldn't find him afterward. I'm worried he may be sick, but I don't know his last name, and there isn't anyone at the rectory today who can help me with the matter. The pastor and housekeeper are both out of town. So, there's no one I can rely on to contact Bobby's family to make sure he's all right."

"There's not much I can do today without knowing the boy's full name," Officer Sommers explained. "All I can do is contact the rectory tomorrow morning. Someone there will know who the boy is and how to contact his family. Good luck with your car, and enjoy your cruise."

As soon as the policeman drove away, Thielemans introduced himself to the tow truck driver, Alarico Reynosa, a quiet Mexican with black, shoulder-length hair and tattoos that covered his tattoos. Reynosa was meticulous about the way he hooked Thielemans' Cadillac to his tow truck, and as he checked and rechecked his tow chains, the usually patient clergyman checked and rechecked his watch.

Thielemans rode in Reynosa's tow truck to the Cadillac dealership and quickly became mesmerized by the collection of magnetized statues and Bobbleheads the driver had on his dashboard. Surrounding statues of Jesus and Our Lady of Guadelupe were Bobbleheads of the Cisco Kid and his sidekick Pancho, wrestler Rey Mysterio, Jr., singer Freddy Fender, revolutionary Emiliano Zapata, actor Danny Trejo, guitarist Carlos Santana, actress Selma Hayek, baseball star Fernando Valenzuela, the San Diego Chicken, a generic Hula Dancer, and the Lennon Sisters. The entire collection was surrounded by a Hawaiian lei.

"That's quite an assortment of statues you have on your dashboard," Thielemans observed.

"*Si, Padre*," the taciturn driver responded.

Upon arriving at the Cadillac dealership, Thielemans tried to quickly fill out the repair requisition forms. Completing the forms took longer than he anticipated, but after he finally signed all the required authorizations, dropped the forms and car keys into the lockbox, and retrieved his luggage, Reynosa drove him directly to the cruise terminal.

"*Vaya con Dios*," the grateful clergyman said, handing the driver a $20 tip and collecting his bags.

"*Vaya con Dios*," Reynosa replied appreciatively.

Carrying his luggage, Thielemans ran through the terminal to a processing station where cruise line personnel rushed him through the various embarkation procedures and security checks. Running up the gangway, he stepped aboard the Eurodam at the precise moment the ship's horn sounded to signal the vessel's imminent departure.

As Thielemans walked into the ship's atrium and reviewed a deck plan to see where his suite was located, he could feel the ocean liner moving. Looking out a window, he could see the ship slowly pulling away from the pier.

Taking the elevator to the Rotterdam Deck, he carried his luggage to the port-side Pinnacle Suite, the ship's largest and most expensive stateroom. Throwing his bags on the suite's king-size bed and quickly surveying the layout of the enormous cabin and contents of its refrigerator, he walked out on to his private balcony with a can of Sprite, sat down, and watched the ship leave the beautiful San Diego harbor.

Intermittently distracted by the sight of jet airliners taking off from the airport, an aircraft carrier preparing to depart from Naval Base San Diego, and the gradually diminishing city skyline, Thielemans thought about the events of the past twenty-four hours. After he recalled the kindness of Mother Murray, rudeness of Father Kittrick, and quirks of everyone associated with his car accident, Thielemans started thinking about Bobby Kucera. As he was analyzing the uncomfortable relationship between Bobby and Kittrick, Thielemans was coaxed out of his deep thought by the sound of a chiming doorbell.

Startled by the loud interruption, Thielemans got up from his balcony chair and quickly walked through his suite. Opening the door, he came face to face with a smiling, well-groomed cabin steward.

"Good afternoon, Father Thielemans," the forty-something native of the Philippines said, extending his hand. "My name is Winston. I am your cabin steward."

"I'm pleased to meet you, Winston," Thielemans replied, returning the dark, handsome cabin steward's handshake and smile. "Please call me, 'Father Paul.'"

Entering the suite, the cabin steward closed the door, opened a closet, and removed a life-preserver. Unclasping its belt, Winston handed the life-preserver to Thielemans.

"Father Paul, have you ever cruised before?" Winston asked politely.

"Yes, of course," the priest answered.

"Then, you know how important the lifeboat drill is and how attendance at the drill is mandatory," Winston stated diplomatically. "Since you boarded the ship after the drill was already conducted, I have been instructed to give you a private lifeboat drill right now."

"Certainly," Thielemans agreed.

Demonstrating how to put on a life-preserver and reviewing the location of the priest's lifeboat muster station from a chart affixed to the inside of the priest's cabin door, Winston effectively explained the ship's safety measures, using impeccable English.

"Is there anything else I can do for you at this time?" the steward inquired, as he returned the life-preserver to its place in the closet.

"There is one thing," Thielemans requested, as he opened the refrigerator. "Could you replace the beer in the refrigerator with bottles of Saint Bavo Witbier?"

"Bavo Witbier," the steward repeated with a hint of unfamiliarity. "Let me see what I can do."

After Winston left the suite, Thielemans returned to the balcony, sat down, and watched the sun start to sink into the Pacific Ocean. Realizing the ship was now at sea and the San Diego skyline was no longer visible, the priest thought again about Bobby Kucera.

Propping his feet on another chair, the tired priest closed his eyes and quickly drifted off into a deep sleep. Somewhere along his journey through a mysterious dream, he found himself frantically searching the Hawaiian Islands for an altar boy he hardly knew and fervently praying for answers to questions he never asked.

CHAPTER THREE

The waitstaff enthusiastically smiled as passengers strolled into the Eurodam's main dining room for their first dinner at sea. Among those who were being shown to their table was a party of two priests and two nuns.

The leader of the group was Father Edmund Prosky, a tall, portly 70-year-old with a pale complexion and healthy head of white hair. Aided by a wooden cane, Prosky slowly walked next to Father William Conyngham whose slender frame hunched over the walker he required for ambulation.

The same age as Prosky but appearing much older, Conyngham was a deeper shade of pale than his traveling companion. Although he handled his walker as adroitly as a septuagenarian might be expected to handle such an appurtenance on a cruise ship at sea, Conyngham's thinning gray hair and thick frameless eyeglasses identified him as someone who had seen better days.

Following closely behind the conventionally-dressed priests were two nuns who wore matching brown pantsuits and veils. Being pushed in a wheelchair was the older of the two nuns, Sister Regina Nelson, a frail, white-haired 75-year-old who rubbed her arms and appeared cold despite wearing a thick sweater under her suit jacket.

Pushing the wheelchair was Sister Michelle Erzengel, an exceptionally beautiful and statuesque 33-year-old whose flowing chestnut hair, mahogany eyes, and alluring smile quickly captured the attention of most passengers and crew members. So many eyes followed Sister Michelle to her table that the ship seemed to be listing in her direction until she was finally seated.

"I arranged for you to have a larger table so you could be more comfortable," Carlo, the Eurodam's middle-aged, Italian dining room captain said, as he snapped his fingers to signal two waiters.

"Thank you, Carlo," Prosky replied, as he sat down at the table and watched the waiters help Sister Regina out of her wheelchair and Father Conyngham away from his walker.

"*Buon appetito*," Carlo crooned with a big smile, helping Sister Michelle with her chair.

"Hey, Carlo," Conyngham yelled, as he settled into his chair with considerable difficulty. "Is this one of the tables they reserve for steerage passengers?"

"*Mi scusi?*" Carlo responded with surprise.

"You said you arranged for us to have this table," Conyngham continued. "Couldn't you have arranged a table closer to the entrance? We walked so far to get to this table I had to stop twice to show my passport."

"*Mi dispiace, Padre,*" the embarrassed dining room captain answered. "I'm sorry for the inconvenience, but the ship is full. As you can see, there are many other elderly passengers who also have special needs. Many of them booked their cruises more than a year ago and put in their dining room requests at that time. It's a matter of, *come si dice*, first come, first served."

"Is that why we didn't get the first-seating dinner reservations we requested?" Conyngham inquired.

"*Si, Padre,*" Carlo confirmed.

"What about your 'As You Wish' dining program that allows passengers to eat dinner whenever they want?"

Conyngham asked. "Could we do that in the future and get a table closer to the entrance?"

"You can dine at your convenience between 5 p.m. and 9 p.m.," Carlo explained. "However, you may have to wait in line to be seated, and you will be seated at whatever table is available at the time, regardless of its location. You may also be seated at large tables with other passengers."

"So, what you're saying is this table is the best you can do for us," Conyngham surmised.

"*Si, Padre,*" Carlo confirmed. "The second seating is at 8:30 every evening, just two and one-half hours later than the first seating. More importantly, you will be dining at the same comfortable table every evening with two of our very finest waiters serving you. If the walk to this table is too much for you, we can arrange for a wheelchair to be available at the dining room entrance every evening and have someone help you to your table."

"Thank you, Carlo," Prosky said with a smile. "I'm sure this table will be fine."

"*Prego,*" Carlo replied, as he nodded and walked away with a look of relief on his face and perspiration evident in his thick crop of curly, black hair.

"I think Carlo got his Italian accent from the movies," Conyngham mumbled, not realizing another waiter was standing behind him. "He sounds like he's from Philly."

As Prosky shook his head and laughed, the waiter emerged from Conyngham's shadow.

"Good evening, good evening," the tall, thin waiter exclaimed with a big smile. "My name is Angel, and my partner and I will be your waiters this cruise."

"I think this table could use an Angel," Prosky quipped to Conyngham's smirk and Sister Michelle's amusement, as the waiter started placing dinner napkins on everyone's laps and handing out menus.

"Good evening, everyone," the second waiter said with a cordial smile. "My name is Mang, and it will be my pleasure to serve you. My partner and I work very hard to always provide excellent service. So, if there is anything you need, just ask. We will be happy to bring you anything you wish to eat and make sure it is always to your liking. If there is something you don't like, please tell us, and we will replace it immediately. Do you have any questions?"

"Where are you boys from?" Sister Regina asked with a quivering voice.

"Angel is from the Philippines, and I am from Bali," Mang answered with a smile.

"So, then, your given name is not Mang, but Komang," the perceptive nun observed.

"That is correct," the surprised waiter acknowledged.

"And you are the third oldest son in your family," she stated authoritatively.

"That is also correct," Mang replied.

"Regina, how do you know so much about this young man?" Prosky inquired. "Have you two previously met?"

"Balinese birth order," Conyngham mumbled, as he reached for a dinner roll.

"What do you mean?" Prosky asked.

"Tell him, Regina," Conyngham requested, as he started buttering his roll.

"Many Balinese people follow a custom of giving their children specific names according to birth order," the nun answered.

"The whole idea is the Balinese can identify the birth order of any male by his first name," Conyngham interrupted. "There are also standard female birth order names."

"Very impressive, Regina," Prosky said.

"Uh, huh," Conyngham concurred, as he reached for another pat of butter.

"Very impressive, indeed," Mang added. "Have you been to Bali before, Sister?"

"Yes, I have – many years ago," the nun confirmed. "Catholicism has always been a minor religion in Bali. There are more Muslims and people of other faiths there. I did missionary work in Bali and helped many Balinese convert to Catholicism."

Mang smiled and acknowledged Sister Regina's familiarity with his country by nodding his approval.

"When we arrive on the Big Island of Hawaii, I plan to visit a missionary sister I worked with in Bali and haven't seen in fifty years," the nun added. "Her name is Alena Opunui, and she lives in Hilo. Father Conyngham also did missionary work in Bali, didn't you, Father?"

"I did biological research in Bali, as well as in Java, Komodo, Sumatra, Borneo, Trinidad, Tobago, and the Galapagos Islands," the priest replied. "I was never a missionary, though."

"What wonderful stories," Mang exclaimed, realizing he already spent a great deal of time at the table and had not yet taken the dinner orders of the passengers. "So, does everyone know what they would like for dinner?"

"I'll have the red snapper, Komang," Sister Regina announced. "I'd like it poached, and not buttered or seasoned. I would also like boiled, unseasoned, and unbuttered vegetables, but no salsa. I don't care for any appetizer, soup, or salad, but I would like sherbet for dessert and a cup of Chamomile Tea at the end of the meal. I'll just have water for now."

"And you, Sister?" Mang asked Sister Michelle.

"I'll have a salad with dressing on the side, prime rib - medium rare, and strawberry parfait for dessert," she replied. "I'd also like iced tea with lemon."

"Father?" Mang prompted, looking at Prosky.

"I'll have the same as Sister Michelle," Prosky answered. "I'd also like a bowl of chicken soup and a cup of regular coffee with dessert."

"And for you, Father?" the waiter requested, looking cautiously at Conyngham.

"I'll have the fruit plate as an appetizer, Caesar Salad without anchovies, New York Strip Steak – well done, vanilla ice cream, and decaffeinated coffee," Conyngham quickly responded.

"Thank you very much," Mang closed, gathering the menus and quickly walking away from the table.

By the time everyone emptied the breadbasket, Mang returned. As he began serving their first courses, Carlo approached the table with another passenger.

"*Mi scusi,*" Carlo interrupted, as he pulled an empty chair away from the table and offered it to another priest who just entered the dining room. "The *padre* just arrived for dinner, and I knew he would be welcome here."

"Of course," Prosky said. "Please join us."

"By all means," Conyngham added. "Any friend of *Carlo Scusi Vusi* is a friend of ours."

"Paul Thielemans," the priest announced, shaking hands with both priests and waving to both nuns.

"I'm Ed Prosky," the elderly priest revealed. "This is Bill Conyngham, Sister Regina, and Sister Michelle."

"Bill Conyngham," Thielemans exclaimed. "Why does your name sound familiar to me?"

"I used to play basketball for the Philadelphia 76ers," Conyngham replied facetiously. "But that was years ago when I was a foot taller and spelled my name differently."

"Don't pay any attention to him," Prosky advised. "The only thing Bill ever played was his record player."

"Seriously, Father, your name is familiar to me," Thielemans insisted, sitting down and folding a napkin over his lap.

"Before my recent retirement, I was on the faculty of Georgetown University," Conyngham revealed. "I was Professor Emeritus of Biochemistry."

"That's why I recognized your name," Thielemans realized. "I read the Georgetown University newspaper whenever I return home to Alexandria, and I remember reading an interview you gave not too long ago."

"It was probably the one about female students on Catholic college campuses using birth control pills," Conyngham surmised.

"That's the one," Thielemans confirmed. "I remember how you condoned the use of birth control pills by female students because of the different medical conditions they can be used to treat, like ovarian cysts and serious acne."

"I also condoned their use as an effective way to prevent young girls from getting pregnant," Conyngham quipped.

Caught off guard by Conyngham's unexpected remark, Thielemans nodded, forced a smile, and opened his menu.

"Well, I guess I'd better pick out something to eat before they start serving breakfast," Thielemans joked. "You'll have to excuse my intrusion here tonight. I'm on the 'As You Wish' dining program, and this was the only available table. I would have come earlier, but I had a long, hectic day and fell asleep while we were leaving San Diego. Fortunately, I woke up before the dining room closed."

"We're delighted to have you join us, Father," Sister Regina said with a smile. "I'll bet you're a member of the Apostleship of the Sea and have been brought on to the ship to say Mass during our cruise."

"I'm afraid I don't belong to that group," Thielemans politely replied. "I haven't been brought on to the ship to say Mass, but I would be happy to do so if asked."

"Regina, I'm surprised you don't recognize Father Paul Thielemans," Prosky interjected. "This man is famous. He writes books that are bestsellers, and is always on television and in the newspapers."

"*Mea culpa,*" Sister Regina whispered, as she bowed her head and lightly touched her chest with her right hand.

"No need for that, Sister," Thielemans said. "Father Prosky is much too kind. I'm not quite the rock star he makes me out to be."

"So, what made you decide to take a cruise?" Sister Regina inquired.

"I'm hoping to combine some business with pleasure," Thielemans revealed. "I'm going to Honolulu to deliver the keynote speech at the American bishops' conference. After that, I plan to get some rest and enjoy the sights."

Hearing Thielemans' revelation, Conyngham lightly elbowed Prosky in the ribs.

"Father, are you ready to order?" Mang asked, as he approached the table.

"I'll have the braised short ribs and cheesecake with raspberry sauce for dessert," Thielemans answered with a smile. "Also, would you please ask the wine steward to come to the table?"

"Very good," Mang exclaimed, signaling a sommelier.

"You didn't order very much," Sister Regina observed.

"I got here late and didn't want to delay your dinner any more than I already have, Sister," Thielemans explained considerately. "If I'm still hungry later, I can always order room service."

"You haven't delayed anything," Prosky insisted.

"Yeah, you haven't delayed much," Conyngham added sarcastically. "It took *Scusi Vusi* thirty minutes to find us the most out-of-the-way table on the entire ship."

As everyone at the table laughed, a short, dark-haired sommelier approached.

"Good evening, everyone," she said. "My name is Penny. May I get you some wine this evening?"

"You certainly may," Thielemans responded enthusiastically.

Quickly perusing the wine list, the priest looked at each of his dinner companions.

"I'm buying," Thielemans announced. "What would everyone like?"

"I could murder a glass of dry, red wine about now," Conyngham revealed.

"That sounds good to me," Prosky added.

"Thank you, Father, but I don't drink," Sister Regina whispered.

Sister Michelle looked at Prosky as if to solicit permission to have a drink. Not receiving any confirmation, she turned toward Thielemans and smiled.

"I'd better not," the young nun answered politely. "Thank you anyway, Father."

"We'll have a bottle of this Cabernet Sauvignon," Thielemans indicated, pointing to a particularly expensive wine on the list before glancing back at Sister Michelle.

"Excellent choice," Penny exclaimed, as she smiled, took Thielemans passenger card for payment processing, and quickly walked away from the table.

"What about you, Father Prosky?" Thielemans inquired. "Were you also affiliated with Georgetown?"

"Are you kidding?" Conyngham interrupted. "The Jesuits have standards, you know."

"I recently retired as a consultant to the National Institutes of Mental Health in Bethesda, Maryland," Prosky explained, ignoring Conyngham's banter. "However, the N.I.M.H. was my second career. I spent the first twenty years of my priesthood with the Congregation of the Servants of the Paraclete and worked at the congregation's main treatment facility in Jemez Springs, New Mexico."

"Why did you leave New Mexico?" Thielemans asked.

"The Jemez Springs facility ceased its treatment operations in 1995," Prosky stated. "So, I returned to school to get my doctorate in clinical psychology. By the time I received my degree, the congregation had already closed most of its remaining facilities. That allowed me to pursue professional activities outside the congregation. I joined the N.I.M.H. in 1998, and retired last year."

"Is that all you did?" Thielemans joked.

"Not quite," Prosky chuckled. "During my tenure with the N.I.M.H., I continued my priestly duties, saying Mass and hearing confessions at understaffed churches in Maryland on weekends. I also maintained a small private practice that was devoted exclusively to the care of priests and nuns."

"Quite impressive," Thielemans exclaimed. "You know, Father, I'm fascinated by the word, 'paraclete.'"

"You and everyone else," Prosky admitted. "The term, 'Paraclete,' which is spelled with an uppercase letter, 'P', is a name given to the Holy Spirit. This is the religious definition of the word. The word, 'paraclete,' which is spelled with a lowercase letter, 'p', describes a person who serves as an advocate or helper. This is the secular or legal definition of the word. So, our congregation served in the name of the Holy Spirit who is **'THE'** Paraclete. Each of us in the congregation served as an advocate or helper of impaired priests and brothers. In that capacity, each member of our congregation was **'a'** paraclete."

"Very interesting," Thielemans said. "What type of impairments did the congregation treat?"

"When the congregation was founded in 1947, it treated priests and brothers who were addicted to alcohol, drugs, or women," Prosky replied. "Eventually, our treatment center became a depository for pedophiles who were unable to be rehabilitated but expected by their dioceses to be treated nonetheless. This led to problems that eventually led to lawsuits and the congregation being forced to close its treatment facilities."

"Were you there when the tide turned against the congregation?" Thielemans asked.

"Not really," Prosky answered. "I first became interested in the congregation while I was attending the Immaculate Heart of Mary Seminary from 1970 to 1974. The seminary was located in Santa Fe, and the congregation's main treatment facility was only a stone's throw away in Jemez Springs. I officially joined the congregation in 1975 and left in 1995. I wasn't there when the tide turned, but I mean to tell you I was certainly there when the floodgates opened and all hell broke loose."

Prosky took a sip of wine and stared at Thielemans who found himself in the unfamiliar position of not knowing what to say. Sensing the uncomfortable silence, Conyngham decided to change the subject.

"So, Father Thielemans, how does one get asked to present the keynote address at a conference of American bishops?" Conyngham asked inquisitively.

"It has a lot to do with who you know," Thielemans conceded. "I have the attention of a few influential bishops who just happen to like what I do."

"When you're not writing or schmoozing with bishops, what do you do?" Conyngham inquired. "I know you used to teach at Catholic University."

"I still do," Thielemans replied. "I lecture there when I'm working on a new book. When the book is published, I go back on the lecture circuit. I answer to the Archdiocese of Mechelen-Brussels but have no obligations there."

"It must be nice," Conyngham quipped.

"It is," Thielemans admitted with a deliberate smile.

As more food and wine were brought to the table, everyone concentrated on enjoying the delicious meal and making small talk with the waiters. By the time everyone was ready for dessert, most of the other passengers had already finished eating and exited the dining room.

"So, what is the theme of the talk you'll be giving at the bishops' conference?" Prosky asked.

"My talk will be based on my latest book, *Catholicism Astray*," Thielemans explained. "I plan to present the findings of my book and invite the bishops to participate in a program I hope to implement in their dioceses. The program calls for participating parishes to cancel Saturday night Masses and offer Latin Masses one Sunday a month," Thielemans said. "It also encourages the members of the parishes to voluntarily refrain from eating meat on the Friday of the same weekend. The goal of the program is to see if non-practicing Catholics will return to the Church when older traditions are restored."

Hearing Thielemans explaining his program, Prosky and Conyngham quietly stared at each other.

"Father Thielemans, I'm afraid I have to disagree with the major premise of your book," Conyngham stated. "Both Ed and I have already read and discussed *Catholicism Astray*. Personally, I don't believe most Catholics who no longer attend Mass or receive the sacraments do so because the Church has become too lax with its rules. Nor do I believe hearing the Gregorian Chant on Sundays once a month is going to bring truly disenchanted Catholics back into the fold. The reason Catholics have turned away from the Church is not because of Mass in the vernacular, Masses on Saturday night, or an insatiable desire to eat steak every Friday night. The reason Catholics have turned away from the Church is because the Church turned its back on these people when they needed God the most."

"Why do you say that?" Thielemans asked.

"The world continues to change, but the Church has failed to change with it," Conyngham replied. "For example, the Church has treated divorce as some kind of grievous offense against the Law of God rather than what has become a societal norm. It has allowed divorced Catholics to come to Mass and put money in the collection basket, but not receive Holy Communion or remarry as Catholics unless they've had their marriages annulled."

"You know the Church's position," Thielemans countered. "Once Catholics marry, they marry for life,"

"Of course, I know the Church's position," Conyngham argued. "I also know no woman should ever have to live in fear of being beaten by her husband or watching her children being abused or neglected. Likewise, no man should ever have to live under the same roof with an unfaithful wife. Our society's answer to serious marital discord is divorce. If divorce is the only protection for Catholics who are in bad marriages, the Church must become more understanding and less punitive. Every time a priest refuses Holy Communion to a divorced Catholic, the Church turns its back on another member."

"But divorced Catholics can receive the sacraments once their marriages are annulled," Thielemans suggested.

"That's true," Conyngham conceded. "Unfortunately, annulments are a separate process from civil divorce, take a lot of time, and until recently, cost a lot of money. What's more, annulments accomplish nothing more than civil divorce other than allowing the dissolution of a marriage to be officially sanctioned by the Church."

"Divorced Catholics are just one group the Church has turned its back on," Prosky interjected. "The Church has also turned its back on homosexuals. The Church has deprived homosexuals of the sacraments, but conveniently allowed other homosexuals to remain in the priesthood."

Thielemans stared at Prosky without disagreeing.

"Would you like to hear more?" Prosky asked.

"Please, continue," Thielemans requested.

"For longer than you've been alive, I've also watched the Church refuse to change," Prosky observed. "There once was a day when large families were the norm rather than exception. Some were so large the children had to raise each other. Those were the same days when a wealthy Catholic man could bury his wife after a dozen pregnancies finally killed her, remarry a younger woman, and do the same thing all over again with the full blessings of the Church. Fortunately, those days are long gone."

"Amen to that," Conyngham exclaimed.

"Unfortunately, the American housewife has become an anachronism," Prosky continued. "Today, most married couples have to work, and while they're still in the early stages of their marriages, starting families may be difficult or impossible for any of a number of valid reasons. Forbidding thoughtful contraception is another way the Church has refused to keep up with the changing times."

"Amen," Conyngham repeated.

"Women are also starting to have babies later in life," Prosky added. "At a certain point, their doctors are recommending tubal ligations because of the potential risks older women face if they become pregnant. Other doctors are recommending the husbands of these older women have vasectomies. By forbidding these procedures, the Church continues to turn its back on its members."

"For the record, the Church recognizes the needs of its members and does allow the Rhythm Method as a means of contraception," Thielemans argued. "It also recognizes the role of doctors in determining the need for medical procedures, such as tubal ligations, and does not try to undermine the authority of the medical profession when a woman's health is at stake."

"I'm glad you said that," Prosky countered. "By endorsing the Rhythm Method as a means of contraception, the Church has formally acknowledged the existence of circumstances in which Catholics may not be ready or able to have children. However, by allowing one method of birth control to the exclusion of others, the Church has been illogical, if not hypocritical. How can the Church teach and sanction the Rhythm Method as a method of contraception when it forbids the use of condoms and birth control pills because they are contraceptives?"

Prosky paused and took another sip of wine.

"Father, abortion is a sin," Prosky continued. "Certain forms of contraception, such as I.U.D.s, achieve the same result as abortion by interfering with the development of an existing conception. Condoms and birth control pills, on the other hand, do not destroy anything. They merely prevent conception from occurring which is the very same thing the Rhythm Method theoretically does."

"During the sacrament of Matrimony, Catholics promise to freely accept children," Thielemans responded.

"Using condoms or birth control pills for limited times during their marriage does nothing to break that promise," Prosky opined. "Neither does obtaining a tubal ligation or vasectomy after a husband and wife have already had their family. The spirit of the promise to freely accept children supports the purpose of marriage which is to procreate. The spirit of the purpose doesn't extend to having more children than a couple can realistically raise or having children at the expense of a mother's health or life."

"This is your opinion," Thielemans suggested.

"Father, I am a follower of Jesus Christ," Prosky proudly stated. "Whenever I'm confronted with an ethical dilemma, I ask myself how Christ would handle the same dilemma if He still walked the earth. I can't imagine Christ advising His followers to start families when they were not ready or able to do so. Nor can I imagine Christ telling a 40-year-old woman to continue having children despite medical conditions that might make carrying another child dangerous for her or the child itself. I don't believe there is anything sinful or immoral about tubal ligations, vasectomies, condoms, or oral contraceptives. I do believe birth control is a matter of the same conscience every individual has the right and obligation to follow."

"There are times when birth control is also a matter of necessity," Conyngham added. "Pope Francis recently supported the use of condoms in countries where Zika epidemics were occurring."

"I know," Thielemans concurred.

"In my not-so-humble opinion, Pope Francis did the right thing," Conyngham said. "Zika can be transmitted through sexual intercourse and cause severe birth defects and retardation in children born to women infected with the virus. By allowing the use of condoms, Pope Francis set a new precedent for the Church that may lead to a complete rethinking of the entire matter of contraception."

"We'll see," Thielemans replied. "The Catholic tradition supports abstaining from sex rather than resorting to any form of contraception."

"Tell me you're joking," Conyngham laughed. "We're living in the 21st century. Like it or not, sex is here to stay, and the sooner the Church leaves the Middle Ages and catches up with the rest of the world, the sooner Catholics will start returning to Mass."

"The Church's teaching on human sexuality is one of the tenets that separate Catholicism from every other religion," Thielemans argued.

"I'm sure you're aware of the fact Roman Catholicism has the most followers of any religion in the United States," Conyngham offered. "I'm sure you also realize non-practicing Catholics represent the second-largest religious group in the country. There are reasons for this."

"I understand what you're saying," Thielemans conceded. "That's why I wrote *Catholicism Astray*."

"Father, you say the purpose of your book is to restore Church membership," Prosky reiterated. "I'll tell you how I'd restore it. First of all, I'd allow priests to marry. This would dramatically increase the number of men entering the priesthood. Many men feel they have a vocation to the priesthood but don't pursue their vocation because of a desire to marry and have families. Allowing such men to marry would expand the priesthood and increase Church membership, as would reinstating the thousands of priests who previously left the priesthood to marry. When these priests returned to the Church with their families, the Church would have the necessary manpower it required to help restore activities it had been previously forced to curtail or abandon. When many of these activities were restored by the Church, many non-practicing Catholics would return to the fold."

"Father, let me also remind you Catholic priests married from the time of the Church's founding through the Middle Ages," Conyngham interjected. "Saint Peter and other apostles were married and had families. Some popes were the sons of popes. The Church tried imposing celibacy on clergymen from as early as the 4th century, but despite numerous Church decrees, priests continued to marry and father children well into the 10th century when the number of married priests reached an all-time high."

"That's right," Prosky concurred.

"In an attempt to increase its wealth during the 11ᵗʰ century, the Catholic Church prohibited clergymen from bequeathing property to their children," Conyngham continued. "A few decades later, the Church underwent the Great Schism which created what are today the Roman Catholic Church and the Eastern Orthodox Churches. In the 12ᵗʰ century, the Roman Catholic Church officially prohibited priests from marrying, but priests once again ignored the decree and continued to marry. It wasn't until the 16ᵗʰ century that priestly celibacy, as reaffirmed at the Council of Trent, finally became the norm throughout the Roman Catholic Church."

"The Council of Trent also recognized celibacy as the sign of a priest's devotion to God," Thielemans argued. "So, there are religious reasons for celibacy."

"Meh," Conyngham mumbled.

"Have either of you ever wished you were married?" Thielemans asked curiously.

Prosky and Conyngham looked at each other, seemingly saddened by Thielemans' inquiry.

"Before we answer your question, I'd like you to answer one of mine," Conyngham requested. "Do you know why Ed and I are taking this cruise to Hawaii?"

"No, I don't," Thielemans admitted.

"We're both dying of cancer," Conyngham revealed. "This is probably the last vacation either of us will ever take. Ed and I have metastatic prostate cancer. We've been undergoing treatment for several years. We both have so many chemicals and so much radiation in our bodies that we can't cross most state lines without first getting written permission from the Environmental Protection Agency."

"The real pity of the whole thing is our cancers probably could have been prevented," Prosky added.

"How?" Thielemans asked.

"If Bill and I had not played by Church rules and not remained celibate, we may have never developed prostate cancer," Prosky replied. "That's why Bill and I believe the Church predisposed us to acquiring our disease by not allowing us to marry or become sexually active. Protestant ministers are followers of Jesus Christ, and most of them marry and have families. So, there's no good reason Catholic priests shouldn't be allowed to marry."

Hearing about the priests' cancers left Thielemans momentarily speechless.

"I'm sorry to hear about your problems," Thielemans responded with obvious sincerity. "It's not my position to question your opinions about the causes of cancer, but I was under the impression medical research had already proved celibacy protected males against cancer of the prostate rather than predisposing them to the disease."

"I wish that was the case," Prosky lamented.

"I have a younger brother who is a medical doctor with a lot of research experience," Conyngham interjected. "I reviewed the study you're referring to with my brother, and he was critical of the study's methodology. It seems the authors of that particular study reviewed death certificates to determine the causes of death of a thousand or so Catholic priests. According to my brother, death certificates frequently cite diagnoses other than cancer as a cause of death, even when the deceased had cancer. In hospitals, death certificates are frequently signed in the middle of the night by tired on-call doctors or residents who never treated the patient. So, even if a priest had prostate cancer, the disease may not have been indicated on his death certificate. Instead, the document may have cited a heart attack, stroke, or something else as the cause of death. Seeing non-cancer diagnoses listed as causes of death could have made the researchers erroneously conclude the priests in the study didn't die from prostate cancer and their celibacy protected them from the disease."

Conyngham paused to take a sip of water, and Thielemans patiently waited for the priest to continue.

"Another problem my brother had with the study was its inability to confirm a lifetime of celibacy from a death certificate," Conyngham added. "He also pointed out a significant number of priests in the study could have had prostate cancer and not known it at the time of their deaths. This would have also affected the statistical outcome of the research. After we reviewed the study you're referring to, my brother showed me several more recent studies that concluded sexual activity actually protects males from prostate cancer. One study even concluded, the more frequently a man has sex, the greater his protection."

"Even though Bill is a trained scientist and understands what makes scientific research valid, neither of us needed any research studies to tell us what we already knew," Prosky suggested. "Through the years, we've seen a lot of prostate cancer in the priesthood. We've lost friends and witnessed a great deal of suffering. Bill and I actually met at a support group for priests with cancer several years ago and have been roommates ever since. Nearly half of the priests who attended the sessions had prostate cancer."

"We've lost many good friends to the disease," Conyngham lamented. "So has the priesthood."

"We don't want to trouble you with our problems," Prosky said, as the dining room's imminent closing was signaled by a dimming of the lights. "The point is sex is a gift from God. In truth, it is one of His most beautiful gifts. The Church acknowledges that sex serves two purposes - to create children and alleviate concupiscence. Unfortunately, the Church conveniently downplays the beauty of sex and its many benefits."

"Does anyone even use the word, 'concupiscence,' anymore?" Conyngham quipped. "Why not just say, lust?"

"I beg your pardon," Prosky chuckled. "What the Church has never seemed to realize is there's a lot more lust in the human condition than desire to procreate. So, to answer your original question, I truly regret I never married and had a family. I'm not saying this just because I have prostate cancer which I attribute to my celibacy. I'm saying this because I missed a great deal in life without the companionship of a woman and love of children. Marriage would have prevented much of the loneliness I experienced as a priest."

"Ditto," Conyngham added, reaching for his walker. "I'm firmly convinced I would have been a better priest and a better man if I had a wife and family. I also regret never marrying. That being said, I guess celibacy is a small price for guys like Ed and me to pay so the Vatican can add to its art collection and real estate holdings."

Prosky put his head down and laughed.

"What about you, Sister?" Thielemans inquired.

"The convent is my family, and no marriage could ever replace that," Sister Regina replied with a trembling voice. "I have been Mother Superior to many young women. They are my children."

"This has been very interesting," Thielemans offered, rising to his feet. "I understand a lot of what you're saying, but I still believe in my research and the program I plan to offer at the bishops' conference."

"You know, it's not a sin to agree to disagree," Prosky suggested, grabbing his cane and wiggling out of his chair.

With Carlo leading the way, a small army of waiters approached the table and carefully escorted the party out of the dining room. As the party slowly exited, Thielemans shook the hands of the two priests and Sister Regina.

Before he could offer his hand to Sister Michelle, the beautiful nun stepped away and showed him the peace sign.

"Peace," the surprised clergyman exclaimed, as he returned the peace sign and smiled at Sister Michelle.

With a final wave to everyone, Thielemans walked away from his new acquaintances.

"See you around campus, Rock Star," Conyngham shouted, as Thielemans turned a corner outside the dining room and quickly vanished from sight.

As the party waited for an elevator, the two priests stared at each other and read each other's minds.

"I'll wager you all my surplus plenary indulgences we won't be seeing Father Paul Thielemans again any time soon," Conyngham remarked, breaking the momentary silence.

"I wouldn't be too sure of that," Sister Michelle said with a demure smile and a mysterious look in her eyes.

"You wouldn't be too sure of what?" Conyngham asked. "Seeing Father Thielemans again or my having plenary indulgences?"

"Both," the young nun replied definitively.

Feeling somewhat frustrated by his recent dining experience, Thielemans returned to his suite with an intense desire to savor an ice-cold bottle of Saint Bavo Witbier. Opening his cabin's refrigerator expecting to find the beer he requested, the thirsty priest's jaw dropped when he saw the spacious refrigerator stocked with wall-to-wall cans of Barq's Root Beer.

Removing a root beer from the refrigerator, Thielemans stared at the can and laughed when he realized how much "Barq's Root Beer" sounded like "Bavo Witbier." Realizing his luxury suite's liquor cabinet was well-stocked with premium booze, he stared at his can of root beer and also realized a carbonated, non-alcoholic beverage was about all he could handle at the present time.

"Heaven help us," he mumbled, as he walked toward the balcony and what promised to be a long night of reflection, soul-searching, and unquenchable thirst.

CHAPTER FOUR

Following a restless night and another bizarre dream about Bobby Kucera, Thielemans awoke to a beautiful day at sea. After he perused the cruise's itinerary and realized the Eurodam would be at sea for a total of six days before arriving in Honolulu, Thielemans called Winston to order breakfast and request having all his meals served in his suite until further notice.

The five remaining days before the Eurodam reached the Hawaiian Islands seemed like sufficient time to edit and rehearse the speech he would deliver at the bishops' conference, but without his sister to review and critique his message and presentation, Thielemans realized he would need time to prepare for one of the most important speeches of his career. Realizing the Eurodam's six days at sea would be followed by two days in Honolulu (Oahu), one day in Nawiliwili (Kauai), one day in Kona (Hawaii) with night passage past the Kilauea Volcano, one day in Hilo (Hawaii), one day in Lahaina (Maui), four days at sea, one day in Ensenada (Mexico), and an overnight return to San Diego, Thielemans began to see the completion of his speech as a means to a badly needed vacation.

For the next three days, Thielemans stayed in his suite, fine-tuning the text and delivery of his speech and becoming unwittingly addicted to Barq's Root Beer. To break the monotony of his recent existence without compromising his continued need for solitude, the resourceful priest took early-morning walks on the

Eurodam's outside decks and late-evening strolls through the public areas of the ship's interior.

Awaking on the fifth morning of the cruise, Thielemans realized his speech needed no further preparation. Feeling an urge to end his self-imposed seclusion and start interacting with people again, he shaved, showered, and decided to experience the Eurodam while passengers were occupying its decks and public areas.

Strolling from deck to deck, the gregarious priest went out of his way to exchange pleasantries with crew members and passengers. Finally arriving on the Lido Deck, Thielemans entered the ship's swimming pool area where he saw a group of pool attendants gathering around an elderly gentleman who had slipped and fallen while trying to get into a hot tub.

Approaching the scene of the accident, Thielemans suddenly realized the injured passenger was Father Bill Conyngham. Seeing the elderly priest being helped to his feet by the pool attendants and the priest's walker being fished out of the hot tub by Father Ed Prosky, Thielemans prepared to offer his assistance.

"Father, are you hurt?" Thielemans asked, taking hold of Conyngham's arm.

"Is that you, Rock Star?" Conyngham mumbled, as he tried repositioning wet eyeglasses on his face.

"Does that answer your question?" Prosky interjected, positioning a dripping walker in front of his traveling companion. "The man could be drowning, and he'd still think of something sarcastic to say."

"You'd be sarcastic, too, if you felt anything like I have for the past week," Conyngham replied.

"*Mea culpa*," Prosky said. "I know it's been tough."

"What's the problem?" Thielemans questioned.

"Bill has not reacted well to all the salt in the ocean air and water," Prosky explained. "He has been retaining fluid, and this has made his pain worse. We thought a nice hot tub would bring him some pain relief, but he almost killed himself trying to get into the thing."

"How about you?" Thielemans asked.

"My pain has also gotten worse," Prosky admitted. "Fortunately, I've been too busy taking care of Bill to worry about my own problems."

"May I help you?" Thielemans humbly offered.

"Sure," Conyngham snapped. "Did you bring enough bullets to shoot both of us?"

"Follow me," Thielemans instructed. "I think I may able to help both of you without firing a single shot."

"We won't be long, will we?" Conyngham inquired, as he slowly walked with the aid of his walker and Prosky's steadying hand. "We have to start walking through the dining room two hours ahead of time if we want to get to our table in time for dessert."

"Maybe I can help you with that problem as well," Thielemans said with a sly smile.

Taking the elevator two floors down to the Rotterdam Deck, Thielemans led the two elderly priests to his suite.

"It's not much, but it's home," Thielemans joked, as he opened the door to his suite and led his guests inside.

"Holy, Sweet, Loving Mother of Pearl," Conyngham exclaimed, as he entered the Pinnacle Suite. "You could fit a half-dozen of our cabins into this place."

"I'd like to take credit for choosing this suite, but my sister reserved it," Thielemans revealed. "It was supposed to be for both of us. She was my secretary until a family crisis forced her to return to Belgium a week before the cruise."

"I didn't realize cruise ships had cabins like this," Prosky admitted. "You have a bedroom, living room, dining room, pantry, and balcony. This is incredible."

"Here's what I think you'll like most," Thielemans suggested, as he led his guests into one of the suite's two bathrooms. "The suite has a whirlpool bathtub in this bathroom, and a hot tub on the balcony."

"Bill, will you look at this," Prosky requested, as he helped his friend into the bathroom. "Talk about a sight for sore eyes."

"Forget the sore eyes," Conyngham quipped, quickly opening his bathrobe. "Help me get undressed so I can start doing something about my sore arse. I tell you, Rock Star, it's all downhill after the Eighth-Grade Picnic."

The two priests laughed as they helped Conyngham remove his bedroom slippers and Georgetown sweatshirt. Filling the tub with warm water, they eased Conyngham into the tub and turned on the air jets.

"How's that?" Thielemans inquired.

"I can't believe how good this feels," Conyngham replied, draping both arms over the sides of the whirlpool bathtub. "All I need now is a stiff drink."

"What can I get you?" Thielemans asked.

"You've got to be kidding," Conyngham exclaimed.

"Rock stars don't kid," Thielemans said with a smile. "What'll you have?"

"I'll have whatever Ed's having," Conyngham answered.

"Is it noon yet?" Prosky joked.

"Somewhere, but not here," Thielemans observed.

"Then, you'd better make it vodka," Prosky suggested.

"Let's see," Thielemans mumbled, as he walked behind his bar and reviewed the different liquors and spirits on the surrounding shelves. "Vodka, vodka, vodka… Here's one you might like. It's called, 'Grey Goose.'"

"That'll work," Conyngham shouted from the bathroom.

"Yeah, don't fuss," Prosky added. "Grey Goose is good enough for the likes of us."

Filling three glasses with ice cubes and premium vodka, Thielemans looked at Prosky and smiled.

"How about you?" Thielemans asked, as he handed Prosky his drink. "Do you feel like a whirlpool?"

"Not really," Prosky replied. "I think I'd just like to sit on your comfortable sofa, savor my drink, and keep an eye on Bill so he doesn't inhale his potato juice and go teats up in your tub."

Thielemans laughed as he walked into the bathroom.

"Drink this slowly," he advised, handing Conyngham a full glass of vodka. "We'll be sitting within earshot. Call if you need anything - and don't drown."

"I won't drown," Conyngham promised. "If I did, I wouldn't be able to come back for another whirlpool and more booze. Besides, I'm wearing buoyant swim trunks."

Taking a long sip of vodka, Conyngham smacked his lips and looked at his host.

"Here's to you, Rock Star," he said, raising his glass.

"Rock on," Thielemans replied with a pumped fist, as he left the bathroom.

Retrieving his glass of vodka from the bar, Thielemans took a seat across from Prosky.

"*Na zdrowie*," Prosky toasted, raising his glass.

"*Na zdrowie*," Thielemans responded in kind.

"We were starting to worry about you," Prosky revealed, embracing his glass. "When we didn't see you at dinner after the first night, Bill and I thought we might have come on too strong with you."

"Not at all," Thielemans laughed. "You guys aren't the first retired, ultraliberal clergymen who've tried to tag-team me during a theological debate. If anything, meeting you has made me feel stronger about my own beliefs. I'm inspired by the way you and Bill have kept the faith, even though you both disagree with several Church rules."

"That's wonderful," Prosky exclaimed. "You know, Paul, every day is a test of faith. If you still believe in God at the end of the day, you pass today's test and qualify for the one you'll have to take tomorrow."

"Amen," Thielemans agreed, raising his glass.

"And never forget, the Church exists wherever two or more people assemble in the name of Jesus Christ," Prosky added. "The people are the Church, Paul, and every single one of those people has the same right to call themselves a Catholic as any sanctimonious bureaucrat who has taken temporary custody of the Church's rule books."

Thielemans and Prosky clinked their glasses and took long sips of vodka.

"So, where have you been eating dinner the past few nights?" Prosky inquired.

"Right here," Thielemans replied. "Since I saw you last, I've been here in my suite, working on my speech. One of the perks of the Pinnacle Suite is the option to have meals served in the suite's dining room. I decided to stay in my suite until I put the finishing touches on my presentation. That finally happened last night."

"Good for you," Prosky exclaimed with a smile.

"So, tell me more about your experiences with the Congregation of the Servants of the Paraclete," Thielemans requested.

"Sure," Prosky agreed. "The congregation initially began treating impaired religious in New Mexico, but eventually expanded its operations to nearly two-dozen different locations throughout the United States, Europe, South America, Asia, and Africa. When bishops started sending pedophilic priests to the facility, it became obvious the same spiritual approach that worked to rehabilitate alcoholics and drug addicts wouldn't work with pedophiles. The congregation notified the bishops of its inability to cure pedophilia and recommended pedophilic priests be defrocked and not allowed to return to their priestly duties. Some bishops accepted the congregation's recommendations, but others disregarded the recommendations and reinstated their pedophilic priests."

"Why?" Thielemans asked inquisitively.

"Not much was known about pedophilia in the late 1940s and early 1950s," Prosky replied. "Compared to today, pedophilia was thought to be a rarity. Back then, the bishops thought they were dealing with isolated cases and had no idea how widespread pedophilia would become within the priesthood. What's more, our congregation had no legal authority to enforce its recommendations. So, the bishops were left with the option of either accepting the recommendations of an organization whose spiritual methods failed to cure pedophiles or searching until they found mental health professionals who were willing to treat pedophiles and authorize their reinstatement to priestly duties."

"If your congregation freely admitted it couldn't cure pedophilia, why did bishops continue sending their pedophilic priests to your treatment facility?" Thielemans inquired.

"First of all, the bishops had nowhere else to send their pedophiles, and to be sure, they had to send them somewhere," Prosky stated. "They couldn't keep transferring them from parish to parish. The congregation was unique in its willingness and ability to work with impaired religious. So, with little alternative, that's where the bishops continued sending their dirty laundry. The next reason had to do with bishops pressuring the congregation to not only accept pedophiles but to also develop more effective ways to rehabilitate them. Because of this mounting outside pressure, the congregation changed leadership and started relying more on scientific and less on spiritual methods to treat pedophilia."

"How did that work out?" Thielemans asked.

"With time, mental health professionals who believed pedophilia could be cured started working at the congregation's main treatment center," Prosky continued. "The congregation followed their lead and eventually changed its position on pedophilia, accepting the premise certain pedophiles might be cured. With this change in philosophy, the congregation stopped recommending every pedophilic priest be defrocked and started recommending certain pedophiles be allowed to return to priestly life."

"So, where did the congregation go wrong?" Thielemans inquired.

"In my opinion, the congregation went wrong by not sticking to its guns," Prosky stated emphatically. "A few of the first priests to work at the congregation in the late 1940s had it right all along. Pedophiles can't be cured. As they used to say, pedophiles were 'beyond redemption,' and had no place in the priesthood, a parish, or proximity to innocent children. Pedophiles are a different breed, Paul. They're created from a broken mold. I've dealt with every conceivable mental and behavioral disorder, and found no abnormality as futile to treat as pedophilia."

Prosky paused and took a healthy swig of vodka.

"When I first joined the congregation, I heard some of the older priests talking about how the congregation once entertained ideas of transporting pedophiles to a remote island and leaving them there for the rest of their lives," Prosky revealed. "At first, I thought the guys were just pulling my cassock. With time, I began to wonder if there was any truth to the idea because it started making perfect sense to me. It may be hard for you to believe, but in my opinion, pedophiles **are** beyond redemption. They **should** be abandoned on a remote island and never allowed to look at a child again."

"Why do you say that?" Thielemans asked.

"Paul, I closely worked with pedophiles for twenty years at the congregation and studied them for just as many years at the N.I.M.H.," Prosky continued. "During that time, I was charmed by them, conned by them, and with time, appalled by them. I watched pedophiles exhibit perfect behavior to earn weekend furloughs from the congregation's treatment center, and while away from the facility, sexually molest innocent children in nearby towns. I watched pedophiles claim to be cured of their afflictions and volunteer to fill in for sick or vacationing priests at local churches, and when given their reprieve, immediately return to their pedophilic ways. I watched pedophiles do all kinds of unnatural and unspeakable things, and when confronted about their aberrant behavior, claim to be misunderstood, falsely labeled, and deprived of the rights they were granted when they were ordained."

Realizing he was starting to sound angry, Prosky paused and took a deep breath.

"So, to answer your question, the congregation succumbed to the pressure of the bishops and deviated from its original game plan," he continued in a calmer tone of voice. "As a result, sexual predators were released into the wild and given more chances to prey on innocent children. When caught with their pants down, the pedophiles were transferred to other parishes where they continued to stalk, molest, and forever ruin the lives of innocent children and trusting families. The congregation was taken to court on multiple occasions for its role in returning pedophilic priests to parish life and eventually sued out of existence. Today, only renewal centers in Missouri and England remain from what was once a noble, unique, and very necessary organization."

"Would you have done anything differently with your time at the congregation?" Thielemans asked.

"For two long decades, I was an obedient servant of the congregation," Prosky stated. "I did exactly what I was told to do. After all, I was a 'paraclete,' and as such, had dedicated my life to helping others who couldn't help themselves. Unfortunately, it took too long for me to realize the individuals who couldn't help themselves weren't the pedophiles I futilely tried to rehabilitate, but the children whose lives those monsters ruined. So, there is something I would have done differently."

Prosky leaned closer to Thielemans.

"Paul, there are a lot of different ways for a person to die in the deserts of New Mexico," he continued. "There are poisonous snakes, scorpions, and spiders, rodents that carry fatal diseases, and wild animals that have a taste for human flesh. There are lightning storms, flash floods, and treacherous terrain that claim the lives of unsuspecting and unprepared visitors who wander too far. There are also the potentially fatal effects of sun poisoning, dehydration, and accidental injury that frequently befall inexperienced desert explorers. So, if I had to do it all over again, I would have made sure every pedophile at the congregation's treatment center had the opportunity to visit New Mexico's beautiful and mysterious desert – but never return from it."

Thielemans carefully watched as Prosky's facial expression dramatically changed.

"You're not serious," Thielemans exclaimed.

"I'm very serious," Prosky replied with a chilling stare. "Paul, the desert is dynamic. It creates life and takes life. Those who study the desert understand where and when the desert is safe, and where and when it's dangerous. I've carefully studied the desert for more than a quarter-century. I could have easily arranged for the pedophiles I met to take a walk in the desert and never come back. The desert would have been their judge, jury, and executioner, countless children and their families would have been spared the sexual molestations that ruined their lives, and no one would have lost any sleep over the death of any priests who violated their sacred oaths and the most basic tenets of human decency."

Thielemans was visibly unnerved by his guest's unexpected comments.

"But what about the commandment that orders us not to kill?" he inquired.

"I'm a big fan of the commandment," Prosky said with a fresh smile. "However, the commandment applies to humans. It doesn't apply to animals or pedophiles who may belong to some race - but not the human race. Even if the commandment did have a provision for pedophiles, I doubt the good Lord would hold against anyone those actions intended to save the life of an innocent child."

Prosky paused and took another sip of vodka.

"Maybe it's the old man in me talking, my subconscious trying to get out, or just the booze, but I'm serious when I say I'd never give another pedophile the chance to hurt a child, a family, or Holy Mother Church," Prosky vowed. "Interpret the Ten Commandments as you will, but always remember there are certain sins that are more contemptible than others. No sin is greater than violating the innocence of a child, not even the elimination of someone who has forfeited the right to live because of their inhuman behavior."

"Let's just say you helped a pedophile get lost in the desert, and as a result, they died," Thielemans proposed hypothetically. "How would you feel if it was later proven the pedophile wasn't a pedophile, but an innocent priest who had been falsely accused?"

"Paul, innocent priests have been falsely accused of being pedophiles, especially since the courts have declared open season on priests and allowed their alleged victims to be awarded huge sums of money in lawsuits against the dioceses," Prosky replied. "Some of these priests did nothing more than innocently hug or touch a child. Fortunately, frivolous claims and lawsuits against innocent priests have a way of ending as soon as the plaintiffs realize they'll have to go to court and convince a jury they were sexually molested by a priest. Innocent priests are usually vindicated when their accusers discover they won't be receiving money for just inventing a phony story and hiring a crooked lawyer. Back in the old days, priests frequently coached parochial school basketball and baseball teams. No one ever thought twice about a priest patting a kiddo on the rump and giving him an encouraging word as the youngster was entering a ball game. Today, the same innocent gesture would be considered pedophilia. So, I would have never had an opportunity to interact with a priest who had been falsely accused of being a pedophile. Innocent priests were correctly identified by their dioceses and never sent to our treatment facility. The characters we treated were five-star perverts whose diagnoses and guilt were never in question."

As Prosky smiled and gave Thielemans a reassuring look, loud cries were heard in the bathroom.

"Help!" Conyngham shouted. "Help!"

Thielemans and Prosky rushed into the bathroom to find Conyngham smiling and shaking his glass.

"Help me, please," the elderly priest requested. "I need a refill."

"You don't need a refill," Prosky argued, as he coaxed his friend out of the whirlpool bathtub. "You need to get out before you start looking more like a prune than usual."

"How are you feeling?" Thielemans asked.

"I feel wonnderrrfullll," Conyngham slurred with a tipsy smile. "What I need now is a nap."

"Let's get him dressed and over to the sofa," Thielemans suggested, reaching for a towel and

Conyngham's clothing. "He can rest here for a while. In the meantime, I want to call my cabin steward and have him send tonight's dinner menus to your room. I'd like the two of you and the sisters to dine with me here tonight. All I need to know is what time you'd like to have dinner and your cabin numbers."

"Paul, you don't have to go through all this trouble for us," Prosky said graciously. "You've already been too kind."

"Ed, let the man go through all the trouble he wants," Conyngham mumbled, clinging to his friend.

"Bill, you're starting to get pickled," Prosky observed.

"But I'm not feeling any pain," Conyngham slurred. "I can't remember the last time I felt this good."

Thielemans smiled as he and Prosky walked Conyngham to the sofa and helped him get comfortable.

"So, what time would you like to eat?" Thielemans asked. "How about 7 o'clock?"

"That would be great," Prosky replied enthusiastically.

"What's your cabin number?" Thielemans inquired.

"Let's see," Prosky stalled. "I think we're in 7121, and the sisters are in 7125. We're at the far end of this deck."

Thielemans nodded and phoned his cabin steward.

"Winston, this is Father Paul in Suite 7036," he began. "I'd like to dine with four guests in my suite this evening at 7 o'clock. Could you arrange this?"

"Of course, Father Paul," Winston responded. "Where would you like me to send the menus?"

"Send a menu and wine list to me, and also send menus to Cabins 7121 and 7125," Thielemans requested.

"Consider it done," Winston promised. "I'll stop by at 6:30 to clean your suite and prepare the dining room."

As soon as Thielemans hung up the phone, Prosky asked to use it.

"I'll need some help getting Bill back to our cabin," he suggested, dialing Sister Michelle's stateroom. "He could probably use a long nap, and I don't want to tie up the rest of your day."

"Nonsense," Thielemans replied. "It's my pleasure to spend time with you. If the whirlpool and drink helped Bill as much as he said, we'll have to do this again."

Prosky smiled and waited for his call to be answered.

"Michelle, it's me," the priest began. "What are you and Regina doing right now?"

"Regina's taking a nap, and I'm dying from heat exhaustion," the nun protested. "She complained of being cold again after breakfast and made me call the front desk. A maintenance man just left. He checked the thermostat and vents for the third time this cruise and told us the heating and air conditioning were working perfectly. It feels like 100 degrees in here right now, and she's still wearing a sweater and complaining of being cold."

"I may have a temporary solution to your problem," Prosky suggested. "If she's sound asleep, bring her wheelchair to Cabin 7036 as soon as you can. It's on our deck, just down the hall from us. We're here with Father Thielemans who has been kind enough to share his whirlpool bathtub and bar with us this morning. Bill is three sheets to the wind, and we'll have to wheel him back to our cabin. Once again, we're in Cabin 7036."

"I'll be right there," Michelle said enthusiastically.

Quickly brushing her hair and covering it with a veil, she quietly exited the cabin with a wheelchair in tow. A few seconds later, she returned and quickly removed her veil.

As she started to leave the cabin for the second time in as many minutes, she looked at herself in the mirror, placed the veil back on her head, and quietly left.

In less time than it took for the young nun to decide whether to wear a veil, she pushed her roommate's wheelchair to Thielemans suite. Ringing the doorbell, she straightened the jacket of her pantsuit and took firm hold of the wheelchair handles.

"Thank you for coming," Thielemans said, as he opened the door to his suite and greeted Sister Michelle.

"Sure," his guest answered, as she entered the suite and appeared dumbfounded by its unexpected ambience.

"Are you all right, Kiddo?" Prosky asked, as he watched the young nun react to the grandeur of Thielemans' suite. "You look like you need a wheelchair."

"I'm fine," Sister Michelle replied, as she continued to study the suite, wide-eyed and at a loss for words. "I just didn't realize there were cabins like this on a cruise ship."

"I'm glad you approve," Thielemans remarked, as he tried unsuccessfully to make direct eye contact with the nun. "Since you seem to like my suite so much, I think your entire party should come back and have dinner with me here this evening."

"Sure," his guest mumbled unemotionally, as she continued inspecting the suite.

"Your invitation hasn't registered with her yet," Prosky observed, as he pulled the wheelchair closer to the sofa and gave Conyngham a gentle tug. "I'm sure it will eventually."

After Prosky helped his groggy roommate into the wheelchair and Sister Michelle finally completed her unguided tour of the Pinnacle Suite, Thielemans held the door for his departing guests.

"Thanks again, Paul," Prosky said gratefully, as he pushed the wheelchair into the hallway. "See you tonight."

"Later, Dude," the inebriated wheelchair passenger added, giving a high-five and missing Thielemans' hand.

As an overwhelmed Sister Michelle walked toward the door with Conyngham's folded walker and Prosky's cane in hand, Thielemans looked into her eyes, smiled, and offered her the peace sign.

"Yeah, peace to you," the anxious nun replied, fumbling the walker and cane, returning the priest's peace sign, and then, awkwardly reaching out to shake his hand.

"Peace," Thielemans responded, as he shook Sister Michelle's hand and watched her leave his suite.

Thielemans spent the rest of the day reviewing his itinerary and realizing he still had to reserve rental cars on each of the islands and go over a few last-minute details with the Hawaii Convention Center, the site of the bishops' conference. Before she returned to Belgium, his sister saw to such things, and Thielemans realized how much he missed the companionship of his sister, as well as the capable assistance she routinely provided.

Promptly at 7 o'clock, Prosky and company, who were all dressed in conventional religious attire, rejoined the casually-dressed Thielemans for dinner. Meals prepared exactly as ordered, impeccable service, and friendly conversation ruled the evening.

Thielemans and his fellow priests also enjoyed different wines with each course. With each new wine service, Sister Regina reminded everyone she didn't drink and Sister Michelle graciously declined, although she appeared willing and able to sample her fair share of fine wine under different circumstances.

Throughout the evening, Thielemans skillfully directed much of the conversation away from the priests and toward the nuns. As a result, he learned Sister Regina had been Mother Superior of her religious order for several decades and only recently agreed to move from Baltimore to a Catholic retirement community in Florida. This cruise and a large nursing home endowment were retirement gifts from a group of generous benefactors who helped maintain her order's financial stability during her years of leadership.

Thielemans also learned Sister Michelle was Sister Regina's niece in secular life and special assistant in religious life. The beautiful, young nun was accompanying her aunt to Hawaii as a part of her religious duties. She was also accompanying Prosky who, as her psychotherapist, had recommended the cruise as a means of her preparing emotionally for an inevitable reassignment by her order. Serving as her aunt's special assistant was the only position Sister Michelle ever held in the convent, and the idea of being ordered to accept a different position, with different responsibilities, expectations, and supervision, proved to be very unsettling for the young nun.

Following dinner, a round of Macallan scotch, and some small talk, Thielemans' guests offered their sincere thanks and enthusiastically accepted their host's invitation for future whirlpools, dinners, and drinks. As they were leaving, Thielemans thanked each of them for coming and liberally flashed the peace sign.

In return, Sister Michelle looked into Thielemans' eyes, returned the peace sign, and made a fist with her right hand. Thielemans bumped fists with the young nun which immediately brought a smile to her face.

For the next few hours, Thielemans sat on the quiet balcony and relaxed with the moon, stars, and ocean for company. Nursing another glass of single malt scotch, he thought about his dinner guests and tried to piece together the seemingly unrelated facts he learned about Sister Michelle.

Thielemans knew Sister Michelle had finished high school before she was talked into joining the convent by her aunt, but couldn't understand why the only position she ever held in the convent was serving as her aunt's special assistant. He also realized Prosky maintained a small psychology practice, limited to the care of priests and nuns, but couldn't understand why Sister Michelle required psychotherapy.

Being an astute observer, Thielemans sensed a profound reliance on Prosky by Sister Michelle, as well as some kind of mutual understanding between Prosky and Sister Regina. Sister Michelle looked at Prosky for permission whenever wine was offered to her and appeared disappointed when she was signaled to decline the offer. In turn, Prosky looked at Sister Regina to seek silent approval in decisions concerning her niece.

As Thielemans finished his scotch and continued watching the moonlight gracefully dancing across the ocean, his mind wandered from thoughts of his dinner guests to concerns about his upcoming speech to recollections of Bobby Kucera. When he finally grew tired of thinking, he propped his feet up on another chair, closed his eyes, and concentrated on the peaceful sounds of the waves and sea breeze.

Just as Thielemans started to get comfortable, he was startled by the chiming of the suite's doorbell. Gently placing his glass on a nearby table, he made his way to the cabin door.

Opening the door, Thielemans discovered Sister Michelle, dressed in a gray tee-shirt, matching jogging shorts, and white flip flops – but no veil.

"Can I sleep with you tonight?" Michelle asked expectantly.

Thielemans quickly looked out into the hallway to see if anyone was watching, gently pulled Michelle into his suite, and promptly closed the door.

"Did you just ask if you could sleep with me tonight?" Thielemans inquired, fully realizing Michelle's query was more innocent than it sounded.

"Uh-huh," Michelle replied.

"Don't you think this is a bit premature, Sister Michelle?" Thielemans suggested facetiously. "Shouldn't we first obtain some sort of dispensation from the Church that allows priests and nuns to marry or otherwise alleviate each other's concupiscence?"

"You're joking with me, aren't you," Michelle observed. "You know I didn't mean what you thought I said. I didn't ask if you wanted to have sex with me. I just asked if I could sleep in your room tonight."

"Let's talk about this," Thielemans recommended.

"Sure," Michelle agreed. "Could I have a drink first?"

"What would you like?" Thielemans asked. "I have root beer, iced tea, sparkling water…"

"How about some of that Grey Goose you and the boys were drinking this morning?" Michelle suggested.

"Are you sure?" Thielemans inquired.

"Would you like to see my driver's license or birth certificate?" Michelle quipped.

"No," Thielemans responded. "It's just that you turned down wine every time we've had dinner together. I thought you were like your aunt and didn't drink."

"It's because of my aunt that I need a drink," Michelle explained. "Grey Goose on the rocks, please."

"So, tell me why you want to sleep here tonight," Thielemans requested, as he filled two glasses with ice and generous pours of Grey Goose.

"Our cabin is 100 degrees right now," Michelle said, as she walked toward the balcony, craving the ocean breeze. "Regina is in our cabin, sleeping with pajamas, a thick sweater, and three blankets, and still shivering like she was in a blizzard on an ice-float during an Arctic winter. I've dealt with it since we got on the ship, but I'm all played out and in desperate need of a friend, a drink, and a few hours' sleep. I've been dreaming of sleeping on your sofa bed with the balcony door open from the moment I walked in here this morning."

"Won't you be missed?" Thielemans asked, as he handed Michelle her glass of vodka.

Before answering his question, Michelle took a healthy swig of Grey Goose, closed her eyes, and savored its delicious taste.

"No, I won't be missed," Michelle guaranteed, quickly taking a second taste of vodka. "Regina sleeps like a rock and wakes up the same time every morning. I'll be back in the cabin before she wakes up and tells me to call the front desk again to complain about how cold our cabin is."

"What would Father Prosky say about your sleeping here tonight?" Thielemans inquired.

"Ed understands me and realizes I wouldn't be asking for this favor if I didn't need it," Michelle answered. "He would let me sleep in his cabin if I asked. Ed is very pragmatic and understands happiness is all about maintaining one's balance in life. He's an independent thinker who sees things for what they are. He tries to understand people within the context of their particular environment."

"Are you sure you don't mind sleeping on the sofa bed?" Thielemans asked. "You can use my bed, and I can sleep on the sofa bed or outside on the balcony."

"The sofa bed will be more than adequate," Michelle insisted. "By the way, thank you for all your kindness. You really are a rock star."

For the next hour, the two sat on the balcony, talking and finishing the bottle of Grey Goose. Thielemans found it very easy talking to Michelle and discussing his concerns about the upcoming conference. Michelle understood Thielemans' need to talk and proved to be a receptive and supportive listener.

When the two finally decided to call it a night, Thielemans retrieved bedding from a closet and opened the sofa bed in the suite's living room. Trading a final smile, peace sign, and high-five with his guest, the tired priest retired to his bedroom.

Once in bed, Thielemans thought about his evening with Michelle before saying a special prayer for her and finally closing his eyes. On the other side of his bedroom door, Michelle was already fast asleep, dreaming of tropical islands, ocean breezes, and a man.

CHAPTER FIVE

After a few hours' sleep, Thielemans awoke to discover an empty living room that had been completely restored to pristine condition. Calling Winston to order breakfast, the priest showered and prepared for the final day before the Eurodam would arrive in Honolulu.

Following breakfast, Thielemans returned to his laptop for another attempt at making rental car reservations over the internet. As in his previous attempts, the technology-challenged priest was able to accomplish little more than locating car rental websites online.

Just as Thielemans realized the futility of his continued efforts and closed his laptop, the doorbell chimed. Looking at the wall clock, he proceeded to the front door.

"Is this a good time for a soak?" Prosky asked from behind Conyngham's wheelchair. "Bill had a rough night."

"Nothing a tub and tonic won't cure," Conyngham added.

"Please, come in," Thielemans responded obligingly, as he watched two priests and one veiled-nun enter his suite.

"I hope you don't mind my inviting Michelle along," Prosky said. "You mentioned all the problems you were having with renting cars online, and I thought Michelle might be able to help you."

"You couldn't have brought help at a better time," Thielemans revealed. "We're one day away from Hawaii, and I still haven't rented any cars or contacted the Hawaii Convention Center to go over last-minute details."

"Just show Michelle what you want her to do, and I'll help Bill get ready for his whirlpool," Prosky advised, as he wheeled Conyngham into the bathroom.

"So, how are you today?" Thielemans asked, as he smiled and looked into Michelle's eyes.

"Never better," Michelle answered confidently.

"Glad to hear it," Thielemans said, as he handed Michelle his laptop. "A good night's sleep is important."

"Tell me about it," Michelle requested. "While you're at it, tell me exactly what you need to have done."

"I need to rent cars for two days in Honolulu, and one day in Nawiliwili, Kona, Hilo, and Lahaina," Thielemans stated succinctly. "I'd like something more formal for Honolulu, and convertibles for the other places. I also have to find a way to contact the Hawaii Convention Center to make sure the beer and glasses arrived. I need the beer chilled and ready to serve when my talk begins."

"Do you have a cell phone," Michelle inquired.

"I do," Thielemans confirmed, as he opened his desk drawer, retrieved an iPhone, and handed it to Michelle. "I've had it set to 'Airplane Mode' since we left San Diego. It's my spare phone, but it's fully charged."

"Where would you like me to work?" Michelle asked, as she opened the iPhone and quickly adjusted the settings.

"The balcony would be fine," Thielemans replied. You can shut the door and have all the privacy you need."

"Cool," Michelle said, as she gathered her equipment and retreated to the balcony.

"How's everything in here?" Thielemans inquired, as he entered the bathroom.

"I've got Bill undressed, and just need some help getting him into the tub," Prosky answered.

Thielemans turned on the water and helped Prosky ease Conyngham into the whirlpool bathtub.

"Fire it up – and don't spare the horses," Conyngham commanded, as he sunk into the tub. "My whole body feels like throbbing cement today."

"Aye, aye, Captain," Thielemans exclaimed, turning on the whirlpool jets. "And what can I get you to drink?"

"Did we finish that bottle of cheap vodka you opened yesterday?" Conyngham joked.

"I'm afraid so," Thielemans confirmed. "Fortunately, the stuff is so cheap, I had my cabin steward throw a few extra bottles into the refrigerator."

"Good idea," Conyngham suggested. "It's better to grab all the cheap booze you can while it's still affordable and there's no Prohibition. It's also better to refrigerate cheap vodka. It improves the taste."

Thielemans poured tall glasses of Grey Goose for Conyngham and Prosky, and after serving the vodka, opened the door to the balcony.

"Ed and Bill are planning to have a drink," Thielemans announced. "Can I get you something?"

Michelle raised her hands to chest level and panted like a puppy.

"I'll have what everyone else is having," Michelle quietly replied with a coy smile.

"Of course, I have Barq's Root Beer," Thielemans loudly proclaimed.

Retrieving two cans of root beer, Thielemans gave one can to his disappointed guest on the balcony, closed the balcony door, and returned to the living room.

"Na zdrowie," he toasted, sitting down and clinking his root beer can against Prosky's vodka glass.

"Na zdrowie," Prosky responded with a big smile. "How come you're not drinking?"

"I've got too much to do today," Thielemans answered. "I'll drink with you tonight when you bring everyone over for dinner."

"Paul, if you're busy, you don't have to entertain us again this evening," Prosky said considerately.

"I know I don't," Thielemans replied. "I'd still like you to dine with me again this evening. I'll be out the next few nights, rubbing elbows with bishops in Honolulu. So, I probably won't be seeing you guys until we leave Kauai a few days from now. We'll have dinner again that night."

"We'll be on and off the ship as well," Prosky revealed. "Michelle handled all our cruise reservations and booked us on tours two days in Honolulu and one day on every other island except Maui. Regina won't be coming on our tours of the Big Island because she'll be spending time with an old friend from her missionary days. The Eurodam docks at piers everywhere but Maui. So, we should be able to get on and off the ship without too much difficulty. Unfortunately, the ship can't dock in Maui, and we won't be able to get on and off the tender passengers have to take to get to Maui. Bill would never make it with his walker, and I'd have a tough time because I rely on my cane."

"I need something," Michelle announced, opening the balcony door. "Do you have a credit card?"

"Of course," Thielemans replied. "Let me get it."

As Thielemans left the living room, Prosky winked at Michelle, and the two bumped fists.

"Use this one," Thielemans advised, as he returned to the living room and handed Michelle a Visa card. "This is a spare card I use for some of my business transactions."

"Cool," she responded, returning to the balcony.

"Paul, you'll never find anyone who has a better business mind or acumen than Michelle," Prosky stated confidently. "She has not only helped Regina take care of their order's business for many years, but she has also helped me with my latest project."

"I thought you were retired," Thielemans quipped.

"Technically, I am retired," Prosky acknowledged. "But, once a paraclete, always a paraclete."

"Why am I not surprised," Thielemans remarked, as he got up from his chair and walked into the bathroom to check on Conyngham.

"How are we doing, Captain?" Thielemans asked, as he watched Conyngham savor a prolonged sip of vodka.

"Better, thanks to you, Rock Star," Conyngham admitted, smacking his lips.

"Just keep your dingy between the navigational beacons," Thielemans said, as he left the bathroom.

"Arrrrrgh," Conyngham grunted.

"So, tell me about your latest project," Thielemans requested, as he returned to the living room and freshened Prosky's drink.

"You know, Paul, I never stopped being a paraclete," Prosky said. "Even while I was at the N.I.M.H., I got involved in various initiatives aimed at identifying sexual predators within the religious community and finding ways to control them. I wasn't the only one, of course. Have you ever heard of *BishopAccountability.org*?"

"No, I haven't," Thielemans admitted.

"The group operates a website that provides a current database of Roman Catholic priests, nuns, brothers, deacons, and seminarians in the United States who have been publicly accused of being sexual predators," Prosky stated. "Type the group's name into any internet search engine to access their website, and you'll be able to read about the offenders, listed by name, diocese, and state."

"Are you personally affiliated with the group?" Thielemans inquired.

"No, I'm not," Prosky replied. "*BishopAccountability.org* provides an internet directory that anyone can access online. What I've done is different. I've helped create a network that allows the reporting of suspicious activity and earlier identification of sexual predators in the Church. *BishopAccountability.org* provides information to the general public. I've been part of a private, underground movement that identifies sex offenders in the Church and removes them months to years before they've had the chance to hurt others and finally become publicly accused of sexual improprieties. Our database is confidential."

"So, how does your group work?" Thielemans asked.

"Through connections with my congregation, law enforcement agencies, Catholic dioceses, members of groups like *BishopAccountability.org*, and the N.I.M.H., I've been able to recruit concerned individuals who agree to share the names of religious who have been suspected, but never publicly accused, of sexual offenses," Prosky answered. "When the name of an individual is forwarded to our group, that name is added to our watch list and surveillance of the individual begins. No member of our group does anything to interfere with the life of the individual under surveillance, violate their civil liberties, or cause others outside our group to become suspicious of the individual. The only thing our members do is notify the group of any current or imminent sexual improprieties. If any impropriety is discovered and substantiated, the matter is turned over to diocesan and law enforcement officials. Our group does not investigate alleged impropriety. We only report such impropriety and allow the diocese and law enforcement agencies to perform the necessary investigations."

"So, your group is a watchdog group," Thielemans suggested.

"We are a watchdog group that has no formal identity, address, or payroll, no public website, and no legal authorities or obligations," Prosky stated. "Our only goal is to get to the sexual predators before they have a chance to hurt more innocent people, especially children."

"How successful have you been?" Thielemans inquired.

"Very successful," Prosky responded with obvious pride. "We have already identified multiple individuals who were in the early stages of pedophilia, as well as multiple attempted cover-ups of pedophilic activity."

"What kind of cover-ups?" Thielemans asked.

"Let me give you an example," Prosky replied. "Our group was recently alerted to a situation in North Carolina. A single mother with five children caught her oldest daughter, a beautiful 14-year-old deaf-mute, having sex with a classmate. She immediately took her daughter to see their parish priest who agreed with the mother that the youngster had committed a mortal sin and appeared to need spiritual guidance and discipline. After a lengthy conversation, the priest, who was skilled in American Sign Language, offered to take the girl under his wing, have her work part-time in the rectory, and attempt to steer her back onto the path of righteousness."

"I see where this is going," Thielemans chuckled.

"Well, the priest, a lonely gentleman in his forties, made it a point to hear the girl's confession every weekend," Prosky continued. "Whenever she confessed another roll in the hay with one of a growing number of boyfriends, the priest granted her absolution, and as a part of her penance, required her to have sex with him to 'return her body to a purified state.' This went on for months until the girl bragged to a younger sister that she had many boyfriends, including the parish priest. When the mother found out about her daughter's unexpected detour from the path of righteousness, she visited the priest and asked him what he planned to do about the situation. Before long, the diocese paid off the mortgage on the mother's home, bought her a new pickup truck, and enrolled the daughter in a school for the deaf in Pennsylvania. The rest of the family got new clothes, and the priest was transferred to a diocese in Florida." '

"How did your group's enhanced surveillance lead to the discovery of the cover-up?" Thielemans inquired.

"For the record, Michelle played a big part in unraveling the cover-up," Prosky revealed. "When our group received a tip about the priest and the young girl, Michelle contacted a nun who used to give C.C.D. religious instructions to public school kiddos who were members of the priest's parish. The nun knew a number of his parishioners, and after making a few phone calls, learned everyone in the small town was surprised to see the deaf child move north, the priest move south, and the financial fortunes of a destitute family suddenly and inexplicably undergo a major reversal. The concerns of our group were shared with diocesan and state officials who investigated the matter and ultimately determined the priest had taken sexual advantage of the young girl. They also determined an individual within the diocese had attempted to cover up the priest's indiscretions. As a result of our work, criminal prosecutions are forthcoming."

"How long has Michelle been aware of your clandestine activities?" Thielemans questioned.

"Michelle has been aware of all my clandestine activities for a very long time," Prosky admitted. "She's also been an important part of them. Why, it was her managerial, computer, and communications skills that helped our group get started. If it wasn't for her, our group would still be in the planning stages."

"Does Michelle share your obvious disdain for pedophiles?" Thielemans asked.

"I certainly hope so," Prosky chuckled.

"What's so funny?" Michelle inquired, entering the living room and closing the balcony door behind her.

"Speak of the devil," Prosky laughed.

"Devil wants a blue dress, blue dress, blue dress," Michelle chanted, as she handed Thielemans a sheet of paper. "Here are your reservations. I've written down each reservation, according to the make of car, rental agency, and location, as well as some important instructions. I did well on the prices because I was able to access a few coupons from the internet, and all prices include unlimited mileage. I made the reservations through a single online discount agency, and although you may be using different rental companies on each of the different islands, all of the companies are located at the same centralized locations."

"This is excellent," Thielemans suggested. "This is just how my sister made all my reservations."

"Pay close attention to the instructions I've written," Michelle urged. "How you'll be getting to the rental car agencies on each island and back to the ship is very important. For example, I got you a Mercedes convertible for two days in Honolulu. You have to take a taxi to the airport to pick up the car at the rental agency and another taxi back to the ship after you return the car. I got you a Camaro convertible in Kauai. Someone from the rental agency will pick you up outside the cruise terminal, and then, bring you back to the ship when you return the car. The same is true for Kona on the Big Island of Hawaii, where I got you a Mustang convertible, and Hilo on the other side of the Big Island, where you'll be getting another Camaro convertible. In Maui, you have to call the rental agency when you get off the tender and arrive at the pier. A van will pick you up and take you to the agency where you'll get your Corvette convertible. Another van will take you back to the pier after you return the car. Got that?"

"Outstanding," Thielemans exclaimed.

"I told you she was good," Prosky boasted.

"Let me call the Convention Center," Michelle said, as she started to leave the living room.

"Can I get you another root beer?" Thielemans asked, tongue-in-cheek.

"No, thanks," Michelle answered with a scowl.

Thielemans chuckled as he walked through his suite.

"How are you doing in here?" he inquired, as he entered the bathroom.

"Surf's Up, Dude," Conyngham slurred.

"Watch out for those sharks," Thielemans advised, as tapped his guest on the shoulder and left the bathroom.

"Will do, Skipper," Conyngham agreed.

Returning to the living room, Thielemans freshened Prosky's drink and sat down.

"With all your experience, can you tell a priest is a pedophile just by looking at him?" he questioned.

"No," Prosky stated succinctly. "I've been wrong many times. The only thing that alerts me to the possibility of a priest being a pedophile or some other kind of sexual predator is not a specific physical feature or type of behavior, but a record of frequent and multiple transfers from parish to parish over a short period."

Prosky paused to take a long sip of Grey Goose.

"Generally speaking, pedophilic priests frequently appear nervous and irritable when they're around unfamiliar people or feel they're being watched," he continued. "Their personalities can also seem to change when they have recently taken advantage of a child. Unfortunately, anxiety, irritability, and personality changes are common problems, and not enough to label a priest a pedophile. What I find much easier to do is identify a child with a history of recent sexual molestation by carefully studying their appearance and behavior."

Thielemans sat back and stared at Prosky. As he thought about the way Father Kittrick appeared and acted at Saint Declan's in San Diego, he realized Prosky could have been thinking about Kittrick when he described some of the features of a pedophilic priest.

"What kind of features make you think a child had been sexually molested?" Thielemans inquired reluctantly.

"Well, there are many different features, and not every child exhibits the same ones," Prosky replied. "As a rule, though, sexually molested children can appear anxious, depressed, unhappy, frightened, listless, shy, unmotivated, quiet, easily distracted, or overly dependent on another person – even the individual who has been sexually molesting them. They can stop taking care of themselves, and appear dirty, disheveled, and poorly dressed. They may even seem unaware they are wearing dirty, malodorous, stained, wrinkled, or torn clothing and shoes."

Prosky paused and took another healthy swig of vodka.

"Children who have been sexually molested can also lose weight, have a poor appetite, experience frequent stomach aches, appear malnourished, and have difficulty urinating or defecating," he continued. "They may also feel the urge to urinate or defecate frequently, experience pain or bleeding with elimination, and spend a lot of time in the bathroom. Sexually molested children may also lose interest in many activities they once enjoyed and show significant declines in their academic performance. These are the features I've seen most often."

Thinking of Bobby Kucera and realizing the young boy had exhibited many of the features Prosky just mentioned, Thielemans sat back and became speechless.

"Are you all right?" Prosky inquired.

"I'm fine," Thielemans said with a manufactured smile. "I just started feeling tired all of a sudden."

"It's probably time for us to head out anyway," Prosky suggested, finishing his vodka with a final sip. "Let me see if Bill is still alive."

As Prosky walked into the bathroom, Michelle walked into the living room from the balcony.

"I'm sorry I took so long," she apologized. "It took me longer than expected to get the convention center manager on the phone. Your talk is still set for 1 o'clock tomorrow. There was some confusion about what you wanted to be done with the beer and glasses. I told the manager you wanted the beer chilled and ready to be served to everyone in attendance at the start of your talk. I also told him to arrange delivery of any unopened bottles of beer and unused glasses to the Eurodam by the end of the day. He assured me any extra beer and glasses would be delivered to the ship as promised."

"Excellent work," Thielemans remarked. "Thank you very much."

"You owe me, big time," Michelle replied with a curious smile and twinkle in her eye.

"Name your price," Thielemans suggested.

"Some other time," Michelle promised, as she handed the grateful priest his credit card, iPhone, and laptop.

"Hold on to these," Thielemans said, handing the credit card and iPhone back to Michelle. "You may need them while you're ashore. Feel free to use them."

"Are we ready to get this show on the road?" Prosky asked, as he led Conyngham out of the bathroom and into his wheelchair.

"Do we have to go?" Conyngham mumbled.

"Just for a while," Prosky replied. "We're coming back for dinner tonight. You'll know it's time when you're fully dressed and not feeling pickled anymore."

As Prosky and Conyngham continued their banter down the hallway, Michelle and Thielemans traded smiles and high-fives.

"Thanks again for all your help," Thielemans reiterated, as he held the door for his departing guest. "I really appreciate it."

"Any time, Rock Star," Michelle responded, as she left the cabin. "Any time at all."

Walking backward, Michelle raised her arms and formed the letters, U and O, and then, pointed to herself.

"You owe me," she verbalized, as she formed the letters again before turning around and continuing down the hall.

CHAPTER SIX

Having traveled extensively, Thielemans beheld some of the world's most beautiful scenery. As he sipped coffee on his balcony and watched the Eurodam approach Honolulu, he wondered if anything was more beautiful than the Hawaiian Islands.

Trying to savor the moment and concentrate on the island's beauty, Thielemans was distracted by thoughts of quickly disembarking the Eurodam as soon as it docked in Honolulu, taking a cab to the airport to pick up his rental car, and driving to the Hawaii Convention Center in time for his keynote address. Taking a final look at Honolulu and a final sip of coffee, Thielemans left the balcony and started to prepare for his imminent disembarkation.

After being forced to wait at the end of a long and slow-moving line of passengers who were exiting the ship, Thielemans finally hailed a taxi van outside the Honolulu cruise terminal. With the meter running, the native van driver, a Sumo wrestler wannabe, who was dressed in a 9XL Hawaiian shirt, beach shorts, and sandals, proceeded to carefully time his drive to hit every red light and navigate every back alley between the cruise terminal and airport.

When he finally arrived at the airport and professed his devotion to the Catholic Church for the third time, the driver made a last-ditch effort to enter the *Guinness Book of World Records* for the longest and most expensive taxi ride through downtown Honolulu. Slowly driving past each of the car rental agencies, the driver suddenly remembered the agency Thielemans needed was located at the opposite end of the airport. This required him to drive to highway H-1, go back an exit, and resume his game of red lights and back alleys until he finally arrived at the right location.

By the time the rental agency located Thielemans' black Mercedes convertible and carefully explained the stack of rental and insurance forms he was required to sign, the anxious priest was finally able to begin his trip to the Hawaii Convention Center. After a long drive in which he unwittingly drove past the facility and had to fight heavy, Saturday morning traffic to return to his destination, Thielemans struggled to find a place to park, raise the convertible top, and lock the Mercedes without setting off its security alarm.

Arriving at the convention center an hour later than he originally planned, Thielemans was able to quickly sign in, set up his PowerPoint, and make sure chilled bottles of Saint Bavo Witbier were ready to be served to each bishop at the start of his talk. With a half-hour left before his speech was scheduled to begin, Thielemans skillfully worked the crowd, renewing acquaintances with several bishops and meeting a few new ones.

As his speech was about to start and Thielemans was being introduced to the large gathering of bishops, waiters served chilled bottles of Saint Bavo Witbier. Teaching the bishops how to get the most flavor out of a bottle of unfiltered beer, Thielemans watched many of the bishops nod their approval, several show signs of confusion when they saw the beer's cloudy appearance, and a few completely abstain from the experiment. Explaining how the second sampling of beer was tastier because the flavorful filtrate was included, Thielemans smiled.

"Even someone who thinks they know everything can always learn something new," he proclaimed.

As most of the bishops laughed, applauded, and took additional sips of beer, Thielemans grinned and prepared to begin his keynote address. When he was sure he had everyone's undivided attention, the renowned speaker began discussing his latest book, *Catholicism Astray,* and plan to renew interest and restore membership in the Catholic Church.

Being a skilled orator, Thielemans knew how to read an audience, and from the very beginning of his speech, he realized he was speaking to a distracted group. Bishops whispering among themselves, looking at their watches, and inspecting their beer bottles and glasses suggested the minds and attention of the bishops were elsewhere.

Although Thielemans received an enthusiastic round of applause at the end of his speech and congratulatory remarks immediately thereafter, he couldn't help but think of Thomas Gray's *Elegy Written in A Country Churchyard.* He wondered if he was one of the flowers Gray described — flowers that were born to blush unseen and waste their sweetness on the desert air. Thielemans felt as though he had just delivered the finest speech of his career, but wondered if his talk had fallen on deaf ears and been wasted, just as the sweetness of Gray's desert flowers.

By previous arrangement, Archbishop Benedetto Palmieri, an official of the U.S. Conference of Catholic Bishops, agreed to meet with Thielemans an hour after his speech to discuss his proposed plan. With time to kill, Thielemans decided to pay a visit to Palmieri's assistant, Monsignor Stanley Janulis, who was in charge of the conference.

Walking inside the convention center's seemingly unoccupied event office, Thielemans smiled as he saw the young monsignor eating a traditional Hawaiian plate lunch of barbecued pork, rice, and beans, and washing everything down with a glass of Saint Bavo Witbier.

"I hope you swirled the bottle and added the spices to that glass of beer," Thielemans joked, as he approached Janulis.

"Of course," the tall, blonde monsignor replied, as he stood up and offered his hand to his unexpected guest. "I learned that trick at your talk today."

"I'm glad someone learned something," Thielemans said sarcastically, as he shook hands with his old friend.

"I think a lot of people learned a lot about their Church today," the monsignor responded.

"How do you think my talk went?" Thielemans inquired with an expectant look on his face.

"Paul, as always, you proved yourself to be one of the most knowledgeable priests in the entire Catholic Church, as well as one of its most gifted writers and skilled orators," Janulis answered convincingly.

"Thank you," Thielemans replied. "I hope my talk lived up to everyone's expectations, but I'm troubled by how pre-occupied many of the bishops seemed."

"Your talk certainly lived up to the expectations of the conference planning committee, and it's obvious you still know how to read an audience," the monsignor observed. "You spoke to a distracted audience today. This sexual abuse mess is the only thing the bishops have been talking about since they got here. Several states plan to release the results of their investigations into sexual abuse by the clergy later this year, and it appears many states plan to go public with the names of guilty clergymen and those who tried to cover up for them."

Janulis paused and stared at Thielemans.

"Understandably, the bishops are worried about the civil and criminal prosecution of those involved, as well as the predictable onslaught of lawsuits against the dioceses," he continued. "So, you can understand why many of the bishops were only listening to you with one ear today. They have so much on their minds that they may not have been able to give your speech the attention it deserved."

Hearing the monsignor talk about sexual abuse, Thielemans immediately thought about Bobby Kucera and Father Kittrick. As he thought about the two, he suddenly remembered Bishop Grannick was Kittrick's uncle.

"Do you know where I might find Bishop Joseph Grannick?" Thielemans inquired.

"He didn't make it to the conference," Janulis replied. "He had urgent matters at home and was forced to cancel at the last minute. In fact, he was the celebrant at the funeral Mass for that altar boy who committed suicide last week in San Diego."

"An altar boy committed suicide in San Diego last week?" Thielemans repeated.

"That's right," Janulis confirmed. "An altar boy, dressed in his cassock and surplice, jumped off a bridge into the San Diego Bay. Haven't you been following the news? The story has been on national television, in the newspapers, and all over the internet."

"No, I haven't been following the news," Thielemans admitted, sitting down at a computer station. "I've been on a cruise ship for the past week. Is there any way you could pull up the story about the boy's suicide on the internet?"

"Sure," the monsignor responded, turning on the computer in front of Thielemans and quickly accessing the internet. "Let's just type in 'San Diego Suicide' on *Google* and see what we get."

In seconds, the links to more than a dozen news reports about the recent San Diego suicide appeared on the computer screen.

"Here are links to the original newspaper story in the *San Diego Union-Tribune,* internet reports, and television news feeds from the Fox, A.B.C., and C.B.S. affiliates in San Diego," Janulis stated. "The television news report at the top of the list is from earlier today."

"Let me see that one, please," Thielemans requested.

As Janulis promptly accessed the television news feed, Thielemans suddenly felt nauseated.

"Could you get me a soda to quiet down my stomach?" the nervous priest asked.

"Certainly," the obliging monsignor replied, leaving the room to find his guest a drink. "I'll be right back."

As a recording of the television news feed began, Thielemans stared anxiously at the computer screen.

"This is Kate Ward, reporting live from Saint Declan's Roman Catholic Church in San Diego," the veteran field reporter with cherry brown hair and a resonating voice began. "Behind me, the casket of young Robert Kucera is being carried from the church, following a concelebrated Mass of Christian Burial. You can see the Mass's celebrant, Bishop Joseph Grannick, standing at the entrance to the church, waiting to receive the boy's casket before it is taken to Holy Cross Cemetery. Standing next to him are the Mass's co-celebrants, Reverend Gordon Kittrick and Reverend Francisco Melendez."

Seeing Kittrick and hearing the name of the deceased, Thielemans became more nauseated, but took deep breaths and continued watching the news report:

"Robert Kucera was the 13-year-old altar boy who jumped from the Coronado Bridge earlier this week. Wearing a cassock and surplice, he unexpectedly jumped out of a taxi cab that stopped in slow-moving traffic, midway across the bridge's two-mile span. Climbing onto the bridge railing, he looked toward heaven, folded his hands as if to pray, and jumped into the San Diego Bay before stunned motorists could intervene. Following the incident, divers from Naval Base San Diego searched the bay for two days before his body was found."

With the imagery almost too much to bear, Thielemans started hyperventilating and paused the news feed. Getting up from his chair, he walked around the room and tried to control his breathing. When he started regaining his composure, he returned to the computer, and with a trembling hand, restarted the news feed:

"The boy's mother, Rebecca Kucera, previously told our station her son never got over his father's recent death. The boy mentioned his father in the suicide note he left on his bed before he began his trip to the Coronado Bridge, a trip that proved to be the last of his all-too-brief life."

The broadcast veteran adroitly moved to allow a different camera angle before finishing her report:

"As we watch the casket being taken down the church steps to a waiting hearse, we can sense sorrow and loss in the faces of the deceased's bereaved family, neighbors, and schoolmates. Seeing this, we must ask, how many more suicides are yet to occur from the railings of the Coronado Bridge? As of July 2017, there were more than 400 known suicides committed from the span. Although the bridge has no sidewalks and is closed to pedestrian traffic, its limited access has not prevented determined individuals from using the bridge to take their own lives. There are plans to install a bird-spike barrier near the bridge railings to thwart future suicide attempts. However, the installation is not scheduled to begin for another year. Until then, we can only watch and wait. From Saint Declan's Roman Catholic Church, this is Kate Ward."

The television screen faded to black, and a photograph of Bobby Kucera, dressed in full religious attire, and Father Gordon Kittrick, dressed in his church vestments, appeared on the screen.

Perceiving a frightened look on Bobby's face and the look of a hunter who had just corned his prey on Kittrick's, Thielemans became physically ill and ran into the restroom. Several minutes later, Janulis returned to the office, just as Thielemans was exiting the lavatory, wiping his face with a paper cloth.

"Paul, what's wrong?" the monsignor asked.

"Something happened last week I'd rather not talk about," Thielemans revealed, accepting a can of Coke from the monsignor. "I saw something happening I should have been able to stop. I failed to act in time, and now, a young boy is dead."

"Paul, I've never seen you like this before," Janulis observed. "You look like you've just seen a ghost."

"I have," Thielemans replied, taking a sip of soda. "Thanks for everything. I have to get to that meeting with the archbishop."

As Thielemans left the room, the monsignor walked over to a computer and accessed the recorded TV news feed Thielemans just watched. Meanwhile, Thielemans walked to a meeting room where he was scheduled to discuss his speech and plan with Archbishop Palmieri.

"Father Thielemans, please come in," the archbishop, a dark-haired, imperially slim man in his seventies, requested.

"Your Eminence," Thielemans said, shaking the archbishop's hand.

"Father, I don't have a lot of time, so I'll cut right to the chase," the archbishop began. "I've consulted with a few other bishops, and we all feel your latest book and plan to invigorate the Church are enlightening. Unfortunately, Mother Church is facing difficult times with this clergy sex scandal hanging over everyone's heads, and the time has come for us to circle the wagons rather than ride off into the sunset. I know you would like me to coordinate your proposed plan with all the bishops, but I'm afraid too many dioceses have other priorities at present. You could not have picked a more inopportune time to present us your plan."

"I understand," the disappointed priest responded.

"However, I am impressed with your plan and would like to offer you the following compromise," Palmieri continued. "You have my permission to present your plan to individual parishes throughout the United States. You may ask your fellow priests to set aside one weekend each month for Sunday Latin Masses and the other alternatives you've suggested. You can monitor the progress of the participating parishes and see if your plan garners the results you predict. All of us would love to see non-practicing Catholics return to the fold, and your plan may be the heaven-sent means by which we can reunite such

Catholics with Mother Church. We're planning another bishops' conference to be held this fall. If you'd like, you can contact Monsignor Janulis in my office before that time and make arrangements to present your research findings at our next meeting. Do you have any questions?"

"Your Eminence, are you suggesting I find the priests and parishes willing to try my plan on my own time, without any guidance or help from the dioceses?" Thielemans asked.

"I'm afraid so," the archbishop replied. "I'm sorry, but it's the best I can do for you. Now, if you'll please excuse me, I have other meetings scheduled."

"Thank you, Your Eminence," Thielemans said.

"By the way, since you're Belgian, you should visit the Cathedral of Our Lady of Peace while you're in town," the archbishop recommended. "I'm sure you've heard of Saint Damien who was also from Belgium. His relic is on display at the cathedral, and seeing it may inspire you."

"I've heard of Saint Damien," Thielemans remarked, somewhat defensively. "He was born in Belgium in 1840 and named Jozef De Veuster. His countrymen call him, *De Grootste Belg,* which honors him as the greatest Belgian of all time. He is also revered for his missionary work with the lepers in Molokai and is the patron saint of both Honolulu and Hawaii. A relic of his right heel bone is on display at the local cathedral. I've planned to view it for quite some time because I've already visited Saint Damien's burial site in Leuven, Belgium. While I'm in town, I also plan to take a look at his statue at the State Capitol Building. I'm sure seeing Saint Damien's relic and his statue will be inspiring."

"Yes, well, very good," the archbishop responded, quickly leaving the room. "God bless you, my son."

As one meeting was ending in Honolulu, another was beginning at Saint Declan's Rectory in San Diego.

"I think it's time we had a long-overdue chat," Bishop Grannick suggested, sitting down in the rectory's living room and lighting a Cuban cigar.

"I'm all ears," Father Kittrick replied, as he handed the bishop, a short, thin 67-year-old with silver hair and metal designer eyeglasses, a glass of Glenfiddich scotch.

"I'm glad you're all ears because I'm beginning to wonder if you have any brain beneath that thick skull of yours," Grannick responded. "I know you can't control this obsession you have with young boys, but you've finally gone too far. The death of this Kucera lad had better be a wake-up call for you, and you'd better pray no one starts snooping around and finding out it was your repeated sexual indiscretions that pushed him over the edge."

The bishop took a sip of single-malt scotch.

"I've covered up for you on countless occasions in the past, but I'm running out of parishes to transfer you to and money to pay off the families of your victims," he continued. "What's more, I can't pull any strings and arrange for you to be transferred any time soon because of how suspicious the move might appear. You'd better understand you'll be living your life in a goldfish bowl for the foreseeable future. You'd better also pray the diocese and archdiocese never find out about how I've been managing your career and redirecting funds to pay for your mistakes. I have just as much to lose as you if your aberrant sexual tendencies are ever made public."

"I hear you, Uncle," Kittrick replied, fidgeting in his chair. "Don't think I'm not grateful for everything you've done. I know I have to be more careful, but I can't change who I am or help the way I react to young boys. It's probably the same way you react to young girls."

"We're not talking about me, Boyo," Grannick shouted. "We're talking about you. Get that into your head. Now, listen closely. I met with Kucera's mother after the funeral today and don't think we'll have any problem with her. She's a little bit slow. She's also impressionable and desperate. Her husband left her nothing when he died, and she doesn't earn much working at Walmart. I think I was able to convince her that her son had severe psychological problems and that you and I are truly concerned about her family's welfare. I told her the Church can refuse to bury a Catholic who has committed suicide, but extenuating circumstances, such as suspected mental health issues, allowed us to give her son a Christian burial."

Grannick took another sip of Glenfiddich.

"Now, she's about to default on her mortgage," he added. "So, I suggested a move north and offered her subsidized housing, full parochial school tuition for her two daughters, and more lucrative employment opportunities. I told her these offerings were to be kept confidential and were being made in recognition of her son's service as a devoted and faithful altar boy. She cried and told me how grateful she was for everything you and I were doing for her."

As Grannick puffed on his cigar, the phone rang.

"Saint Declan's," Kittrick announced.

"May I speak to Mother Murray?" the caller requested.

"She no longer works here," Kittrick replied nervously. "May I ask who is calling?"

"This is Paul Thielemans," the caller said. "I didn't know you'd be answering the phone, Father Kittrick. I know you're probably busy, and I hate bothering you. I just wanted to thank Mother for all the hospitality she showed me while I was at Saint Declan's."

Kittrick distanced the phone receiver from his ear and took a deep breath.

"Let's be honest with each other," Kittrick yelled. "You didn't call here to thank Mother Murray for her roast beef and peach pie dinner. You called to pump her for information about Bobby Kucera. So, let me tell you something. You, Father Paul Thielemans, are the reason the boy is dead. That's right. You are the reason. You sent a San Diego police officer to the rectory to check up on Bobby. Unfortunately, the boy was here with me when the police officer showed up at the front door. Bobby didn't understand why a policeman was looking for him. He thought he was in some kind of trouble. He went home scared, even after being reassured he wasn't in any kind of trouble, and that was the last time I saw him."

Kittrick held his hand against the receiver and took another deep breath.

"You may not realize it, but Bobby had serious psychological problems," he continued. "That's why I was working with him. Because of you and your need to be everything to everybody, all my hard work has been wasted. If you had only minded your own business and not sent that police officer here, Bobby would still be alive."

"For your information, I was in a motor vehicle accident shortly after I left Saint Declan's," Thielemans explained. "After the policeman finished investigating the accident, I asked him to do me a favor and contact the rectory to make sure Bobby was all right. Bobby appeared ill and left the altar while I was saying Mass at your church.

I didn't know Bobby's last name or how to get in touch with his family before I left San Diego, and I couldn't contact you or Mother because you were both out of town. I only asked the police officer to contact your rectory and make sure you knew about Bobby's possible illness. I thought he would just call your rectory rather than visit it in person."

"Well, he didn't do what you expected, did he now?" Kittrick shouted. "As a result, an innocent boy is dead."

"Father Kittrick, I've had enough of your nonsense," Thielemans responded. "I have a different theory about Bobby's death, and I'll be happy to discuss it with you in person if you ever get past your absurd notions. I plan to be back in San Diego in twelve days, and you have my cell phone number to contact me if you want to meet."

"It'll be a cold day in hell before you're allowed to come into my rectory again," Kittrick screamed.

"Father Kittrick, I think you'd better start praying for cold days in hell," Thielemans advised. "It sounds like you're going to need them."

Kittrick quickly became so angry and flustered he was unable to verbally respond to Thielemans.

"Regardless if I ever meet with you again, I'd still like Mother's phone number," Thielemans insisted. "Despite what you may think, I want to thank her for her kindness."

"I told you Mother Murray is no longer here," Kittrick reiterated. "I don't know where she's at or how to get in touch with her. She's gone - and that's the end of it."

Kittrick hung up the phone and returned to his seat.

"Who were you talking to?" Grannick inquired, flicking the ashes off his cigar. "Did I hear you mention Paul Thielemans' name?"

"That was Thielemans," Kittrick replied. "I wish you never sent him here. He told me he has a theory about Bobby Kucera's death. Can you imagine that?"

"Oh, no," Grannick exclaimed, putting down his cigar and cradling his face in his two hands. "I can't believe it."

"You can't believe what, Uncle?" Kittrick asked.

"I can't believe how stupid you are," Grannick shouted, taking his hands away from his face and staring at his nephew. "And I can't believe you'd talk to an influential priest like Paul Thielemans with such disrespect. Do you have any idea how influential he is? He's in Honolulu right now, rubbing elbows with every bishop in the United States and lecturing to them about what they have to do to save the Catholic Church. I can't believe it."

"I'm sorry, Uncle," Kittrick said. "I lost my head."

"You'll lose a lot more than just your head if you don't meet with Thielemans and find out how much he knows about you and Bobby Kucera," the bishop warned. "You have to meet with him and hope he hasn't already talked to anyone about you and your history of raping orphans. I hope you realize the Kucera kid did you a favor by drowning and staying underwater for two days. The autopsy shouldn't be able to reveal sexual abuse in a waterlogged corpse. So, no one will be able to prove anything, but they can still be suspicious of you."

"So, you're serious about my arranging a meeting with Thielemans," Kittrick reiterated.

"I've never been more serious," Grannick answered. "You not only have to meet with Thielemans, but you have to change his mind about things. That won't be easy to do, but you could try showing the guy you're sorry for any misunderstandings and want to be friends with him."

"How am I supposed to do that?" Kittrick asked.

"He opens his talks and meetings by giving everyone a bottle of beer and showing them how to pour the beer into a glass to improve its taste," the bishop replied. "He enjoys performing the same act every time he meets with someone, and if you smarten up, you'll pretend to enjoy his act and drink his beer just like everyone else. Thielemans can be the end of both of us if you don't handle him right."

"I understand," Kittrick responded. "Do we have to worry about Mother Murray?"

"I don't think so," Grannick said. "We're making her comfortable in an assisted living facility in the desert. I convinced her son she was demented and needed assisted living. He didn't care about her condition as much as he cared about our picking up the tab for her new apartment. I told him her new living arrangement was our way of rewarding her for her many years of service to the parish."

"We should have gotten rid of her a long time ago," Kittrick argued.

"Maybe, you should have stopped fondling altar boys a long time ago," Grannick advised.

Grannick finished his Glenfiddich.

"So, tell me, are you sorry for your sins and ready to make a good confession?" the bishop inquired.

"Yes, I am, Uncle" Kittrick replied sheepishly.

"Then, kneel down and prepare to receive forgiveness for your sins," Grannick instructed.

Kittrick knelt in front of the bishop and laid his head on his confessor's lap.

"That's a good Boyo," Grannick said, gently stroking his nephew's hair.

CHAPTER SEVEN

As a full moon rose over Honolulu, Thielemans drove his open-top convertible to the North Shore of Oahu. With a container of takeout barbecue and six-pack of local microbrew for companions, he left what had become a world gone mad in favor of the quiet and solitude of the night, moonlit ocean, and incomparable feeling of spending quality time with one's self.

Feeling the ocean breeze caress his face and blow through his hair, Thielemans drove to a secluded scenic overlook. There, he nibbled pieces of barbecue, sipped beer, and tried to lose himself in his surroundings.

The mentally fatigued priest had experienced worse days in his life, but he could count those days on the fingers of one hand. The reluctance of the bishops to implement his ambitious plan, suicide of Bobby Kucera, and accusations of Father Kittrick were a lot to handle in a single day, even for a strong and phlegmatic man like Thielemans.

Hoping the cool ocean breeze, aroma of mixed tropical vegetation, and sound of crashing waves could penetrate his brain and erase the day's bad memories, the exhausted priest closed his eyes and drifted off into a deep sleep. Awaking three hours later, Thielemans realized it was 3 a.m., removed his only remaining beer from a small cooler, and reluctantly began his long drive back to the ship.

Trying unsuccessfully to savor the tranquility of pre-dawn Oahu, Thielemans couldn't stop thinking about

Kittrick. The more he thought about him, the more he understood why Prosky had such unabashed hatred for pedophiles.

Thielemans realized Prosky was right about a lot of things, including his belief that every day was a test of faith. He remembered Prosky saying, "if you still have faith and believe in God at the end of the day, you pass that day's test and qualify for the one you'll have to take tomorrow."

The theologian firmly believed nothing could make him lose his faith in God, not even the short-sightedness of bishops, death of an altar boy, or false accusations of a pedophile. Knowing he had successfully passed the test of yet another day, he prepared for his next set of challenges.

Arriving at the cruise terminal at 5:15 a.m., Thielemans found a parking space about a half-mile from the ship, and after experiencing less difficulty securing the convertible top and locking his car, he walked through the terminal and on to the Eurodam. Calling room service for a breakfast sandwich and pot of strong coffee, Thielemans shaved, showered, and tried to get motivated for the start of another busy day.

After his short respite aboard the cruise ship, Thielemans attended Sunday Mass at the Cathedral of Our Lady of Peace and remained immediately thereafter to view the relic of Saint Damien. Following a short detour to the State Capitol Building where he viewed Saint Damien's statue, Thielemans returned to the Hawaii Convention Center.

There, he tried enlisting the help of several bishops he felt were enthusiastic about his plan to renew interest in the Catholic Church. Able to get a dozen bishops to agree to send him the names of priests he could contact about his plan, Thielemans left the convention center and embarked on an abbreviated tour of Honolulu.

The Eurodam was set to leave Honolulu and sail to Kauai at 4 p.m. which left Thielemans only three hours to sight-see, return his rental car, and take a cab back to the ship. Realizing he had to stay within close driving distance of Honolulu, Thielemans decided to drive twenty minutes and visit the Pearl Harbor National Memorial.

Arriving at Pearl Harbor, Thielemans was informed tickets to watch a short documentary and take a shuttle to the U.S.S. Arizona Memorial were given away each morning until the 1,300 free tickets were distributed on a first-come, first-served basis. The tickets were stamped for use at specific times, with each documentary and boat trip to the Arizona Memorial lasting ninety minutes.

By the time Thielemans arrived at Pearl Harbor, there were no tickets left. With little alternative, he decided to walk around the park and view several exhibits.

Realizing he needed approximately one hour to drive from Pearl Harbor to the airport car rental agency, return his car, and take a cab back to the ship, Thielemans decided to leave Pearl Harbor by 2 p.m. Doing so, he drove on to H-1 and started following the signs to the airport.

Having driven one mile on H-1 and being another mile from the next exit, Thielemans sensed trouble as traffic in front of him was stopped as far as he could see. A multi-car accident, with a car fire and multiple injuries, occurred on the highway a few minutes earlier, and as police cars, ambulances, and fire engines tried to squeeze through and around the hundreds of cars that were stopped behind the accident, Thielemans realized his ability to return to the Eurodam before it set sail was in serious jeopardy.

Not being able to drive his car in any direction until the accident was cleared or rely on roadside assistance to get him around the logjam, Thielemans turned off his car. Opening the cooler to see if, by some miracle, he had overlooked a final bottle of beer while still parked on the North Shore scenic overlook, Thielemans saw only empty bottles and began to doubt if he would be witnessing any miracles in the foreseeable future.

Realizing it was already 2:30 p.m., Thielemans decided to call Michelle to explain his dilemma and see if anything could be done to hold the ship. As he removed the iPhone from his belt, he realized he turned off the phone just before his speech, and being consumed by the remaining events of the day, forgot to turn it back on.

Having called Kittrick from a landline inside the convention center, he wondered if his iPhone was still charged. Dialing the number of the spare iPhone he loaned Michelle, Thielemans was amazed his iPhone was still working and Michelle was waiting for his call.

"Paul, where are you?" Michelle inquired frantically. "I've been trying to call you all night and all morning."

"It's a long story," Thielemans replied. "Unfortunately, it's not a very good story."

"Where are you?" she repeated.

"I'm about three miles away from the car rental agency at the airport," Thielemans revealed. "Unfortunately, there are hundreds of cars stopped in front of me on the highway because of a multi-vehicle accident. You can probably hear the sirens in the background. I can see quite a few fire trucks, ambulances, and cop cars that are still trying to get to the scene of the accident. Therefore, I think I'm going to be here a while."

"How long?" Michelle asked.

"To be honest with you, I may be here until moonlight returns to Waikiki," Thielemans answered. "So, I need you to do me a favor. Could you call the customer service desk on the ship and alert them to my situation? Could you also ask them if there is any way they can hold the ship until I get there?"

"Give me a few minutes," Michelle said. "I'll call you right back."

Fifteen minutes later, Thielemans' iPhone rang.

"What were you able to find out?" Thielemans nervously inquired.

"Here's the deal," Michelle began. "It's 3 o'clock now, and passengers are supposed to be on board by 3:30. The ship plans to leave on time at 4 p.m. sharp. The girl at the customer service desk made a few phone calls, and it appears you're the only one who is caught up in traffic. All other passengers who have not yet returned to the ship are on tours and expected to return to the ship momentarily. The girl also said you're going to be sitting in traffic for a few more hours until the accident is completely cleared from the highway. So, there's no way you'd be able to return your car to the rental agency and make it back to the ship in time. Because of its tight schedule, the ship can't wait for just one passenger."

"So, what do I do now?" Thielemans questioned with obvious frustration.

"Give me a few minutes," Michelle requested. "I'll call you back as soon as I put together a game plan."

Twenty minutes later, Michelle called back.

"So, here's what you do," she began. "I made a reservation for you on Hawaiian Airlines. Your flight leaves the Honolulu Airport at 5:26 a.m. tomorrow and arrives at the Lihue Airport in Kauai at 6:03 a.m. The flight only takes thirty-seven minutes. So, you'll arrive in Kauai before the ship which is supposed to dock at 7 a.m. When you get to Kauai, take a cab to the car rental agency, rent your Camaro convertible, and do whatever you originally planned to do for the day. We're going on a tour to see where the movies, *South Pacific* and *Jurassic Park*, were filmed. The ship leaves Kauai tomorrow at 5 p.m. sharp. Passengers have to be on board by 4:30. Whatever you do, make sure you return the rental car by 3:30 so you have enough time to get back to the ship in time. The rental agency will provide return transportation. Got it?"

"Loud and clear," Thielemans acknowledged. "I can't believe how good you are at handling emergencies and scheduling things. Thank you very much. Now, listen. Call Winston and tell him I'd like to have dinner with you and your gang in my suite tomorrow at 8 p.m. He knows the drill. Also, tell him I'm all right and explain why I wasn't able to board the ship in time today. Finally, ask him to check if the ship received the Saint Bavo Witbier the Hawaii Convention Center was supposed to send. If the ship received it, ask Winston to put a few six-packs in my refrigerator. Okay?"

"Okay," Michelle agreed. "How did your speech go?"

"The speech went great," Thielemans replied. "Unfortunately, every bishop in the United States is more concerned about how the clergy sex abuse scandal is going to affect their dioceses than what they have to do to save the Church. So, the U.S. Conference of Catholic Bishops will not implement my program on a national scale as I requested. However, I have been given permission to test my program in parishes I can enroll myself. Fortunately, a few of the bishops have agreed to send me the names of priests they feel might be interested."

"So, yesterday wasn't that bad a day for you," Michelle suggested.

"Forgive me if I misled you in any way," Thielemans argued. "My speech was just about the only thing that wasn't completely tragic yesterday. Following my talk, I learned about an altar boy's suicide, one which I may have been able to prevent. If that wasn't enough, I also got blamed for the kid's death by the pedophilic priest who was sexually abusing him."

"What?" Michelle exclaimed.

"When you get a chance, search for 'San Diego Suicide' on the internet, and check out the television feeds and newspaper reports," Thielemans advised. "The feeds and news reports will give you a better idea of what I'm talking about before we have a chance to discuss the entire matter. The bottom line here is I saw a priest, Father Gordon Kittrick, and an altar boy, Bobby Kucera, together at the rectory of Saint Declan's Church in San Diego. I failed to detect a pedophilic relationship, even though all the telltale signs were right in front of me. A few days later, Bobby Kucera committed suicide."

"You've got to be kidding," Michelle said in disbelief.

"Last night, I called Saint Declan's to try to get some information from the housekeeper, but Kittrick answered the phone and blamed me for the boy's death," Thielemans added. "I'll talk with you and Ed about the whole matter when I get back to the ship. In the meantime, run Gordon Kittrick's name by Ed, and ask him if he knows anything about the guy."

"Will do," Michelle agreed. "I also have access to our group's private website and data bank that contains the names of priests suspected of sexual abuse. So, I'll do some snooping myself."

"You're unreal," Thielemans said. "You'll never know how much I appreciate your help."

"Just remember one thing, Rock Star," Michelle replied. "You owe me."

"I've heard that somewhere before," Thielemans chuckled. "See you tomorrow night, and thanks again."

As he could see emergency vehicles and tow trucks starting to leave the scene of the accident, Thielemans thought about Michelle and how she would make a great secretary. Realizing such an arrangement was unlikely because of her obligations to the convent, he thought about some of her antics and smiled.

Sitting in traffic for an additional two hours, Thielemans also thought more about Bobby Kucera and Kittrick. Every time he saw another ambulance leaving the accident scene, he pictured Bobby's body being placed in an ambulance and taken away for an autopsy.

Recalling the photo of Bobby and Kittrick from the television news report, Thielemans wondered how he could have failed to realize Bobby was being sexually abused. The more he wondered, the more he blamed himself for not being able to prevent the youngster's tragic and unnecessary death.

Thielemans silently prayed to Bobby for forgiveness, and as he prayed, he closed his eyes and was able to imagine the young boy in his arms and the feeling of the truly loving embrace a father might share with his son. Thielemans was suddenly coaxed out of his daydream by a concerned motorist who got out of his car and approached Thielemans when he saw the priest crying.

When the highway finally reopened at 6 p.m., Thielemans drove to a nearby Walmart to purchase a change of underwear and some toiletries. As he left the store and realized the sun had already set over Honolulu, he decided to drive past Waikiki and Diamondhead, and explore a few of Oahu's famous shore points.

Stopping briefly at scenic overlooks at the Maunalua Bay, Wawamalu, Makapuu, Kaiona, and Waimanalo Beach Parks, Thielemans picked up a Hawaiian Pizza and bottle of Zinfandel and proceeded to the Kailua Beach Park. There, he ate, drank, and watched the moonlight dance off the ocean and nearby Popoia Island.

After he ate half of his pizza, finished his bottle of wine, and managed to forget his problems for an hour, Thielemans closed his eyes and took a brief nap. Awaking at 1 a.m., he decided to retrace the path of his recent adventure and drive leisurely back to the airport.

Returning his Mercedes to the rental agency at 3:30 a.m., he took a shuttle to the airport terminal. There, he freshened up and sampled local pastry and coffee before reporting for his 5:26 a.m. flight to Kauai.

Arriving on time in Kauai, Thielemans took a cab to the car rental agency, picked up his blue Camaro convertible, map of the island, and complimentary coffee, and set out for the Waimea Canyon. On his way to the attraction frequently referred to as the "Grand Canyon of the Pacific," Thielemans drove past large farms and watched haggard workers exiting old, dilapidated cars, trucks, and vans to begin their days in the heat of the Hawaiian sun.

After he made a stop at the Hanapepe Lookout, Thielemans continued his drive to the canyon. Along the way, he noticed a small church that was tucked away on the side of a hill. Wondering how many Catholics attended the remote church, he proceeded to Waimea.

Arriving at the Waimea Canyon State Park, Thielemans got out of his car and viewed the breathtaking scenery of the canyon from several different vantage points. Although he tried to concentrate on the extraordinary beauty of the natural wonder, he couldn't help but think about Bobby Kucera.

As images of the altar boy jumping from the Coronado Bridge suddenly raced through his mind, Thielemans became depressed. No longer able to concentrate on the beauty of the canyon, he decided to return to the ship.

Driving back to the car rental agency, Thielemans once again noticed the small church on the hillside. Curious about the church's location and structure, he drove off the main road and on to the narrow road that led to the unusual house of worship.

Parking his car in an unpaved lot, Thielemans entered the empty church and blessed himself with holy water from an old wooden font. Gingerly walking toward the altar on the old church's bare, rickety, wooden floor, the priest genuflected and sat down in a narrow, wooden pew.

Lowering the flimsy, wooden kneeler, Thielemans got on his knees, lowered his face into his hands, and began to pray. Using words of his own composition, he silently prayed and asked both God and Bobby Kucera for forgiveness.

After several minutes of intense prayer and the shedding of more tears, Thielemans removed his hands from his face, dried his eyes, and looked at the pew in front of him. There, he noticed an unusual rosary.

Picking up the rosary, he studied its unique construction and realized it was fashioned from some kind of exotic seeds. Bright red with a black band covering one end, the oval seeds differed in appearance from one another, but when combined with a small wooden crucifix and silver attachments, created an exotic work of art.

Feeling strangely empowered by the blessed string of beads, Thielemans remained on his knees and prayed the rosary with profound devotion. When he finished praying, he sat down in the pew and felt an unexpected level of peace and contentment.

Suddenly, the troubled clergyman felt hopeful about being able to solve his problems. Looking at his newly-found rosary, he wondered if the Blessed Mother was answering his prayers.

Clutching the rosary in his right hand, Thielemans got up from the pew, genuflected, and started to leave the church. Suddenly realizing the person who inadvertently left the rosary in the pew might regret its loss, Thielemans kissed the rosary and reluctantly returned it to the pew.

As he started to leave the church again, he looked inside a room used for confessions and found a table with rosaries for sale. Picking up five rosaries that were identical to the one he just prayed, he placed a $100 bill in the slotted, wooden lockbox that was used for donations.

With his new acquisitions in hand, he returned to the middle of the church. Retrieving the first rosary he discovered, he replaced it with one he had just purchased.

Returning to his car, Thielemans realized he didn't know the name of the church. As he started walking around the grounds, looking for a sign with the church's name, a teenage girl approached him.

"Good morning, Father," the Kauai native with long, dark hair and ebony eyes, said. "Did you just buy those rosaries in the church?"

"Yes, I did," the priest replied. "I left a donation in the wooden box. I wish there were more to buy."

"If you'd like to buy more, I may be able to help," the teen suggested. "My mother makes the rosaries for the church. She picks the seeds from the vines, whittles the crucifixes out of wood, and buys the connectors and varnish from our local hardware store. We don't have any rosaries made right now, but if you'd like, I could sell you fresh seeds my mother just picked. I could also sell you everything else you'd need to make your own rosaries. It's easy to do. I live in that house at the end of the road. It would only take me five minutes to get everything for you."

Looking down the road at the small shack the teenager called home, Thielemans realized her family could use the money. He also realized he could find someone to assemble the rosaries, and then, use them as special gifts.

"I'd be happy to buy the supplies," Thielemans announced. "How much will everything cost?"

"Would $50 be too much?" the teenager asked.

"How about $100?" Thielemans countered.

With a big smile on her face, the young girl ran to her home and quickly returned with enough supplies to make a dozen rosaries.

"I put the seeds in a closeable freezer bag," she indicated, handing a large shopping bag full of supplies to the priest. "That will keep them fresh longer. You can also freeze them."

"Thank you very much," Thielemans responded, handing the teenager a $100 bill.

"Thank you very much, Father, and God bless you," the teenager said, as she smiled and carefully studied the currency.

"God bless you," Thielemans replied, as he got back into his convertible, added a smaller bag with his recently-acquired underwear and toiletries to the larger shopping bag, and resumed his trip.

Thinking about the small hillside church and realizing he never learned its name, Thielemans drove to the car rental agency, returned the convertible, and took the agency's shuttle back to the Eurodam. As he walked through security to board the ship, he was asked to run his shopping bag through the ship's large scanner.

The security guard who operated the scanning device seemed to momentarily balk when he saw the contents of the priest's shopping bag. Ultimately deciding nothing in the bag represented any security risk to the Eurodam, he allowed Thielemans to retrieve his bag and board the ship.

Looking in his refrigerator and seeing Winston was able to add six-packs of Saint Bavo Witbier, Thielemans sat on his balcony and enjoyed a sandwich and a beer while he watched the Eurodam leave port. An hour later, he shaved, showered, and prepared for his dinner guests.

Arriving on time, Fathers Ed and Bill, and Sisters Regina and Michelle entered Thielemans' suite. As they sat at the dining room table and waited for Winston to arrive with dinner, Thielemans gave each of his guests one of the rosaries he purchased earlier in the day.

"I can't believe it," Conyngham exclaimed. "Why, I haven't seen these since I was in Trinidad."

"Rosaries?" Thielemans' inquired incredulously.

"Rosary peas," Conyngham answered. "That's what they call the red seeds they used to make these rosaries. In different parts of the world, the seeds are also called jequirity beans, crab-eye seeds, Jumbie beads, and a few other names I don't remember off-hand. Scientifically, the rosary pea is *Abrus precatorius.*"

"You seem to know a lot about the rosary pea," Thielemans observed.

"As a scientist, you have to learn everything you can about anything that can kill you," Conyngham replied.

"What do you mean?" Thielemans asked curiously.

"What we are holding in our hands are rosaries made of seeds that contain one of the deadliest poisons known to man," the former Georgetown University biochemistry professor stated authoritatively and dramatically. "The rosaries can be safely handled now because they were varnished after they were assembled. The varnish sealed the seeds. The seeds come from invasive plants that grow in warm climates all over the world. You can find the plants growing wild in Hawaii, the Caribbean, Central America, the South Pacific, and even in the United States in places like Florida and Alabama. I worked with them in Trinidad where the natives used to string red, green, white, and black rosary peas into bracelets they believed would ward off *jumbies*, the name for their evil spirits, and the *mal yeux*, or evil eye."

"What makes them so toxic?" Prosky inquired.

"The toxin in the rosary pea is abrin, a chemical that is many times more toxic than ricin," Conyngham revealed. "The fatal dose of abrin is roughly the amount contained in a single pea."

"If abrin is so toxic, how are people able to safely pick the seeds from the vines?" Sister Regina asked.

"The hard shell of the rosary pea can completely contain the abrin, unless it's cracked," Conyngham replied. "So, picking seeds is usually safe, especially if you're wearing gloves. You can swallow an intact rosary pea without being poisoned. If you swallow the complete contents of an opened rosary pea, however, you'll probably be dead in three or four days. Inhaling abrin powder can also lead to death by causing respiratory failure. Getting abrin on your hands can cause a severe skin reaction, but it won't kill you. Getting the chemical in your eyes won't kill you either, but it can cause severe eye irritation that can progress to hemorrhaging and even blindness."

Conyngham's assertions left the group speechless.

"Interestingly, death from the oral ingestion of abrin can closely resemble death from acute illnesses, such as gastrointestinal bleeding, shock caused by severe dehydration, prolonged seizures, kidney or liver failure, and myocardial infarctions," Conyngham continued. "Even more interesting is the fact abrin cannot be detected by routine lab analysis, such as those used in hospitals. So, a person could poison someone by slipping the contents of a rosary pea into their drink, and the chance of anyone finding out would be extremely remote. The victim would appear to die of an acute illness, and routine hospital tests would not reveal the real cause of death."

Without saying a word, Thielemans got up from his chair and walked into his bedroom. He quickly returned, holding the bag of rosary peas he just purchased.

"Can I safely carry these around?" the concerned priest asked. "I bought them earlier today, along with the crucifixes, connectors, and varnish used to make rosaries. I bought them from a young girl whose mother made the rosary I just gave you."

"Since they're in an airtight freezer bag, you shouldn't have any problem safely transporting them, but you may have a problem getting them off the ship," Conyngham stated, as he inspected the bag. "You're not supposed to bring seeds from outside the country into the United States. If you really want to take the rosary peas home, carry them off the ship in an attaché or small bag. It's doubtful anyone will check bags you're carrying off the ship yourself. I wouldn't pack the rosary peas in luggage you plan to have carried off the ship for you. That luggage could be inspected on the dock."

"Thank you, Bill, for sharing your insights," Prosky said. "This has been quite a revelation. Who would have ever thought the same beads we pray with could kill us?"

"Paul, there is one more thing I should tell you," Conyngham added. "If you plan to make rosaries out of the rosary peas or have someone do it for you, make sure you do your homework and learn how to safely handle everything. There have been cases where individuals have unwittingly handled rosary peas that had minute cracks in them and developed painful skin or eye conditions after the abrin leached out of the rosary peas and penetrated openings in their skin or got into their eyes. So, please be careful if you plan to work with rosary peas. They can be dangerous. Also, don't forget the varnish."

As everyone continued heeding Conyngham's admonitions, Winston entered the suite with the evening's dinner. For the next several hours, the group thoroughly enjoyed their meals and each other's company.

After everyone left, Thielemans retired to the balcony with a large snifter of cognac. Relaxing to the sounds of the ocean and gentle stimulation of the sea breeze for more than an hour, Thielemans started thinking about Michelle and wondering if she would pay him a late-night visit.

Hearing the front doorbell chime, Thielemans realized the answer to his question was standing outside his cabin. Opening the door, he saw her waiting expectantly.

"Can I sleep with you tonight?" Michelle inquired, looking into Thielemans' eyes.

"Only if the temperature in your cabin is 100 degrees," Thielemans joked.

"Why do you think I wear a tee-shirt, jogging shorts, and flip flops when I come here?" Michelle asked, as she entered the suite. "This is what I wear when I'm in the cabin with Regina. It's 100 degrees in there right now."

"It sounds like you could use a drink," Thielemans observed.

"What are we drinking?" Michelle questioned.

"Courvoisier," the obliging host announced.

"Make it a large," she requested.

"So, how were your excursions?" Thielemans inquired, as he poured his guest a large snifter of cognac.

"The Pearl Harbor Memorial Park was impressive, but I got tired of listening to Regina complain," Michelle revealed. "At the end of our tour of the Arizona Memorial, she spoke to a young sailor who was just visiting the park and insisted he arrange for the Memorial to be closed until the unsteady dock was fully repaired."

"Was the dock unsteady?" Thielemans questioned.

"Probably," Michelle chuckled. "Ed and Bill nearly fell, and Regina experienced vertigo."

"So, maybe Regina was right," Thielemans suggested.

"Regina usually is right," Michelle admitted. "Unfortunately, she suffers from, what Bill calls, 'diabetic dosidosis.' He invented the syndrome. He says it's when a diabetic person blames every conceivable symptom or problem in their life on diabetes."

"Is Regina diabetic?" Thielemans asked.

"That's the problem," Michelle exclaimed. "Several years ago, she had a fasting blood sugar of 107 which is practically normal. Her sugar hasn't been over 98 since. The doctor told her she was pre-diabetic and should watch her diet. Since then, Regina has attributed her cold intolerance, arthritis, diverticulosis, angina, and COPD to diabetes. Not a day goes by that she doesn't wake up and go to sleep complaining of different ailments she blames on an imaginary disease. As Bill said, the woman suffers from diabetic dosidosis, and she's allowed it to ruin her life, and mine as well."

"Now, Sister Michelle, is that any way to talk about your Mother Superior?" the priest joked.

"Don't get me wrong," the young said. "I'm grateful for everything my aunt has done for me. What gets to me, though, is how she just can't complain about something without going off on a tangent. You ask her the time, and she tells you how to make a clock."

Thielemans shook his head and laughed.

"Tonight, she went to bed complaining about lightheadedness and blaming it on her diabetes," Michelle continued. "Last night, she went to bed complaining about shortness of breath and blaming it on her diabetes. The night before, it was diabetes-induced chest pain. Like I told you, it's constant with her. After she was through complaining tonight, she went off on a tangent about changing her funeral arrangements. Even though she last saw Anela Opunui, the friend she'll be visiting on the Big Island, a half-century ago, she's stayed in close contact with her ever since their days as missionary nuns. 'Nellie,' as Regina calls her, has several burial plots in a Catholic cemetery outside Hilo, and recently offered Regina one of them. Ever since I've known her, Regina has talked about wanting to be buried next to other nuns in Baltimore. As of last night, she wants to retire and die in Florida, but be buried next to her old friend in Hawaii."

"Being buried in Hawaii sounds pretty good to me," Thielemans said, taking a sip of cognac. "It beats jumping off the Coronado Bridge."

"I'm glad you mentioned that," Michelle offered. "I read the newspaper story about Bobby Kucera on the internet but wasn't able to download any of the television feeds. I know how you must feel."

"I'm doing all right now, but I was a basket case the night after I learned about his death," the priest revealed.

"I can imagine," Michelle empathized. "By the way, I looked into Kittrick and discussed him with Ed. There have been multiple unsubstantiated reports of him sexually abusing young boys and being transferred from one parish to another with alarming frequency. Unfortunately, the families of the children he allegedly abused have been unwilling to report him to the diocese or police. Ed thinks someone is getting to these families, paying them to look the other way, and demanding silence and confidentiality in return for the hush money. Several of the families whose young boys were supposedly molested by Kittrick moved away from San Diego at the same time Kittrick changed parishes or was given a very long sabbatical leave. Interestingly, every child in every family that moved from San Diego received full-tuition scholarships to attend different parochial schools. What's more, the new schools claimed they granted the scholarships because of financial hardship or academic excellence. So, Kittrick, and whoever is working with him, really know how to cover their tracks."

"Kittrick is a real toad," Thielemans insisted. "He went out of his way to make me feel like a penny waiting for change the day I first met him. He came up from his gym, where he claimed to be teaching Bobby Kucera how to wrestle, and talked down to me before he finally left the rectory. I only wish I had met Ed before seeing Kittrick and Bobby together that night. I would have known how to identify a pedophilic relationship. More importantly, I may have been able to intervene and prevent Bobby's death."

"You can't blame yourself for Bobby's suicide," Michelle stressed.

"Kittrick certainly did when I called his rectory from Honolulu," Thielemans argued. "I never told you this, but my car was broadsided by a pickup truck last Sunday, shortly after I left Saint Declan's Church. While the police officer was investigating the accident, I told him about Bobby leaving the altar during Mass and asked him to contact the church rectory to make sure Bobby was all right. Instead of calling the rectory, the policeman paid a visit the next day while Kittrick was there, doing who knows what with Bobby. Kittrick claimed seeing the police officer scared Bobby and made him think he was in some kind of trouble. According to Kittrick, if I hadn't asked the policeman to contact the rectory, Bobby's suicide would have never occurred. I told Kittrick I had a theory about Bobby's death and would be glad to discuss it with him in person when I returned to San Diego, but I doubt if he'll call to schedule a meeting."

"What would you do if Kittrick did call you?" Michelle asked.

"I'd meet with him as soon as possible," Thielemans replied. "During our meeting, I'd back him into a corner and carefully observe how he reacted. I know how to interpret body language pretty well, and I would know when he was lying. I'd confront him about any lies, and hope he would decompensate and unwittingly say something he shouldn't. If he did and he incriminated himself, I'd go to the authorities and tell them everything I knew."

"Where did you learn about body language and interviewing techniques?" Michelle inquired.

"At Harvard," the priest answered. "I took a course in criminal justice one semester and learned a lot. I even learned about polygraphs and how to beat lie detector tests. It was a great course."

After another hour of cognac and conversation, Thielemans and Michelle decided to get some sleep and continue their discussion the following night after dinner and the Eurodam's evening cruise past the Kilauea Volcano. As Thielemans turned down the sofa bed for Michelle, he thanked her again for all her help while he was in Honolulu.

Following his expression of gratitude, Michelle looked into Thielemans' eyes. Without warning, she kissed him on the cheek.

Not sure how to react, the surprised priest just smiled and walked into his bedroom. Closing the door, he stood still and felt the warmth of Michelle's kiss spread through his entire being.

CHAPTER EIGHT

Hearing his bedside telephone ring, Thielemans emerged from a deep sleep and looked at his watch. Seeing it was 5:30 a.m., he wondered who would be calling at such an early hour.

"Paul, please come to my cabin as soon as possible," Michelle said anxiously. "Something's wrong with Regina. I'm in Cabin 7125, down the hall. Please hurry."

Quickly dressing, the priest left his bedroom, and seeing the living room already returned to its original condition, exited the suite. When he arrived at Michelle's cabin, he found Michelle, Prosky, and Conyngham hovering over Regina's bed.

"Bill thinks she's having a heart attack," Michelle revealed, as Regina clutched her chest and struggled to breathe. "Help is on the way."

As Michelle wiped perspiration off the elderly nun's forehead, a team of emergency medical personnel arrived. Placing Regina on a gurney, taking her vital signs, starting an I.V., connecting her to a portable cardiac monitor, and placing an oxygen cannula in her nose, the team quickly transported her to the ship's medical facility.

With Michelle informing the emergency response team of Regina's medical history and Thielemans running ahead to open doors, the elderly nun was whisked from one end of the large ship to the opposite end. Arriving at the Eurodam's emergency treatment area, Regina was transferred to a bed and met by the ship's physician.

"I'm Dr. Tito," the tall, middle-aged physician with curly, brown hair and thick, tinted eyeglasses, announced with a tired voice. "Are you still having chest pain?"

"Yes, right here," Regina answered, holding a clutched right fist against her sternum. "My diabetes is acting up."

"Give her an aspirin and sublingual nitroglycerin, and get an E.K.G., chest x-ray, and routine blood work," the physician ordered, as he began listening to her heart and lungs with his stethoscope. "I think we're dealing with more than just diabetes here."

As a nurse and technician followed Dr. Tito's orders, the physician finished his examination, and then, asked Thielemans and Michelle to join him in another room.

"I'll wait for her tests to come back, but it looks like she's having a heart attack and could be in congestive heart failure," the concerned doctor said, as he removed an Earl Gray tea bag from his cup and took a sip. "I don't think we're dealing with a pulmonary embolism or lung infection. If we can't slow down her heart rate and increase her blood pressure in a hurry, she may not make it."

"What's the long-term game plan?" Thielemans inquired.

"It's 7:15 a.m.," Dr. Tito began. "We're scheduled to dock in Kona at 9 o'clock. If we're able to stabilize her, we'll transfer her from the ship to the Kona Community Hospital as soon as we dock. An ambulance will be waiting for her, and she'll be taken off the ship before passengers are allowed to go ashore. What happens after that will be up to the doctors in Kona. They may choose to treat her at their hospital or transfer her to a larger hospital in Hilo."

"My aunt has a living will and doesn't want C.P.R. or life support," Michelle informed the physician.

"That's important to know," Dr. Tito responded. "We'll respect her wishes and pass the information along to the doctors in Kona if it comes to that."

"What would happen if my aunt didn't want to be transferred to a hospital, but wanted to remain on the ship?" Michelle asked.

"The decision to transfer her would be made according to the ship's protocols," the physician answered. "Your aunt or family wouldn't have any say if we decide to transfer her to a hospital."

"What if she wanted to die at sea?" Michelle inquired.

"It's a popular misconception that a ship will allow one of its passengers to die at sea once medical treatment has begun," the physician explained. "If a sick passenger wants to die at sea on a cruise ship, they have to stay in their cabin, and do so without seeking medical attention."

"What influences your decision-making process when it comes to passengers presenting with life-threatening illnesses or injuries?" Thielemans questioned.

"If we're at sea, several days away from land, we will treat a critically ill or injured passenger to the best of our ability and transfer them to a hospital as soon as we reach the next port." Dr. Tito replied. "If the passenger happens to die at sea despite our best efforts or because they refuse resuscitation, so be it. Depending on the number of days left in the cruise and available morgue space, the body of a dead passenger will either be removed from the ship at the next port or placed in our morgue and removed from the ship later. When we're close to a port, however, as in Sister Regina's case, we treat the passenger and transfer them as soon as possible, even airlifting them from the ship when necessary."

"Who pays the bills if an ill or injured passenger has to be transferred from the ship?" Thielemans asked.

"An ill or injured passenger has to pay all their own expenses once they've been transferred from the ship," the doctor replied. "Friends or family members who leave the ship and stay with the passenger also have to pay their own expenses."

"What kind of expenses are we talking about?" the curious priest questioned

"Ill or injured passengers, and any passengers staying ashore with them, have to pay their own transportation, medical bills, and food and lodging, as well as any incidental charges," Dr. Tito remarked. "In many cases, if they have to be airlifted from the ship, they have to pay for the helicopter ride. If they have to take a commercial flight home after they are hospitalized, they have to pay for their airplane ticket. If they are in serious condition and require a medevac flight, they have to pay for the flight and crew which usually consists of a pilot, copilot, nurse, and respiratory therapist."

"How much does a medevac flight cost?" Michelle inquired.

"A medevac flight to the United States from a different continent can cost $50,000 or more," the physician replied. "Closer flights from Hawaii to California can cost considerably less but are still in the five-figure range. That's why cruise lines advise passengers to take out comprehensive trip insurance that pays for emergency hospitalizations and medevac flights."

The nurse walked into the room and handed Dr. Tito Regina's E.K.G. and chest x-ray. As the doctor reviewed the diagnostic studies, Michelle stared at Thielemans.

"Regina doesn't have trip insurance," she whispered with concern. "None of us do."

"Don't worry about any expenses," Thielemans said reassuringly. "I'll pay for anything she needs."

Hearing the priest's offer, Michelle stared at him in disbelief.

"She's definitely having a heart attack and is already in congestive heart failure," the physician stated. "If you'll excuse me, I have to reexamine your aunt and order additional treatment. You can stay here or return to your cabin. If you leave us your cabin number, we'll call you as soon as you can visit her."

"When can I administer the Anointing of the Sick sacrament?" the priest inquired.

"Let me do a few things first," the doctor requested. "I'll call you as soon as I'm finished. Don't worry. I won't let her die without being blessed and anointed. I must be getting old. I remember when they used to call the sacrament, Extreme Unction."

Thielemans gave the nurse his suite number and left the facility with Michelle. As they walked away, Thielemans called Prosky and Conyngham with his iPhone and invited them to come to his cabin. He also called Winston and requested continental breakfast for four.

Arriving at his suite, Thielemans met Prosky and Conyngham who both appeared unnerved by the events of the morning.

"They're going to call when we can see Regina," Michelle said, watching Thielemans walk into his bedroom.

Returning to the living room, Thielemans opened a small, leather case from which he removed containers of holy water, anointing oil, and communion wafers. Then, he unfolded and inspected the purple stole he wore around his neck while anointing the sick, hearing confessions, and administering other sacraments.

"It looks like you come prepared for everything," Prosky observed.

"Doctors travel with their black bags," Thielemans replied. "I travel with this. I never leave home without it."

As Winston entered the suite and started serving coffee and pastries, a nurse called and told Thielemans he and Michelle could see Regina. Returning to the ship's medical facility, they found the elderly nun more alert and not experiencing as much chest pain or shortness of breath.

After Thielemans heard Regina's brief confession, gave her Holy Communion, and anointed her with oil, she smiled and reached out for Michelle who showed very little emotion.

"I hope you realize I'm dying," the elderly nun stated with a tremulous voice. "So, I have a few last requests. As my only living relative, I trust you to handle all the details. Nellie is supposed to meet me when the ship docks. Find her, and ask her to ride with me in the ambulance to the hospital. Look at her recent photo in my prayer book so you can recognize her. When you come to the hospital, bring my formal habit and the new rosary Father Thielemans gave me. If I die, I want to be buried in Hawaii. I don't know how long it will take for me to get from my grave to heaven. In case it takes a while, I don't want to be cold."

With tears in her eyes, Regina touched Michelle's stoic face before looking at Thielemans.

"Father, thank you for everything you've done for us," Regina said in choppy phrases. "You're a good man and a true priest. I know I can trust you with my niece. That's why I give you my permission to have her work with you. Father Prosky knows my successor, Sister Consuela, and will be able to convince her Michelle is not ready to return to convent life. Hopefully, after some time with you, she will be. I would never want to see her leave the convent, but I don't want her consumed by it either."

"Thank you, Sister," Thielemans replied. "God willing, you'll survive this illness and be able to make the call to Sister Consuela yourself."

As Dr. Tito returned to Regina's bedside, Thielemans and Michelle returned to Thielemans' suite where Prosky was sipping coffee and watching Conyngham take a badly-needed whirlpool. Without any discussion, Michelle got on the phone and quickly canceled the reservations for Thielemans' rental cars in Kona and Hilo, and made new reservations for passenger vans in both locations.

Next, she called the ship's customer service desk and informed a representative of Regina's heart attack. After she provided all the details, she canceled her group's shore excursions for the remainder of the cruise.

Excusing herself, Michelle returned to her cabin to change her clothes and collect the items Regina requested. Following her lead, Prosky helped Conyngham out of the whirlpool bathtub, and the two returned to their cabin to prepare for what promised to be a very long day.

At 8:30, Thielemans received a call from the medical facility, informing him Regina would be taken off the ship at 9 o'clock. He was instructed to bring those going ashore with Regina to the treatment area before that time.

As directed, Thielemans, Michelle, Prosky, and Conyngham reported to the treatment area and accompanied Regina off the ship. Waiting on the dock was Regina's friend, Nellie Opunui.

Recognizing Nellie from her photo, Michelle approached her, apprised her of the situation, and invited her to ride in the ambulance with Regina. With a smile on her face, Nellie, a short, plump 72-year-old Hawaiian with satin skin and long gray hair, gladly obliged.

Michelle accompanied Regina and Nellie to the hospital, while Thielemans and the two other priests rode a shuttle bus to a car rental agency. After Thielemans picked up a white Ford passenger van, he drove the other priests to the hospital.

Walking into the hospital emergency room, the priests were greeted by Michelle and Nellie.

"Regina died a few minutes ago," Michelle announced stoically. "The E.R. doctor said her heart attack led to heart failure, cardiogenic shock, and complete heart block, and there wasn't much anyone could do if she wouldn't agree to be placed on a ventilator or have a pacemaker inserted."

"I've waited for Regina to visit me in Hawaii a half-century," Nellie, a peaceful woman with a perpetual smile, stated. "Being able to spend the last hour of Regina's life with her made my long wait worthwhile. Now, the two missionary sisters who went to Bali as young girls will be able to rest, side-by-side, at the Paauilo Cemetery before we walk through the gates of heaven together."

"I'd like to see Regina one last time," Prosky requested.

"Me too," Conyngham added.

As the two priests disappeared behind the curtain surrounding Regina's bed, Thielemans sat down with Michelle and Nellie.

"So, where do we go from here?" Thielemans asked.

"Regina wants to be buried at the Paauilo Cemetery, outside Hilo," Michelle replied. "Thanks to Nellie, Regina already has a cemetery plot. Unfortunately, the timing may be a problem. The ship will be in Kona today and sail to Hilo overnight. Hilo is a few hours from here by car. The ship will be in Hilo tomorrow, and then, sail to Maui for one day before it begins its return trip to San Diego. I don't know if we could arrange a funeral in time, but if we could, we could probably stay here for the next few days, have the funeral, and then, fly to Maui and catch the ship before it leaves."

"Don't overthink everything," Nellie calmly advised. "We do things differently here. By Hawaiian law, embalming is not required if a body is buried within thirty hours of death. If you'd like, I could arrange Regina's funeral today, and we could bury her tomorrow. I'm good friends with a funeral director and the pastor of the Immaculate Heart of Mary Church. So, I should be able to expedite things. At the very least, I know I could get a casket for Regina and have her body moved to the church today, and schedule a Mass of Christian Burial for tomorrow. If the pastor is unable to perform the service, I'm sure he would grant permission for Father Thielemans or one of the other priests to officiate."

"That would be great," Michelle said.

"Absolutely," Thielemans concurred.

"Let me call the priest and funeral director right now," Nellie suggested. "I should be able to arrange the entire funeral within the next few minutes."

As promised, Nellie returned thirty minutes later and confirmed Regina's funeral would be held the following morning at 11:30 a.m. from the Immaculate Heart of Mary

Church, with Father Thielemans celebrating the Mass. While everyone waited for a funeral director to come to the hospital and transport Regina's body to the other side of the island, Michelle and Nellie returned to Regina's bedside and helped a nurse dress her in the formal brown habit and veil of her order.

When the funeral director finally left the hospital with Regina's body at 1 p.m., Nellie left to return home, and Thielemans convinced everyone else to go for a ride. Having until 9 p.m. before the Eurodam sailed from Kona, the priest piled everyone into the rented passenger van, and after quickly perusing a map of Hawaii, drove off to explore the Big Island.

After stopping for lunch at a roadside stand, Thielemans drove everyone to Punaluu for a brief look at the black-sand beach. From there, he continued his two-hour trek to the Hawaii Volcanoes National Park.

Arriving at the park, Thielemans drove the van to the parking lot adjacent to the Kilauea volcano. There, he and Michelle helped Prosky and Conyngham out of the van and up to the volcano's closest vantage point.

"I always wanted to see this," Prosky revealed, as he carefully studied the volcano. "We were scheduled to come here on a shore excursion tomorrow but had to cancel. Coming here with you is so much nicer. Thank you, Paul."

As Thielemans smiled at Prosky and nodded, a perplexed look came to Michelle's face.

"There's something I don't understand," she admitted. "If Kilauea is an active volcano, what are we doing standing right next to it? Couldn't it erupt at any moment?"

"There are many sensors that warn of increasing pressure and activity inside the volcano," Conyngham revealed. "The sensors are monitored around the clock, and any data suggesting a possible eruption over the next few days or weeks would give the park sufficient time to close and surrounding communities sufficient time to evacuate. You can't see it from here, but lava is flowing out of the volcano's side vents as we speak."

"So, I shouldn't worry," Michelle suggested.

"Would it help?" Prosky joked.

Following their visit to the park, the group returned to the Eurodam. Boarding the ship at 7:45 p.m., everyone retreated to their cabins to freshen up before their scheduled 9 o'clock dinner in Thielemans' suite.

At dinner, the mood was somber as everyone tried to comfort each other over Regina's loss and find some meaning in her unexpected death. Not even one of the highlights of the cruise, the ship's evening passage past the Kilauea volcano, was able to significantly change the group's mindset.

As everyone sat on Thielemans' balcony and watched the spectacle of red, hot lava pouring into the sea from the side vents of the volcano, Conyngham's extensive scientific knowledge continued to amaze. Commenting on everything from the possibility of volcanic eruptions causing rivers of lava to flow from fissures on the sides of the volcano to the legal ownership of any new land created after lava flowed into the sea and solidified, the retired biochemistry professor held everyone's attention and was able to answer their most difficult questions.

Shortly after the Eurodam cruised past Kilauea, Conyngham and Michelle complained about being tired. As Michelle wheeled Conyngham back to his cabin, Prosky remained in Thielemans' suite for a nightcap.

"To Sister Regina," Thielemans said, toasting the late nun's memory with a glass of Bushmills Irish Whiskey.

"To Sister Regina," Prosky replied, clinking glasses with his host.

"How do you think Michelle will handle Regina's death?" Thielemans asked.

"Oh, she'll do just fine," Prosky answered reassuringly. "Michelle still has some unresolved issues with Regina, but tincture of time heals all."

"I was surprised by what Regina said to me before she died," Thielemans admitted. "She permitted Michelle to work for me. That was surprising because I never discussed the possibility with Michelle. Truthfully, I never seriously entertained the idea because I didn't think Sister Regina or Michelle's convent would allow it."

"Michelle probably kicked the idea around with Regina after she realized how much help you needed," Prosky surmised. "Would you want her to work for you?"

"Absolutely," Thielemans replied. "Since my sister returned to Belgium, I've been helpless. I need to find another secretary in a hurry, and Michelle has already shown she can handle the kind of things I need to have done. What's more, I like Michelle a lot."

"Don't take this the wrong way, Paul, but would Michelle be a distraction to you or those you'll be meeting during your travels?" Prosky inquired. "After all, she is a stunning woman, and people could get the wrong idea."

"My sister is also a stunning woman, and we never had any problems traveling together," Thielemans answered. "We always stayed in separate hotel rooms, and my sister never accompanied me to any of my speeches or meetings. When we went out to dinner, my sister and I dressed casually. So, we never gave strangers the chance to question why a beautiful woman and Catholic priest were having dinner together, not that it should matter."

"Don't you think working in proximity to a beautiful woman who was not your sister could present some problems?" Prosky asked.

"Not at all," Thielemans responded. "I've been working around beautiful women my entire life and have never had any problems. I, for one, still believe celibacy in the priesthood is non-negotiable. I have been celibate throughout my priesthood and plan to remain that way."

"Paul, you're a true priest," Prosky said, raising his glass to Thielemans, smiling, and nodding his approval. "From one true priest to another, I think it's time for some shuteye. Tomorrow's going to be a long day."

"That's for sure," Thielemans agreed. "It's been a long time since I conducted funeral services."

"Don't worry," Prosky chuckled, finishing his drink. "Besides Bill, Michelle, Nellie, and me, I doubt anyone else will be attending the Mass. With so many cataracts in the church, I don't think anyone will notice any mistakes."

Thielemans laughed and showed Prosky to the door.

"You know, Paul, we'll be in Maui the day after tomorrow," Prosky observed. "Bill and I won't be able to get on the tender to go ashore, but you and Michelle will. With Regina gone, there's no reason for Michelle to stay on the ship all day. Why don't you take her with you to Maui? That will give you a chance to talk with her about working with you. Give it some thought."

"I will, Ed," Thielemans replied.

As Prosky hobbled down the hallway with his wooden cane in hand, Thielemans watched and wondered what the old priest was thinking. Realizing Prosky was probably pondering the successful passing of another day's test of faith, Thielemans smiled and closed the cabin door.

The family and friends of Sister Regina were among the first to disembark the Eurodam when it docked in Hilo the next morning. Taking a shuttle bus to a car rental agency at the airport, they picked up another Ford passenger van and drove to the church.

Arriving at the empty church thirty minutes before the funeral Mass, the group met Nellie. Together, they walked toward Sister Regina's casket at the foot of the altar.

Sister Regina looked peaceful, dressed in the brown formal habit and veil of her order and holding the rosary Thielemans gave her just a few days before her unexpected death. Her longstanding friends, Fathers Prosky and Conyngham, appeared stoic as they silently prayed over her, while her niece, also dressed in her formal habit and veil, appeared pensive, but unemotional.

As Nellie took Thielemans into the sacristy and helped him prepare for Mass, Michelle and the two priests took their places in the front pew and quietly talked about the many baskets of beautiful native flowers that adorned the altar and surrounded Sister Regina's casket. A few minutes later, the group watched in disbelief as four altar boys, the church's organist and choir, a group of retired nuns, a busload of parochial school children, and dozens of Nellie's friends and relatives started arriving at the church.

To Thielemans' utter amazement, he was about to celebrate a funeral Mass in front of an unexpectedly large crowd. What surprised him most was the number of people who came to honor an elderly Catholic nun they never met.

Walking from the sacristy to the front pew with her perpetual smile locked firmly in place, Nellie waved to everyone in the church and watched as most in attendance smiled and waved back. Inspired by the kind of funeral Nellie had been able to arrange for her friend in a few hours and perceptible faith and love that filled the church, Thielemans proceeded to celebrate the funeral Mass.

During the service, he delivered an inspiring homily and touching eulogy. As he did, he showed Sister Regina the kind of respect a woman who had devoted her entire life to God and the service of others truly deserved.

Following Sister Regina's funeral Mass and interment at the Paauilo Cemetery, Thielemans handed Nellie a check and his business card. The check was a generous donation to Nellie's church, and the business card contained the address where Nellie was instructed to have the bills for Regina's funeral sent.

Seeing Nellie hugging Thielemans and thanking him for his extraordinary generosity, Michelle smiled. Watching the touching scene, Prosky and Conyngham silently nodded their approval.

Later that evening, everyone gathered in Thielemans' suite to enjoy dinner, watch the Eurodam sail away from Hilo, and reminisce about Sister Regina. When the group suddenly realized no one informed Sister Regina's convent about her death, Prosky volunteered to call the convent's new Mother Superior.

After Thielemans made arrangements with Winston to allow Prosky and Conyngham to use his suite for the day while he explored Maui with Michelle, the group called it a night. An hour later, as Thielemans sat comfortably on his balcony, thinking about Maui and wondering how Michelle would like to spend the day there, the front doorbell chimed.

"Let me guess," Thielemans said, opening the door for Michelle. "You want to sleep with me tonight."

"Can't," Michelle answered, walking toward the bar and tugging on her tee-shirt. "Have to get ready for Maui."

"Would you like to talk about it?" Thielemans asked.

"Nope," Michelle replied, picking up a bottle of Belvedere. "I could use a drink, though. How's this stuff?"

"It's Polish vodka," Thielemans revealed, walking toward the bar.

"Make it a large," Michelle requested.

Carrying their drinks, Thielemans sat down next to Michelle on the sofa.

"To Sister Regina," Thielemans toasted.

"To Regina," Michelle responded reflexively.

As Thielemans was taking his first sip of vodka, Michelle leaned over and kissed him on the cheek.

"Thank you for everything you did for Regina," Michelle said softly, but unemotionally. "You were always nice to her, and you went out of your way to include her in our group conversations. With Ed and Bill in the same room, that couldn't have been easy. You celebrated the most beautiful funeral Mass I've ever attended today, and the check you gave Nellie, as well as your offer to pick up the tab for Regina's funeral, were the most generous gifts I've ever seen. Thank you."

"You're welcome," Thielemans replied modestly.

"That having been said, you still owe me," Michelle continued with a hint of an imminent smile.

"Could you please explain exactly what it is I owe you?" Thielemans requested.

"You owe me a day in Maui," Michelle stated succinctly. "The tenders start taking passengers ashore tomorrow at 9 a.m., and the last tender returns to the ship tomorrow at 10:30 p.m. You owe me everything between those hours. I have an entire day and evening planned. Are you game?"

"Michelle, it sounds really great, but I'd like to know a little more about what you have planned," Thielemans explained.

"Everything tomorrow will be on a need-to-know basis," she revealed. "I'll explain each new step of our day in Maui as we get to it. What you need to know right now is I still have your spare iPhone and the credit card you gave me when we docked in Honolulu. I plan to pay for tomorrow's expenses by charging a thousand bucks to your card. Are you with me so far?"

"I guess," Thielemans agreed somewhat hesitantly.

"You're too generous a man to hoard your enthusiasm," Michelle quipped. "So, I'll call you tomorrow morning, somewhere after 9 o'clock. I'll have to wear my nun clothes off the ship, but you could dress casually. Everything else will make sense when we get to it. Okay?"

"I guess," Thielemans repeated, even more hesitantly.

"Let's work on that enthusiasm," Michelle encouraged, finishing her drink and getting up from the sofa.

As Thielemans started walking Michelle to the door, she turned around and gave him another kiss on the cheek.

"Later, Rock Star," Michelle said with a seductive smile, as she left the suite. Walking backward down the hall, she raised her arms and formed the letters, U and O, and then, pointed to herself. "You owe me," she quietly verbalized.

"I guess," Thielemans mumbled, as he closed the door and retreated to his bedroom for the kind of sleep that usually precedes a trip to the unknown.

CHAPTER NINE

Following a restless night's sleep, Thielemans awoke and immediately checked his email. Gratified by encouraging messages from two bishops and the names of several priests interested in his program, Thielemans ordered a hearty breakfast and retreated to his bathroom to prepare for his big day in Maui.

As Thielemans sat on his balcony, finishing his breakfast and watching the first tenders taking passengers to Lahaina, his iPhone rang.

"Hey, Rock Star, are you ready for some fun in the sun?" Michelle asked enthusiastically.

"I'm just about ready," Thielemans replied. "Come to my suite in ten minutes, and we'll leave from here."

"No can do," Michelle said. "I'm already in Lahaina. I hopped on the first tender and just got here. So, get a move on, and I'll meet you at the pier."

Rather than trying to understand the mysterious workings of the day's event planner, Thielemans just smiled, quickly dressed in his wardrobe *du jour* - a navy blue golf shirt, khaki slacks, and brown boat shoes, and headed for the nearest tender. An hour later, the priest arrived in Lahaina and began searching the crowded pier for his traveling companion.

Unable to immediately locate a young nun, dressed in the brown pantsuit and veil of her religious order, Thielemans moved with the crowd into an adjacent courtyard and quickly reached for his iPhone. As he began to call Michelle, the priest witnessed the quasi-miraculous parting of the crowd and emergence of a beautiful, young woman who, dressed in a white shirt, shorts, and baseball cap, strapped wedge sandals, and fashionable sunglasses, gave new meaning to the phrase, "Maui Wowie."

"Why, Sister Michelle," the surprised clergyman exclaimed, as he watched the gorgeous woman slowly approach and a mesmerized crowd grow fat on eye candy. "When did your convent adopt the new look?"

"When Father Thielemans loaned us his credit card," Michelle replied. "All my buds at the convent asked me to thank you for their new outfits."

"I can just imagine," Thielemans chuckled, as he removed his sunglasses and wiped them clean.

Carrying a few shopping bags filled with new clothing and old religious attire, Thielemans and Michelle boarded a shuttle bus and soon arrived at a fashionable resort.

"There's the car rental agency," Michelle observed, pointing to an office directly across from the resort's lobby. "You get the car, and I'll get us a room."

Thielemans removed his sunglasses and stared in disbelief at Michelle.

"Trust me," she said reassuringly. "No rock star will be harmed during the filming of this motion picture."

Before Thielemans could say a word, Michelle kissed him on the cheek, picked up her shopping bags, and disappeared into the lobby of the beautiful resort. With little alternative, the bewildered priest walked into the car rental agency and retrieved the red Corvette convertible Michelle reserved in his name.

Picking up Michelle at the lobby, Thielemans followed her instructions and drove to an oceanside building.

"We're in Room 247," Michelle said, as she exited the convertible with her shopping bags. "We'll only be here a minute. I just want to drop off the bags and make sure the room is all right."

Without commenting, Thielemans followed Michelle into the room.

"What a beautiful view," Michelle exclaimed, as she threw her bags on the sofa and opened the balcony door.

"It is beautiful," the priest agreed, carefully studying the ocean and beach. "So, what's the game plan?"

"After I powder my nose, I'd like to drive to Haleakala and check out the volcano," Michelle replied. "I heard the view from the crater is breathtaking. There's supposed to be a few roadside-stands along the way that serve great barbecue and fish tacos. I thought we might stop at one for lunch. After we visit Haleakala, I'd like to drive to the beach. The surf is supposed to be spectacular. Then, I thought we'd watch the sunset before driving back here for dinner. I've already arranged for us to have dinner served in our room at 8 o'clock. The last tender returns to the ship at 10:30, and it's about a fifteen-minute cab ride to the pier. So, we should have plenty of time to enjoy a nice quiet dinner together."

"I've got to hand it to you," Thielemans admitted with a smile. "You certainly know how to plan things."

"You have no idea," Michelle answered with a twinkle in her eye.

Hopping into the Corvette convertible, Thielemans and Michelle toured Maui, dining at a local fish shack, looking down at the clouds and air traffic from 10,000 feet above sea level at the Haleakala crater, and even taking a walk along the beach. Before returning to the resort, the two visited a different shore point and drank rum punch as they watched the sun gracefully sink into the ocean.

Following a beautiful day on Maui, Thielemans drove Michelle back to their room before reluctantly returning the Corvette to the rental agency. Michelle used the time to shower, put on a new dress she bought upon arriving in Lahaina, and drape the Hawaiian shirt she bought for her traveling companion over a bedroom chair.

Returning to the room and seeing Michelle wearing a plumeria over her left ear and dressed in a floor-length, white dress with a multicolored Hawaiian floral pattern, Thielemans could do little more than stare.

"Does everyone at the convent look like you tonight?" Thielemans asked.

"I seriously doubt it," Michelle replied with a smile.

Thielemans continued to stare at Michelle and slowly shake his head, side to side.

"Don't just stand there, gawking," Michelle said, pulling Thielemans inside the room and closing the door. "Dinner's on the way. So, go shower and think of something nice to say when you get back."

Nodding in agreement, Thielemans let out a loud sigh and walked into the bathroom.

While the priest was showering, a Hawaiian waiter delivered dinner and two bottles of Asti Spumante to the room. Distributing several covered dishes across the dinner table and placing both bottles of Asti into a large, ice-filled punch bowl, the young waiter took a final look at Michelle, mumbled something in Hawaiian, and quietly left the room with a smile that extended from ear to ear.

As Michelle started rearranging the various dishes on the dinner table, Thielemans returned, wearing a white

Hawaiian shirt with a tropical bird pattern. Before he could say anything, Michelle handed him a long-stem, pink rose.

"This flower is the lokelani," Michelle said with a smile. "It's the official flower of Maui."

"Thank you," Thielemans responded, smelling the fragrant flower. "What is the name of the flower you're wearing in your hair?"

"It's a plumeria," Michelle answered, repositioning the flower over her left ear. "A woman wears a plumeria over her right ear when she is single, and over her left ear when she is already taken."

"You're single," Thielemans observed. "So, why are you wearing the flower over your left ear?"

"Because I'm already taken," she whispered lovingly, kissing the unsuspecting priest on the cheek.

As Michelle uncovered the dishes that contained their sumptuous feast, Thielemans opened a bottle of Asti Spumante and filled two champagne glasses.

"To our beautiful day in Maui," Thielemans announced, as he raised his glass.

"And to beautiful days that never end," Michelle replied, clinking glasses with Thielemans.

Following their toast, Thielemans refilled their glasses with Asti, and Michelle filled their plates with perfectly prepared samples of red snapper, ahi tuna, and mahi-mahi, as well as native fruits and garnishes. As the two dined, they talked about Maui, highlights of the cruise, and the prospect of working together after the Eurodam returned to San Diego.

Throughout dinner, the two laughed, teased, and thoroughly enjoyed each other's company. After they finished a dessert of pineapple cheesecake and Kona coffee, Thielemans poured what was left of the second bottle of Asti into their champagne glasses and walked with Michelle out on to the balcony.

"We'll always have Maui," he suggested, raising his glass for a final toast.

"To days that never end," Michelle replied, taking a sip of Asti and savoring her final taste.

Taking Thielemans' glass from his hand and placing both glasses on a balcony table, Michelle threw her arms around the surprised priest's neck and kissed him tenderly on the lips.

"Father, is it a sin to kiss someone you love?" Michelle whispered in Thielemans' ear.

"Let me check," Thielemans answered, gently returning Michelle's kiss. "No. Kissing someone you love is not a sin."

Laughing out loud, Michelle hugged Thielemans and dried a few joyful tears in his shirt. Trying to memorize the feeling of Michelle in his arms, Thielemans closed his eyes and incorporated the sound of the pounding surf and smell of the tropical air into his memory.

"I've never felt so content," Michelle revealed, still locked in Thielemans' embrace. "Could we stay here forever?"

"I'm not sure the ship would wait that long," Thielemans said. "What time do we have to leave here?"

"By 10 o'clock," Michelle sighed.

"It's 9:45," Thielemans observed, looking at his wristwatch. "I'd better call a cab."

Without saying a word, Michelle returned to the room. While Thielemans phoned the front desk to request a taxi, Michelle went into the bathroom.

A few minutes later, she returned, dressed in her religious attire. Consolidating Thielemans' golf shirt and the shoes, clothing, and flowers she purchased in Maui into a single shopping bag, Michelle stared at the priest, nervously smiled, and patiently waited for the cab.

Catching the last tender, the two boarded the Eurodam just minutes before its 11 p.m. departure. Exchanging a quick kiss, each went to their respective cabins.

Grabbing a snifter of Courvoisier, Thielemans took a seat on the balcony and prepared to watch the Eurodam leave Maui and begin the final leg of its trip home. As he watched the ship depart, he thought about the events of the day and realized he was starting to venture outside his comfort zone with Michelle.

Thirty minutes later, Thielemans returned to the bar with an empty glass, and as he started refilling it, the front doorbell chimed. Opening the door, Thielemans made immediate eye contact with Michelle who was dressed in a white bathrobe and carrying the lokelani she gave him in Maui.

"Can I sleep with you tonight?" she asked seductively, as she returned Thielemans' pink rose, adjusted the plumeria behind her left ear, and entered the suite.

Before Thielemans could answer, Michelle walked into his bedroom and turned on the light. The priest returned to the bar and poured a second glass of Courvoisier before joining her.

As Thielemans entered the bedroom holding two snifters of cognac, Michelle removed her bathrobe and dropped it to the floor. Adjusting the top of her strapless, white bikini, she sat on the side of the bed and slowly unfastened the straps of her wedge sandals.

Handing Michelle her snifter of Courvoisier, Thielemans sat down next to her on the side of the bed. Looking into her eyes, he clinked glasses with her and took a sip of cognac.

"Since you're in my bed, I think a bedtime story would be appropriate," Thielemans said with a nervous grin. "Once upon a time, there was a teenage boy who was spoiled rotten by two wealthy parents. His parents were wonderful people who spent a lot of time away from home because of their thriving business. So, unsupervised and left to his own devices, the lad became sexually active while still in high school. By the time he got to Harvard, he was a regular James Bond. Like 007, the young man had it all – the sports car, the expensive clothes and jewelry, the line, the technique, and most of all, the willingness. Young girls and older women threw themselves at him – and he let them. Having sex with beautiful women quickly became his major extracurricular activity in college."

Thielemans paused and took a sip of Courvoisier.

"The young man majored in international studies and planned to take over his father's thriving export business," Thielemans continued, as he put his head down and stared at the floor. "Midway through college, he met Barbara, a Harvard classmate whose background was similar to his. She came from money and planned to make more of it as an international business lawyer. The two started having sex on their second date, and by their third date, Barbara was already planning their wedding reception. Within a few weeks, she had lists of potential bridesmaids and wedding guests, stores that sponsored bridal registries, and honeymoon destinations."

Thielemans took another sip of cognac.

"The young man had no plans to get married while he was still in college, and no plans to ever marry Barbara," he continued. "He didn't love her, but he hung out with her because they had a lot in common. The more he got to know Barbara, the more he started disliking her. Getting filthy rich seemed to be her only goal in life, and she seemed to lack real character. When she talked about marriage, the young man tried convincing her he wasn't interested. True to her nature, she never listened to anything he had to say. So, she continued making plans for both of them, even though she began wondering if his plans for the future and hers were the same."

Thielemans raised his head, repositioned himself on the side of the bed, and took a deep breath.

"The young man decided to see Barbara one final time and tell her their affair was over," he continued. "When he arrived at her apartment, she took his hand, led him over to the couch, and delivered an Academy Award-winning performance. Holding his hands, she looked into his eyes, smiled, and announced she was pregnant. After he finally managed to get his heart out of his throat, the young man stared at Barbara in disbelief. He asked her to explain how she could be pregnant when he always used a condom during sex and she was taking birth control pills. In response, Barbara just shrugged her shoulders and smiled weakly. Giving the young man a few minutes to walk around her apartment and think, Barbara informed him of her desire to get married as soon as possible. When he asked her if she had seen a doctor and confirmed her pregnancy, she told him she tested positive on two different over-the-counter pregnancy tests and planned to see a doctor later in the week. Not knowing what else to do, the young man told her to call him after she saw the doctor and quickly left her apartment."

Michelle took small, nervous sips of scotch, but remained silent and continued listening.

"A few days later, Barbara called the young man," Thielemans revealed. "She informed him she didn't appreciate his lack of support when she told him she was pregnant, and after giving the matter some thought, decided she was going to have an abortion. Hearing she wanted to terminate the life of his child, the young man dropped the phone, jumped into his car, and raced over to Barbara's apartment. He spent the rest of the night pleading with her to change her mind about having an abortion. Through it all, she enjoyed watching him squirm and suffer. Sensing she would forget about the abortion if he got down on his knees and begged her to marry him, he suddenly realized her pregnancy story might be a scam and just a way to facilitate a wedding. Carefully looking at her, he suddenly saw a person who was quite capable of faking a pregnancy, marrying an heir to a large fortune, and shortly thereafter, filing for divorce and walking away with one-half of a large inheritance."

Thielemans paused, took a sip of cognac, and looked into Michelle's eyes.

"The young man asked Barbara if she had seen a doctor yet and had her pregnancy confirmed," he continued. "When she gave some lame excuse about her appointment being canceled, he asked to see the pregnancy tests she took. Claiming she already disposed of them, she freaked out when he offered to go to the pharmacy and buy another pregnancy test. In response, Barbara told him she couldn't stand looking at him any longer, would never marry him, and couldn't wait to get rid of his child. When she started screaming and throwing things, he decided to get out of harm's way until she regained her composure. Stepping into the bathroom, he noticed an open box of tampons and an open sleeve of Midol resting on top of a hot-water bottle. Touching the hot-water bottle, he realized it had recently been used because it was still warm. Seeing empty tampon wrappers sticking out of a full wastebasket, he looked inside the basket and found a pharmacy receipt. Perusing the receipt, he noticed tampons and Midol among the items that were purchased that morning. Since she lived alone, he realized Barbara was having a menstrual period and couldn't be pregnant. Returning to the living room, he confronted her with his discovery. Throwing herself on the couch, she cried hysterically. The young man left and never returned."

"You were the young man," Michelle correctly observed, looking out into the distance.

"Yes, I was," Thielemans conceded. "That experience changed my entire life. Becoming sexually active at an early age, I never gave any serious thought to the consequences of sex. With time and experience using condoms, pregnancy was the farthest thing from my mind when I made love to a beautiful woman. Fortunately, Barbara's fake pregnancy made me realize pregnancy is a consequence of sex, and the result of a successful pregnancy is God's most loving gift, the gift of life. I can't tell you how distraught I became when I envisioned my child inside Barbara and heard Barbara threatening to have my child killed by an abortionist. Every time I thought of the possibility, I became physically ill."

Thielemans and Michelle stared at each other.

"From the moment I left Barbara's apartment for the final time, I started praying," he revealed. "The more I prayed, the more I sensed a direction in life. I realized I was already rich and didn't have to expand my father's business. I also realized I needed to share God's message. That's when I started studying theology and planning to become a priest. I can't tell you how ashamed I was of the gratuitous sex I had with so many women I didn't love. I prayed and offered my celibacy in exchange for God's forgiveness. Barbara was my last sexual encounter. I have been celibate ever since, and choose to remain that way. I've had many chances to have sex since I broke up with Barbara and more chances to have sex since I became a priest. I truly miss the feeling of being one with a woman, but not as much as I would miss being able to do the things only a priest can do. Michelle, I love you with all my heart, but I can't be intimate with you. I hope you understand."

"If you'll buy me another drink, I'll tell you a bedtime story," Michelle replied unemotionally.

Thielemans obliged and left the bedroom to retrieve more Courvoisier. When he returned, Michelle fluffed a pillow, swung her legs into his bed, and positioned the pillow between her back and the bed's headboard.

Seeing Michelle sitting comfortably in bed, Thielemans returned her snifter of Courvoisier, kicked off his boat shoes, and joined her in bed.

"So, let's hear your bedtime story," he requested, adjusting his pillow and sitting next to Michelle.

"My father died when I was in fifth grade," Michelle began. "My mother raised me until my junior year in high school. When she was diagnosed with metastatic lung cancer, our roles suddenly reversed. With no brothers or sisters, I became my mother's caregiver. Aunt Regina was our only living relative, and to her credit, she sent a constant stream of nuns through our house to help me take care of my mother. Obviously, I didn't have a normal high school experience. I never dated, attended proms, or participated in any important high school events. The nuns became my sisters and helped me care for my mother. When my mother died a month before my high school graduation, Regina became my new parent. She took care of my mother's funeral and financial affairs, and at the same time, convinced me to join the convent. With little alternative, I went directly from high school to the convent where Regina, who was Mother Superior of the entire order, personally supervised my religious development."

Michelle paused and stared out into the distance.

"Midway through my novitiate, Regina encouraged me to participate in a summer outreach program for native Americans and Mexican migrant workers in Arizona," she continued. "The program lasted six weeks, and during that time, hundreds of different priests, nuns, native Americans, migrant workers and television, newspaper, and magazine reporters commingled in the desert. The nuns were the easiest to identify because a large sporting goods chain donated blue jeans, tee-shirts, and western boots for all of us to wear. During the program, everyone shared canned surplus food and bottled water, and slept in huge teepees. Religious services and campfire singalongs were the highlights of the program. Most participants only stayed for a few days or a week. So, there was a constant infusion of new faces into the program every day, and a constant game of musical teepees every night."

Michelle paused and took a sip of cognac.

"Early one morning, a priest who I had never seen before appeared out of nowhere and told me he needed my help," Michelle revealed. "Telling me he had already gotten the permission of the program director, he asked me to go with him into town to pick up supplies. Not thinking anything of it, I got into his car. Telling me I appeared dehydrated, he offered me a cold bottle of orange juice which I gladly accepted. Feeling thirsty, I drank the juice in a hurry and quickly started feeling woozy. I fell asleep, and other than briefly opening my eyes during a stop at the Mexican border station, didn't wake up until we arrived at a large home that overlooked the ocean. There, he invited me to cool off in the shower before we sat down and ate Mexican food and drank lemonade."

Michelle paused for a few seconds, took another sip of cognac, and loudly sighed.

"Shortly after lunch, I began feeling woozy again and took a nap in his large bedroom," she continued. "As soon as I fell asleep, he removed my clothes and sexually abused me for the rest of the day and throughout the entire night. I awoke when he first climbed on top of me but was too weak and confused to resist. After he took my virginity, he kissed me for a very long time. Then, he turned me over and started having sex with me from behind. For what seemed like an eternity, he punished me with painful intercourse, pausing occasionally to make me take sips of drugged cocktails. This put me to sleep and allowed him to briefly nap beside me. Twice during the night, he pulled me out of bed and took me to the bathroom. He was a little man who tried to make up for his physical inadequacy by being rough with me in bed. Hurting me seemed to excite him sexually."

As her anger mounted, Michelle paused for a moment.

"The next morning, I was drowsy and could hardly walk," she continued in a calmer voice. "My abductor dragged me into the bathroom and threw me into the shower. Then, he helped me dress before spoon-feeding me some cereal and milk. As he led me out of the house, I could see the ocean, but no other houses, buildings, or landmarks of any kind. I fell asleep in his car, and hours later, woke up under a tree in the Arizona desert. A migrant worker and his wife found me and drove me back to the program site."

Michelle paused again and took another sip of cognac.

"As soon as I arrived at the program site, the nun who was in charge gave me something to drink, and unable to understand my garbled speech, put me to rest in a teepee before calling my aunt," she revealed. "Regina immediately flew from Baltimore and arrived at the program site later that night. She brought with her a nun who was also a licensed nurse practitioner. By the time they arrived, I was still drowsy, but more coherent. After they listened to my detailed account of what had happened, the nurse practitioner thoroughly examined me. Then, she gave me shots of penicillin in both my cheeks, rubbed antibiotic cream into the lacerations I had in my vagina and rectum, and gave me a pill that was some kind of sedative. Early the next morning, we got on a plane and flew to Philadelphia. From there, we drove to a psychiatric facility where I spent the next few months of my life taking various combinations of mind-altering medications that turned me into a zombie."

"Did Regina visit you while you were in the psychiatric hospital?" Thielemans inquired.

"Every weekend," Michelle replied. "During those visits, she tried convincing me she left no stone unturned in her investigation of what happened to me in Arizona. It was her belief someone slipped me some of the peyote that was later discovered at the program site, and the combined effects of the peyote and intense heat caused me to wander off into the desert and start hallucinating. She insisted my being abducted by a priest, driven to Mexico, and raped was a hallucination, and my being taken from Arizona to the Pacific coast and back in twenty-four hours, while not impossible, was highly improbable. She even went so far as to bring in photos of every priest that participated in the outreach program. When I couldn't identify my abductor from the photos, Regina insisted the priest wasn't in the photos because he only existed in my imagination."

"Did anyone at the program site report you missing while you were gone?" Thielemans asked.

"Apparently, no one realized I was missing," Michelle said angrily. "That's not surprising, though. Every nun participated to some degree in each of the program's many different events. Every nun also slept with a dozen or so different program participants in different teepees every night. There were no formal schedules of events, sleeping assignments, or roll calls. Nuns leaving the program site and driving into town with other program participants was an everyday occurrence. So, no one ever worried about a nun who was temporarily away from the program site."

"Did you ever ask Regina why you required penicillin shots, treatment of your vaginal and rectal lacerations, or sedatives if you were never raped?" Thielemans asked.

"Of course," Michelle exclaimed. "Regina remembered bringing a nurse practitioner to examine me, but didn't remember my being given injections or other treatments. She also remembered my needing a sedative because of the prolonged effects of my purported peyote ingestion and altered mental status. Regina cited the altered mental status as the reason she decided to fly me to Philadelphia instead of Baltimore and have me driven directly from the airport to the psychiatric facility."

"I can understand patients being observed in a hospital for a few days because of the unpredictable effects of a hallucinogen, but why did they keep you institutionalized for several months?" Thielemans questioned.

"The psychiatrists claimed the peyote caused an acute psychotic episode, which in turn, unmasked a previously undiagnosed bipolar condition," Michelle stated. "They claimed it took them several months to bring my illness under control and regulate the medications required to control my manic-depressive disorder."

"Have you been on medications since you left the psychiatric hospital?" Thielemans inquired.

"When I first left the psychiatric facility, Regina watched me like a hawk," Michelle revealed. "She dispensed my pills three or four times a day and watched me swallow every last one. With time, I saw different psychiatrists, the medications were changed, and I was placed on meds that only had to be taken once or twice daily. When this happened, Regina started backing off and trusting me to manage the pills on my own. That's when I stopped taking all the medications. I discarded a few pills every day so Regina wouldn't get suspicious if she checked my bottles and counted the pills. They used to check blood tests on me during my psychiatric evaluations to make sure my drug levels were adequate. Knowing this, I would restart the medications a week before my visits so the drugs would show up in my blood, and stop taking them immediately after I saw the psychiatrist."

"When was the last time you took any medications?" Thielemans asked.

"Six months ago," Michelle answered. "That was the last time I met with my psychiatrist. Before that, I didn't take any medications for nearly a year."

"How did your psychiatrist feel you were doing?" the priest inquired.

"He told me the drugs were working so well no one would ever suspect I was bipolar," Michelle chuckled.

"What about Ed?" Thielemans questioned. "As your psychologist, how does he feel you're doing?"

"Considering Ed and I mostly discuss our secret desires to kill sex offenders, I'd say he thinks I'm probably doing as well psychologically as he is," Michelle joked. "He still thinks I'm bipolar."

"Does he think you're still taking your medications?" Thielemans queried.

"Of course," Michelle answered. "That's why he still advises me not to drink wine or liquor when we dine with you. He realizes mixing psychogenic medications and booze is a no-no."

"There's one last thing that's still bothering me about your story," Thielemans argued. "Why did Regina go through all the trouble of turning you into a mental case when she could have just as easily taken you to an emergency room, had any reputable doctor determine you had been raped, and called the police?"

"Father Thielemans, you still have an awful lot to learn about this Catholic Church of ours," Michelle stated sarcastically. "First of all, Regina was an 'Old School' nun. Her Church was one that put priests on top of the heap and trained nuns to keep them there. She was taught to cover up a priest's indiscretions and make sure nothing ever allowed an outsider to question the sanctity of the Church or its priests. Today, people are shocked when they read news reports about priests raping nuns or nuns getting pregnant. Don't people realize these things have been going on for centuries? Very few priests are rapists and very few nuns ever get pregnant, but the human condition doesn't change just because a person takes theology courses or starts wearing religious garb."

Michelle paused and took another sip of Courvoisier.

"I think Regina discovered the identity of my abductor and realized he was a priest," she continued. I don't know why she chose to protect him instead of me, but she must have had her reasons. I've often wondered if she tried to save his career as a priest, spare the Church any embarrassment, or take advantage of a situation that allowed her to keep me close and under her control. I've even wondered if Regina did what she did to protect me and have a reason to keep me by her side as her assistant. In truth, Regina probably did what she did for all those reasons. I'll never forgive her for sacrificing me to protect the career of a priest or reputation of the Church, but I realize her training caused her to do the things she did. Pope Benedict forced a French convent, the Community of Saint Jean, to disband in 2005 when he discovered their nuns were being used as sex slaves by priests. If untold numbers of sexual abuses in a convent could be successfully covered up for years, why couldn't a one-day abuse of a young novice?"

"Do you remember what your abductor looked like?" Thielemans asked.

"I'll never forget what he looked like," Michelle replied. "He was short - about 5'4", and thin. He had meticulously cut, light brown hair and perfect teeth. He wore standard priest attire and aviator eyeglasses. He drove a small, black sports car, but I don't know the make or model. He didn't speak much, but I did hear him answer the phone a few times. I thought I heard him tell someone on the phone he was a bishop, but I'm not sure I understood him correctly. He looked too young to be a bishop, and didn't dress or act like one."

"He doesn't sound like any priest or bishop I know," Thielemans admitted.

"He's not the kind of priest or bishop anyone should know," Michelle insisted.

Thielemans and Michelle both stared out into space before looking into each other's eyes.

"Alrighty, then," Michelle swooned, as she got out of bed and put on her bathrobe. "I want you to know I feel like a fool right now... I apologize if I made you feel uncomfortable... I've got to go."

Taking a few steps, Michelle suddenly stopped.

"There is something else I should tell you," Michelle added, as she turned and walked toward Thielemans. "I had something very important stolen from me when I was raped and never thought I could ever feel like a woman again. I've lived my life in shame and never associated love or sex with anything that wasn't painful. That was before you came along. From the moment I met you, something came alive inside me. I tried ignoring my feelings, but every time I saw you, my feelings grew stronger. I've fantasized about making love to you every night for the past week and planned our day and night in Maui to make my fantasy come true. I thought you and I had something between us, but after hearing your story, I realize I made a mistake and underestimated your dedication to the priesthood."

Michelle paused, reached into the pocket of her bathrobe, and removed a small, wrapped gift.

"Paul, you're fortunate to be wealthy and not have any obligations," she continued. "You're also lucky you had your parents for as long as you did and to still have a sister. With Regina gone, I don't have any family. For a while, I thought you and I could be a family, but I was wrong. I'll find out in the morning if Ed talked to Mother Superior today, and if she'll allow me to work with you. If she orders me to return to the convent, I'll probably be teaching science at a parochial school in Southeast Nowhere by the end of the month. As you've probably surmised, I never wanted to become a nun. I was pulled into the convent by my aunt when I was 18 years old, vulnerable, and without other options. I'm 33 years old now, just as vulnerable as I was when I entered the convent, and still without options. You were my one chance to find love, and I'm sorry I handled our brief love affair so poorly. Thank you for telling me you loved me. Unfortunately, the world is full of slow learners like me who have to be shown everything. I really love you, Paul. I'm sorry if I offended you."

Tossing the gift to Thielemans, Michelle walked out of the bedroom. Hearing the front door close, Thielemans sat up and unwrapped his gift – a box of condoms.

Throwing the condoms on his night table, Thielemans got out of bed and walked to the balcony. Standing against the railing, he studied the vastness of the sea and night sky, and realized he was not only in the middle of the Pacific Ocean but also in the middle of an existential crisis.

Struggling with an overwhelming flight of ideas, he thought about the separate realities of loneliness, sacrifice, and celibacy that were part of most Catholic priests' lives. As he revisited the events of the preceding hours and started feeling tired, the front doorbell chimed.

"I forgot my shoes," Michelle said with an embarrassed look on her face, as she entered the suite and slowly walked past Thielemans into the bedroom.

Instead of retrieving her shoes, Michelle removed her bathrobe, adjusted her bikini top, and climbed back into bed. Seeing Michelle getting comfortable, Thielemans shut off the light, and without undressing, joined her.

"I hope you realize I was just testing you before," Michelle whispered, moving toward the middle of the bed.

"I knew it all along," Thielemans said, pulling Michelle into his arms. "Did I pass the test?"

"I forgot to keep score," Michelle replied.

"Maybe, next time," Thielemans suggested, as he quickly fell asleep with the young nun in his arms.

"Maybe, next time," Michelle whispered, as she closed her eyes and joined Thielemans in his dream.

CHAPTER TEN

Thielemans awoke the next morning and found himself still dressed in his Hawaiian shirt and khaki slacks, but alone in bed. After he showered, ordered breakfast, and put on a golf shirt, walking shorts, and boat shoes, he checked his email and was disappointed to find no new messages from priests interested in his program.

Checking the latest internet news, he read about the U.S.S. Arizona Memorial being closed for repairs. He smiled when he thought about Sister Regina approaching a sailor at Pearl Harbor and complaining to him about the poor condition of the Memorial's dock.

While Thielemans was perusing other news reports on the internet, he suddenly thought about Bobby Kucera and considered reopening the television news feed that reported the altar boy's death and funeral. Picturing Bobby and still blaming himself for not being able to prevent the youngster's death, the conscientious priest thought better of revisiting the unsettling news report, immediately closed his laptop, and walked out on to the balcony.

As he waited for his breakfast to be delivered, Thielemans reviewed the Eurodam's itinerary and realized it was Day 13 of the cruise, with Days 13 through 17 to be spent at sea, and Day 18 to be spent in Ensenada, Mexico before the ship returned to San Diego. It was hard for him to believe two-thirds of the cruise was already over, and harder for him to predict what still might happen before the cruise came full circle.

Thielemans enjoyed a leisurely breakfast and was just about to take his last sip of coffee when Prosky and Conyngham showed up at his front door.

"Are we too early for a soak?" Prosky questioned, as he pushed Conyngham's wheelchair into the suite.

"Not at all," Thielemans replied.

"How was your day in Maui?" Conyngham inquired.

"Fit for a rock star," Thielemans answered.

As Prosky helped Conyngham into the whirlpool bathtub, Thielemans poured everyone a glass of Bailey's Irish Cream Liqueur.

"So, how did yesterday go for you and Bill?" Thielemans asked, sitting down on the sofa next to Prosky.

"We had a wonderful day, thanks to you," Prosky revealed. "We spent most of the day here in your suite, using your whirlpool and drinking your booze. Winston was even kind enough to serve us lunch and dinner here."

"I'm glad you had a nice day," Thielemans said. "Did you have a chance to call the Mother Superior?"

"Yes, I did," Prosky confirmed. "I had a nice, long chat with Sister Consuela, and I think I sold her on the idea of Michelle working with you for the foreseeable future."

"That's wonderful," Thielemans exclaimed, raising his glass to salute Prosky.

"I'm surprised she didn't give me a hard time," Prosky admitted. "I've known Consuela for many years. Before I called her, I realized she trusted my judgment and would probably follow my recommendations, but I expected some kind of tussle. I told her Michelle was having a tough time handling Regina's unexpected death and wasn't ready for a return to convent life. Consuela liked the idea of Michelle working with a renowned theologian on a project of importance to Mother Church. I think I sealed the deal when I told her you would be taking care of Michelle's living expenses and donating her pay to the convent."

"I never really talked finances with you, but I have money," Thielemans revealed with an air of genuine humility. "My sister and I inherited our parents' fortune, and neither of us will ever be able to spend anywhere near the amount of money we have earning interest and dividends in banks and brokerage houses all over the world. So, paying Michelle's convent for her work won't be a problem. I'll also be glad to pay for anything Michelle needs, even health insurance."

"This suite and your generosity gave you away a long time ago," Prosky suggested. "I knew you probably came from money, but didn't realize the extent of your wealth."

"I don't flaunt my wealth, but I don't make excuses for it either," Thielemans stated. "My father worked very hard to earn the money my sister and I inherited. It would be an insult to him for me not to enjoy a small portion of what he left me, especially since I give most of my earnings back to the Church in one way or another."

"Paul, there is no doubt in my mind Michelle would be safe working with you and profit from the experience," Prosky remarked. "I'm not worried about Michelle, but I am worried about you."

"I don't understand," Thielemans said.

"How well do you know Michelle?" Prosky asked.

"Not very well," Thielemans admitted.

"That's what I thought," Prosky answered, as though his worst fears had just been realized. "I make it a policy to never violate doctor-patient confidentiality, but this is one time where I feel the need to make an exception. That's because the futures of two people I care about very much are at stake. What I'm about to tell you is highly confidential, and I need your assurance you'll never repeat anything I tell you to anyone, especially Michelle."

"You have my word," Thielemans promised.

Prosky gulped down the remainder of his liqueur. Putting down his glass, he stared into Thielemans' eyes.

"Paul, Michelle is bipolar," Prosky revealed. "Her disorder is under optimal control and will most likely remain that way as long as she continues to take her medications and receive regular counseling. In addition to having me as her psychologist, she also has a psychiatrist in Bethesda who has done a nice job with her. He talks with her every month via video teleconferencing over the internet and renews her prescriptions as necessary. Once or twice a year, he sees her in his office. When I'm not with Michelle, I talk with her on the phone. Because we're both involved in the clergy sex abuse monitoring program, we communicate with each other a few times a week, and usually see each other once or twice a month."

Seeing his guest needed a refill, Thielemans poured another glass of Irish Cream.

"What's important for you to realize is Michelle decides to stop taking her medications every so often," Prosky added. "When that happens, all bets are off because she's capable of doing the most unexpected things."

"Like what?" Thielemans inquired.

"Well, a few years ago, she stopped taking her medications for a week and decided to go for a drive," Prosky continued. "She's usually a very good driver, but on this one occasion, she tried to beat a traffic light that was about to change. She thought she could make it through the light before it turned red, so she floored it. Unfortunately, the drivers of the three cars in front of her didn't think they could make it through the light. Need I say more? The convent's insurance company is still paying off car repair bills and medical claims."

"Does Michelle feel she needs to be on medication?" Thielemans asked.

"Michelle feels she has never needed medication," Prosky replied. "She also feels she has been misdiagnosed by every psychiatrist and psychologist who has ever treated her. That includes me. This brings up another important point. Michelle has a history of delusional thinking, as well as a history of inpatient psychiatric treatment."

"Tell me more," Thielemans requested, although he already knew where the story was headed.

"While she was still a novice, Michelle went to some small town between Phoenix and Tucson to take part in a summer outreach program," Prosky continued. "A few weeks into the program, Sister Consuela, who was the program director at that time, called Regina and told her Michelle was in a bad way. Michelle was found delirious in the desert by migrant workers. After being rehydrated and allowed to rest, she reported being abducted by a priest who drove her to Mexico and forced her to have sex with him. Michelle said she tried to resist the priest's advances, but was unable to do so because she had been drugged."

Prosky paused and took another sip of his liqueur.

"When she heard the news, Regina immediately flew from Baltimore to Arizona, bringing with her another nun who was a nurse practitioner," he continued. "As soon as they arrived in Arizona, Regina had the nurse practitioner thoroughly examine Michelle. The nurse practitioner told

Regina there was no evidence of forceful sex or spermatic fluid. Allowing for the possibilities Michelle could have been drugged and coaxed into having non-violent sexual intercourse and the male could have worn a condom, the nurse practitioner told Regina there was no physical evidence of rape."

Prosky looked directly at Thielemans.

"Giving Michelle the benefit of the doubt, Regina initiated a full-scale investigation," Prosky revealed. "Unfortunately, she couldn't find anything that supported Michelle's story. No one could substantiate that Michelle left the program site and spent a night in Mexico. No one could remember seeing her leaving the program site or being absent from it. What's more, Michelle couldn't give the name of the priest who allegedly abducted her or the coastal town in Mexico where she was taken. What's more, she was unable to identify the priest from photos of every priest associated with the program. Michelle claimed the priest was about 5'4" and may have even been a bishop. That part of the story seriously hurt her credibility because there aren't many 5'4" bishops in the Catholic Church."

"So, what happened," Thielemans asked.

"With little alternative, Regina confronted Michelle about her story and told her she hallucinated and imagined everything," Prosky replied. "Regina blamed the entire episode on Michelle unwittingly ingesting some of the peyote that was later found to be present at the program site. What you have to understand is Regina and Michelle were each other's only family while all this was happening. Michelle had no siblings, and both of her parents were dead. So, when Regina told Michelle she was imagining things, Michelle went off the deep end. She became hysterical and had to be sedated. Before the dust settled over the Arizona desert, Michelle found herself hospitalized in a Southeastern Pennsylvania psychiatric facility. That's where she was diagnosed as being bipolar and the rift between Michelle and Regina began. I doubt if Michelle ever forgave Regina for not believing her story or having her committed."

"That's an incredible story," Thielemans suggested, not revealing he had already been told a different version of the same story by Michelle.

"It is an incredible story," Prosky agreed. "It's also a story I felt you had to hear before making your final decision about Michelle. You need to give the entire matter some careful thought before you commit to taking on Michelle as your secretary. Don't forget, she'll be traveling with you, working with you, and sharing food and lodging with you. So, she'll be your full-time companion."

"Where did you leave the matter with Sister Consuela?" Thielemans asked.

"I told her I'd get in touch with her when we arrived in San Diego," Prosky replied. "She wants to talk with Michelle and start planning a memorial service for Regina at the Mother House. The scheduling of the service is flexible, but Consuela feels Michelle should return to Baltimore to attend it."

"I understand," Thielemans answered. "By the way, Michelle told me you have Gordon Kittrick on your clergy sex abuse watch list."

"Kittrick was added to our group's watch list and placed under enhanced surveillance a month before the altar boy's suicide," Prosky confirmed. "We just learned the altar boy's mother and two sisters moved from San

Diego to a suburb of Los Angeles. This indicates someone is attempting to cover up Kittrick's sex crimes. Unfortunately, we're still not sure who that someone is. We've also recently learned Kittrick appears to be grooming his next victim – another fatherless 13-year-old. There's no telling how many more young boys Kittrick will irreparably harm before the Church admits he has a problem and the police arrest him. Ironically, it may take years for Kittrick to finally get put behind bars, and even if he goes to prison, he'll still be able to thrive as a sex offender. I can just picture him hearing the confessions of young male prisoners and giving them penances that require their direct participation in one of Kittrick's sexual perversions. I only wish I could show guys like Kittrick the New Mexico desert. They'd never come back."

As Thielemans studied the dramatic changes in Prosky's facial expression, Conyngham started shouting.

"I need another milkshake," he yelled.

Retrieving the bottle of Bailey's Irish Cream, Thielemans walked into the bathroom.

"Thank you, Rock Star," Conyngham said, as Thielemans refilled his glass. "You'll never know how much you've meant to all of us on this trip. It would have been a disaster without you. All I need now is to figure out a way to take this whirlpool bathtub home with me."

"Has the whirlpool bathtub helped you that much?" Thielemans inquired.

"The tub and the booze," Conyngham responded. "They've both helped me deal with my pain and allowed me to cut way down on all the pain pills I was taking."

"Make sure to leave me your address and phone number before the cruise is over," Thielemans advised.

"I'll make arrangements to have a hot tub installed where you live. That way, this cruise will never end."

Conyngham looked at Thielemans and started sobbing.

"You're serious, aren't you," he cried in a broken voice, wiping tears from his eyes. "You'd do that for me."

"That's what rock stars do," Thielemans joked, as he mussed Conyngham's wet hair. "Elvis used to buy Cadillacs for people he liked. I buy hot tubs."

"Here's to takin' care of business, Rock Star," Conyngham toasted, raising his glass.

"To takin' care of business," Thielemans agreed, raising the bottle of Irish Cream. "Thank you very much."

"Hey, Paul, there's one other thing," Conyngham added. "Don't forget what I told you about your rosary peas. Be very careful with them. There's enough poison in that bag of rosary peas to wipe out a small village."

"I won't forget," Thielemans promised, as he topped off Conyngham's drink and walked out of the bathroom.

One hour and a bottle of Bailey's Irish Cream later, Thielemans' guests departed. Feeling fatigued and looking forward to an extended afternoon nap and light supper from room service, the elderly priests courteously declined Thielemans' dinner invitation before leaving.

Sensing restlessness and the early signs of hunger, Thielemans decided to take a walk around the ship before grabbing lunch. After walking for an hour, he arrived on the Lido Deck and promptly selected a sandwich, bowl of soup, and slice of pie from the ship's buffet.

As he carried his lunch through the congested dining area, he saw several empty tables toward the back of the room. Sitting alone at one of the tables was an elderly Catholic priest who Thielemans didn't recognize.

Conventionally dressed in aging priestly attire, the clergyman had wavy, white hair and a matching chinstrap beard that gave him the appearance of an Amish Colonel Sanders. A friendly smile came to his face as he saw Thielemans walking toward his table.

"Well, hello, there," the elderly priest said, as he made eye contact with his unexpected guest, and pointed to one of the many empty seats at the table. "Please join me."

"Thank you," his guest replied, as he placed his lunch on the table and extended his hand in friendship. "Paul Thielemans."

"Richard Frost," the elderly priest announced, shaking Thielemans' hand.

"This is the first time I've seen you on the ship," Thielemans observed, as he folded his hands, looked at his lunch, and quickly offered a silent prayer of grace.

"I just joined the ship in Maui," Frost revealed, reacting favorably to Thielemans' prayer with a nod. "I was just asked to take over as the Eurodam's priest a few days ago. I'm a member of the Apostleship of the Sea and get called occasionally to fill in as a ship's priest whenever there's an emergency. I'm 80 years old and retired. So, I don't get called that often anymore. I just happened to be visiting my son in Oahu when the ship's former priest became ill and had to return home for surgery."

"I'm sorry to hear about your predecessor," Thielemans stated, as he finished tasting his first spoonful of chicken noodle soup. "Did you say you were visiting your son in Oahu?"

"That's right," Frost answered confidently. "My youngest son is a naval officer, stationed in Pearl Harbor."

"How many children do you have?" Thielemans asked.

"Three," Frost replied with obvious pride. "My oldest son is a marine biologist, my daughter is with the F.B.I., and my youngest son is the naval officer. Their mother died last year, shortly after our 57th wedding anniversary."

"I'm sorry to hear about the loss of your wife," Thielemans said. "It sounds like the two of you shared a beautiful family and many happy times."

"We did," Frost acknowledged. "I'm sure you're wondering how a Catholic priest wound up with a wife, three children, and many happy times."

"To be honest, I'm wondering if you became a priest through Pope John Paul II's 'Pastoral Provision' or Pope Benedict XVI's 'Personal Ordinariate of the Chair of Saint Peter,'" Thielemans chuckled. "Both programs allowed Protestant clergymen, mainly from the Episcopal Church, to become Catholic priests and remain married. Based on your age, I'm leaning toward the Pastoral Provision as your entry into the Catholic priesthood."

Frost stared at the young man who, dressed in a golf shirt and walking shorts, continued to slurp chicken noodle soup and take large bites out of a thick deli sandwich. Taking a sip of tea, Frost shifted his seemingly perpetual smile into a higher gear.

"You realize, of course, you've only known me for ten minutes and already know more about me than most of my former Catholic parishioners," Frost said with a twinkle in his eye. "So, tell me, how do you know so much about the process that allowed a former Episcopalian presbyter like me to spend more than forty years in the Catholic priesthood?"

"Well, I did read the *Baltimore Catechism* from cover to cover as a child," Thielemans teased.

"I'd say you read more than just a catechism to acquire your level of knowledge," Frost laughed.

"Do the theology books I read at Harvard or classes I attended at the North American Pontifical College count?" Thielemans inquired with a sly grin.

"I knew you were a priest from the moment I laid eyes on you," Frost exclaimed, tongue-in-cheek.

"Guilty as charged," the second oldest priest at the table declared. "I'm Father Paul Thielemans."

"Why does the name, Thielemans, sound so familiar to me?" Frost asked with a curious expression on his face.

"Maybe you recognize my name from the books I've published," Thielemans offered modestly.

"No," Frost disagreed. "I haven't read any of your books, but I know why your name sounds so familiar. There's a jazz musician named Thielemans. I think he's Belgian. That's where I've heard the name."

"You're thinking of Toots Thielemans," his namesake confirmed. "He is Belgian, and many say he's the finest harmonica player in the world."

"Maybe you and Toots are related," Frost suggested.

"I don't think we're related," Thielemans said. "However, we did go to different schools together."

As Thielemans took another bite out of his sandwich, Frost finally got the joke and started laughing.

"That's a good one," Frost exclaimed, picking up a cookie from his tray. "So, tell me about your books."

"I've written several," Thielemans answered. "My latest is *Catholicism Astray*, an analysis of how changes in the Church since the Second Vatican Council have affected Church membership and attitudes."

"It sounds interesting," Frost commented.

"Father, I've met a few priests who entered the Catholic Church through the Personal Ordinariate in 2012, but I've never a priest who entered earlier through the Pastoral Provision," Thielemans revealed. "How were you received when you entered the Church in 1980?"

"Most of the priests Pope John Paul II brought into the Church in the 1980s were initially assigned to positions that kept them out of the public eye," Frost admitted. "I spent a few decades working as a chaplain in Catholic hospitals, colleges, high schools, societies, and retirement homes for priests and nuns. When the Church discovered it was about to embark on a profound priest shortage, guys like me were finally given parishes. There were more than 59,000 priests in the United States in 1970 and barely 35,000 in 2017. So, with so many priests retiring and vocations to the priesthood at historical lows, the Church started promoting people."

"I guess your situation was a lot different from that of the priests who entered the Church through the Personal Ordinariate in 2012," Thielemans surmised.

"It was," Frost agreed. "Through his Personal Ordinariate, Pope Benedict XVI created a diocese without borders. Today, there are more than 100 priests who entered the Church through this pathway and are serving as parish priests. As the media started informing people about married Catholic clergymen, most Catholics became aware of and accepted the concept of married priests. However, certain Catholics refused to accept the concept and wound up leaving their parishes or the Church. When I first started working as a Catholic chaplain in hospitals and schools, very few people knew I was married. Years later, when I started working as a parish priest, very few parishioners realized there were married Catholic priests. So, it took a while to explain the entire process to my parishioners. Fortunately, most parishioners were more interested in my abilities as a spiritual leader than my marital status."

"I'm sure they were," Thielemans agreed.

"By the time priests started entering the Church through the Personal Ordinariate, a married Catholic priesthood wasn't as much of a novelty as when I entered and was probably more easily accepted," he continued. "A priest's family can influence how easily a priest is accepted. In my case, most parishioners loved my wife and children. This tremendously helped me gain their acceptance."

"So, I take it you favor a married Catholic priesthood," Thielemans suggested.

"I favor a priesthood that gives the individual the option of being married or remaining single," Frost answered. "Although marriage isn't for everybody, there are many advantages to a priest being married and having a family. I can honestly say I'm proud of what I accomplished as a priest and feel marriage and fatherhood made me a better one."

"I think the movement toward a married priesthood may be gaining significant momentum within the Church," Thielemans said. "I recently spoke to a friend who is a Belgian bishop, and he told me the bishops in Belgium plan to petition the Vatican for a married priesthood."

"If they do, they'll have an ally in Pope Francis," Frost opined. "The Church in South America currently has a critical shortage of priests. Some Catholics there only get to attend Mass twice a year. Fortunately, their bishops are looking for ways to correct the shortage. One of the quickest ways would be a married priesthood. Many of the bishops from Argentina and the other South American countries have known Pope Francis since he was Archbishop of Buenos Aires. So, they have his ear, and I'm sure his empathy and support as well. A married priesthood may return to the Church sooner than many people realize."

"How do you feel about the Church reinstating Catholic priests who left the priesthood to marry?" Thielemans asked.

"I'd do it in a heartbeat," Frost replied. "You know, a man is a man before he becomes a Catholic or a priest. He is born with many traits that are inherent to manhood, including sexuality. For the Church to deprive a man of his God-given sexuality as a requirement for the priesthood is one of its most short-sighted decisions. This is especially true since celibacy is a reversible Church regulation rather than irreversible dogma, and was imposed for reasons that were more economic than religious. The Church created the regulation of Catholics not eating meat on Fridays as a way to allow Europe's struggling fishing industry to become profitable and give fishermen the chance to earn more money and increase their contributions to the Church. For similar economic reasons, the Church initially imposed celibacy on its priests as a way to acquire the personal property married priests had been previously bequeathing to their children."

"Don't you feel there were religious reasons for these Church regulations that were more important than the economic benefits you mentioned?" Thielemans asked.

"I don't," Frost replied. "Greed is a strange motivator. It changes the way a man thinks and causes a man to lose perspective. I believe this is what happened when Church leaders imposed such ridiculous regulations on Catholics. Honestly, do you believe God will refuse a place in heaven to a Catholic who lived an exemplary life but ate meat on Friday before they died? I don't. If I ever saw any value in Catholics not eating meat on Friday, I changed my mind the day the Archdiocese of New York granted Irish Catholics dispensation to eat ham on Good Friday because the day was also the feast day of Saint Patrick, Ireland's patron saint. How important could abstinence from meat be if the Church could offer a single ethnic group dispensation on the most solemn day of the entire Church year? I also don't believe God will look harshly on a priest who falls in love with a woman and leaves the priesthood to have a family with her. In my eighty years on this planet, I've learned there are people who enter your life that you are incapable of not loving."

"People who enter your life that you are incapable of not loving," Thielemans quietly repeated. "What a profound observation."

"Thank you," Frost answered modestly. "You know, in my many years as a priest, I've also learned most young men enter the priesthood not knowing who they are. They enter the priesthood with the best of intentions, but without sufficient information or experience to anticipate their future needs. To a celibate priest, life can become lonely, and when this happens, someone's love can become a life-changing event. Like I said before, a man is a man before he becomes a Catholic or a priest. When a hierarchy of needs presents itself, it's unrealistic to think every man can ignore his basic instincts and rely on blind faith to unravel his life's disarray."

"I agree," Thielemans said.

"What I find curious is how Church leaders could have been so short-sighted when they decided to impose celibacy on priests," Frost continued. "The Church could have greatly strengthened itself by allowing its priests to reproduce and add to the fold more Catholics who had the potential for the same morality, intelligence, and inherent goodness as their fathers. By forbidding this, the Church significantly limited its membership and gave its enemies and detractors a major advantage."

"I've never heard that argument before," Thielemans revealed. "I don't know quite how to say this without sounding self-serving, but I've personally discussed theology with the last three Popes, a hundred cardinals and bishops, and many theologians. Throughout all those discussions, I've never heard that argument."

"I tend to look at things differently," Frost admitted. "I know I can be long-winded, but I try to keep my opinions to myself until I feel I can adequately defend them. My ideas are not always popular, but they do get people thinking."

"I'd agree with that," Thielemans replied. "So, tell me more about why you'd reinstate former Catholic priests."

"As you know, the Church is not only experiencing a critical shortage of priests in South America and Belgium," Frost continued. "It is also experiencing a critical shortage in the United States. Catholic parishes all across America used to have three or four priests in their rectories, churches where multiple religious services were being held daily, parochial schools that provided quality education, public services that extended beyond the religious realm, and activities that allowed the Church to be the focal point of every Catholic family. Today, many churches have either closed or been forced to consolidate because of a shortage of priests. Parochial schools have either closed or consolidated, church services have become sparse, and church-related activities have dramatically decreased. Regrettably, older priests will be retiring by the droves over the next few years, and there are nowhere near enough seminarians to replace them. So, the shortage of priests in the United States will get worse before it gets better."

"It's inevitable," Thielemans said.

"Reinstating American priests who left the Church to marry would immediately restore the manpower the Church needs to get back on its feet," Frost argued. "The precedent of a married priesthood would also encourage a tremendous number of new vocations to the priesthood from men who felt they had a calling to the priesthood but were unwilling to live celibate lives. A rejuvenated priesthood would also allow the Church to do something about its problem with sexually abusive clergymen."

"Do you believe marriage would cure a priest's pedophilia or sexual perversion?" Thielemans asked.

"Not at all," Frost quickly answered. "Marriage would not prevent a predisposed priest from being a pedophile or sexual predator, but with adequate manpower, the Church would be able to greatly improve the screening procedures that precede acceptance into seminaries. Pedophiles and sexual predators would be weeded out before they were allowed to study for the priesthood, and perverts who fell between the cracks and entered the seminary would be more quickly identified and dismissed."

"Is there anything else you'd do to bring non-practicing Catholics back to the Church?" Thielemans asked.

184

"There is," Frost replied. "I'd substitute general absolution for traditional confession. I'd also make general absolution a part of the Mass. Before a priest began Mass, he would ask everyone to silently confess their sins to God. After a minute of silent prayer, he would have everyone recite an Act of Contrition for their penance, grant general absolution, and begin the Mass. The entire process would only take five minutes and ensure everyone arrived at Mass on time. Catholics who requested traditional confession would certainly be allowed to do so. I think general absolution would bring many non-practicing Catholics back to the Church because many Catholics find it difficult or embarrassing to confess their sins to a priest. By not being willing to confess or able to receive Holy Communion regularly, these individuals feel incomplete as Catholics and stop going to Mass."

"I know quite a few Catholics who stopped going to Mass for the reasons you mentioned," Thielemans revealed. "Several of them had been in the military where they received general absolution before Mass. They argued, if they received general absolution on a battlefield or ship, they should be able to receive it in Church."

"I've also heard Catholic veterans say the same thing," Frost concurred. "It's a shame the Vatican can't understand that Catholics who no longer attend Mass or receive the sacraments are still Catholics. They're still individuals who were baptized and continue to have spiritual needs that can't be conveniently forgotten by the Church. By changing just a few regulations, the Church could bring most of these souls back into the fold and create the greatest religious assembly ever known to mankind. I think God would like to see this."

"No doubt," Thielemans agreed.

"At the end of the day, most non-practicing Catholics are not at odds with Church dogma, but with Church regulations that could be changed by a signature from the Pope," Frost opined. "I think the time has come for the Vatican to create a more user-friendly Church. God understands human frailty and wouldn't hold a less-than-perfect Church against those who tried to make it more understanding and forgiving. I know some people say anyone who doesn't want to follow the regulations of the Catholic Church should just leave and join a religion that better suits their needs. Those who would say such a thing seem to forget the Church is all its members and not just one person or group. Because of this, every Catholic has the right to question the regulations that might be interfering with their pathway to God, and no Catholic has the right to tell another to love the Church or leave it."

"Father, what made you leave the Episcopal Church to become a Catholic priest?" Thielemans asked.

"The acceptance of homosexuality and the ordination of women were why many clergymen left the Episcopal Church in the 1970s," Frost stated. "However, my reason was much more personal. In essence, I was forced out of the Episcopal Church by parishioners who tried using me as a front for their criminal activities. I was the pastor of an Episcopal Church in upstate New York. The church's treasurer was a popular, young woman who was a third-generation member of the church and community. On the outside, she seemed personable, but on the inside, she was a true con artist. She had the unique ability to join different school, civic, and recreational groups in the community and always manage to get elected or appointed treasurer of every group she joined. In addition to being treasurer of our church, she was, at one time or another, treasurer of the high school sports booster club, girl scout troop, and volunteer ambulance company."

Thielemans shook his head in disbelief.

"This woman came from a politically active family and had an older sister who worked as a police dispatcher," Frost continued. "The sister was well-known by many of the prominent businessmen and public officials in the community, and when I say well-known, I mean it in the biblical sense. Unbeknownst to her milquetoast husband, the sister tried seducing anyone who had any kind of influence in town. She slept with most of the police force and many of the businessmen and politicians in town, and even threw herself at me on more than one occasion."

Frost paused and took a sip of tea.

"So, with a politically active family and sister who was having sex with many of the town's more influential men, the woman I'm telling you about felt she was able to take certain liberties," he continued. "One of those liberties was her taking unauthorized loans from the treasuries of my church, as well as other groups I've mentioned, and using the money to pay her family's bills. When I caught her with her hand in the church's till, she told me I was only the appointed pastor, but as treasurer, she was an elected official of the church. She also informed me she was elected to actively manage the church's treasury which gave her the freedom to take money out of the treasury as long as the money was fully returned at any time the church needed it. As it turned out, she was borrowing money from every treasury under her control and regularly robbing one treasury to repay another."

Frost paused and looked into Thielemans' eyes.

"When I discovered her illegal activity and attempted to dismiss her as church treasurer, I got a lot of opposition from a few high-ranking members of the church council and threats from the town's sleaziest lawyer," Frost revealed. "With little alternative, I handed the entire matter over to my bishop who took very little time declaring the issue an overreaction and failure to communicate on my part and issuing an apology to the woman on behalf of the parish and diocese."

"Unbelievable," Thielemans exclaimed, as he slumped into his chair and carefully studied Frost's aging eyes.

"Of course, the bishop's intervention was only the beginning of the end for me and my family in the Episcopal Church," Frost lamented. "It didn't take very long for the woman's entire family to use their political influence and spread their seeds of dissension throughout the entire community. While I was being quietly harassed by the woman's lawyer, my wife, who was the high school music teacher, was notified her untenured position was being unexpectedly eliminated by the school district at the end of the school year. Next, my daughter lost her starting position on the varsity volleyball team even though she was the team's leading scorer, and my youngest son failed to make the honor roll for the first time in his life. The final straw came when my oldest son started getting detentions for ridiculous reasons like not reporting to the principal's office when paged over the high school intercom, even though he was away from school on an honor society field trip the day he was paged."

"It's hard to believe anyone could have treated a clergyman's family this way," Thielemans said.

"With time, greater numbers of parishioners started leaving the church," Frost continued. "As soon as the church revenues started plummeting, I was transferred to another church in a much smaller community. The town had limited employment opportunities for my wife and sparse educational advantages for my children. My entire family struggled with my new assignment for a few grueling years, and during that time, I prayed fervently for God's guidance. That guidance came when I became aware of Pope John Paul II's Pastoral Provision and applied to become a Catholic priest. The rest is history."

"Thank God," Thielemans exclaimed.

"I do every day," Frost answered enthusiastically.

"So, how do you like serving as a cruise ship chaplain?" Thielemans inquired.

"I enjoy it," Frost admitted. "You know, people come on cruises for many different reasons. Interestingly, many people come on a cruise searching for God and not realizing it. That gives me a chance to help them find who they're looking for. I've met Catholics who hadn't been to Mass in years but attended every Mass while they were on their cruise. I've met Catholics who hadn't been to confession in decades but unwittingly confessed all their sins to me while we strolled around the deck, never realizing I planned to grant them absolution after we finished our walk. I've met widowed and divorced Catholics who were lonely and unable to see God offering his comfort through strangers. I've met all kinds of people on cruise ships and found most of them searching for meaning in their lives."

"You're a remarkable man, Father, and I feel closer to God just by being in your presence," Thielemans said.

"Thank you for the beautiful sentiment, Father," Frost responded. "A priest could go years without hearing such a nice compliment. Strangely, you're the second member of the religious community to say such nice things to me in the past few hours."

"You're kidding," Thielemans exclaimed.

"No, I'm not," Frost replied, shifting his smile into overdrive. "Just before lunch, I was walking on the Promenade Deck and saw this beautiful, young nun, standing by the deck railing and staring out into space. I approached her, and after introducing myself, invited her to walk with me. We walked around the ship, and by the time we finished, I learned a lot about life in the convent. At the end of our stroll, the young nun thanked me for inspiring her, although she did most of the talking."

"Sometimes, it's what you say and not how much you say," Thielemans suggested.

"I guess," Frost chuckled.

"So, what did this nun teach you about the convent you didn't already know?" Thielemans asked.

"For one thing, I knew many nuns left the convent over the past few decades, but I didn't realize how many," Frost answered. "From what Sister Michelle told me, there were more than 160,000 nuns in the United States in the early 1970s. As of last year, there were only about 45,000. That's almost twice the attrition the priesthood has experienced. I also didn't realize nuns who received their educations in the convent before deciding to leave were required to pay back the cost of their entire education before their convent would provide them with their academic records. Sister Michelle told me she had both a bachelor's and master's degree, but wouldn't be able to use her academic credentials to get a job if she left the convent unless she repaid the cost of her entire schooling."

"I didn't realize that," Thielemans admitted.

"I felt bad for Sister Michelle," Frost added. "I didn't get to discuss much of her personal life with her, but she seemed unhappy to me. She told me she wondered what it would be like to go on a cruise and actually enjoy all the activities and entertainment. She told me she was on the cruise with two elderly priests and her aunt, an elderly nun who died unexpectedly while the ship was in Hawaii. When she said such events made her question the purpose of life, I told her the purpose of life is to live it. After I told her that, she smiled, gave me a big hug, and thanked me for inspiring her."

"The purpose of life is to live it," Thielemans repeated with an impressed look on his face. "I can see why you inspired Sister Michelle. You've also inspired me. I think it's wonderful you have been blessed with a family and the priesthood. You've been given the best of all possible worlds, realized your purpose in life, and lived life to the fullest. That's what gives you the ability to inspire others."

"I am blessed," Frost admitted. "Not many Catholic priests have been blessed with children, and I must admit my children have always been my greatest priority in life. The way I look at things, we're all just stepping stones in evolution, and we've fulfilled our most important purpose in life if we can entrust our children to leave the world a better place than we did."

"When you talk about us being stepping stones in evolution, I can't help but think you've read the works of the renowned French Jesuit philosopher, Pierre Teilhard de Chardin," Thielemans suggested.

"I've read his books, *The Divine Milieu* and *The Phenomenon of Man*, but quite honestly, I can't say Teilhard de Chardin's writings really influenced my thinking to any great degree," Frost remarked. "I find his writing too abstract at times. I understood his concept of the 'Omega Point,' but I always felt his writing was too academic."

"Teilhard de Chardin was a brilliant philosopher and truly independent thinker," Thielemans explained. "He was the classic Renaissance Man, but many readers didn't understand or agree with his writing. In fact, the Church was critical of much of his work and even issued a *monitum* which cautioned Catholics not to accept a number of his controversial ideas."

"Did the Church ever condemn any of his work to its forbidden books list?" Frost asked.

"So, you've heard about the Church's infamous *Index Librorum Prohibitorum*," Thielemans chuckled. "The Church never added any of his books to the list, but it wasn't until Pope Benedict XVI came into office that Teilhard de Chardin's writing ever received any official praise from the Church. Posthumously, his books became centerpieces of theology courses in the vast majority of Catholic colleges and universities."

"I once made the mistake of telling a parishioner any rewards for my life's work would probably come posthumously," Frost said with a grin. "Not knowing what the word, 'posthumously,' meant, the well-meaning woman replied, 'And the sooner, the better!'"

"That's funny," Thielemans admitted. "So, tell me more about your stepping stones philosophy."

"It's quite simple," Frost continued. "My three children are better than me in every conceivable way.

They're healthier, smarter, more creative, more successful, and probably even more spiritual than I am. So, my children have evolved into better human beings than I could ever become, and what's important, I allowed it all to happen by accepting my role in life and nurturing the growth and development of my children. As I said, we're all just stepping stones in evolution, and I fulfilled my purpose in life by living my life the best way I could and showing my children how to live their lives even better."

"That's a truly remarkable philosophy," Thielemans observed. "You really know how to lay a lot on a person over lunch."

"If you liked my lunch act, you should catch my dinner show," Frost joked.

Getting up from the table, Thielemans shook hands with Frost.

"Thank you for allowing me to spend this time with you," he said. "I'll look forward to talking with you again."

"The feeling's mutual," Frost replied. "God bless you."

Leaving the dining area, Thielemans decided to continue his stroll through the ship. Walking down six flights of stairs, he arrived on the Promenade Deck where the ship's retail shops were located.

As Thielemans moved from one shop to another, looking at the various window displays of expensive jewelry, designer watches, and fashionable menswear, he suddenly noticed Michelle window-shopping on the opposite side of the deck. Watching her admiring elegant evening gowns and cocktail dresses through the window of a women's apparel store, Thielemans recalled Frost's comment about Michelle wondering what it would be like to actually experience the many luxuries of a cruise.

Not realizing she was being watched from afar, Michelle took one last look at the dresses, sighed, and walked away from the dress shop. As she did, Thielemans thought about his recent lunch with Frost.

He remembered Frost saying, "there are people who enter your life that you are incapable of not loving." As Thielemans watched Michelle walk through the ship and get on an elevator, he realized Frost was right.

Walking toward the women's apparel shop and looking at the beautiful dresses in the store's window, Thielemans also remembered something else Frost said. "The purpose of life was to live it," Thielemans thought to himself, as he took a final look at the dresses and walked into the shop.

CHAPTER ELEVEN

Before returning to her cabin, Michelle decided to check in on Prosky and Conyngham. Seeing a "Do Not Disturb" sign on their door and hearing both priests snoring loudly inside their cabin, Michelle surmised both priests were resting comfortably.

After listening to her elderly aunt sleep for many years, Michelle learned how to gauge wellness by the nuances of snoring. Prosky usually snored as though he was being gently rocked to sleep by Gregorian Chant, while Conyngham snored as though he was playing lead guitar in a heavy metal band.

Confident Prosky was snoring along with Benedictine monks and Conyngham was sawing logs to the music of Metallica, Michelle walked toward her cabin. Knowing the priests planned to spend a quiet day and evening in their stateroom, Michelle opened her cabin door, wondering how she was going to spend her own time.

Removing her veil and kicking off her shoes, Michelle sat at the edge of her bed and turned on the television. As she started channel-surfing, she thought about Thielemans and wondered if he had recovered from her recent amorous advances.

Michelle realized he was a dedicated priest with high moral standards, but he was also a virile man who seemed to relish the feeling of a beautiful woman in his arms and the taste of a woman's lips. She felt a connection with Thielemans but didn't know if her love was unrequited.

As she continued channel-surfing, watching five or ten minutes of one movie before losing interest and switching to another, Michelle was startled by restrained knocking on her cabin door. Quickly jumping to her feet, she opened the door to discover a salesgirl holding three gift boxes.

"These are for you, Miss," the tall, dark Indian salesgirl revealed with a decidedly British accent. "There is a card inside the large box, and you can feel free to exchange any of the items at our store if they don't fit perfectly. We're open until 9 p.m. this evening."

Taking the gift boxes from the salesgirl and placing them on her bed, Michelle appeared embarrassed.

"I'm afraid I don't have any money for a gratuity," she apologized.

"That's quite all right, Dear," the salesgirl responded. "The gentleman already took care of that."

"Thank you," Michelle said, closing the cabin door.

Quickly untying its ribbon, Michelle opened the largest box, set aside the enclosed card, and removed the very cocktail dress and matching scarf she admired in the dress shop window an hour earlier. Carefully laying the elegant brown dress and scarf across her bed, she unfolded the card and read its hand-written message:

"Please wear this dress tonight when you join me for dinner. I'll call for you at 9 p.m. A Secret Admirer."

Laying the card on the bed next to her dress, Michelle opened the second gift box and smiled when she saw a pair of metallic-brown high heels with thin ankle-straps. Removing the shoes from the box, she placed them next to her dress and opened the final gift box to discover three pairs of nylons in different shades, a container of soft plum lip gloss, and a bottle of Obsession perfume spray.

Quickly undressing and trying on her new ensemble, Michelle looked at herself in the mirror and realized how perfectly her new dress, scarf, and shoes fit and complemented each other. Thinking her not-so-secret admirer must have been paying closer attention to her than she realized, Michelle posed in front of the mirror, smiled, and savored feeling beautiful.

While Michelle spent the rest of the day preparing herself for dinner with an admirer, Thielemans spent his time arranging the kind of dream date very few passengers had ever experienced on the Eurodam or any other cruise ship. With Winston's help, Thielemans spared no expense planning the night of Michelle's young life.

Thielemans wanted Michelle to experience all the ambience and entertainment of the Eurodam but didn't want to be overly conspicuous while they were enjoying the Eurodam's Gala Night as a couple. By having Winston pull a few strings with several of the ship's entertainers and management of the Pinnacle Grill, Thielemans hoped to provide Michelle the perfect date while playing a veritable game of shadows.

As the magic hour approached, Michelle interspersed sessions staring at the clock with longer sessions checking her appearance in the mirror. Precisely as the clock struck 9 p.m., Michelle heard a knock on her door, and answering it, discovered Thielemans, dressed in a white dinner jacket, and holding a plumeria.

"You look beautiful," Thielemans said with a smile.

"How did you ever find a plumeria on a cruise ship at sea?" Michelle giggled.

"Sometimes, it's not what you know, but who you know," Thielemans replied, as he adjusted his bow tie.

Retreating to the mirror, Michelle carefully positioned the flower behind her left ear.

"I thought women wore a plumeria behind their left ear when they were already taken," Thielemans suggested.

"I am already taken," Michelle answered, as she approached Thielemans and kissed him softly on the lips.

Speechless, Thielemans took Michelle's arm and escorted her to his cabin.

"Do I hear violins playing?" Michelle inquired, as Thielemans opened the door to his suite.

"Just these," Thielemans said, as he led Michelle inside and watched her eyes light up at the sight of the ship's string trio playing live music.

"This is the same group that performs on the ship at the Lincoln Center Stage," Michelle whispered, as she watched the three beautiful blondes, dressed in formal black gowns, playing a classical piece with confident smiles on their lovely faces. "I think they're from Poland."

"They are from Poland, but they only perform on the ship until 8:45 each night," Thielemans responded, as he watched the violin, viola, and cello players performing in perfect synchrony. "For the next hour, they're ours."

"But how did you get them to play for us?" Michelle questioned, as she sat down on the sofa with Thielemans.

"As they say, sometimes, it's not what you know, but who you know," Thielemans jokingly reiterated, as he signaled for Winston to bring over two glasses of Veuve Clicquot and a silver tray filled with *hors d'oeuvres*.

"To life, and living it," Thielemans toasted.

"To nights that never end," Michelle sighed.

For the next hour, the two drank champagne, ate caviar, salmon mousse, and bacon-wrapped shrimp with assorted breads and toppings, and listened to the string trio play a variety of classical compositions, Broadway favorites, and popular romantic ballads. All the while, Thielemans smiled as he watched Michelle, seemingly awestruck by the food, wine, and entertainment.

At 10 p.m., as the trio finished playing *All I Ask of You* from *Phantom of the Opera*, Thielemans stood up and helped Michelle to her feet. As the musicians rose to their feet and carefully laid down their instruments, Thielemans and Michelle applauded, and Winston prepared to serve Veuve Clicquot to everyone.

"*Na zdrowie,*" Thielemans exclaimed with a smile, as he raised his glass to toast the musicians.

"*Na zdrowie,*" the three performers responded enthusiastically, raising their glasses.

"Thank you for the wonderful concert," Thielemans added. "*Dziękuję.*"

"*Dziękuję, Dziękuję,*" the performers, Nicola, Marta, and Roksana, chimed, as they watched Winston approach with a fresh tray of *hors d'oeuvres*.

"*Nie ma za co,*" Thielemans replied, as he watched the musicians become wide-eyed at the spectacle of the gourmet *hors d'oeuvres* being carried in their direction.

"What does that mean?" Michelle inquired.

"It means, 'don't mention it,'" Thielemans answered, as he held Michelle's hand and walked toward the door.

Opening the door, Thielemans turned toward the entertainers and waved.

"*Dobranoc,*" he exclaimed with a smile. "Good night,"

"*Dobranoc,*" the musicians replied in unison.

As Thielemans quickly walked down the hall, leading Michelle toward the elevator, he felt a quick tug.

"Paul, where are we going?" Michelle asked curiously. "And why are we leaving the party just when everyone was getting all, *'Dziękuje, Dziękuje'* with each other?"

"We're going to the Mainstage Theater," Thielemans stated, as he helped Michelle on to the elevator. "We're going to see the stage show tonight. It should be good."

"But why the rush?" Michelle questioned.

"The show already started," Thielemans explained.

"So, you mean you and I are stepping out in public tonight like two real human beings?" Michelle suggested, as the elevator arrived on the Promenade Deck.

"It's time we took a break from being troglodytes and joined the human race for a night," Thielemans proclaimed, as he exited the elevator and started walking with Michelle toward the theater.

"What if passengers who know you're a priest and I'm a nun recognize us and see us all dressed up like this?" Michelle inquired.

"So, what if they do?" Thielemans countered. "Just tell them you're wearing a new habit your convent designed for soirees and other social occasions. After all, it is brown, just like everything else the nuns in your order wear."

"I'd like you to name one convent that designs cocktail dresses for soirees and other social occasions," Michelle insisted.

"If anyone asks, just tell them you belong to the Sisters of Saint Laurent," Thielemans quipped.

"The Sisters of Saint Laurent?" Michelle repeated.

"That's right," Thielemans chuckled. "The Sisters of Yves Saint Laurent."

As Michelle smiled and hugged her date's arm, the two approached the theater's rear balcony entrance. Hearing music, singing, and applause, Thielemans led Michelle into the dark theater and quickly selected two aisle seats close to the exit. Quickly forgetting about being recognized, Michelle sat back and enjoyed the show, laughing and applauding with the rest of the audience.

While the singers and dancers were finishing their final number and preparing to take their curtain calls, the theater's house lights were turned up, and Thielemans sprang up from his seat and took Michelle's hand.

"Time to go," Thielemans announced, as he quickly led Michelle out of the theater and down a flight of nearby stairs. "We have a special dinner reservation at the Pinnacle Grill for 11 p.m."

"What makes the reservation special?" Michelle asked.

"The Pinnacle Grill closes at 10 o'clock," Thielemans explained. "Very few passengers ever get to eat there after 11 p.m."

"So, how were you able to get such a late reservation?" Michelle inquired.

"Well, sometimes, it's not what you know, but who you know," Thielemans chuckled, as the two arrived on the Lower Promenade Deck and walked toward the restaurant.

Passing the Billboard Onboard Piano Bar and B.B. King Blues Club, Michelle was surprised to see both lounges preparing to close.

"Why are the lounges closing already?" she asked.

"Most of the lounges that have entertainment have been closing around 11 p.m.," Thielemans answered. "There's an older crowd on the ship, and most older passengers are already partied out by 11 o'clock. A few bars and the Lido deck buffet stay open until midnight or so, but the entertainment venues have already closed by then."

Arriving at the Pinnacle Grill, Thielemans and Michelle were immediately shown to a table toward the back of the restaurant. As they walked to the table, a few remaining diners smiled approvingly at the attractive couple.

"This restaurant is beautiful," Michelle said, as she was seated by the Maître D' and handed a menu.

"I thought you'd like it," Thielemans replied.

"Like it," Michelle exclaimed. "Paul, I love everything about this night. I feel like I'm dreaming."

While Thielemans called over the sommelier and ordered red and white wine to be served with each course, Michelle got lost in the menu. After giving the menu the once-over twice and still not knowing what to order, she finally gave up and asked Thielemans to order for her.

As the two leisurely dined on Tomato Broth with Spicy Lemongrass Chicken, Spinach and Arugula Salad with Gorgonzola Dressing, Rack of Colorado Lamb with Whipped Potatoes and Sautéed Mushrooms, and Crepes Suzette, they spoke of things that didn't matter, laughed, and carefully studied each other's eyes, lips, and words. Complementing their dinner selections with glasses of Chateau Pape Clement and Puligny Montrachet, Thielemans and Michelle eased into levels of contentment seldom reached by mere mortals.

After they finished their coffee and chocolates, Michelle reached for Thielemans' hand across the dinner table and thanked him for the beautiful evening. Explaining their evening was just beginning, Thielemans took his date by the hand, left the Pinnacle Grill, and walked toward the nearby B.B. King Blues Club.

Entering the vacant club and sitting down at a front-row center table, Thielemans held Michelle's hand and smiled without saying a word. As Michelle gazed at a wall clock and realized it was nearly 1 a.m., she was suddenly startled by a waiter who appeared out of nowhere.

"And what would the lady like to drink?" the bald, middle-aged Jamaican asked with a big smile.

"What would the lady like to drink?" Michelle repeated, looking at Thielemans for an answer.

"We'll both have a Mojito," Thielemans replied.

As the waiter left to fetch their rum, lime juice, and mint concoctions, Michelle seemed to be confused.

"Paul, we're the only two people here," she observed. "Except for the few people still in the casino, I think we're the only two people on the entire deck. How do we rate drink service so late?"

"Michelle, my dear, sometimes, it's not what you know, but who you know," Thielemans said with a smile.

As Michelle pondered Thielemans' pronouncement, the footlights suddenly turned on, stage curtain opened, and entire B.B. King Blues Club Band started playing The Friends of Distinction's upbeat rhythm and blues classic, *Grazing in the Grass.* Michelle watched and listened in disbelief as the group's male and female singers, guitarists, bass player, piano player, drummer, and horn section sang, danced, and played full-throttle to their private audience.

"Let me guess, it's not what you know, but who you know," Michelle quipped to Thielemans' amusement.

While the band was finishing its first number, the waiter arrived with the Mojitos.

"To life, and living it," Thielemans toasted.

"To who you know," Michelle giggled.

Thielemans and Michelle applauded as the band finished its first song, and without missing a single beat, continued with its second number, The Blackbyrds', *Walking in Rhythm,* and third, George Benson's, *Breezin'.* As the energetic group followed with a Stevie Wonder medley of *You Are the Sunshine of My Life, Overjoyed,* and *My Cherie Amour,* Thielemans and Michelle enjoyed their Mojitos, never missing a word, note, or beat of the dynamic music.

As the band decided to slow things down with Nat King Cole's, *Unforgettable,* Thielemans got up from the table and led his partner onto the dance floor. Taking Michelle into his arms, Thielemans surprised her with his agility as a dancer.

"Where did you learn to dance so well?" she asked.

"My mother made me take ballroom dancing lessons when I was a teenager," Thielemans replied. "I didn't argue with her because I quickly learned there were other things you could do with a girl in your arms."

Thielemans and Michelle remained on the floor, slow dancing to The Stylistics', *You Make Me Feel Brand New,* and Johnny Mathis', *Misty,* which Thielemans sang to Michelle as they danced. As soon as the band finished playing *Misty,* Thielemans applauded and waved to the group before leading Michelle off the dance floor and out of the lounge.

As they were leaving, the band's vocalists, Jalen and Shanice, waved and returned Thielemans' applause. One by one, the rest of the band quickly followed suit.

Taking the stairs up one flight, Thielemans and Michelle walked outside on the Promenade Deck and strolled around the ship. Pausing frequently to study the stars and waves, feel the salubrious sea breeze on their faces, or share a kiss, the couple walked, arm-in-arm, as though they were the only two passengers on the ship, if not in the entire universe.

"I wish tonight would never end," Michelle sighed. "This has been the most beautiful night of my entire life, and I'll never forget a single minute of it."

"What was your favorite part?" Thielemans asked.

"Ask me tomorrow," Michelle replied seductively.

As a sudden gust of wind blew through Michelle's hair, Thielemans took her into his arms and kissed her until she was nearly breathless. Keeping her in his embrace, he took a final glance at the ocean and heavens before taking her by the hand and walking with her to his suite.

When they entered his cabin, Thielemans closed the door, turned on the lights, and started walking toward the bar. Having other ideas, Michelle removed her scarf, wrapped it around Thielemans' waist, and pulled him into the bedroom.

Without objection, Thielemans smiled, closed the bedroom door, and embraced his captor. Gently kissing her on the neck and right earlobe, he adroitly unzipped her dress and coaxed it off her shoulders.

As soon as her dress hit the floor, Thielemans swept Michelle off her feet, carried her across the room, and eased her into bed. Looking into her eyes, he kissed her on the lips, and then, slowly moved away.

Taking off his dinner jacket, loosening his bow tie, and opening the top two buttons of his dress shirt, Thielemans got into bed. Methodically removing Michelle's bra and panties, he covered her body with kisses.

Moving to the foot of the bed and positioning himself between her legs, he unbuckled the straps on her high heels and tossed the shoes on the floor. As he proceeded to remove her stockings, he could feel Michelle trembling under his hands.

Watching Thielemans lean forward, Michelle removed the plumeria from behind her left ear and symbolically handed it to him. Accepting the flower and placing it on the bed, Thielemans moved closer, gently touched her face, and kissed her tenderly on the lips.

With a final embrace, Thielemans got out of bed. Looking at Michelle as he undressed, he could feel himself being pulled back into bed by her eyes.

Returning without hesitation, Thielemans passionately kissed Michelle and caressed every inch of her body until her trembling finally gave way to ecstasy. As Thielemans became one with Michelle, he loved her in a way he had never loved any other woman before, and in the exact way Michelle had long dreamed of being loved.

CHAPTER TWELVE

As the Eurodam cruised toward Mexico, Thielemans and Michelle lived different lives by day and night. By day, they lived the industrious lives of a priest and nun who were using the internet to acquaint clergymen with Thielemans' program to restore Church membership. By night, they lived the passionate lives of two lovers whose only concern was discovering everything they could about their new love.

On the same night Thielemans and Michelle made love for the first time, Kilauea unexpectedly erupted on the Big Island. Any other Catholic priest and nun who had just broken their religious vows and become lovers might have read some ominous symbolism into Kilauea erupting shortly after they did. However, such was not the case for Thielemans or Michelle whose growing preoccupation with each other caused them to temporarily disregard anything they couldn't find in each other's embrace.

Six days after the Eurodam left Maui, it arrived in Ensenada to give its passengers a brief taste of Mexican culture. Since the ship was only scheduled to spend four hours in the coastal resort town, Thielemans and Michelle decided to take a brief sightseeing tour of the town and its nearby surroundings.

With Prosky and Conyngham in tow and everyone dressed in appropriate religious attire, Thielemans and Michelle enlisted the services of tour guide, Raul Gutierrez, a thin, dark and unprepossessing native of Ensenada, to escort their party around town in his aged, but reliable, Chevy conversion van. Fluent in English and renowned for being able to ensure the safety of his passengers, Gutierrez relied on Ensenada's natural beauty, rather than excessive narration, to provide his guests an enjoyable and memorable tour.

Avoiding the sections of downtown Ensenada where old native women, wearing dark, hooded shawls, begged tourists for money to feed the deformed and malnourished children they held in their arms, Gutierrez drove his van down a few busy streets where bars, clothing stores, food vendors, novelty shops, and discount pharmacies competed for tourist dollars. Stopping at one bar to purchase a round of takeout margaritas which were made with local tequila, limes, and sea salt, Gutierrez allowed the drinks to entertain his passengers while he drove along the seashore and called out the names of the various resorts.

After he had shown his guests Ensenada's commercial district and resort area, Gutierrez stopped at a roadside food truck and bought seafood tacos for his guests to eat while they were driven through the hills that surrounded Ensenada. As they carefully surveyed the surprising number of beautiful homes that were ensconced in the hills, as well as incomparable views of the Pacific Ocean from Ensenada's higher elevations, the group savored their afternoon repast and enjoyed a careless afternoon.

As Gutierrez began to drive back to town, Michelle spotted a large home overlooking the ocean.

"Raul, could you please drive closer to that big house over there?" she nervously requested.

"Michelle, what's wrong?" Prosky asked, as he watched fear quickly blanket the nun's face.

As Gutierrez stopped, Michelle opened the van's side door and slowly walked toward the house.

"Michelle, what's wrong?" Prosky yelled.

Without answering, Michelle approached the house the same way a cautious hunter approaches a dangerous animal that has been shot but not yet proven dead.

"Michelle, talk to me," Thielemans said, as he joined Michelle and put his hand on her shoulder.

"Paul, this is the house where I was raped," Michelle answered, as she pulled Thielemans' hand away from her shoulder and walked alone toward the front door.

Ringing the doorbell, Michelle quickly took a step backward, as though she was expecting to see a ghost, the devil, or the rapist who continued to appear in her dreams. When no one came to the door after two more rings, Michelle looked inside the house through its large front windows but was unable to see any activity.

"Is everything okay?" Raul inquired, as he approached Michelle who continued to walk around the property and look into every window.

"Raul, do you know who owns this house?" Michelle asked, as anger began to replace fear in her voice.

"A rental company, I think," Raul surmised. "Tourists come here and usually stay for a week or two, but there hasn't been anyone here for the past month. I think maybe they booked their rentals online, but I don't know the name of the rental company. I'm sorry I don't know the address of this house either. There are no street signs."

With tears in her eyes, Michelle threw her arms around Thielemans and buried her face in his chest.

"I knew this house was somewhere in Mexico, but I never dreamed I would be able to find it again," Michelle cried. "I knew I wasn't imagining it. I told you I wasn't crazy."

"I never thought you were," Thielemans replied, gently pressing Michelle's head into his chest.

"I want Ed to see this," Michelle insisted, quickly pulling away from Thielemans.

Walking back to the van, Thielemans informed Prosky his presence was requested at the house. With some difficulty, Prosky got out of the van with his cane and limped toward the property.

"This is the house where I was raped after that priest kidnapped me from the program site in Arizona," Michelle stated, looking directly at Prosky. "This is the house everyone has been telling me I've been imagining for the past twenty years. Take a good look at it, Ed. It's just as I originally described it to you, ocean view and all. Tell me you see it or tell me you're imagining it along with me, but tell me something. I think I deserve that much."

"Of course, I see it," Prosky conceded. "I know you're upset, but we'll have a long time to talk about everything."

"Ed, we've been talking about everything for as long as I've known you," Michelle screamed. "I don't want to talk about this place anymore. Now that I've located it, I want to find out who rented this torture chamber and used it to prove to me hell really exists."

"I understand," Prosky calmly replied, as he slowly returned to the van.

Borrowing Thielemans' iPhone, Michelle took photos of the house and grounds from every conceivable angle.

"I told you I wasn't crazy," Michelle angrily reiterated, as she handed the iPhone back to Thielemans, took a final look at the house, and sighed.

As soon as everyone was in the van, Raul returned to the ship, resisting the urge to interrupt the van's silence, even while driving past a coastal embankment and dozens of barking, malodorous sea lions. Raul's saying, *"Gracias,"* after being paid by Thielemans, was the only time anyone spoke during the final half-hour of the tour.

Once aboard the ship, Thielemans invited everyone back to his suite. When they arrived, Michelle immediately borrowed his iPhone and iPad, excused herself, and quickly returned to her cabin to do some investigative work.

"So, what do you think about Michelle finding that house today?" Thielemans asked, as he removed three bottles of Saint Bavo Witbier from the refrigerator and carefully poured the contents into tall glasses. "Do you think finding the house makes her story about being kidnapped more credible?"

Seated on the sofa, Prosky and Conyngham stared at each other and pondered Thielemans' question.

"No," Prosky answered. "Michelle has been acting differently ever since we left Maui, and with Regina no longer around to watch over her, I wouldn't be surprised if she stopped taking her medications. When she's skipped her meds in the past, her personality and thinking changed perceptively. Michelle claimed the house she found today was the same house where her alleged rape took place years ago. This could be nothing more than a manifestation of the kind of delusional thinking bipolar patients exhibit when they stop taking their medications."

Thielemans handed his guests their glasses of beer and sat down in a chair facing the sofa.

"To Regina," Thielemans said, raising his glass.

"To Regina," Prosky and Conyngham responded.

"I wouldn't worry about Michelle," Prosky continued. "She'll be fine once she settles into a new routine. She'll be flying back to Baltimore with Bill and me tomorrow after we dock in San Diego. Her order is planning a memorial service for Regina next week. After the service, I guess she'll be flying back here to start working with you. I should be able to get her in to see her psychiatrist in Bethesda sometime next week. When the psychiatrist sees her, I'm sure he'll order blood tests to make sure the levels of her drugs are within a therapeutic range. I'm sure he'll also make any new recommendations he sees fit after he hears the story about her finding the house."

"So, what about you, Rock Star?" Conyngham asked. "What's on your agenda?"

"After we dock tomorrow, I'm going to check into the Wyndham, across the street from the cruise terminal," Thielemans answered. "Once I'm settled, I have to retrieve my car from the Cadillac dealership. From there, I plan to drive to the beer distributor in town and get the cases of Saint Bavo Witbier and glasses I ordered."

"Pick up an extra case for me," Conyngham joked.

"Sure thing," Thielemans agreed. "I'll have them bring it when they deliver your hot tub."

"What are your long-term plans?" Prosky inquired.

"I plan to stay in San Diego this week because I have talks scheduled at the University of San Diego and John Paul the Great Catholic University," Thielemans replied. "Next week, I'll be in Rancho Palos Verdes for a talk at Marymount Catholic University and in Los Angeles for talks at Loyola Marymount University and Mount Saint Mary's University. The week after that, I'll be in Santa Paula to speak at Thomas Aquinas College. Michelle will join me in San Diego, and we'll drive to Los Angeles together. When I'm not lecturing, I plan to discuss my program with priests throughout Southern California. After that, we're headed to Texas by way of Nevada, Arizona, and New Mexico."

"How's enrollment in your program been going?" Prosky questioned.

"I don't know," Thielemans admitted. "Michelle has been handling most of the enrollment over the internet. She told me not to worry because she has a few resources that will lead her to more prospective participants than we'll need to make the program successful. So, we'll see."

"That wouldn't surprise me a bit," Prosky said confidently. "If anyone can get a job done, it's Michelle."

Thielemans got up and retrieved a pen and paper.

"I'd like contact information for both of you," he requested, handing the pen and paper to Prosky. "Give me your addresses, phone numbers, and email info. Bill, if you don't hear about the hot tub in a week, call me."

"You're really serious about buying me a hot tub, aren't you?" Conyngham said, with tears in his eyes.

"I've got to spend my money somewhere," Thielemans answered, grabbing Conyngham's shoulder.

"I really don't deserve such a gift," Conyngham cried.

"Don't think of it as a gift," Thielemans advised. "Think of it as a contribution to religious education and a tax deduction. Besides, I owe you something for teaching me about rosary peas."

"As I told you before, please be careful with them," Conyngham reiterated. "Orally ingesting the poisonous contents of just one pea can kill you in a matter of days. Also, be smart about taking them off the ship."

"Will do," Thielemans replied. "Thanks again for the advice. So, Ed, what can I do to repay you for all you've taught me on this cruise?"

"You've got to be kidding," Prosky chuckled. "You're the one we should be repaying for all you've done for us. You fed us, got us drunk, comforted us, took us on adventures, and even inspired us. Besides, we could never begin to repay you for all you did for Regina, giving Michelle a new purpose in life, and putting up with Bill."

"Ed, there must be something I can do for you," Thielemans insisted.

"Well, actually, Paul, there is one thing," Prosky revealed. "I'd like you to keep me in the loop about Kittrick and any other sex offenders you come across. My group still has a lot of work to do to clean up the priesthood, and with the continued input from people like you and Michelle, our work will be considerably easier and more productive."

"I'll do everything I can," Thielemans promised, as he shook the elderly priest's hand. "I'll never be able to repay you for all you taught me about sex offenders in the clergy and the importance of being a paraclete."

While still holding Thielemans' hand, Prosky rose to his feet and looked into Thielemans' eyes.

"Paul, I hope you realize I have accepted you into my inner circle, and now consider you to be a paraclete," he said with obvious sincerity. "I pray you will always recognize those who deserve your protection and strive to keep them out of harm's way."

"I'm honored," Thielemans responded.

Prosky smiled at Thielemans, and glancing out the balcony window, he realized the ship was moving.

"Looks like we're pulling out," he correctly observed. "Next stop, San Diego."

"And reality," Conyngham interjected. "You know, I'm not happy this cruise is coming to an end, and I'm not even happy to be leaving Ensenada. However, if I never see, hear, nor smell another sea lion again, I think I'll die a happy man."

"Well, since I'm already on my feet, I think this would be a good time to leave," Prosky announced, as he pulled Conyngham's walker closer to the sofa and extended his hands to his feeble friend. "We still have to pack and get ready to disembark tomorrow morning. We have an early flight. So, I think we're just going to order some food from room service tonight and get a decent night's sleep. It will be a long flight tomorrow."

"I understand," Thielemans said, as he moved closer to the sofa to help Prosky hoist Conyngham to his feet. "God bless you both. I sincerely hope we'll have the chance to meet again in the not-too-distant future."

"When you're home again, look us up," Conyngham requested. "Maybe we could check out the sea lions at the National Aquarium in Baltimore."

"Maybe," Thielemans chuckled. "By the way, let me know when your hot tub arrives."

"Thanks, Rock Star," Conyngham answered with tears still in his eyes. "I'll never forget you."

"Neither will I," Prosky added, as he shook Thielemans' hand. "Congratulations on becoming a paraclete, and thanks for everything you've done for us."

Holding the door for his departing guests, Thielemans watched them hobble toward their cabin. While he was watching, Michelle suddenly appeared in the hall, and after speaking briefly with the priests, continued toward Thielemans' suite.

"How did your investigative work go?" Thielemans asked, holding the cabin door for Michelle.

"Not too well," she answered, as she removed her religious veil and placed a shopping bag and Thielemans' iPad on the bar. "The house has evidently been a rental property for the past twenty years. I spoke with a secretary at the realty office but didn't get very far. She told me rental records are confidential and cannot be released without the written permission of the individual renters."

"That's not surprising," Thielemans remarked, as he approached the bar. "What's in the bag?"

"The dress and shoes I bought in Maui, and the ones you bought me," Michelle replied. "I was hoping you could carry them off the ship and hold on to them until I see you next week. I don't want to show up at the convent, carrying the latest fashions of the Sisters of Saint Laurent."

"I'll carry them off the ship for you," Thielemans responded. "I just hope no one inspects my luggage while I'm passing through customs."

"If anyone does, just tell them the truth," Michelle advised. "Tell them you're having a love affair with a nun, and she asked you to carry her dresses and shoes for her."

"You don't think it would be better if I told them I belonged to a foreign congregation of priests called the Order of Holy Transvestites?" Thielemans joked.

"Maybe you should," Michelle agreed. "After all, 'transvestite,' sounds religious. By the way, what do you want me to do with your spare credit card and iPhone?"

"Keep them for now," Thielemans advised. "You'll need a credit card to buy new clothes and a cell phone for travel. When you get back, I'll get you a new credit card, newer model iPhone, and laptop of your own."

"Cool," Michelle exclaimed.

"What can I get you to drink?" Thielemans requested.

"I'd love something tall and cold, but I'll have to pass on anything with alcohol in it," Michelle answered. "Knowing Ed as well as I do, I'm sure he'll insist I see my shrink when we get back to Baltimore, especially since I carried on when I saw the house today. Ed probably thinks I've become delusional. Knowing my psychiatrist as well as I do, I'm sure he'll order blood tests to make sure I'm taking my medications and have therapeutic drug levels. So, to avoid all kinds of inevitable problems, I started taking my meds again. I took the first of my regular doses before I came to see you and I'll probably take extra doses over the next few days to get my blood levels up faster. So, I'd better avoid booze until I'm off medications again."

"How about a Barq's?" Thielemans suggested.

"Okay," Michelle agreed.

Pouring root beer into a glass for Michelle and Saint Bavo Witbier into his personal beer glass, Thielemans walked with Michelle to the sofa.

"The Saint Bavo Witbier glasses really are beautiful," Michelle observed, as she admired the one Thielemans was holding.

"Yes, they are," Thielemans concurred. "Now that you've mentioned it, my sister used to clean the glasses, cover their tops with cellophane wrap, and chill a six-pack of beer every night before I visited a priest. If it's not too much trouble, I'd like you to take over the job."

"No problem at all," Michelle said. "By the way, what do you do if a priest doesn't drink beer?"

"That's never been a problem," Thielemans replied. "Even priests who aren't beer drinkers will usually take a sip of beer just to be sociable. On a few occasions, I have visited priests who didn't want to drink beer because they were reformed alcoholics or had illnesses, like diabetes. In those cases, they filled their new glasses with iced tea or soda, and we were still able to enjoy a drink together. Do you have any other questions?"

"Not really," Michelle answered. "So far, I've been able to fit your meetings with priests in between the lectures your sister scheduled before she returned to Belgium. I've tried to limit the driving time between the venues of your events and the priests' residences to an hour or less. I may not be able to do that as easily when we get to Texas or some of the other states, but I'll try."

"I can't believe how you do everything the same way my sister did when she worked with me," Thielemans observed enthusiastically.

"Everything?" Michelle asked, as she leaned toward Thielemans and placed a hand on his thigh.

"Well, almost everything," the priest replied, as he watched Michelle smile and withdraw her hand. "So, what do you want to do about dinner tonight?

"I hope you don't mind, but I told the boys I'd order room service with them in a few hours," Michelle said apologetically. "Believe it or not, I still have an awful lot to do tonight. I still have to pack my bags and my aunt's bags and help the boys pack theirs. I also have to run down to the Customer Service desk and get special shipping tags. I have to fill out the tags and place them on Regina's bags before I put them out in the hall tonight for pick-up. Then, the ship will arrange for her bags to be shipped back to the convent. So, once I leave here, I probably won't be seeing you again until I fly back to San Diego next week. I'll call you in a few days with the flight information."

Michelle leaned toward Thielemans and threw her arms around him.

"I love you so much, and I thank God for you every day of my life," she whispered, as she hugged him and kissed him gently on the lips.

"I love you too," Thielemans responded, as he embraced Michelle. "I also thank God for you every day of my life."

Michelle hugged Thielemans and kissed him again.

"I'll miss you," Thielemans said softly.

"I'll miss you too," Michelle replied. "The boys are probably waiting."

Michelle got up from the sofa and retrieved her veil.

"When are you disembarking tomorrow?" Thielemans inquired.

"We're with the first group to get off the ship," Michelle answered. "We have to catch an early flight."

"I'm in the first group too," Thielemans stated. "If I see you in the morning, I'll walk off the ship with you."

"Sounds good," Michelle sighed, throwing her arms around Thielemans and kissing him again on the lips.

"See you soon," Thielemans promised, as he gave Michelle a final hug and opened the cabin door.

"See you soon," Michelle echoed, as she placed her veil on top of her head, stepped outside the cabin door, and with a final wave, walked down the hall.

After Michelle turned the corner at the end of the hall, Thielemans closed the door, retrieved his glass of beer, and walked on to the balcony. Looking at the sea, he recalled sitting on the balcony on the first day of the cruise and watching the Eurodam sail away from San Diego. He also recalled thinking about Bobby Kucera and Father Kittrick at that time, never realizing Bobby's life was about to tragically end or Father Prosky's tutorials were about to introduce him to the sordid world of pedophilia.

Thielemans had been a passenger on the Eurodam for eighteen days, and as he watched the ship cut through the waves, he wondered how so many days could have passed by so quickly. Reflecting on each of those days, he wondered how he could have experienced so many life-changing events in such a short time.

The renowned theologian and best-selling author boarded the ship a celibate priest who wrote a book he was confident would restore interest in the Catholic Church. As he prepared to disembark from the ship, he wondered if his book would ever fulfill its original purpose, love affair with a nun would affect his priesthood, or new affiliation with a secret society of paracletes would allow him to protect the innocent from sexual predators in a way he wished he had been able to protect Bobby Kucera.

As Thielemans watched the night slowly take the ocean into its hands, he realized there were a few things he still had to do. He had to run down to the Customer Service desk to settle his account, meet with Winston, and figure out what he was going to do for dinner.

After Thielemans showered and dressed in casual attire, he took a walk through the ship to the Customer Service desk. Joining a long line of passengers waiting for customer service, he suddenly felt a tap on his shoulder.

"Why, hello, there, young man," Father Frost said enthusiastically.

"Good evening," Thielemans replied, as he extended his hand to the elderly priest. "Welcome to the long line of passengers who all wish they came here yesterday."

"Better late than never," Frost suggested, as he ratcheted up his perpetual smile a notch.

"So, are you disembarking tomorrow or staying on as the ship's chaplain?" Thielemans inquired.

"I signed up for another tour of duty this morning," Frost replied. "I've been asked to stay on through the Alaska run."

"That's wonderful," Thielemans exclaimed. "Seeing both Hawaii and Alaska from the same ship should be something you'll remember for a long time."

"I would say so," Frost agreed.

"What are your plans for dinner tonight?" Thielemans inquired.

"You know, I haven't had time to think about it," Frost admitted. "I've been busy all day, and haven't had a single moment to think beyond the here and now."

"I know what you mean," Thielemans agreed. "Well, if you don't have any other plans, would you like to join me for dinner? I can arrange for us to have a leisurely dinner at the finest restaurant on the entire ship."

"I'd enjoy having dinner with you very much," Frost responded. "Unfortunately, I don't think I have enough spare cash to eat at the Pinnacle Grill."

"I know a better place, and it won't cost you a pauper's penny," Thielemans promised.

"Well, the price certainly sounds right," Frost laughed.

"What do you feel like eating?" Thielemans inquired.

"I can usually make a meal out of anything," Frost replied. "It's a funny thing, though. After I eat a lot of fancy food for a week or so on a cruise, I usually start craving something simple like a cheeseburger and french fries."

"It's funny you should say that," Thielemans chuckled. "I could go for a cheeseburger and plate of fries myself."

Seeing Frost smiling and nodding his approval, Thielemans excused himself, walked over to a wall phone, and called Winston with his dinner order.

After both priests finished their business at the Customer Service desk, they walked through the ship to Thielemans' suite.

"Welcome to Steerage," Thielemans announced, opening the cabin door.

"Steerage?" Frost exclaimed, as he marveled at the size of the suite. "Why, the Titanic didn't have cabins this big."

"It certainly has been a comfortable place to hang a hat for a few weeks," Thielemans admitted. "It has also been a great place to dine and entertain guests."

"I can imagine," Frost concurred.

"So, what can I offer you to drink?" Thielemans asked, as he walked behind the bar. "Beer? Wine? Something stronger?"

"To be honest with you, I'm not much of a drinker," Frost politely explained. "A soft drink, coffee, or even water would be fine. What are you having?"

"I'm going to have a cold beer," Thielemans responded. "If you'd care to join me, I think you might enjoy a glass of Saint Bavo Witbier, the Belgian beer my father introduced America to many years ago."

"All right," Frost agreed. "I'll try one."

Sitting down on the sofa, Frost continued to marvel at the suite's many features. As he did, Thielemans opened two bottles of beer.

"So, was your cruise everything you hoped it would be?" Frost inquired, as Thielemans handed him a bottle of Saint Bavo Witbier and a glass.

"I think you'll have to ask me that question a few months from now after I've had time to process everything that's happened in the past several weeks," Thielemans replied, as he sat down in a chair facing the sofa and showed his guest the proper way to pour a glass of unfiltered Belgian beer.

"To your health," Thielemans toasted, raising his glass.

"To your health," the elderly priest exclaimed, as he savored the taste of his beer. "This beer is really delicious. So, tell me more about your cruise."

"If anything, the cruise turned out to be a test of reality and an even greater test of faith," Thielemans continued. "I delivered my talk in Honolulu to a group of distracted bishops, discovered a few issues that made me question some of my deepest-rooted religious beliefs, and unexpectedly learned about the tragic death of a child – a death I may have been able to prevent. Conversely, I was able to learn other ways to restore interest in the Church, gain a better understanding of Catholicism, and discover a subculture of the Church I never knew existed."

"It sounds like your vacation was more work than play," Frost observed. "I hope you did have some time to relax and enjoy the cruise."

"Politics and religion notwithstanding, I did have a very nice vacation," Thielemans admitted. "I thoroughly enjoyed the ship, the Hawaiian Islands, and many of the people I met along the way."

"I guess there's no getting away from politics or religion," Frost opined.

"You're right about that," Thielemans answered. "You know, I've been thinking about our discussion at lunch the other day. I think you had some good insights about the Church moving toward a married priesthood in the near future."

"I think it's inevitable," Frost replied. "You know, Paul, you and I are both Catholic priests. We have both devoted our lives to the service of God and our fellow man. However, there is a significant difference between the two of us. For most of the forty years I've been a Catholic priest, I was able to love a woman and cherish the three children she gave me. During that time, there was never a single moment when I had any mental reservations or qualms of conscience about the intimate life my wife and I shared. For most of the years you have been a Catholic priest, you willfully sacrificed the opportunity to have an intimate relationship with a woman and share the love of your own children. In doing so, you forfeited the right to a kind of happiness very few Catholic priests ever experience in their lifetimes. Honestly, I can see no good reason why Catholic priests have to make such a sacrifice."

"A lot has to do with economics," Thielemans said.

"It does," Frost agreed. "But here's the rub. If the Church's only concern is having to financially support a priest's wife and family, there is no concern. The wives of most protestant ministers work and frequently make more money than their husbands. In most cases, they also get health insurance and other benefits from their employers that also cover their spouses and children. So, a priest being married could actually save the Catholic Church a lot of money."

"You may be right," Thielemans conceded.

"What all this boils down to is the fact celibacy is a man-made regulation and not a sacred dogma," Frost emphasized. "So, without beating a dead seahorse for the few remaining hours we have left on this cruise, let me just say two things. First of all, in the history of the Catholic Church, priests have been allowed to marry and engage in sexual activity longer than they've been required to be celibate. So, the Catholic Church has allowed its priests to express their God-given human sexuality for more centuries than it has prohibited them from doing so. What's more, the Church has allowed me – a man who converted to Catholicism relatively late in life, to not only serve as one of its priests but to also enjoy all the benefits of married life at the same time. However, the moment my wife died, the Church took away my sexual freedom and required me to become celibate. Can you imagine that? I'm 80 years old, and for the first time in my adult life, I'm celibate. This shows how inconsistent, unfair, and illogical man-made rules can be, regardless of what church or institution creates them."

Thielemans quietly nodded his head in agreement.

"The second thing you have to understand is, under certain circumstances, it may be a greater sin for a priest to deprive a woman of his love than share it with her," Frost added. "You won't find that written in any Catholic theology book, but you will find it in the *Book of Life*."

"You may be the most original human being I've ever met," Thielemans observed. "You've said things I've never heard anyone say before, and everything you've said has been thought-provoking. For example, you just said, 'by sacrificing the opportunity to have an intimate relationship with a woman and share the love of my own children, I forfeited the right to a kind of happiness very few Catholic priests ever experience in their lifetimes.'"

"Yes," Frost acknowledged. "That's right."

"Then, tell me more about your children," Thielemans requested with sincere interest. "I'd like to know what kind of happiness they've brought to your life."

"Well, my oldest son, Michael, is a marine biologist in Key West," Frost began. "My daughter, Joanne, is a special agent with the F.B.I. in Los Angeles, and my youngest son, Charles, is a naval officer in Honolulu. My three children are all married and have two children each."

"What kind of work does your daughter do with the F.B.I.?" Thielemans asked.

"Mainly homicide investigations," Frost laughed.

"What's so funny? Thielemans inquired.

"Joanne's field office is in Los Angeles," Frost replied. "Her married name is Faraday, but instead of calling her, Joanne Faraday, her coworkers call her, 'Jo Friday,' after the detective in the television series, *Dragnet*, which took place in L.A."

"That is funny," Thielemans acknowledged.

"You asked what kind of happiness my children brought to my life," Frost continued. "There's not enough time to tell you all the ways my wife, children, and grandchildren have filled my life with happiness. They were, are, and will always be the true blessings in my life. When I die, I plan to picture each one of them smiling, and with my last breath, just say, 'Thank You, dear God.'"

"That's beautiful," Thielemans said. "Do you still spend a lot of time with your children and grandchildren?"

"Not as much as I'd like," Frost admitted. "My children are all busy with their work, but I do see them semi-regularly and spend a lot of time talking with them on the phone. They still call me and pretend they're asking for advice. They really call to make sure I'm still ticking."

"I hear you," Thielemans remarked. "And I can see why few Catholic priests ever experience the unique kind of happiness your family has brought you."

As Frost's smile expanded, the doorbell chimed, and Winston entered with dinner. After he finished placing plates of cheeseburgers, hot dogs, french fries, chili, buns, condiments, and pepperoni pizza on the dining room table, Thielemans walked his cabin steward to the door.

Thanking Winston for his outstanding service, Thielemans quietly informed him that, in addition to his standard gratuity, he would also be receiving a bonus of one-thousand dollars which Thielemans already deposited in his shipboard account. As the grateful cabin steward left, Thielemans rejoined his guest, and the two embarked on an evening of beer, junk food, and poignant conversation.

As one conversation continued in Thielemans' suite on the Eurodam, another was ending at Saint Declan's Rectory in San Diego.

"What do you mean you still haven't talked to Thielemans?" Bishop Grannick shouted angrily.

"I've tried calling him a dozen times in the past two days," Father Kittrick insisted. "Every time I call, I get a message that says, 'the wireless customer you are calling is not available. Please try again later.'"

"The ship he's on doesn't arrive in San Diego until tomorrow morning," Grannick stated with a calmer voice. "He's probably got his cell phone set to 'Airplane Mode.' He probably won't change the settings until he's ready to get off the ship."

"I'll keep trying to call him, Uncle," Kittrick said. "As soon as I get him on the phone, I'll arrange a meeting. I promise."

"See that you do," Grannick demanded. "And when you finally meet with him, make sure you find out everything he knows about you and the Kucera boy."

"I will," Kittrick replied.

"The last thing either of us needs is for someone as prominent Father Thielemans to go blabbing to the police," Grannick emphasized. "And don't forget what I told you about that beer gimmick he uses. Make sure to ask him to bring you some of that good Belgian beer of his, and go along with his act like you're really interested in what he has to say. Convince him your only interest in Bobby Kucera and all the other orphans was platonic. Then, apologize for your previous behavior and get on the man's good side. Understand?"

"Yes, Uncle," Kittrick answered. "But what if he sees through me and won't let me get on his good side?"

"You're right to suspect Thielemans may see right through you," Grannick acknowledged. "If he does, he'll give you all the rope you need to hang yourself. He's a sly one, for sure. If he sees what you're doing and you've pulled out all the stops, you may have to give the man exactly what he's looking for."

"And what's that, Uncle?" Kittrick asked.

"Your confession, Boyo," Grannick replied deviously. "You may just have to give Thielemans exactly what he's expecting to hear – that you sexually molested Bobby Kucera and many others before him."

"Are you crazy?" Kittrick shouted. "Do you really expect me to admit to Thielemans I'm attracted to young

228

boys and not always able to control my behavior when I'm alone with them?"

"Remember this about your uncle, Boyo," Grannick responded. "He is crazy – crazy like a fox. He's also the smartest person you'll ever know. So, let's say you decide to confess to Father Paul Thielemans. Well, if you do, go the whole nine yards with the man. But before you admit to anything, tell him you want to receive the Sacrament of Reconciliation, and ask him to hear your confession. If he agrees and puts the purple stole around his neck, get down on your knees and confess your little heart out. After he gives you penance and absolves you of your sins, look him in the eye, give him a hearty handshake, and thank him. After he leaves, you can thank me for showing you how to use religion to your advantage."

"What do you mean?" Kittrick inquired.

"What I mean is, once Father Thielemans hears your confession, he can never reveal anything you told him during the confession to anyone," Grannick explained. "Even if you confirm his suspicions about you and the Kucera kid through confession, Thielemans can never tell anyone what you confessed to him. He can't repeat a word of your confession to the authorities or anyone else. I'd use the confession ploy only as a last resort, but if you use it, make sure it's convincing."

"I understand, Uncle," Kittrick said.

"Make sure you do," Grannick warned, getting up from his chair and handing his nephew a bag containing two pairs of new shoes. "I'm flying to Rome tomorrow morning. I'll be at the Vatican for several weeks, handling legal affairs for the archdiocese. While I'm gone, take these shoes to Silvestri the shoemaker downtown, and have him fit both pairs with three-inch lifts and thick heels like he usually does for me. He'll call you when they're ready to be picked up."

"Anything else, Uncle?" Kittrick asked.

"There is," Grannick replied, as he walked toward the rectory door. "Be careful with this new 13-year-old you're trying to recruit. If you're not careful, this obsession you have with young boys will be the end of you."

"I understand, Uncle," Kittrick mumbled, as he watched Grannick leave the rectory and hurry to his car.

CHAPTER THIRTEEN

Upon arriving in San Diego, Thielemans left the Eurodam, checked into the Wyndham San Diego Bayside, and shortly thereafter, retrieved his newly repaired Cadillac. Following a hectic day of running errands and intentionally ignoring phone calls from Father Kittrick, he relaxed in his hotel room and reviewed the talk he would be giving in two days at the University of San Diego.

As he relaxed, he thought about the many different things that happened during his cruise and smiled every time he thought about Michelle. He laughed out loud when he recalled accompanying her off the ship, past a long line of entertainers who smiled, waved, and offered best wishes to disembarking passengers. He couldn't forget the stunned looks on the faces of the Polish violinists, Nicola and Marta, and the B.B. King Blues Band singers, Jalen and Shanice, when they suddenly realized the attractive man and woman who they entertained on the Eurodam a few days earlier were, in real life, a Catholic priest and nun.

While Thielemans continued working on his speech and thinking about his recent cruise, he received a text message on his iPhone:

"Pot roast and peach pie like Mother used to make. Oasis Visitor Center, Joshua Tree National Park, Twentynine Palms. Tomorrow at 3 p.m. sharp."

Reading the cryptic message, Thielemans tried texting the sender several times, but his attempts were all unsuccessful. Realizing the message could be coming from

Mother Murray, he added a trip to Joshua Tree National Park to his busy itinerary.

The next morning, Thielemans, wearing a San Diego Padres baseball cap, Hawaiian shirt, khakis, boat shoes, and sunglasses, embarked on the three-hour drive from his hotel to Twentynine Palms. As he drove, he wondered if it was Mother who sent him the text message, and if it was, how she obtained his cell phone number, knew he would be in San Diego, and had to meet him under an apparent veil of secrecy. Sensing she probably needed to talk with him about her sudden departure from Saint Declan's, Father Kittrick, and Bobby Kucera, Thielemans drove the scenic route from the Pacific Ocean to the Mojave Desert.

Arriving at Joshua Tree National Park at 2:45 p.m., Thielemans parked his car and walked into the Oasis Visitor Center. Realizing two park rangers were the only people inside the building, he returned outside and sat down on a bench.

As he was admiring the beauty of the park, a passenger van from a local assisted living facility pulled up to the Visitor Center entrance. One by one, a dozen senior citizens slowly stepped off the van and walked into the facility.

The final passenger to exit the van was an elderly woman with silver hair and an apparent need to visit a restroom. As the van driver pointed to the restrooms which were located in a separate building a few hundred feet away, the woman started hobbling in that direction.

Realizing the woman was Mother Murray, Thielemans got up from his bench and nonchalantly walked toward her. Seeing Thielemans approaching, Mother Murray slowed down and started walking with a noticeable limp.

"May I help you?" Thielemans inquired loudly, in the manner of a courteous stranger who didn't appear to know the elderly woman.

"Why thank you, Sir," Mother gratefully replied, as she allowed Thielemans to take her by the arm. "These old bones aren't what they used to be."

As the two slowly walked, arm-in-arm, toward the restrooms, onlookers smiled at Thielemans' apparent act of chivalry. Once the two were out of earshot, Mother squeezed Thielemans' arm.

"Thanks for coming, Honey," Mother said *sotto voce*. "I don't have much time, but there's a lot I have to tell you."

"Before you start, tell me how you got my cell phone number and knew I'd be in San Diego," Thielemans requested.

"I got your phone number from a business card you left at Saint Declan's," Mother revealed. "I knew you were in San Diego because the diocesan newspaper mentioned you'd be speaking at San Diego's two Catholic colleges this week. They won't let me have a cell phone of my own. So, I had to use another resident's phone to text you. I borrowed it after she fell asleep in our community room."

"So, where's my pot roast and peach pie?" Thielemans joked.

"Probably the same place my Saint Bavo Witbier is," Mother quickly retorted, squeezing the priest's arm again. "So, I guess you've heard about Bobby Kucera by now. Heaven help us."

"Unfortunately, I have," Thielemans confirmed. "I called Kittrick a few weeks ago from Hawaii after I heard the news about Bobby. Kittrick was very defensive on the phone, and when I asked to speak with you, he told me you were no longer at Saint Declan's. He also claimed he didn't know where you were living."

"He knows where I'm living," Mother insisted angrily. "Just so you understand, my son came to see me at Saint Declan's a few days after Bobby died. He told me to pack my things because I was being officially retired by the parish and given a rent-free apartment at an assisted living facility about fifteen minutes from here in Twentynine Palms. The apartment was supposed to be a part of a retirement gift from the parish, but it's more like a prison cell if you ask me. Kittrick knows where I'm living because he and Little Joe were the ones who had me exiled to the desert. They're worried about the police investigating Bobby's suicide, and me saying something I shouldn't."

"Who is 'Little Joe?'" Thielemans asked.

"Little Joe Grannick," Mother answered emphatically. "He's the bishop who asked you to say Mass at Saint Declan's. He's also Kittrick's uncle."

"Now I know who you mean," Thielemans conceded. "Why do you call him 'Little Joe?'"

"The man is a dwarf," Mother chuckled. "He's a veritable leprechaun. He's only 5'4", standing tippytoe. If he seemed taller when you met him, it's because he wears elevator shoes in public. The shoes have lifts and big heels that make him appear 5'8" or so."

"I didn't realize that," Thielemans admitted.

"Oh, I could tell you stories," Mother swooned.

"So, when I talked with Kittrick, he blamed me for Bobby's suicide," Thielemans continued. "Bobby walked off the altar during the second Mass I said at Saint Declan's. I was concerned he might be sick. So, I looked for him after Mass, but couldn't find him. As I was about to board my ship, I asked a policeman to call the rectory and make sure someone was aware Bobby might be ill. Instead of phoning, the policeman came to the rectory the next day, and Kittrick claimed seeing the policeman frightened Bobby who thought he might be in some kind of trouble. Kittrick claimed Bobby's suicide was my fault because I sent the policeman to the rectory."

"Bobby's suicide wasn't your fault, Father Darling," Mother said in a comforting tone. "His suicide was the fault of that monster, Kittrick, who used Bobby and too many others like him for his own sexual gratification. Kittrick lured Bobby and several other carefully-selected altar boys who wanted to become priests into his gym. He taught them how to wrestle, and after he gained their confidence, he convinced them seminarians were required to become sexually submissive to their superiors as a secret rite of passage into the priesthood. The boys he recruited to become his sex slaves were in desperate need of a father figure. They trusted Kittrick, believed everything he told them, and allowed themselves to be sworn to secrecy. Before they knew it, they were being sexually abused by Kittrick, offering up their pain for the poor souls in Purgatory, and praying for the day they would become ordained priests and have altar boys of their own to sexually abuse. Kittrick ran his junior high sex tutorial as some kind of Head Start program for future seminarians. The pity of the matter is the young boys of Saint Declan's weren't the first children Kittrick duped and molested."

"That is the most disgusting thing I've ever heard," Thielemans stated angrily.

"Poor Bobby's suicide was Kittrick's fault, but it was mine as well," Mother whispered, as tears filled her eyes. "I

235

saw what was happening, but was afraid to say anything to anyone. I didn't think anybody would believe an old woman like me. Besides, the rectory was my home, and I had nowhere else to go. None of my children could take me. So, I had to keep my mouth shut or risk losing the roof over my head. I still have to be careful what I say to anyone because Grannick has diverted funds from the archdiocese to pay the rent at my new bug-infested residence. If I say the wrong thing to the wrong person, I could find myself sleeping under a rock in the desert."

"How did you discover Kittrick was sexually abusing Bobby and the other boys?" Thielemans inquired.

"I got suspicious when the boys started coming up from the cellar with stiff upper lips, fear in their eyes, and pain everywhere else," Mother answered. "That's when I decided to hide a tape recorder downstairs and start listening to what was happening."

"Do you still have the tapes?" Thielemans asked.

"I only had one cassette and had to tape over earlier encounters between Kittrick and the boys to record newer ones," Mother revealed. "I got nervous after Bobby died. So, I destroyed the cassette. I was worried about what might happen if Kittrick found out I was taping him."

"Is the bishop aware of Kittrick's exploits?" Thielemans questioned.

"Aware?" Mother exclaimed. "The bishop has been aware of Kittrick's antics ever since the pastor entered the priesthood and started raping altar boys. Who do you think has been paying off the families of all the children Kittrick has molested? Why it's been Grannick who has been stealing money from the archdiocese and handing out hush money all along. And who do you think arranged Kittrick's transfers from town to town and parish to parish every time he got caught with his pants down? Why, it's been Grannick, of course. I've seen and heard a lot at Saint Declan's over the years. I also know people from other parishes who could tell you stories about Kittrick. So, I swear everything I'm telling you is the eyewitness truth. Heaven help us."

"What about Grannick?" Thielemans asked, as he watched a few of Mother's traveling companions exiting the Visitor Center and returning to their van.

"Grannick is even dirtier and more perverted than his nephew," Mother insisted. "He's also a lot smarter. I'm told he sticks to young women for sex and doesn't crap where he eats. He does most of his fornicating in towns where no one knows him, and then, triumphantly returns home where he is revered as one of the leaders and staunchest defenders of Holy Mother Church."

"Does Grannick go after consensual sex with girlfriends or prostitutes, or is he a sexual predator like his nephew?" Thielemans inquired.

"I understand he's a real predator, that one," Mother answered. "I hear he doesn't get nearly as excited about sex as he does about plucking forbidden fruit from the tree."

As the two arrived at the restrooms, Thielemans could see the last members of the tour group getting on the van and the driver looking in Mother's direction.

"Your van is getting ready to leave," Thielemans warned, as held the restroom door for Mother.

"I hope you understand I contacted you so you would know what happened to me and be able to hear the truth about Bobby, Kittrick, and Grannick," Mother suggested with trepidation in her voice. "I'm living at the 'Saints of the Desert Assisted Living Villa' in Twentynine Palms if you need to get in touch with me. I think I'm safe for the time being, but I'm truly worried about what might happen if the police do a proper investigation of Bobby's death and come looking for me to question. Forgive me for not sounding like a good Catholic, but I'd feel a lot safer if someone punched Kittrick and Grannick's one-way tickets to hell already."

Realizing the van was approaching the restrooms, Mother squeezed Thielemans' hand, smiled, and winked.

"Be gone with you, Father Darling, and may the road rise up to meet you," she said, closing the door to the restroom. "Now, let Mother go tinkle. Heaven help us."

"God bless you," Thielemans replied, as he walked behind the restrooms and out of sight.

Shortly after the van left the parking lot, Thielemans returned to his car and drove to several of the park's scenic views. After he studied the unique beauty of the desert preserve and its namesake Joshua Tree, he drove back to San Diego. As he did, he digested Mother's comments.

Early the following morning, Thielemans looked up the address of the Kucera family in the telephone book and drove to their residence. When he arrived there, he discovered a vacant home.

Seeing a neighbor sweeping her front porch, Thielemans inquired about the family and was told Mrs. Kucera and her two daughters left their home a few days after Bobby's funeral. He also learned the members of the family left the house with only two suitcases each, and Mrs. Kucera appeared uncharacteristically tight-lipped and purposefully vague when asked where the family was going.

With a great deal on his mind, Thielemans drove to the University of San Diego where he delivered another well-received lecture. Following his talk, as he was leaving the university's auditorium, he saw a short, stocky man waiting for him at the main exit. As he walked closer to the exit, he realized the man was Father Kittrick.

"Bravo," Kittrick exclaimed facetiously, as he smiled and clapped his hands. "That was some speech. Now I know why you drive a Cadillac."

"After our last phone conversation, I didn't think I'd ever see you again," Thielemans admitted.

"You'd improve your chances of seeing people again if you answered your phone more often," Kittrick advised.

"I've been very busy," Thielemans replied.

"I'm sure," Kittrick agreed sarcastically. "Rubbing elbows with all those bishops in Honolulu and eating nine meals a day on a cruise ship probably took a lot of time."

"I've also been very busy since I returned to San Diego," Thielemans emphasized.

"I'm sure," Kittrick repeated. "Well, look, I didn't come here to have you explain yourself. I came here to make peace. I know our phone conversation didn't go well, but I was still trying to deal with Bobby's death and didn't choose my words as well as I should have. For that, I am sorry. So, if you'll accept my apology, I'd like to sit down and talk with you about Bobby. I'd like to start our relationship all over again, the way I should have started it the night you visited the rectory. To this day, I regret not having a beer with you or showing more gratitude for the book you brought me."

"I'll be happy to sit down with you, have a beer, and talk about whatever is on your mind, but I can't do it today," Thielemans replied emphatically. "I have to prepare another talk, and I already have appointments to meet with several other priests."

"So, when do you think you'll have time to meet with me?" Kittrick inquired impatiently.

"I'll probably have some time in a few days before I leave San Diego," Thielemans answered. "I'll call you as soon as I know when I can meet with you, and I'll start chilling a six-pack of beer for you as soon as I get back to my hotel room."

"So, you'll definitely meet with me before you leave town?" Kittrick reiterated.

"You have my word," Thielemans guaranteed. "By the way, did you ever find out where Mother Murray is living? I'd still like to thank her for all her hospitality."

"As I told you when we spoke on the phone, I have no idea where she is," Kittrick stated nervously. "Her son showed up at the rectory one day, helped his mother pack her bags, and whisked her away. Neither one of them offered any thanks, gave a reason for leaving, or left a forwarding address. They just got in the son's truck and hit the road. I've been told the son is a construction worker and does a lot of work in Mexico. So, if I had to guess, I'd say he probably moved Mother south of the border where the air is warmer and drier, and it's much cheaper to live. Mother has arthritis and emphysema, you know. So, Mexico would probably be a healthier place for her to spend her last years anyway. If you'd like, I can make a few inquiries and give you a better idea of Mother's whereabouts the next time we meet."

Hearing the lame response, Thielemans just stared at Kittrick.

"I'll call you," Thielemans said unemotionally, as he quickly left the auditorium.

For the next few days, Thielemans visited several priests in the San Diego area, taught them how to properly drink Belgian beer, and acquainted them with his program to restore Church membership. Between visits, he lectured at John Paul the Great Catholic University and continued thinking about a dead altar boy and the sanctimonious pedophile who caused the boy's death.

As the weekend arrived, Michelle returned to San Diego in religious attire, hailed a cab at the airport, and checked into her own room at the Wyndham. Following a shower and exchange of a religious habit and veil for tight-fitting jeans and a loose-fitting top, the eager nun hurried to Thielemans' suite.

Hearing an energetic knock, Thielemans opened the door and beheld his new secretary.

"Can I sleep with you tonight?" Michelle asked sheepishly with an innocent look on her face.

Without answering her question, Thielemans quickly pulled Michelle inside his suite, kicked the door shut, and took her into his arms. Not giving her the chance to speak, Thielemans kissed her passionately.

"I'll take that as a 'yes,'" Michelle panted, as she took a deep breath, looked into Thielemans' eyes, and smiled.

After another embrace and short smooch, Michelle grabbed Thielemans' hand and led him to the sofa.

"Ed sends his regards, Bill thanks the Rock Star for his new hot tub, and Mother Consuela blesses you for everything you did for Regina," Michelle announced, as the two sat down.

"And it's nice seeing you again," Thielemans replied.

"So, what have you been up to?" Michelle inquired, as she squeezed Thielemans' hand.

"I've been busy," Thielemans answered, as he continued to study Michelle's beautiful face. "My two talks went well, and I presented my program to a half-dozen priests. We'll have to wait and see if any of them decide to give the program a try."

"Let's hope," Michelle said encouragingly. "If they don't, I've enlisted other priests who might be interested. So, what else have you been doing?"

"A few days ago, I took a drive to the Mojave Desert in response to a cryptic text message I received from Mother Murray, Kittrick's former housekeeper at Saint Declan's," Thielemans continued. "If being contacted by her wasn't surprise enough for one week, I also got paid an unexpected visit by Gordon Kittrick who attended my lecture at the University of San Diego and waited afterward to speak with me. I wasn't quite ready to talk with him and had a few other things to do. So, I told him I'd meet with him before I left town. Since we're leaving for Los Angeles in two days, I guess I'll have to set some time aside tomorrow to see him."

"So, what did you make of Kittrick?" Michelle asked.

"Guilty as charged," Thielemans exclaimed. "You can see guilt in his eyes and read it in his body language. Kittrick told me he wants to make peace and start our relationship all over again. He wants to sit down and have a beer with me because he thinks there are things I need to know about Bobby Kucera. I didn't tell him I met with Mother. When I asked if he knew where she was living, he said he had no idea. Of course, Mother had an entirely different story. She told me it was Kittrick and his uncle,

Bishop Joseph Grannick, who arranged for her to be sent to an assisted living facility in the Mojave Desert immediately after Bobby committed suicide. Evidently, they're worried Mother might say something to the police that could put nooses around both their necks."

"Wouldn't that be a shame," Michelle said facetiously.

"Mother also told me Kittrick has been a pedophile for as long as he's been a priest," Thielemans added. "Evidently, his uncle, who works in the same archdiocese, has been instrumental in covering up Kittrick's sexual indiscretions, having Kittrick transferred to different towns and parishes every time he got caught sexually molesting altar boys, and even providing hush money to the families of Kittrick's victims. The Kucera family might be the latest to receive hush money from Grannick because they moved out of town a few days after Bobby's funeral. Mother told me Grannick is also a sexual predator who, unlike his nephew, rapes young women instead of boys."

"So, just like Ed suspected, someone is covering Kittrick's tracks, and that someone is Bishop Grannick," Michelle suggested. "Ed will be grateful for this piece of news. It will help him connect a lot of dots."

"Mother told me she thought she was safe for the time being, but would feel a whole lot safer if, in her words, 'someone punched Kittrick and Grannick's one-way tickets to hell,'" Thielemans said.

"I really like Mother Murray," Michelle remarked. "I like the way she thinks, and I'm sure Ed would too. You know how Ed feels about priests who are sexual predators. He thinks they're beyond redemption, and anyone who punches their tickets to hell should be immediately canonized and have a church named in their honor."

"When you look at Kittrick, you get the feeling he is beyond redemption and capable of hurting people without feeling any remorse," Thielemans observed. "This makes me wonder just how safe Mother really is."

"Does she plan to go to the police and tell them about Kittrick and Grannick?" Michelle inquired.

"I think she would if she could, but there are a few extenuating circumstances that are keeping her from doing so," Thielemans replied. "To begin with, she never actually witnessed Kittrick sexually abusing any boys or Grannick making any hush money payments. So, it would be the word of an old woman who lost her job against that of two clergymen who are generally respected by the Church and their communities. Mother tape-recorded Kittrick while he was sexually molesting several altar boys, but she became frightened and destroyed the tape after Bobby committed suicide. So, she knows what Kittrick has been doing, but has no proof that would hold up in court. Additionally, Mother believes Grannick is diverting funds from the archdiocese to pay her monthly rent. If she went to the police, she would probably lose her apartment, and because none of her children are willing to take her in, she's afraid she could wind up homeless."

"Don't you wish we could go back to the days of the Old West and carry six-shooters?" Michelle quipped. "Why, bad guys like Kittrick and Grannick wouldn't stand a chance."

"So, where would you wear your gun belt?" Thielemans asked. "Under your habit or over it?"

"I wouldn't wear a gun belt," Michelle answered. "I'd wear fancy garters over my fishnet stockings, and carry a derringer under the garter on each leg."

Thielemans laughed and pulled Michelle closer. Kissing her, he ran a hand up and down her leg.

"I don't feel any derringer," Thielemans joked. "I guess you're just not packing today."

"Actually, I'm unpacking," Michelle retorted. "By the way, what did you do with my clothes?"

"Try the bedroom closet," Thielemans replied.

"I'll be right back," Michelle promised, as she got up from the sofa and walked into the bedroom.

In turn, Thielemans walked over to the refrigerator, retrieved a chilled bottle of Riesling, and opened it. After he poured wine into two water glasses, he returned the bottle to the refrigerator and walked back to the sofa.

"What did you do with my nylons, perfume, and lipstick?" Michelle shouted from the bedroom.

"Check the dresser," Thielemans hollered.

Michelle walked over to the dresser and opened each of the drawers. As she searched for her items, she saw the freezer bag filled with rosary peas and another bag filled with the crucifixes, silver attachments, and varnish needed to make rosaries. Temporarily mesmerized by the rosary peas, she retrieved her personal belongings.

"What's keeping you?" Thielemans yelled. "Are you praying a novena?"

"I'm writing a novella," Michelle screamed.

As Thielemans continued to wait patiently, Michelle finally returned from the bedroom, wearing only her nylons and metallic brown high heels.

"I missed you," she said softly, as she climbed atop Thielemans on the sofa.

"I missed you," Thielemans repeated, as he kissed her and caressed every aspect of her magnificent body.

Moving their reunion to the bedroom, Thielemans undressed and made love to Michelle without removing her nylons or high heels. After a session of passionate love-making, followed by a glass of wine and second session of passionate love-making, they remained in bed and basked in the warmth of each other's afterglow. Following a reaffirmation of their love, the two showered together, dressed, and returned to the living room.

"This is for you," Thielemans announced, handing Michelle a large cardboard box.

"Oh, wow," Michelle exclaimed, removing a new laptop, iPad, and iPhone from the container.

"And here's a credit card in your name," Thielemans added, handing her a Mastercard. "The iPad and iPhone have already been set up. All you have to do is activate your Mastercard over the phone and transfer the information you have stored on my laptop to yours. All the cables and other accessories you need are in the box. Give me the iPad and iPhone I previously loaned you. I'll store them in case we ever need backups. As far as the Visa card you still have, hang on to it. You may need two different credit cards."

"So, how do you want me to handle financial matters from here on out?" Michelle asked.

"As simple as possible," Thielemans answered. "Buy whatever you need. Keep a ledger with all business purchases, and hold on to all receipts. Whenever you buy anything for the business, use the Visa card. It's attached to my account. Whenever you buy anything for yourself, use the Mastercard. That includes paying for your hotel room and meals. I'll pay for my room and meals separately to make our tax write-offs seem more reasonable. When you're booking a hotel, book a suite in my name and pay for it with the Visa card, and book a separate room in your name and pay for it with the Mastercard. We'll both be spending most of our time in the suite, but the second room will come in handy if you need some private time. Also, having credit card records proving you had your own hotel room in each city should keep Mother Consuela off our backs. My sister always had a room of her own when we traveled together, and having two rooms provided a number of business and tax advantages. It even helped us rack up a lot of bonus points. Got all that?"

"Absolutely," Michelle replied. "Where are the beer glasses you want me to clean before you visit the priests?"

"The glasses and a roll of cellophane wrap are in the case, next to the fridge," Thielemans revealed. "My personal glass is in the kitchen cabinet. I already put two six-packs of beer in the fridge and threw in a few bottles of white wine."

After she retrieved the open bottle of Riesling from the refrigerator and refilled their glasses, Michelle kissed Thielemans on the cheek and carried her glass of wine and new laptop to the kitchen table. Using the appropriate cables, she started transferring information from Thielemans' laptop to her own.

"Paul, what's in this 'San Diego Suicide' folder you have on your laptop?" Michelle inquired.

Getting up from the sofa and walking into the kitchen, Thielemans looked at his laptop.

"There are links to internet newspaper reports and a television news feed about Bobby Kucera's suicide inside the folder," Thielemans explained. "I downloaded them to my laptop after I watched the televised report in Honolulu. I haven't had the nerve to watch the television news feed again. Seeing the photo of Bobby and Kittrick at the end made me physically ill."

"Would you mind if I watched it?" Michelle asked. "I'd like to see what Kittrick looks like."

"Not at all," Thielemans said. "In fact, I think I'm angry enough to finally watch it again."

Accessing the television news feed from the Fox affiliate in San Diego, Thielemans and Michelle closely watched as the conclusion of Bobby Kucera's funeral was being televised.

"Behind me, the casket of young Robert Kucera is being carried from the church, following a concelebrated Mass of Christian Burial," reporter Kate Ward began. "You can see the Mass's celebrant, Bishop Joseph Grannick, standing at the entrance to the church, waiting to receive the boy's casket before it is taken to Holy Cross Cemetery. Standing next to him are the Mass's co-celebrants, Reverend Gordon Kittrick and Reverend Francisco Melendez."

From the moment the report started, Michelle stared at Bishop Grannick as though she knew him. When the television camera took a closeup of Grannick's face, Michelle suddenly gasped and appeared frightened.

"What's wrong?" Thielemans asked.

"Oh, nothing," Michelle answered. "For a second, I thought I recognized Bishop Grannick, but he couldn't be the same person I thought he was."

As Michelle continued staring at Grannick, she remained frightened and uncomfortable.

"Are you all right?" Thielemans inquired.

"I think I'm all right," Michelle explained. "I just got frightened when I saw Bishop Grannick because he looks like an older version of the priest who raped me. It couldn't be him, though. Grannick is taller than the other guy."

"How much taller?" Thielemans queried.

"At least four or five inches," Michelle replied.

As the news feed ended and a photo of Bobby and Kittrick was displayed, Thielemans sighed.

"Are you all right?" Michelle questioned, as she watched Thielemans starting to appear uncomfortable.

"Not while I'm looking at that photo of Bobby and Kittrick," Thielemans emphasized. "That photo will haunt me for the rest of my life."

Thielemans and Michelle stared at each other and studied the uncertainty in each other's faces.

"Go to *Google*, and see if you can pull up any other photos of Grannick," Thielemans requested.

Entering "Bishop Joseph Grannick" in the *Google* search space, a few dozen images of Grannick quickly appeared on the laptop screen. As Michelle viewed photos of Grannick taken at an earlier age, she started to panic.

"Paul, I don't know how this could be possible, but the man in these photos is the man who raped me," Michelle exclaimed, as she started shivering and hyperventilating.

Thielemans quickly embraced Michelle and held her in his arms until her panic attack stopped.

"Michelle, I have something important to tell you, but before I do, I have to ask you something," Thielemans said calmly. "Did you tell your psychiatrist about the house you found in Ensenada?"

"I did," Michelle sighed. "And as I predicted, he immediately checked the level of medication in my blood. The level was therapeutic. So, he attributed my experience in Mexico to therapeutic failure."

Michelle paused and reached for her glass of wine. With her hands shaking, she nervously took a sip.

"The psychiatrist told me I became delusional because my medication was no longer working optimally," Michelle continued. "He said I imagined the house in Mexico to be the house in which my imaginary rape took place. After we argued for a few minutes, he put me on a newer medication which he felt would prevent future delusional episodes."

"Did you start taking the new medication?" Thielemans inquired.

"I took the pills while I was in Baltimore," Michelle revealed. "I stopped taking them the moment I left."

Thielemans stared at Michelle and once again sighed.

"Michelle, I want you to know I have always believed your explanation of everything that ever happened to you in Mexico," Thielemans emphasized. "I have always believed you were raped by a priest and correctly identified the house in which the rape took place. What's more, I have always believed you were misdiagnosed by all the psychiatrists and psychologists who treated you, including Ed. I have never believed you were bipolar or had any other major psychiatric disorder."

Michelle forced a smile and hugged Thielemans' arm.

"With this in mind, there's something you have to know about Grannick," Thielemans said. "The man is only 5'4". He appears four or five inches taller in public because he wears elevator shoes. So, you're probably right. Bishop Grannick could very well be the man who raped you."

"How did you find this out about Grannick?" Michelle asked expectantly, as tears filled her eyes.

"Mother Murray told me about Grannick's shoe lifts when I met her at Joshua Tree," Thielemans answered.

"She also told me Grannick has a long history of sexually molesting young women."

"From the way Grannick treated me, I knew I wasn't the first woman he ever raped," Michelle offered.

"And far from his last," Thielemans added. "So, where do we go from here?"

"Paul, I think I should go straight to the police and have Grannick put away for the rest of his life," Michelle stated angrily, as she wiped tears from her eyes. "Maybe getting raped by a 300-pound cellmate every day for the next decade will change his perspective on things. His being imprisoned would also be a kick in the pants to every shrink who ever tried telling me I was crazy."

"Michelle, I understand what you're feeling and saying, but the police and courts might not be able to help you," Thielemans suggested. "To begin with, all your medical records have identified you as a patient who has been delusional in the past and treated with psychiatric medications for a bipolar condition. Even records of your most recent psychiatric evaluation will probably state you are still delusional. So, if multiple mental health professionals have recorded that your rape and house sighting were delusions, how can you prove they weren't? It would be your word against Grannick's, with his archdiocese and the entire psychiatric community taking sides with him."

"I hear you," Michelle agreed. "The fact he raped me in Mexico could also be a problem in a United States court. Even a statute of limitations could work to his advantage. About the only thing I can do now is share this new information with Ed and hope our group's enhanced surveillance catches Grannick with his pants down in the not-too-distant future. Every dog has his day, and I have a feeling Grannick will have his."

Thielemans nodded in agreement.

"You know, Paul, Ed calls everyone in our surveillance group a 'paraclete,'" Michelle continued. "I'm sure he's told you before the term isn't meant to suggest any affiliation with his former congregation. It's only intended to identify individuals who help others who can't help themselves, as the definition of the word implies. Ed continues to remind me I'm a paraclete, and I heard he also told you that you were a paraclete. So, even though the police or courts may not give us all the help we need identifying pedophiles and other sexual predators in the clergy, our group of paracletes may still be able to bring a few of these perverts to justice."

"You're right," Thielemans agreed. "Just minutes ago, you identified Grannick as a clergyman who is also a rapist. So, chalk another one up for the paracletes."

Michelle stood up and threw her arms around Thielemans.

"Thank you for today, Paul," she said softly, as she buried her head in his chest. "You helped me clear up an important issue. I'm angry but relieved, and I feel like today may be the start of a new life for me."

Looking into Thielemans' eyes, she kissed him softly.

"Paul, if you don't mind, I need some time for myself," she requested. "I could go back to my room if you have work to do."

"No, stay here," Thielemans advised. "I feel like going outside for a walk."

As Thielemans left his suite, Michelle kept staring at Grannick's internet photo. When she could no longer stand looking at it, she pulled up the photo of Bobby and Kittrick, and carefully studied their faces.

Leaving his hotel and starting to walk on East Harbor Drive, Thielemans could see the Coronado Bridge in the distance. Realizing it was the Coronado Bridge Bobby jumped from to take his own life, Thielemans decided to walk toward it.

Arriving at the foot of the bridge and reading the sign that prohibited pedestrian traffic, Thielemans pictured Bobby, dressed in the cassock and surplice he wore as an altar boy, getting out of the cab and climbing to the bridge railing. As he studied the bridge at the spot where Bobby committed suicide, Thielemans could imagine the young boy looking toward heaven, folding his hands as if to say a final prayer, and then, jumping into the bay.

Troubled by the imagery, Thielemans sat down on a nearby bench where he immediately prayed to Bobby to forgive him for not recognizing the life circumstances that led to the youngster's suicide. He also prayed to God to forgive Bobby for taking his own life and allow him to spend eternity in heaven.

Still troubled by everything he was seeing and thinking, Thielemans got up from the bench and started walking back to his hotel. Removing the cell phone from his belt, he paused and phoned Gordon Kittrick.

"Saint Declan's Rectory," Kittrick answered.

"This is Paul Thielemans," the priest announced. "What time would you like to meet tomorrow?"

"Would 3 p.m. be convenient?" Kittrick asked.

"That will be fine," Thielemans confirmed.

"See you then," Kittrick closed. "And don't forget to bring some of that good Belgian beer of yours."

"I won't forget," Thielemans promised.

Pushing the button to end the call on his cell phone, Thielemans looked back at the Coronado Bridge.

"I'll never forget," he vowed, as he imagined the spirit of a winged altar boy hovering over San Diego Bay.

CHAPTER FOURTEEN

"Welcome to Saint Declan's," Kittrick exclaimed with a nervous smile, as he greeted Thielemans at the rectory door. "Thanks for coming, Paul. It's good to see you."

As Kittrick led the way to his office, Thielemans, carrying a chilled six-pack of Saint Bavo Witbier and an attaché, followed closely behind. Walking through the rectory, he noticed two shoeboxes on a table. Attached to one box was a receipt from Silvestri Shoe Repair, which read: "Grannick – Lifts and Heels." Seeing this, Thielemans realized Mother's stories were true.

Entering the office, Thielemans placed the six-pack on the pastor's large metal desk where a photo of Kittrick and Bobby Kucera was prominently displayed.

"Paul, I'm truly grateful for the chance to start our relationship all over again," Kittrick stated, extending his hand in friendship.

Trying hard to hide his mounting anger and underlying disdain, Thielemans shook Kittrick's hand and sat down across the desk from his anxious host.

"So, what say we have a toast to the start of our new friendship," Kittrick suggested, as he removed two bottles of beer from the six-pack's cardboard container.

Taking two glasses out of his attaché and removing the protective cellophane wrap from both glasses, Thielemans handed Kittrick a signature Saint Bavo Witbier glass.

"This is a gift from me to you," Thielemans said cordially. "It will be something to remember me by."

"Now, that's proper," Kittrick exclaimed, as he inspected the ornately-etched beer glass. "It's also a work of art, if you ask me, with the beautiful inscription, colorful crest, and likeness of old Saint Bavo himself."

Reaching across the desk for Thielemans' glass, Kittrick stared at his guest.

"To show my gratitude, let me teach you something about drinking Belgian wheat beer," Kittrick teased, as he poured beer into Thielemans' glass, swirled the remaining beer in the bottle to free up the precipitate, and then, poured the residual contents from the bottle into his glass.

Handing the glass to Thielemans, Kittrick poured beer into his own glass, using the same method.

"You see, the true flavor of wheat beer is in the filtrate at the bottom of the bottle," Kittrick explained with an arrogant smile. "Belgian beer is fine by itself, mind you, but you don't get the full taste without adding the filtrate. I'll bet you didn't know that."

Accepting the feeble attempt at stealing another man's thunder for what it was, Thielemans smiled at Kittrick without saying a word.

"To new beginnings," Kittrick proposed, raising his glass of beer into the air.

"Whatever," Thielemans replied, raising his glass.

Kittrick waited for Thielemans to take the first sip, and then, he chugged his entire glass of beer, pounded the glass on the desktop, and quickly ran his hand across his lips.

"Now, that's good beer," Kittrick proclaimed, as he quickly opened two more bottles of beer and placed one next to Thielemans' half-empty glass. "Paul, you don't know how long I've waited to drink a beer with you."

"The feeling's mutual," Thielemans replied.

Nodding his head, Kittrick poured beer into his glass, remembering to add the precipitate. Taking another healthy swig, he smiled and stared at Thielemans.

"So, Paul, I did as you requested and tried to find the whereabouts of Mother Murray," Kittrick claimed. "Unfortunately, no one has seen hide nor hair of the dear woman since her son took her away from us. You know, it's a terrible thing when a person gets old and senile. Even their own flesh and blood want little to do with them."

"Do you have the addresses or phone numbers of any of her children?" Thielemans asked.

"Not a one," Kittrick answered. "None of them are parishioners any longer, and I believe they've all moved away from the area."

"Didn't you have an emergency phone number in case anything happened to Mother while she was working for you?" Thielemans inquired.

"You know, Paul, it's a funny thing," Kittrick stammered. "Mother was an institution at Saint Declan's. She was here many years before I came on board. So, you're probably right that there was an emergency phone number for the woman somewhere in the rectory at one time or another, but I wouldn't know where to start looking for it. You see, Mother handled everything here. If I needed something, she'd find it for me. It's sort of ironic that, if Mother ever became incapacitated while she was still working in the rectory, I probably wouldn't have been able to ask her where her emergency phone number was. So, that's the long and short of the matter. I'm sorry I couldn't be of more help, but if I ever run into any of her kids, I'll be sure to ask them where Mother is living and send you the information A.S.A.P."

Kittrick took another gulp of beer and repositioned the photo on his desk.

"So, what was it you wanted to tell me about Bobby?" Thielemans asked, watching Kittrick stare at the photo.

"It's still difficult for me to talk about the lad," Kittrick answered, quickly changing his affect from jovial to distraught. "I took him on as a reclamation project shortly after his father died. The boy was a total basket case. He had no joy, no ambition, and no self-respect. He always was a smart boy, but after his dad passed, he lost all interest in school and went from the honor roll to the academic endangered list. He also lost all interest in himself. He stopped taking care of his hygiene, his clothing, and even his belongings. He used to ride his bicycle to church when he was scheduled to serve Mass. He kept his bike all shiny. After his dad died, he stopped taking care of the bike and even rode it to church on underinflated tires."

Kittrick took another sip of beer and shook his head, back and forth, in an attempt to project dismay.

"When Bobby's mother came to visit me after her husband's death, she begged for my help," Kittrick continued. "She's a very intelligent woman and deeply-concerned mother, and she realized a lack of strong male guidance was one of her son's biggest problems. Bobby lived in a house with a mother and two sisters, you see. He was very close to his father, and with the father gone, the lad found himself living in a strange new world with no other male presence. So, the mother begged me to take the boy under my wing, try to renew his interest in life, and give him a father figure to emulate."

Kittrick sighed, took another sip of beer, and for several seconds, struggled to regain his train of thought.

"Now, Bobby once expressed an interest in the priesthood," Kittrick eventually continued. "So, I tried to include him in a greater number of liturgical services and discuss the significance of each service with him afterward. I encouraged him to pursue his vocation and offered to become his religious mentor. Since he stopped eating regularly and was losing weight, I tried taking him out for things like ice cream and pizza after religious services. When he started eating better, I brought him over to my gym in the rectory basement and taught him calisthenics and the basics of wrestling. All the while, I tried to be a friend to him and fill in for his dad. Unfortunately, my best efforts weren't quite good enough."

"Do you have Mrs. Kucera's address and phone number?" Thielemans inquired, knowing she moved.

"I'm sure I do," Kittrick answered, fumbling through a Rolodex on the top of his desk and finally locating the Kucera family's information. "I'll write her address and phone number on an index card for you."

"Do you think she's home now?" Thielemans asked.

"She might be," Kittrick replied. "But then again, she works and might not be home just now. If she's not home, her two daughters might be. But they're involved in extracurricular activities at school and also babysit. So, they may not be home just now either. I'll tell you what. Let me call them and see who's on first and what's on second if you get my meaning."

Dialing the phone number, Kittrick heard a recorded message stating the phone was no longer in service. As soon as he heard the message begin, Kittrick handed the receiver to Thielemans to allow him to hear for himself the Kucera's phone had been disconnected.

"I'm not a bit surprised," Kittrick claimed. "With all the newspaper and television reporters snooping around for a story, Mrs. Kucera probably disconnected the phone to preserve her sanity. I'll give you her address. After we're through today, you can scoot over there and express your condolences in person. If no one's home when you get there, you can wait a bit until someone arrives. It may take a little while, but I'd wait if I were you."

Staring at Kittrick and growing tired of the priest's foolish grin, inane remarks, and thinly-veiled lies, Thielemans poured the second bottle of beer into his glass without including the filtrate, chugged the entire glass, and calmly returned the glass to the desktop.

"Father, I must say, everything you've said here today has been truly enlightening," Thielemans said. "What makes your comments all the more remarkable is the fact Bobby Kucera was probably not the first troubled boy you've taken under your wing here at Saint Declan's or any of a number of other parishes."

"That's a fact," Kittrick responded proudly. "I've never turned my back on a young boy in need."

"That's wonderful," Thielemans exclaimed, looking directly into Kittrick's eyes. "But what I'd still like to know is, at what point in Bobby's reclamation did you start molesting the boy and turning him into your sex slave?"

Outraged, Kittrick got up from his chair and pounded his desk with both fists.

"How dare you come into my rectory and make such an egregious accusation?" Kittrick shouted.

"For that matter, at what point in your reclamation of all those other young boys did your wrestling tutorials turn into acts of sexual abuse?" Thielemans asked.

"How dare you?" Kittrick yelled, once again pounding the desk with his fists.

"How dare I?" Thielemans screamed, rising to his feet and scowling. "No, Reverend. How dare you? How dare you betray God, His Church, the priesthood, humanity, and even yourself by taking advantage of defenseless children and robbing them of their innocence?"

Grabbing an empty beer bottle by the neck, Kittrick broke the bottle on the table, and with rage written across his face, brandished the jagged edge at Thielemans.

"Go ahead," Thielemans dared. "Cut me with that broken bottle. You won't be able to hurt me any more than you've already hurt those young boys or their families. Face it, Reverend, you're a pedophile, a liar, and a disgrace to everyone you've ever known."

Thielemans stood defiant in front of Kittrick. Realizing Thielemans had somehow discovered his deepest, darkest secrets, Kittrick weakly tossed the broken bottle into a trash can, sat down, and buried his face into his hands. In turn, Thielemans sat down and continued to stare at the exposed priest who sat quietly for the next few minutes.

"So, where do we go from here?" Kittrick inquired, as he removed his thick eyeglasses and cleaned them with a tissue. "Are you going to call the police, the diocese, or what?"

"Why would I call the police or the diocese?" Thielemans countered. "I know you've sexually abused young boys but I can't prove it. What's more, the role your sexual abuse played in Bobby Kucera's suicide would be difficult to establish in court. As far as notifying the diocese, let me remind you that you have an uncle who is a bishop in the same archdiocese that governs your priestly activities. So, who in the archdiocese is going to believe me when your uncle is going to do everything he can to defend and protect you?"

"Paul, this obsession I have with young boys is a terrible affliction," Kittrick admitted. "It's a disease I don't know how to control. I'm a sick and lonely man, and I've allowed my illness and loneliness to get the best of me. I'm lost. So, tell me, what do we do now?"

"The correct question is, 'what do you do now?'" Thielemans argued. "What you do to make things right with your victims and their families is completely up to you. No one else can help."

Kittrick remained quiet for another minute as he pondered Thielemans' comments.

"Paul, would you hear my confession?" Kittrick requested, looking at Thielemans through sad, repentant eyes. "I should square things with God before I try to make things right with anybody else."

"If you feel the sudden need to confess, why don't you call your uncle, the bishop?" Thielemans recommended.

"I'm sure that would be the right thing to do," Kittrick agreed. "Unfortunately, my uncle has been called to the Vatican on important Church business. He won't be back for a few weeks. So, would you please hear my confession? I'm truly ashamed of myself and ready to repent."

"In case you haven't heard, the Church is still trying to figure out what to do with guys like you," Thielemans stated emphatically. "The way I see it, the Church would have been better off if more priests refused to hear the confessions of their pedophilic colleagues. With confession and absolution comes an expectation the sinner will amend his ways and sin no more. Unfortunately, within the priesthood, too many priests hear other priests' confessions and absolve their sins, knowing the sinful priests will temporarily repent, and then, go right back to repeating the same sins they just confessed. Pedophilic priests confess to other priests and continue molesting children because they can. They know another priest will hear their confession and absolve their sins."

Kittrick stared at Thielemans without speaking.

"So, if you are truly repentant, why don't you and I agree to take a major step toward eradicating pedophilia in the priesthood," Thielemans suggested. "Why don't I just refuse to hear your confession, and let you think about things for a while. If we do this, your next confession may have greater meaning and actually last a little longer."

"You can't refuse to hear my confession," Kittrick argued. "I'm a fellow priest, and I'm sorry for my sins."

"You know, Gordon, when Jesus appeared to the disciples, He gave them specific instructions about the Sacrament of Confession," Thielemans explained. "Jesus told the disciples, 'Whose sins you shall forgive, they are forgiven, and whose sins you shall retain, they are retained.' So, let's just say, I will not forgive you for what you've done. Instead, I will retain your sins for as long as Bobby Kucera remains in my memory."

Unnerved by Thielemans, Kittrick lowered his head.

"Paul, please hear my confession," Kittrick requested. "I'm begging you."

Tired of Kittrick's theatrics, Thielemans got up from his chair and walked over to the window. Quickly considering his options, he turned and stared at Kittrick.

"Gordon, if you're truly sorry for your sins, I want you to kneel, facing the crucifix on the wall, and with your head bowed, make a thorough examination of conscience," Thielemans demanded.

"Yes, of course," Kittrick agreed, as he quickly got up from his chair, turned, and knelt in front of the crucifix.

"By the way, where is your bathroom?" Thielemans inquired, as he quietly retrieved his attaché and beer glass, as well as the photo on Kittrick's desk.

"Down the hall and to your left," Kittrick answered, as he continued to kneel and bow his head.

"I need a few minutes," Thielemans said, leaving the office. "So, continue examining your conscience."

"Yes, of course," Kittrick obliged.

Walking into the bathroom, Thielemans removed the photo from its frame and carefully tore the photo into two pieces. Placing the portion of the photo with Bobby's likeness into his coat pocket, he returned the portion of the photo with Kittrick's likeness to its frame and placed the frame on the bathroom vanity. As soon as he finished, he gathered his belongings and quietly left the rectory through the kitchen door.

One minute later, Kittrick's solitude was interrupted by the sound of a car door closing. Lifting his head and springing to his feet, he looked out the office window and watched Thielemans' Cadillac leaving the driveway.

CHAPTER FIFTEEN

Following his meeting with Kittrick, Thielemans drove back to the Wyndham. After he changed into casual attire and loaded Michelle's bags into his car, the priest and his secretary began their trip to Los Angeles via Interstate-5.

With the recent meeting still weighing heavily on his mind, Thielemans quietly listened to Michelle talking about the beauty of the Pacific Ocean and allure of the seaside towns they were driving past. Forgetting to compliment Michelle on how beautiful she looked in her white pantsuit and pearl necklace, Thielemans seemed to be listening to Michelle but not hearing anything she was saying.

Realizing Thielemans' body was in the car, but his mind was elsewhere, Michelle asked her companion what was bothering him. As he reluctantly reviewed the salient events of his meeting with Kittrick, Thielemans seemed to be having second thoughts about the way he handled the encounter.

"I can't believe the nerve of the guy," Michelle exclaimed, as an ocean breeze rushed through the Cadillac's open windows and caressed her hair. "After you backed him into a corner, he begged you to hear his confession. He was probably banking on you're never being able to discuss his confession with anyone, especially the police or his diocese."

"I don't think discussing Kittrick with the police or his diocese would change anything," Thielemans replied. "Kittrick has his influential uncle running interference for him and covering his tracks. I could go to the police or diocese and tell them what I know, but without proof, I'd only be wasting my time. Refusing to hear Kittrick's confession had nothing to do with any future plan I might have to turn him over to the authorities or the Church. I refused to hear his confession because I didn't want to give him another chance to abuse the Sacrament of Confession. He's already abused the sacraments enough for one lifetime."

"Who do you think hears Kittrick's confessions?" Michelle inquired.

"If anyone does, it's probably his uncle," Thielemans answered. "I even confronted Kittrick about asking me to hear his confession when his uncle was probably a better choice. He told me his uncle is currently at the Vatican on Church business and won't be back for a few weeks."

"His uncle should be getting raped in prison and not visiting the Vatican," Michelle insisted angrily.

"Be patient," Thielemans advised. "As you've said before, 'every dog has his day.'"

"Listen to you," Michelle exclaimed. "It sounds like you're starting to hate pedophiles and rapists almost as much as Ed and I do."

"If they're all like Kittrick, I can hardly wait to meet every last one of them," Thielemans remarked.

"You know, Paul, I'm glad you feel that way," Michelle chuckled.

"Why is that?" the priest asked.

"Because you're going to be meeting every last one of them in California, Arizona, Texas, Florida, and a whole bunch of other states," Michelle revealed.

"I don't understand," Thielemans said.

"As you know, I've been working very hard to convince as many priests as possible to talk with you about participating in your program," Michelle explained. "Unfortunately, a lot of priests I've talked to are retiring. So, there are fewer priests available to recruit for your program at present, and of the available priests, not many are all that excited about increasing their current workloads. Some of these priests used to serve one parish with one or two other priests, but are now serving two or three churches by themselves."

"I hear you," Thielemans sighed. "When I was giving my talk at the bishops' conference, Archbishop Palmieri told me I couldn't have chosen a more inopportune time to introduce my program. I've been trying to prove him wrong, but I'm starting to sense more disinterest in my program than I would have anticipated."

"I don't think priests are disinterested in your program," Michelle argued. "I think they're disinterested in increasing the amount of work they have to do."

"You may be right," Thielemans conceded.

"I've scheduled meetings with quite a few priests, but I still need to schedule more," Michelle revealed. "The more priests you talk to, the quicker your program will get recognized, and the sooner the Church will start implementing it. Unfortunately, I started running out of priests to contact in the states we'll be visiting in the next few months. So, with little alternative, I tapped our watchdog group's database for additional names. I hope you don't mind, but I've scheduled meetings with several of the priests in our database over the next few weeks."

"So, what you're saying is you expect me to discuss my program with other pedophiles," Thielemans complained.

"Most of the priests you'll be meeting are really good guys," Michelle remarked. "However, several are suspected sex offenders. That's why they're in our database and currently under surveillance by our group. When you think about it, these guys are perfect for your program. If they really are pedophiles or rapists, they'll be on their best behavior and probably more cooperative than priests who have nothing to hide. Sex offenders live their lives in goldfish bowls and are afraid people are watching them."

"Tell me one thing," Thielemans requested. "If I'll be meeting a combination of saints and sinners, how will I be able to tell the good guys from the bad?"

"We'll discuss each priest from our database before you visit them," Michelle answered reassuringly. "In fact, let me tell you about the meetings you have scheduled in the Los Angeles area this week. You have six meetings with priests scheduled between your talks at Loyola Marymount University and Mount Saint Mary's College. Three meetings are with reputable priests and three are with suspected sex offenders.

"Be honest," Thielemans asked. "Are you adding the sex offenders to my schedule so I can spy on them and give you feedback you can share with your group?"

"Absolutely not," Michelle replied. "I'm adding the sex offenders to your schedule so you can spy on them and give me feedback I can share with **our** group. Don't forget, Sherlock, you're one of us now. You're a full-fledged paraclete."

"I guess I'd better order more beer and glasses," Thielemans said facetiously.

"I already have," Michelle quipped. "By the way, how did Kittrick like his Saint Bavo Witbier?"

268

"He chugged two glasses while I was there and will probably finish the rest of the six-pack when he finally gets up off his knees," Thielemans answered.

As Michelle chuckled, Thielemans' cell phone started ringing. Looking at the caller I.D. and seeing Kittrick was calling for the third time in the past hour, Thielemans let the phone ring without answering it.

"As I was saying, three of the priests you'll be meeting with this week are suspected sex offenders," Michelle continued. "They are the Reverends John Iagi, Ryan Poser, and Peter Pauley. Iagi is a Kittrick clone who has allegedly molested several altar boys. Poser reportedly had a fling with a 13-year-old girl in Mexico, got her pregnant, and then, paid for her abortion. Pauley is thought to have sexually abused young boys while he was in charge of an orphanage. Just in case you're wondering, our group is 99.99% certain each of these guys is guilty as sin. Unfortunately, they've all managed to evade detection and prosecution by carefully selecting their victims, having their assignments frequently changed by guys like Grannick, or paying off the families of their victims."

"Sounds like a fun week," Thielemans quipped. "I may need another cruise."

"Be careful what you wish for," Michelle warned.

Assuming Michelle's driving directions were leading him to a Los Angeles hotel, Thielemans suddenly found himself parked in front of The Queen Mary. Once a famous ocean liner, the vessel docked in the port of Long Beach in 1967 and started operating as a hotel in 1972.

"Okay, I give up," Thielemans conceded, as he stared at the floating hotel. "Where are we cruising to?"

"Long Beach," Michelle quickly replied.

"And where are we now?" Thielemans questioned.

"Long Beach," Michelle answered promptly.

"Are there any other ports on the itinerary?" Thielemans inquired.

"That would be North Long Beach and South Long Beach," Michelle responded.

"I don't get it," Thielemans complained.

"You can see North Long Beach from the back of the ship and South Long Beach from the front," Michelle explained. "And since you'll be getting on and off the ship, you'll also be able to visit East Long Beach and West Long Beach as often as you like."

"So, what you're telling me is we'll be cruising to and from Long Beach for the rest of the week," Thielemans suggested. "But the ship won't actually be moving."

"Think of it this way," Michelle advised with a big smile. "Getting there is half the fun."

"How far are we from Rancho Palos Verdes and L.A.?" Thielemans asked, as the two got out of the car.

"Rancho Palos Verdes is about ten miles north of here, and downtown L.A. is about twenty-five miles north," Michelle replied. "That's the nice part about staying in Long Beach. Most of your scheduled meetings are south of L.A. So, you'll be able to drive to most of them without spending a lot of time in L.A.'s bumper-to-bumper traffic."

"Is there anything else I should know?" Thielemans inquired, as he removed their suitcases from his car trunk.

"Well, our cabins are supposed to be shipshape," Michelle boasted. "They've been restored to their original nautical condition and even have portholes that actually open and close."

"Sounds nice," Thielemans said. "Anything else?"

"The Queen Mary has several different restaurants, and the food is supposed to be spectacular," Michelle added.

"Great," Thielemans responded. "Anything else?"

"Well, there is one other thing," Michelle admitted.

"What's that?" Thielemans asked.

"The Queen Mary is supposed to be haunted," Michelle answered hesitantly.

"I'll have to check with the Vatican to see if there's a special prayer for haunted hotels near Los Angeles," Thielemans remarked facetiously, as he and Michelle started walking to their hotel with luggage in hand.

"See if they have a special prayer for haunted hotels near Los Angeles with elegant accommodations and fine dining," Michelle requested.

"I'll do just that," Thielemans promised.

Entering the lobby of the hotel, Thielemans and Michelle acted as though they had just met for the first time. Registering separately, they located their own cabins, unpacked, and showered before meeting for dinner at the hotel's Chelsea Chowder House.

After a satisfying seafood dinner and two bottles of local Sauvignon Blanc, the two left the hotel and took a leisurely walk around the hotel grounds. Taking in the beauty of the ship and Long Beach Harbor by night, they fetched a bottle of Calvados, two six-packs of Saint Bavo Witbier, and container of beer glasses from Thielemans' car before returning to the hotel.

Settling in for the night in Thielemans' suite, the two sipped Calvados, made love, and searched for some semblance of contentment. Relaxed by the French apple brandy, refreshed by a crisp ocean breeze that flowed into the cabin through an open porthole, and reinvigorated by their sexual intimacy, the lovers spent the night reconnecting with sensual pleasures and each other.

In the days preceding his talk at Loyola Marymount University, Thielemans visited several priests, including Father John Iagi. Having placed the photo of Bobby Kucera in the mirror compartment of his car's sun visor, Thielemans began a ritual of looking at the photo and saying a silent prayer before meeting each of the priests.

Entering the rectory office of Our Lady of the Sea Roman Catholic Church in El Segundo, Thielemans met the 47-year-old Iagi, a fat, balding man with a nervous grin and bulging eyes. After the two shared a glass of Saint Bavo Witbier and some small talk, Thielemans tried to explain his program to the easily distracted priest.

Frequently glancing at the watch on his left wrist without moving his head, Iagi gave the appearance of a preoccupied individual who was late for a rendezvous. At one point, Thielemans jokingly confronted Iagi about his fascination with time, causing Iagi's nervous grin to become firmly locked in place for the rest of the meeting.

Midway through the meeting, Iagi excused himself to answer the phone. When he realized who was calling, he put the call on hold, hung up the phone, and moved to an adjacent room to take the call.

Although Iagi continued his phone call from the living room, his loud voice could be heard throughout the small rectory. Thielemans heard Iagi talking on the phone to a concerned mother whose son was an altar boy.

"I don't understand why your son is afraid of me," Iagi said to the mother. "I know I'm a big man, but he certainly has no reason to be frightened. I think you and your son should come into the rectory to discuss this matter. Since your husband left home, your son has been having a difficult time and may have grown a bit sensitive and confused. I think having a positive male role model like a parish priest is very important for a 12-year-old boy, and I'm sure I'll be able to allay any fears you or your son might have when we meet. Please keep in mind what an honor it is for your son to serve on God's sacred altar."

After he finished his phone call, Iagi returned to the office. Nervously wiping perspiration off his brow with a handkerchief, he sat down, and after having to be reminded of what he and Thielemans were discussing, continued the meeting.

Following his uncomfortable conference with Iagi, Thielemans left the rectory, looked at Bobby Kucera's photo, and started driving back to The Queen Mary. As he drove and watched the afternoon sun turn the Pacific Ocean into a mirror, Thielemans continued to ignore repeated calls from Kittrick.

Michelle identified Iagi as a Kittrick clone, and as Thielemans drove to Long Beach, he could see similarities between the two priests. One of the similarities was the probability neither Kittrick nor Iagi would be brought to justice for their pedophilic crimes anytime soon.

Two days after his meeting with Iagi, Thielemans delivered an inspiring lecture at Loyola Marymount University. As he was leaving the university campus following the talk, his cell phone rang and the caller I.D. displayed the name, "Scripps Mercy Hospital."

Answering the phone, Thielemans could hear cardiac monitors beeping in the background.

"Father Thielemans, my name is Nancy Patch," the young woman began. "I'm an intensive care nurse at

Scripps Mercy Hospital in San Diego. We have Father Gordon Kittrick in our coronary care unit. He was admitted last night with a myocardial infarction, and he asked me to call you at this number and request you come to the hospital as soon as possible. Father wants you to administer Last Rites to him."

"I'm very sorry to hear about Father," Thielemans replied unemotionally. "How severe was his heart attack?"

"He sustained a large myocardial infarction and has been running very low blood pressures," the nurse answered succinctly.

"Nurse Patch, I'm in Los Angeles right now, and I have no idea how long it will take me to drive to San Diego through heavy traffic," Thielemans revealed. "It will take at least three or four hours. Isn't there any way you could call a priest who is already in San Diego to see Father?"

"Oh, sure," the nurse admitted. "I could have another priest here in a few minutes, but Father doesn't want any other priest. He wants you."

"I don't want to seem heartless or disinterested, but getting to San Diego anytime soon is going to be very difficult for me," Thielemans stated diplomatically.

"I understand," the nurse answered. "Unfortunately, I'm not sure Father will. This phone has a long extension cord. If I took the phone into Father's room, would you explain things to him?"

"Uh, sure," Thielemans reluctantly agreed.

"Great," the nurse squeaked, as she took the phone into Kittrick's room. "Father Thielemans is on the line."

"Thank you," Kittrick mumbled, as he took the phone from the nurse. "Now, could you please close the door and give me a bit of privacy?"

As the nurse left, Kittrick cleared his throat.

"I see you still haven't learned how to answer the phone," Kittrick remarked sarcastically.

"I've been very busy," Thielemans replied.

"You'd better start thinking up better excuses," Kittrick advised with a weak voice. "I've been trying to get you on the phone for days, and while you've been ignoring my calls, I've been doubled over with abdominal pain and puking my guts up. By repeatedly refusing to take my calls, you got me so worked up I had a severe ulcer attack. Now, they tell me the attack weakened my heart."

"I'm sorry to hear that," Thielemans apologized. "I'm also sorry you continue to blame me for everything that goes wrong in your life."

"Forget about all that for now," Kittrick demanded. "Get in that limousine of yours and drive to the Scripps Mercy Hospital in San Diego as soon as possible. I want you to hear my confession, give me communion, and anoint me, just in case I don't make it."

"I'm in Los Angeles, three or four hours away from you," Thielemans explained. "The nurse tells me she can have a priest at your bedside in ten minutes. So, do the smart thing and ask the nurse to call a priest who's nearby."

"Listen to me," Kittrick shouted. "If I die and go to hell because you refused to give me the sacraments, I'll see to it hell unleashes all its fury. I'll make sure everything biblical heads your way. I'm talking floods, pestilence, and a plague like the world has never seen. So, get here now or prepare to suffer the consequences. Do you hear me?"

"I understand you've had a serious heart attack and the pain medication they're giving you is starting to make you say crazy things," Thielemans countered. "So, please ask the nurse to call you another priest. I'm not coming."

Waiting for a heated response, Thielemans suddenly heard Kittrick's phone hit the floor and a cardiac monitor alarm start clamoring. As health care providers rushed into the room and initiated cardiopulmonary resuscitation, Thielemans listened to the proceedings for several seconds until someone finally hung up the phone.

Driving off the campus of Loyola Marymount University, Thielemans quickly found himself stuck in heavy traffic. Moving a mere five miles in one hour, he thought about the events of the day and wondered if Kittrick survived his cardiac arrest.

As he continued driving at a snail's pace and wondering how California residents did the same on a daily basis, his cell phone rang. Looking at the caller I.D., he realized the call was coming from Scripps Mercy Hospital.

"Father Thielemans, this is Nancy Patch calling you back from the coronary care unit at Scripps Mercy Hospital," the nurse began. "I realize your phone call with Father Kittrick was unexpectedly terminated. I'm just calling to let you know Father had a cardiac arrest while you were talking with him. Unfortunately, our efforts to resuscitate him were unsuccessful. I'm terribly sorry. I know you and Father were probably close friends which is why he wanted you to be the one to administer the sacraments to him."

"Actually, I didn't know Father Kittrick that well," Thielemans admitted. "We only met about a month ago. I'm sorry he asked you to call me instead of a priest who was already in San Diego. I would have never gotten there in time."

"Considering the outcome, neither would have any priest in San Diego," the nurse observed. "I guess it really doesn't matter. I'm sure Father was a good person and is now in heaven."

Not knowing where Kittrick was at the present time but reasonably sure it wasn't heaven, Thielemans decided to end the conversation rather than risk being pulled into an existential debate.

"Thank you for calling me back," Thielemans said with a hint of gratitude in his voice. "And thank you for everything you did for Father."

Thinking about Kittrick all the while, Thielemans drove back to The Queen Mary. Entering his cabin, he found Michelle working on her laptop.

"So, how was your day at the office, Dear?" Michelle asked enthusiastically, as she walked toward Thielemans and threw her arms around him.

"Better than Gordon Kittrick's," the priest replied. "He had a heart attack and died a few hours ago."

Momentarily speechless, Michelle stared at Thielemans and took a step backward.

"A nurse called and told me Kittrick wanted me to come to the Scripps Mercy Hospital to give him Last Rites," Thielemans continued unemotionally. "When I explained I was in L.A. and wouldn't be able to get to San Diego for three or four hours, she put Kittrick on the phone. He was obviously drugged, but that didn't stop him from being his old obnoxious self. When I told him I wouldn't be coming, he started talking crazy. He told me, if he went to hell because he died without receiving Last Rites, he'd see to it hell unleashed all its fury and send floods, plagues, and all kinds of biblical stuff my way. As he was ranting, he had a cardiac arrest and died. I lost the phone connection, but the nurse called me back an hour later and told me what happened."

"So, other than that, how did you enjoy the play, Mrs. Lincoln?" Michelle joked.

"The rest of the play was fine," Thielemans answered. "My talk went well, and I may have recruited a few additional priests for my program."

"Me, too," Michelle revealed. "I spent the entire day trying to locate more priests for you to meet."

"Good guys or bad guys?" Thielemans inquired.

"You've got to take the good with the bad," Michelle advised with a smile.

"I guess," Thielemans conceded. "You can never have too many floods, bug infestations, or plagues."

For the rest of the day, neither Thielemans nor Michelle spoke much. After a quiet dinner and evening stroll, they went to bed and quietly studied the stars through the porthole in Thielemans' cabin.

"Paul, have you ever heard of Saint Margaret Mary?" Michelle asked out of the blue, breaking a long silence.

"Sure," the renowned theologian answered. "Saint Margaret Mary Alacoque was a French monastic nun who lived in the 17th century. She reported several visions, including one in which Jesus appeared to her and promised certain benefits to anyone who received communion on the first Friday of nine consecutive months."

"Do you remember the benefits Jesus promised?" Michelle queried.

"There were twelve benefits," Thielemans began. "Most of them were general promises of grace, peace, consolation, refuge, and blessings. The one notable benefit was a promise of final repentance before dying, or not dying without first receiving the sacraments."

"Do you think Kittrick received communion on the first Friday of nine consecutive months anytime in his life?" Michelle inquired.

"Considering his many years in Catholic education, the seminary, and priesthood, I'm sure he did," Thielemans replied. "I'm sure you're also wondering why he died without receiving Last Rites if he fulfilled the requirements of the First Friday devotion."

"Sort of," Michelle admitted.

"I'm sure there were many Catholics who completed the First Friday devotion and still died without receiving Last Rites," Thielemans surmised. "This could lead one to question the validity of the devotion. Many theologians of the 17th century certainly doubted the legitimacy of Saint Margaret Mary's visions. They questioned if Jesus really appeared to Saint Margaret Mary, and even if He did, if He actually guaranteed final repentance for those who received communion as directed. It is uniformly accepted by the Church that sins can be forgiven without confession if a person makes a sincere Act of Contrition just prior to death, as in the hypothetical case of someone who is in an airplane about to crash into the ocean. Quite possibly, many Catholics who completed the First Friday devotion had the time to make a good Act of Contrition and have their sins forgiven before they died, thereby obviating the need for Last Rites. This would fulfill the promise of final repentance."

"Maybe," Michelle said skeptically.

"Saint Margaret Mary wrote an autobiography before she died," Thielemans revealed. "I've read it and found it very interesting. In her book, she talked about a vision in which Jesus allowed her to rest her head on His heart. At that time, Jesus supposedly told her His Sacred Heart was consumed with love for mankind, but shown contempt, ingratitude, and sacrilege by many individuals, even during the celebration of the eucharist. Jesus also supposedly told her that what pierced his Sacred Heart most deeply was being subjected to such insults by persons especially consecrated to His service."

"So, what does that mean?" Michelle asked.

"It could certainly mean, just receiving communion on nine consecutive Fridays may not be enough to guarantee final repentance, especially if a person lives a sinful life after they complete the First Friday devotion," Thielemans surmised. "In the case of a sinful and pedophilic priest who receives communion when he is not in a state of grace, all prior guarantees could become null and void."

"Do you think we're sinners because we've broken our vows and become lovers?" Michelle inquired.

"In my heart, I feel we truly love each other, and because of extenuating circumstances, are not doing anything wrong in God's eyes," Thielemans explained. "Unfortunately, the Church would disagree. So, accepting that I've previously agreed to follow Church law and live a celibate life, I won't be a hypocrite and receive communion. Nor will I go to confession until I'm absolutely sure what I need to confess. The day may come when the Church reverses its stand on celibacy. If and when it does, we'll have options that allow us to love each other and still remain in the good graces of the Church."

"Promises, promises," Michelle mumbled, as she leaned toward Thielemans and tenderly kissed his lips.

The next morning, Thielemans drove a half-hour to Rancho Palos Verdes and delivered a well-received speech at Marymount California University. Following his lecture, he drove twenty minutes to nearby Torrance to visit Father Ryan Poser, a reputed molester of teenage girls.

On his way to meet Poser at Saint Conrad's Roman Catholic Church, Thielemans drove past the beautiful Saint Margaret Mary Alacoque Catholic Church. Seeing the church, Thielemans thought it ironic he and Michelle had just been talking about the church's patron saint.

Arriving at Saint Conrad's Rectory, Thielemans was welcomed by Father Poser, a short, slim 37-year-old with wavy red hair and a matching pencil mustache. Wearing a white designer shirt, perfectly-tailored black slacks, and black leather loafers of Italian descent, Poser looked more like a European gigolo than a Catholic priest.

After Thielemans went through his introduction on how to properly drink Saint Bavo Witbier, Poser carefully inspected the color and clarity of the beer, put his nose in the glass and smelled it, swished the beer around his gums and through the spaces between his perfect teeth, savored the taste of the beer, and loudly smacked his lips.

"Not bad," Poser said in a patronizing tone.

Continuing to drink beer and discuss Thielemans' program, Poser asked questions and offered suggestions he felt would improve the program and its marketability. Using a slow, deliberate laugh to denote agreement or understanding, Poser left Thielemans with the impression it was Poser who was promoting the program and Thielemans who was learning about it for the first time.

Thielemans read Poser as a five-star narcissist who considered the world, and everything in it, his oyster.

Analyzing Poser's mannerisms, allusions, and liberal use of double entendre in his speech, Thielemans saw him as a corruptible priest who could have impregnated a 13-year-old girl, and then, paid for her abortion as alleged.

Leaving the rectory with Poser's offer to give sound financial advice or legal counsel whenever requested, Thielemans started driving away. As he did, he noticed a beautiful teenage girl, sitting alone on a swing in an otherwise empty church playground.

"Hi, Father," the girl shouted, as she smiled and waved to the priest.

Filled with curiosity, Thielemans drove into the playground and got out of his car.

"Good afternoon, young lady," Thielemans said politely, as he smiled and approached the girl. "I'm Father Paul Thielemans. I just left Saint Conrad's Rectory after a visit with Father Ryan Poser."

"I know," the dark-complected girl replied with a slight Mexican accent. "Father Ryan called me and told me to wait here until you left."

"What's your name, Sweetheart?" Thielemans inquired.

"Leticia Soto," the brown-eyed beauty answered, running a hand through her long black hair.

"What a beautiful name," Thielemans exclaimed. "Are you from Torrance?"

"Father, I know it's a sin to tell a lie," the 14-year-old acknowledged, as the smile left her face and she looked away from the priest. "I'm supposed to tell people I was born in Torrance, but I was really born in Mexicali. My mother, younger sister, and I were brought here six months ago. My father and two brothers are still in Mexico."

"I understand," Thielemans remarked, as he sat down on an adjacent swing. "Tell me, will you be meeting with Father Ryan after I leave?"

"Yes, Father," Leticia admitted. "He told me to come into the rectory after you left."

"That was considerate," Thielemans suggested. "I just left the rectory through the front door. Is that the door you use to go into the rectory?"

"No, Father," the young girl explained. "Father Ryan keeps the front door locked. I go around back and go in through the kitchen."

"I see," Thielemans said.

Responding to Thielemans' gentle ways, Leticia raised her head, looked at the priest, and smiled again.

"You know, you are one of the most beautiful young ladies I've ever met," Thielemans admitted. "But I'm sure you hear that all the time."

"Father Ryan tells me I'm pretty whenever I visit him," Leticia acknowledged with a proud smile.

"How often do you visit him?" Thielemans inquired.

"Whenever he calls me on my cell phone," the teenager answered. "I come to see him once or twice during the week, but never on weekends."

"Is there ever anyone else in the rectory when you visit Father Ryan?" Thielemans asked.

"Oh, no," she replied. "It's just us."

"You must really like Father Ryan," Thielemans observed.

"I love Father Ryan," the young girl exclaimed. "I know he also loves me because he tells me how much he does whenever I visit him. He's very kind to me, and he gets things for me I don't have the money to buy myself.

He gave me money to buy the blue dress I'm wearing and my new sandals."

"Leticia, I have to ask you a very important question, and I'll understand if you don't want to answer it," Thielemans emphasized. "Does your mother worry about you or anyone else in your family ever being sent back to Mexico?"

"Yes, Father," she confessed. "I know you won't tell anyone that we're illegals. My father paid a man all the money he had to drive us across a friendly border crossing into Texas. From there, another man drove us to Torrance where a job as a housekeeper was waiting for my mother. She doesn't get paid very much, but we have been used to being poor our entire lives. We pray together every night and ask God to reunite us with the rest of our family very soon and never give anyone in the United States a reason to make us go back to Mexico."

"Leticia, does your mother know you come to visit Father Ryan?" Thielemans asked.

"No, Father, she doesn't," the teenager admitted. "She works so many hours that she's usually too tired at the end of the day to ask my sister or me what we do when we're not in school. If she did know, I don't think she'd mind. Father Ryan teaches me a lot, and my mother wants me to get a good education so I can get a job that pays a lot of money someday."

"I see," Thielemans said. "What would happen if your mother asked you not to visit Father Ryan anymore?"

"That would make me very sad," Leticia revealed. "But I obey the commandments and honor my father and my mother. So, I would listen to my mother and obey her, even if doing so made me unhappy."

As the two continued talking, Leticia's cell phone rang.

"Leticia, this is Father Ryan," the caller began. "I've just been called out on an emergency. So, I can't see you today, but I'll call you soon. Okay?"

"Yes, Father," the young girl sadly replied.

Glancing at the rectory, Thielemans could see Poser looking through a window with a cell phone in his hand. Thielemans didn't know how long Poser had been watching his conversation with Leticia, but he knew Poser had seen enough to call off his planned visit with her.

"That was Father Ryan," Leticia announced, pointing to her cell phone. "He can't see me today."

"I'm sorry to hear that," Thielemans said, as he watched the smile leave the teenager's face. "By the way, that's a very nice cell phone you have. May I see it? I'd like to see what kind of features it has."

Holding the cell phone and searching for the phone numbers of Leticia's contacts, Thielemans saw a phone number next to the name, "Mama," and quickly memorized the number. Handing the phone back to Leticia, he got up from the swing.

"Can I give you a ride home?" Thielemans offered, as disappointment continued to grip the teenager's face.

"Yes, thank you," Leticia replied with a faint smile.

Thielemans drove the young girl to a rundown apartment building. Giving her some last words of encouragement and reasons to always obey her parents, Thielemans dropped off the teenager and left.

As he continued driving, the priest set his cell phone to make an anonymous call. With his identity concealed, he dialed the phone number of Leticia's mother.

"Hello," the 60-year-old Mexican woman answered.

"Is this Leticia Soto's mother?" Thielemans inquired.

"Yes," the mother cautiously confirmed.

"*Señora* Soto, I'm a friend who wants to help you and your family," Thielemans began. "Do you understand?"

"I'm not sure," Mrs. Soto admitted.

"*Señora* Soto, please listen to me carefully," the priest requested. "Your daughter, Leticia, is a good girl. She has not done anything wrong, but she goes to Saint Conrad's Roman Catholic Church a few times a week to visit a priest, Father Ryan Poser. Do you go to Saint Conrad's Church or know Father Poser?"

"No, I don't," Mrs. Soto answered with a moderate Mexican accent. "I go to Saint Margaret Mary Alacoque's Church, but don't know any Father Poser."

"I see," Thielemans said. "So, *Señora* Soto, I'm calling to ask you to stop your daughter from going to Saint Conrad's Church and seeing Father Ryan Poser anymore. Some people are closely watching the church and Father Poser. They're looking for illegal aliens they can send back to Mexico. Now, I'm not saying you or your children are illegal aliens. What I am saying is it could be dangerous for illegal aliens, or American citizens of Mexican descent who could be mistaken for illegal aliens, to be visiting Saint Conrad's Church or Father Poser. Do you understand?"

"Yes, I understand," Mrs. Soto replied hesitantly.

"Remember, *Señora* Soto, you don't know me, but I really am your friend," Thielemans reiterated. "I don't want to see you or your daughters being hassled by anyone. That's why I'm calling you today. So, tell me, *Señora* Soto, what do you plan to do when you see Leticia tonight?"

"First, I plan to tell her I know she hasn't done anything wrong," Mrs. Soto began, her Mexican accent becoming more pronounced. "Then, I plan to ask her not to visit Saint Conrad's Catholic Church or Father Poser anymore because certain people are spying on the church and the priest. These people are trying to make life difficult for illegal aliens or American citizens who could be mistaken for illegal aliens. Leticia is a good girl and an obedient daughter. I'm sure she'll listen to me."

"I know she will," Thielemans agreed. "God bless you, *Señora* Soto. *Dios te bendiga.*"

"*Dios te bendiga,*" Mrs. Soto exclaimed. "And *muchas gracias,* whoever you are."

As he drove back to The Queen Mary, Thielemans felt proud of his recent intervention on Leticia's behalf. Arriving at the hotel, he walked to his cabin where Michelle continued to be hard at work on her laptop.

"So, how did you make out with the lecture and the lecher?" she asked, as she approached Thielemans and threw her arms around him.

"Quite well," the priest responded. "My talk was a big hit, Poser liked his cold beer, and I may have saved a young girl's life."

Proceeding to tell Michelle the story of Poser and Leticia, Thielemans felt a sense of accomplishment. Listening to his story, Michelle congratulated him on becoming the consummate paraclete.

In the days that followed, Thielemans gave another successful talk at Mount Saint Mary's College and met with two priests who enthusiastically supported his program. The last meeting on his Los Angeles agenda was with the alleged orphan abuser, Father Peter Pauley.

Driving seventy-five miles northwest to Redlands, Thielemans arrived at Saint Daniel's Catholic Church.

Entering the rectory, he met Father Pauley, a wiry 42-year-old with a gray crewcut and lifeless eyes.

From the moment he walked into the rectory, Thielemans felt uncomfortable in Pauley's presence. Pauley stared at Thielemans throughout their entire meeting, grinning whenever his guest stared back and answering questions in monosyllabic sentences.

Although Thielemans' introduction to Saint Bavo Witbier amused Pauley, it failed to interrupt his menacing stare. As he drank glass after glass of beer, the strange priest who looked like a regular participant in all-night pub brawls never took his eyes off Thielemans.

Sensing Pauley's lean and hungry look, and not knowing what the bizarre priest was thinking or capable of doing, Thielemans remained on-guard throughout their entire meeting. Although he realized Pauley's behavior could be an act intended to intimidate unwanted visitors, Thielemans also realized such behavior could only be demonstrated by an individual who was a few knights short of a roundtable.

Pauley impressed Thielemans as the kind of religious sociopath who would rather self-flagellate than attend a personal audience with the Pope, but who would also be a welcome addition to a secret fight club or local brotherhood of cow-tippers. As he constructed a psychological profile of the man in his mind, Thielemans believed Pauley capable of sexually molesting orphans as had been alleged.

As he was returning to Long Beach, Thielemans realized this would be the last night he and Michelle would be staying on The Queen Mary. Having gotten used to the eerie sound of wind blowing through the hallways of the old ship at night, Thielemans thought about Michelle's admonition The Queen Mary was haunted and wondered if the howling wind was one of the reasons people believed the vessel was possessed.

Finally arriving at The Queen Mary after a long drive, Thielemans showered and changed into smart casual attire before preparing to dine at the hotel's premier bistro, Sir Winston's Restaurant. With his fashionably-attired lover taking his arm, the two walked to the restaurant and an evening of choice steaks, decadent desserts, and bottles of California's finest Cabernet Sauvignon.

Following dinner and a final stroll around the hotel grounds, Thielemans and Michelle retired to his cabin, made passionate love, and drifted off to sleep. Although Thielemans was exhausted from his long day on the road and quickly slipped into a deep sleep, Michelle awoke after a short catnap.

Like Thielemans, Michelle had gotten used to the nocturnal sound of wind howling through the hallways of the ship. Unlike Thielemans, however, Michelle seriously entertained thoughts of the ship being haunted.

As a large storm front passed through Long Beach, the wind picked up over the Pacific Ocean, and the howling wind rushed through The Queen Mary with increased intensity. Cabin doors and cabinets started shaking, toiletries started falling off bathroom shelves, and the floating hotel felt as though it was moving.

Having been through storms at sea before, Michelle understood that woodwork shakes, items fall, and ships pitch and roll during inclement weather. What she didn't understand was why someone seemed to be calling her name in the hallway outside Thielemans' cabin.

Shaking Thielemans but unable to wake him from his deep sleep, Michelle continued to listen, and quickly went from being curious to concerned to frightened. Thinking she heard her name being called again, she got out of bed, and with little alternative, opened the cabin door and looked down the hall.

Seeing a vague outline at the end of the hall, she placed a doorstop under the door to keep it open and cautiously walked toward the object of her concern. As the wind started howling with greater force through the hallway and the lights began to flicker on and off, Michelle thought she could detect a human face on the moving object. Upon closer inspection of the face, she feared her name was being called by the ghost of Gordon Kittrick.

Running back into the cabin, Michelle vigorously shook Thielemans with both hands.

"Paul, wake up," she screamed. "Wake up."

"What's wrong?" Thielemans asked, as Michelle continued shaking him.

"It's Gordon Kittrick's ghost," Michelle shouted.

"What?" Thielemans exclaimed.

"Kittrick's ghost is in the hallway," Michelle repeated.

Jumping out of bed, Thielemans followed Michelle outside his cabin.

"Look," Michelle yelled, as she pointed toward the end of the hall. "It's Gordon Kittrick's ghost."

Straining his eyes to see who or what Michelle was trying to identify, Thielemans walked down the hall a few steps. As the wind continued to howl and flickering lights continued manipulating shadows on the walls, Thielemans turned around, took Michelle by the hand, and returned to his cabin.

"Go to sleep," Thielemans advised, as he climbed back into bed and closed his eyes. "That's not Kittrick's ghost."

"Then, what is it?" Michelle demanded.

"Someone else's ghost," Thielemans mumbled, as he drifted off to sleep.

Getting into bed and pulling the covers over her head, Michelle tossed, turned, and listened to someone else's ghost calling her name for the rest of the night.

After bidding a fond farewell to The Queen Mary and all its ghosts the next morning, Thielemans and Michelle began their trip north. Following a short car nap necessitated by an evening of distracted and interrupted sleep, Michelle awoke refreshed and eager to review the week's itinerary with Thielemans.

"So, here's the deal," Michelle began. "We're on our way to Ventura where we'll spend this evening at a seaside hotel. We'll leave tomorrow morning and drive to Santa Paula where you'll be lecturing at Thomas Aquinas University in the afternoon. Following your lecture, we'll drive to Santa Clarita where we'll spend the night. The next morning, we'll leave Santa Clarita and drive to Bakersfield. Between the two cities, you'll be meeting with three priests - one in Santa Clarita, one in Gorman, and one in Mettler. I think you're really going to like the guy in Santa Clarita."

"I wonder why," Thielemans said facetiously.

"His name is Father Timothy Elliot," Michelle continued. "He's a 39-year-old outdoorsman and nature educator. I hear he's tall and muscular with shoulder-length black hair. He's a full-time pastor who also runs nature programs for juvenile delinquents. He takes groups of troubled kids on camping trips into the nearby mountains and teaches them how to hunt, fish, and live off the land.

Unfortunately, Father Elliot shows love in different ways to different children. The love he shows a group of youngsters he's teaching how to fish is not the same kind of love he shows an unsuspecting boy he's able to lure into the woods whenever the opportunity presents itself."

"Haven't any of the kids complained about being sexually abused?" Thielemans inquired.

"Sure," Michelle quickly answered. "Unfortunately, juvenile delinquents don't have as much credibility as a highly-respected priest who is volunteering his time to help kids who have gone astray. Only a few kids have actually complained about Elliot's sexual improprieties, but without witnesses or physical evidence of sexual abuse, their complaints have been disregarded as the kind of lies delinquents typically fabricate when they don't like someone. In truth, most of Elliot's victims have been afraid to tell anyone they were sexually abused. Ed recently told me Elliot is so experienced, he can take a boy into the woods, have his way with the youngster, and return the kid to his group before anyone ever realized they were gone."

"Wonderful," Thielemans exclaimed. "How many other perverted priests will I be meeting in California?"

"Elliot's the last one," Michelle promised.

"Promises, promises," Thielemans mumbled.

"We'll be staying in Bakersfield two nights," Michelle continued. "You'll be meeting three priests who are all good guys at different parishes in Bakersfield our second day there. The following day, we'll drive to Las Vegas. Along the way, you'll have meetings with three more good guys - one in Tehachapi, and two in Barstow."

For the next week, Thielemans and Michelle finished exploring the natural beauty of California and studied the state's many different faces. As they traveled along the state's seashore, over its mountains, and through its desert, Thielemans continued lecturing and meeting with clergymen, while Michelle continued scheduling meetings.

As Thielemans continued meeting with priests, he engaged in several rituals. He always looked at Bobby's photo before and after he met with any priest, always taught priests the correct way to drink unfiltered beer, and always prayed the rosary when his workday was finished.

Whenever he held the special rosary he found in Kauai, he felt as though he was connected to heaven. Whenever he prayed the rosary, he continued to ask God to forgive Bobby for taking his own life, and to forgive him for not doing more to save Bobby's precious existence.

After he finished praying the rosary each day, Thielemans briefly thought about Kittrick and the other pedophilic priests he met. Thielemans understood the concept of forgiveness, but try as he might, he was unable and unwilling to ask God to forgive the likes of Kittrick.

Following more than a month of lecturing, meeting priests, and enjoying California's abundant food, wine, and scenery, Thielemans drove his Cadillac across the state line into Nevada. As he did, he listened to Michelle discuss their Las Vegas itinerary.

"So, we'll be staying three nights in Vegas where I've arranged to pick up a trunkful of brew at a beer outlet. On our second day in Vegas, you'll be meeting three priests at different parishes. The third priest you'll be meeting there is Father Norman Drew, a 45-year-old veteran of the Pedophilic Wars. Following our stay in Vegas, I thought we'd take a week off from work and drive to the Grand Canyon and Monument Valley."

"Sounds great," Thielemans exclaimed. "So, what's this Father Drew's claim to fame?"

"Drew was exiled to a small parish in Las Vegas a few years ago because of drug addiction and gambling with church money," Michelle explained. "He only uses marijuana these days and gambles with monetary gifts from rich parishioners. Those charged with monitoring his drug and gambling addictions have been so impressed with his recovery, they've overlooked his longstanding addiction to teenage boys. He especially likes the lonely and neglected teenage male offspring of drug addicts who work in the casinos and spend more time with their pushers and loan sharks than their children. Drew has been able to form a certain kinship with such kids and teach them how to get stoned and boned at the same time. Over the years, there have been suspicions of sexual improprieties on Drew's part, but no complaints from the kids he turned on and over. Hence, Drew has been able to remain a pedophile and pothead who prefers to trip and strip under the radar."

While Thielemans and Michelle were looking forward to their time in Las Vegas, another man and woman were preparing to board the Eurodam as it prepared to sail from Seattle to Alaska. As the husband and wife entered the cruise terminal and approached the embarkation desk to pick up their boarding passes, they were asked their names.

"My name is Steven Faraday," the husband answered politely. "And this is my wife, Joanne."

As Steve signed several forms, his wife looked around the spacious cruise terminal. Near the door that opened to the Eurodam's gangway, she could see the ship's chaplain, Father Richard Frost, smiling and patiently waiting to welcome his daughter and son-in-law aboard.

CHAPTER SIXTEEN

After they boarded the Eurodam and checked out their cabin, Jo and Steve Faraday walked to the Lido deck where they met Jo's father for a buffet lunch. For the Faradays, who were both graying 55-year-olds with a penchant for cardigan sweaters and retro-style eyeglasses, the cruise was a long-awaited and overdue departure from the monotony that had become their everyday lives.

Jo, a special agent who was highly regarded as one of the F.B.I.'s top profilers of serial killers, and Steve, an overworked and underappreciated mathematics teacher in the Los Angeles School District, desperately needed a vacation. Fortunately, Father Frost's invitation to join him on a cruise came at a time when their demanding jobs, growing time apart, and unresolved personal issues warranted an immediate change of pace and venue.

Following lunch and a brief reunion, Steve excused himself and went back to his cabin to unpack. Still a full hour away from the lifeboat drill and sail away activities, Jo accepted her father's invitation to walk through the ship.

"Is Steve all right?" Frost politely asked his daughter, as they began their walk through the ship's interior. "He seemed a bit tense and preoccupied at lunch."

"He's all right physically, but he's become an emotional wreck," Jo admitted. "That's why I forced him to take this cruise. We're both too busy at work and never seem to have any quality time to spend together. We thought we'd have a life of our own once the kids were finally grown and out of the house, but things haven't worked out as expected. We live in two different worlds, and things only appear to be getting worse."

"Why is that?" Frost inquired.

"The Bureau has offered me a big promotion," Jo replied. "I'd be teaching and leading my own research team at the F.B.I. Academy, but the promotion would require a move from Los Angeles to Quantico, Virginia. The problem is we're 55 years old. I wouldn't move without Steve, and even if he did agree to move, he's not sure he could find a teaching job or any other kind of employment that could match his current salary. School districts try to buy out the contracts of teachers Steve's age and employ younger teachers who they can pay a lot less. Teachers like Steve are not old enough to retire but too old to land new teaching jobs."

"Could you decline the promotion and stay in Los Angeles?" Frost asked.

"I could," Jo confirmed. "Unfortunately, if I stay in L.A., I'll still be doing much of the Bureau's serial killer profiling, doing a lot of it away from home, and doing it without any chance for a significant raise in pay or future promotion. I've worked myself into an enviable position, but my only chance to cash in on that position is to take the promotion and move to Quantico while the job is still available. If I do, my life will become easier, I'll take home a much higher salary, and I won't have to spend much time away from home. As you can imagine, the whole situation has put Steve between a rock and a hard place. If he balks at moving to Quantico, he risks depriving me of my one big chance to move up in the Bureau. If he agrees to move, he risks the loss of his own career and becoming a house husband. That would be fine with me, but we can't afford it. We're still paying off a house mortgage, two different car loans, and a portion of our kids' school loans."

"I can understand your dilemma," Frost said empathetically. "Is your job situation Steve's only problem or are there other factors contributing to his stress levels?"

"Dad, please keep what we say just between the two of us," Jo requested. "Okay?"

"Of course," Frost agreed.

"I don't want Steve to think I'm talking behind his back, but he has other issues that are currently affecting our marriage," Jo admitted. "As you know, Steve was sexually abused by a priest when he was 12 years old. Well, just when it appeared that he had completely recovered from the unfortunate events of his childhood, a sudden recall of the events has come back to haunt him and thoroughly disrupt both our lives."

As the hint of a tear came to Jo's stoic eyes, Frost reached for his handkerchief and handed it to her.

"Thank you," she mumbled, as she kept the handkerchief in her hand and sighed.

"Through most of our married life, we have enjoyed a healthy sex life," Jo continued. "Even while the kids were growing up, we went out of our way to make time for each other and keep our romance alive. Unfortunately, something happened two years ago. One of Steve's junior high math students was sexually abused by a priest. The priest was eventually prosecuted, but the child never recovered from the abuse. Despite timely psychotherapy, the kid lost interest in everything, including himself. Seeing the child failing so miserably, Steve stepped in and offered to counsel the young boy. To do so, Steve had to get the permission of the boy's family. To get their permission, he had to reveal his own history of sexual abuse."

Jo paused and stared at her father.

"I can't tell you how proud I am of Steve for how much he helped that boy," Jo continued. "Although it took some time, Steve helped the kid regain his self-respect and eventually resume normal life activities. Today, the boy is doing well in school and showing renewed interest in his favorite activities. Steve saved that child's life."

"That's wonderful," Frost exclaimed.

"It is wonderful," Jo agreed. "Unfortunately, his work with the youngster forced Steve to recall his own childhood, including his episodes of sexual abuse. Reliving those painful experiences has made Steve lose all interest in sex. As soon as Steve started working with the child, our sex life started to wane. What was once a weekly event turned into a monthly event, and then, an occasional event. Today, it is an impossible dream."

"I'm sorry to hear that," Frost said.

"We have been really struggling with sex for the past six months," Jo continued. "Despite all kinds of interventions, every attempt at sex has been a complete failure. Romantic music, scented candles, and sexy lingerie haven't helped, nor have cocktails, massages, or even Viagra. Steve's continued frustration has turned into a fear of failure and an aversion to sex. He saw a urologist who carefully examined him, put him through various diagnostic tests, and then, reassured him his impotence was not being caused by anything physical. Then, he saw a cardiologist who performed more tests and told him he had the heart of a 20-year-old. Finally, Steve saw a psychiatrist who felt his problem was psychosomatic and prescribed several medications that only made his impotence worse. Since Viagra helps Steve get an erection but not sustain one long enough to have an orgasm, our primary care physician suggested higher doses of Viagra, a vacation, and spontaneous attempts at sex under more relaxing conditions. Your call inviting us on this cruise was a Godsend. It couldn't have come at a better time."

"Hopefully, this vacation will bring the two of you closer," Frost said reassuringly.

"I hope so," Jo replied, handing the unused handkerchief back to her father. "I also hope it will bring us closer to God. I've never told you this, but Steve has avoided priests and the Church ever since he was molested as a child. You're the only priest he trusts, and the only one he would consider receiving the sacraments from. He went through all the motions with the Church when the kids were growing up and receiving the sacraments for the first time, but after that, he stopped going to Mass completely. He goes to church with the rest of the family at Christmas and Easter. He also goes for weddings, funerals, and the like, but that's been the extent of his religious involvement. I'm on the road a lot and have not been a model Catholic myself in recent years, but I haven't lost my faith."

"That's important," Frost stressed, as the two sat down on a bench outside the ship's vacant casino. "I say Mass every day on the ship. I can hear Steve's confession whenever it's convenient. I've just heard yours, and there's no one around. So, make an Act of Contrition now, and when you get back to your cabin, say three Hail Mary's and ask the Blessed Mother to guide you."

After Jo quickly whispered her Act of Contrition, Frost placed his hand on her head and whispered a prayer of absolution. Making the Sign of the Cross, he smiled and kissed his daughter on the cheek.

"And who said you couldn't go to confession outside a casino on a cruise ship?" Frost chuckled.

As Jo laughed and hugged her father, she looked at a wall clock and realized it was 3:45 pm.

"What time is the lifeboat drill?" she asked.

"In fifteen minutes," Frost answered, as he glanced at the same clock. "What deck is your cabin on?"

"Rotterdam," Jo replied, helping her father to his feet.

"I'll walk you to your cabin," Frost said. "There's something I want you to see on the way."

Taking an elevator to the Rotterdam Deck, Frost and his daughter walked down the hall to the portside Pinnacle Suite. As they approached the suite, Winston was opening the cabin's front door.

"Good day, young man," Frost cheerfully exclaimed.

"Good afternoon, Father Frost," Winston responded.

"Winston, this is my daughter, Joanne Faraday," Frost boasted. "She'll be cruising with us to Alaska."

"Good afternoon and welcome aboard," the steward exclaimed with a gracious smile and nod of the head. "It's so nice to meet you."

"It's nice meeting you," Jo answered politely.

"I was just about to tell my daughter about the Pinnacle Suite and the evening I had dinner here with Father Thielemans," Frost mentioned.

"Father, a picture is worth a thousand words," Winston stated. "Instead of telling your daughter how beautiful this suite is, bring her inside and let her see for herself. The couple scheduled to be in this suite canceled their cruise. Since it's vacant, I can show it to you."

As Frost and Jo entered the suite, Jo's eyes opened widely and her jaw dropped.

"I can't believe this," Jo exclaimed, as she walked through the suite. "I've been on cruise ships before, but I've never seen anything like this. The closets in this suite are bigger than our entire cabin."

As Winston laughed, the signal for the lifeboat drill sounded loudly throughout the ship.

"I'd better go," Jo suggested, as she took one last look at the suite. "My husband is waiting for me. Fortunately, our cabin is just down the hall. Nice meeting you, Winston. See you at dinner, Dad."

As Jo quickly departed, Frost thanked Winston for the impromptu tour of the Pinnacle Suite.

"By the way, have you heard from Father Thielemans lately?" Winston inquired, as Frost began to leave.

"I haven't heard from him since he left the ship in San Diego," Frost admitted.

Later that evening, Frost rejoined his daughter and son-in-law for dinner.

"Dad, tell me more about the dinner you had in the Pinnacle Suite," Jo requested, as everyone started sampling their appetizers. "Didn't you say another priest was present at the dinner?"

"Father Paul Thielemans wasn't just present at the dinner," Frost laughed. "The Pinnacle Suite was his cabin for the entire Hawaiian Cruise. He not only dined there for eighteen days. He also lived, worked, and slept there."

"Sounds like he had some wealthy friends," Steve said.

"He did – his mother and father," Frost chuckled. "You see, his father was a wealthy Belgian exporter. He introduced a beer named after Saint Bavo to America.

When he and his wife died, their entire fortune went to Father Thielemans and his sister. This allowed Father Thielemans to live a charmed life. He studied in Rome, was ordained in Belgium, and after a few years teaching at one of their seminaries, left Belgium to write, teach, and lecture in the United States."

"How did he pull that off?" Jo inquired.

"Although his name may not be familiar to the average person, his theological writing is known all over the world," Frost replied. "His books are all best sellers, and he is in high demand as a lecturer. He spends his time traveling the country and lecturing at one Catholic college after another. When he is done promoting a book, he returns to the Catholic University of America where he lectures until he finishes writing his next book. He's currently promoting his latest book which is about restoring membership in the Church. He's currently visiting priests to promote a program his book introduces."

"Doesn't he have any religious duties like most other priests?" Steve asked. "Isn't he required to say Mass and administer the sacraments?"

"His only religious duty is to continue being one of the world's most renowned theologians," Frost answered. "He is so wealthy that he donates all the money from his book sales to the Catholic Church in Belgium. The Belgian Church is grateful for the steady stream of income it receives from his books, and proud such a highly respected theologian is of Belgian ancestry."

"What kind of person is he?" Jo inquired.

"You'd really like him," Frost said confidently. "He's confident, attractive, and despite all his success, only in his mid-forties. He's also very personable, extremely intelligent, and not the least bit affected. He's generous, funny, and really interested in what others have to say. From every indication, he's a good man and a good priest."

"You should get a job as his P.R. man," Steve joked.

"He doesn't need a public relations man," Frost countered. "He's the kind of rare person who can sell himself without any help. As I understand it, he's currently lecturing and visiting priests in California. If he's ever in the Los Angeles area, you should go to one of his talks."

"So, enough about Thielemans," Jo insisted. "Tell us what you had to eat in the Pinnacle Suite."

"To show you how considerate Father Thielemans is, he asked me what I wanted for dinner and told me I could order anything my heart desired," Frost explained. "I told him I was getting tired of the ship's rich food, and really had a craving for a cheeseburger and french fries. Instead of ordering a burger for me and surf and turf for himself, he told me he was also getting tired of rich food and ordered cheeseburgers, chili dogs, and fries for the two of us. We had pepperoni pizza for dessert and washed everything down with a few bottles of his Saint Bavo beer. I'm not much of a beer drinker, but I enjoyed Saint Bavo. The beer's sediment is what gives it such great flavor."

For the next week, Jo and Steve attended each Mass Frost celebrated on the Eurodam and received Holy Communion daily. At dinner each night, the three talked about the wonders of Alaska and their favorite features of each town and attraction they visited.

Following their visit to Juneau, they relived their experiences taking the tramway to the top of Mount Roberts where they came face-to-face with a caged, bald eagle named Lady Baltimore, hiked the trail that led to

Father Brown's Cross, and enjoyed the breathtaking view from the mountain's summit. They also relived their visit to the Red Dog Saloon where Wyatt Earp's pistol still hangs over the bar.

In the evenings that followed, the three relived their cruise to the Hubbard Glacier, where they watched large segments of the glacier calving into the sea; Sitka, where they marveled at the town's early Russian architecture; and Ketchikan, where they studied the native totem poles. As they talked about the many whales, eagles, and bears they saw on their journey, the many different seascapes, and the many buildings of different age, style, and construction that continued to exist side-by-side in the Alaskan towns, they realized how fortunate they were to be experiencing so many different natural wonders and man-made attractions.

With only Victoria, British Columbia, yet to visit before the Eurodam returned to Seattle, the three sat down to enjoy one of their final dinners at sea. As they reviewed the events of the day, Steve brought up an article he just finished reading on the internet.

"There's a website I visit regularly on the internet because it features unusual stories about life in California," Steve began. "Before dinner, I looked at the site and read an article about twelve Catholic priests dying in California in the past two weeks. The author of the article used the deaths to emphasize how California's shortage of Catholic priests was becoming more severe. The article mentioned that half of the priests who died were elderly and being cared for in nursing facilities and one was a middle-aged priest who died in a motor vehicle accident. What really interested me was the fact the remaining five priests died of acute medical illnesses, but were only between the ages of 37 and 49."

"Did the article mention what kind of medical illnesses caused the priests' deaths?" Jo asked curiously.

"It didn't, but the article did mention where the priests resided," Steve replied. "The priests were in residence in Catholic parishes in San Diego, El Segundo, Torrance, Redlands, and Santa Clarita at the time of their deaths."

"It seems the Archdiocese of Los Angeles can't catch a break these days," Jo remarked. "That's quite a few young priests the archdiocese will have to replace, especially since their deaths were unexpected."

"If Holland America doesn't require my services after the Eurodam's Alaska run, I may have to come out of retirement and take over a parish near L.A.," Frost joked.

"Let us know if you need any character references," Steve responded.

Although cruising to Alaska provided the Faradays with a much-needed vacation and allowed them to reunite with Father Frost, the trip did little to remedy their problems in bed. Even though Jo and Steve attended daily Mass, caught up on lost sleep and meals, and allowed themselves to be rejuvenated by the grandeur of Alaska, neither their temporary return to a relaxed lifestyle nor a bottle of Viagra were enough to cure Steve's impotence.

While Jo and Steve were completing their Alaskan cruise, another member of the law enforcement community was learning about the unexpected deaths of young priests in the Los Angeles area. From the comfort of her own bed, Los Angeles Sheriff's Department Detective Irene "Reenie" Behan, chewed almonds, sipped iced green tea, and read about the recent deaths of a dozen California priests on her iPad.

Reenie was a diminutive 40-year-old with mousey auburn hair, pale skin, and oversized eyeglasses that appeared to be epoxied to her face. Inside her 5'6", 130-pound frame, however, lurked an indefatigable crimefighter who considered the few hours' sleep she allowed herself every night as a necessary evil in her constant pursuit of truth, justice, and all things legal.

So devoted was Reenie to her job that she had no time for boyfriends, hobbies, or the kind of personal luxuries most other people her age considered bare necessities of life. Her unprepossessing appearance, spartan lifestyle, and profound absence of any sense of humor made Reenie the brunt of many jokes at the L.A. Sheriff's Department. However, a unique combination of other traits made her a highly intuitive crime investigator whose obsessive-compulsive approach to solving crime gained her widespread, but quiet, respect throughout California's law enforcement community.

The following morning, Reenie walked into Sheriff Hector Aguilar's office to discuss the recent deaths of Catholic priests in California. As she wondered out loud about the feasibility of investigating the deaths of the younger priests who resided within the jurisdiction of the Sheriff's Department, Aguilar, a patient 60-year-old of Mexican descent, just stared at the detective.

"Reenie, what was the first thing I ever taught you about police work?" the stocky sheriff with aging dark eyes and thinning black hair, asked. "The first thing I ever taught you was to not go looking for zebras every time you heard hoofbeats. But I've got to tell you, in the few years you've been working in this department, you've chased more zebras than Tarzan ever did in all his movies."

"With all due respect, Sheriff, I did manage to catch a few zebras over the years," Reenie argued.

"I guess you did, Reenie," Sheriff Aguilar admitted. "I guess you did. What I don't understand is why the deaths of three local priests from acute medical illnesses are bothering you such much."

"Sheriff, I recognized the names of two of the deceased priests from the county," Reenie stated. "One was Father John Iagi, a 47-year-old from El Segundo, and the other was Father Ryan Poser, a 37-year-old from Torrance. I first heard Iagi's name when he was assigned to Our Lady of the Sea Roman Catholic Church. One of our informants at the shore mentioned that Iagi had been an assistant pastor at a list of churches a mile long. He kept getting mysteriously transferred from one parish to another. The informant felt Iagi was a pedophile who was being protected by someone influential in the Church. Whenever Iagi molested another child, that someone arranged for Iagi to be transferred and the parents of the molested child to be paid to keep quiet about the incident."

"What about the other guy?" the sheriff inquired.

"Another informant claimed Poser used to spend a lot of time chasing young girls in Mexico," Reenie answered. "Something or someone scared him away from Mexico a few years ago but didn't change his penchant for underage females. Just before he died, he was rumored to be luring teenage girls into his church rectory and having sex with them. Two of the girls were thought to be illegal aliens."

"So, what does any of this have to do with homicide?" Aguilar asked.

"I don't think we can completely ignore the possibility of relatively young priests, who may have been pedophiles or statutory rapists, being murdered in retribution for their crimes," Reenie replied. "Need I mention how the Catholic Church and law enforcement community have both been very unsuccessful in bringing sex criminals in the priesthood to justice."

"You got me there," the sheriff admitted. "If any of the priests were murdered, do you think they were murdered independently or by a single individual?"

"It could be either," Reenie surmised. "However, the deaths of a 37-year-old, 39-year-old, and 47-year-old priest within the span of a few days implies we may be dealing with a serial killer."

"All right, Reenie, go on safari if you must," Aguilar conceded. "But limit your initial inquiry to the three younger priests from the county, and don't waste a lot of time doing it. Take a look at their hospital records, but don't go any further before you touch base with me. If the records show no possibility of foul play, that's where the investigation stops. All I need is to be wasting my time on the phone with the archbishop and trying to explain why I want the bodies of three of his dead priests exhumed."

"Thank you, Sheriff," Reenie said unemotionally.

"*Adios*," the sheriff responded, as he watched the ambitious detective leaving his office.

While the Faradays continued analyzing their individual and collective problems and Reenie began analyzing the hospital records of three dead priests, Thielemans and Michelle continued their long trip through the southwest. As they did, they discussed some of the more interesting people and places they had seen.

After they finished reminiscing about their time in Las Vegas, the Grand Canyon, and Monument Valley, they recalled Father Arthur Groover, a parish priest from Scottsdale. In his spare time, Groover also served as a retreat master, traveling throughout Arizona to officiate at religious retreats held at parochial high schools.

As a part of these spiritual awareness programs, students received private religious counseling which allowed them to ask personal questions, including queries about sex. A teenage boy who was counseled by Groover and felt to be gay, or on the way, would be invited to another private session where his sexual awareness would be tested, sexual orientation determined, and sexual experience immediately enhanced.

Thielemans and Michelle also recalled Father Eugene Yesjack. The parish priest from Tucson served as the director of a nearby Catholic youth hostel.

Frequented by traveling students and youth groups, the desert hostel also served as a refuge for young immigrants and runaways, as well as a safe house for endangered teenagers. Ensconced in a cactus forest, the hostel was comprised of a few dozen, socially-distanced tents of various sizes, three outdoor community kitchens, and a large stone building that housed restrooms and showers.

Hostel fees were by donation or free to anyone who needed shelter from a storm or safety from the world. The free tents were off the beaten path, separated from the rest of the hostel, and always visited by Yesjack when occupied by a young teenager who aroused his curiosity.

Yesjack knew how to gain the trust of a displaced immigrant, frightened runaway, or teenager who was traveling alone. He understood what a shower, hot meal, and friendly conversation could do for a soul, and quickly provided any and all necessary items for his special guests.

The opportunistic and bisexual priest also knew how to get inside the confused mind of a teenager who felt they were alone in the world. Knowing exactly what to say, what to do, and what to expect allowed Yesjack to seduce and bed many of his special guests, regardless of their sex, age, or level of consensuality.

Many of Yesjack's special guests quickly left the hostel after being sexually abused. For different reasons, every one of his special guests kept silent about the abuse because they were in no position to report it.

During their recollection of New Mexico, Thielemans and Michelle talked about the Land of Enchantment's stunning vistas and memorable priests, including Father Ronald Cazuka. Assigned to assist at multiple churches in the southwest corner of New Mexico, Cazuka was always traveling from one town to another, and not the easiest priest to locate or contact.

The ambitious priest's license to disappear helped him participate in a profitable industry that brought illegal aliens into New Mexico and hid them until they could be safely transported to other states. Although Cazuka knew how to hide illegals, the name of the syndicate that employed him, and his whereabouts on most days, he was unable to hide his obvious lust for young boys.

Cazuka lived his secret criminal life not for the money as much as the ability to borrow a young boy from a family of illegal aliens whenever he so desired and use the child as the object of one of his perverted sexual fantasies. He always returned the nearly-intact youngster to the child's family which is why his perversions were tolerated.

As Thielemans and Michelle left New Mexico and drove through the oil-laden Permian Basin of Texas, they talked about the sites they wanted to see in the Lone Star State. When they started running out of attractions to add to their list, Michelle outlined Thielemans' Texas itinerary.

"So, we'll be arriving in Dallas later today and staying there three nights," Michelle began. "Tomorrow morning, you have a talk at the University of Dallas in nearby Irving, followed by meetings with two priests in the afternoon. The next day, you have a morning lecture at the College of Saint Thomas More in nearby Fort Worth, followed by afternoon meetings with two priests."

"Will I be meeting any priests of special interest?" Thielemans asked.

"Tomorrow afternoon, you'll meet with Father Clyde Farmer, a real cowboy who supposedly likes riding young altar boys hard and putting them away wet," Michelle replied. "After Dallas, we drive to Austin for two nights. You'll speak at Saint Edward's University the afternoon of our arrival, and have meetings with three priests the next day. Of special interest is Father Jamie Zerocks, thought to be a procurer and distributor of child pornography."

"Alas, my dear Watson, the chowder thickens," Thielemans exclaimed.

"Whatever you say, Sherlock," Michelle chuckled. "So, after Austin, we drive to San Antonio for three nights. You have a talk on the afternoon of our arrival at Our Lady of the Lake University. The following morning, you lecture at the University of the Incarnate Word, and that afternoon, you have meetings with two priests. The final morning, you speak at Saint Mary's University, and in the afternoon, you meet with one priest, Father Henry Munches. After your meeting with the priest, we drive to Houston. Munches' specialty is treating fatherless teenage boys to holidays in San Antonio. After Munches surprises a lucky boy by showing him secluded areas of the historic sites not commonly visited by most tourists, he gives the youngster a special reason to 'Remember the Alamo.'"

"Where's Davy Crockett when you need him?" Thielemans joked. "So, tell me about Houston."

"We'll be in Houston two nights," Michelle answered. "You'll be meeting with two priests the afternoon we arrive. The following morning, you lecture at the University of Saint Thomas, and that afternoon, you'll meet with Father Richard Pritchard, an assistant pastor and parochial high school biology teacher. He teaches Sex Education to sophomores and is also reportedly teaching Sexual Technique to precocious female students who show an aptitude for the subject and can fit Pritchard into their busy extra-curricular schedules."

After they arrived in Dallas, checked into their own rooms, and enjoyed a steak dinner, Thielemans and Michelle settled into Thielemans' suite for the night. Following some tender passion, the two relaxed and Michelle started yet another desultory conversation.

"Paul, you've met quite a few good priests in the past month and also a few bad ones," she observed. "Would you be able to tell the good guys from the bad if I didn't tell you which ones were sex offenders ahead of time?"

"Not really," Thielemans admitted. "You can learn a lot about a man over a glass of beer, but some guys are better than others at concealing their inner feelings or hiding their demons from someone they just met for the first time. I'm good at interpreting body language, but some people don't give you enough to interpret. I think the premise of our meetings has also put many priests, both good and bad, on edge. I thought priests would be welcoming my program with open arms, but very few have shown the kind of enthusiasm I expected."

"Don't blame yourself," Michelle advised.

"I don't," Thielemans replied. "To finish answering your question, I'm not sure I'd be able to identify every pedophile or sexual predator in a group of priests. In retrospect, I feel confident you identified every child molester and rapist in the group correctly. There was something about a few of these guys that gave them away. At the same time, some of the other sex offenders actually seemed friendly, personable, and trustworthy. This might explain why their unsuspecting victims initially felt comfortable with them and why these guys have been able to con so many people for so many years."

"Not to change the subject, but did you see how I organized your schedule in spreadsheet form on your laptop?" Michelle asked. "It shows every lecture and meeting in chronological order, and has space for commenting on which priests are joining your program."

"I've looked at the spreadsheet and think it's a great way to keep track of things," Thielemans answered. "Thanks for doing such a nice job. It's too bad there are so few priests ready to join."

"It's still early," Michelle said reassuringly. "Give it some time. By the way, what was that waiter's problem in the restaurant tonight? He was okay until you told him we wanted two separate checks. Then, he started to decompensate. We've always asked for separate checks in restaurants before and never had any problems."

"He probably didn't expect people our age asking for separate checks," Thielemans replied. "If I took the time to explain my income taxes and the need to properly record deductible business expenses, maybe he'd understand."

"Well, I'm glad we had the opportunity to have this enlightening conversation," Michelle yawned, as she leaned toward Thielemans and tenderly kissed him before drifting off to sleep.

Following more days of lectures, meetings, and enlightening conversations, Thielemans and Michelle bid farewell to Texas. As they drove toward Florida and an extended stay in the Sunshine State, they looked forward to the leisurely stops they scheduled in Louisiana, Mississippi, and Alabama.

In New Orleans, they planned to spend three days sampling the city's famous cuisine and listening to Jazz. Thielemans also planned to pick up more beer and visit a few priests, including Father Raoul Chamadham.

A tall and lean parish priest with martial arts training and epicurean tastes, Chamadham took a day off each month to spend time at his secluded hunting cabin which was located in a forest an hour outside of town. The cabin was small but comfortable, had one door and no windows, and was miles away from the nearest neighbor.

While at the cabin, Chamadham, allegedly listened to classical music, drank fine wine, ate gourmet food, smoked expensive cigars, and sexually abused a teenage boy who was brought to the cabin and retrieved later the same day by a corrections officer from a nearby juvenile detention center. Chamadham never saw the same boy twice, and none of his victims ever learned his name, discovered he was a priest, or determined the location of his hideaway.

Following their stay in the Big Easy, Thielemans and Michelle planned two-night stays in Mississippi and Alabama, where Thielemans had meetings scheduled with parish priests. Their stop in Biloxi was to be highlighted by Thielemans' meeting with Father Ebby Richwine and stop in Mobile by his meeting with Father John Manchete. Richwine and Manchete were two young pedophiles who studied from the same playbook as Gordon Kittrick and were similarly addicted to young boys with angelic faces.

As their drive along the bayou was progressing as planned, Thielemans received an unexpected phone call.

"Father Thielemans, this is Bishop Joseph Grannick," the caller began.

Hearing Grannick's voice being transmitted so clearly through his car's sound system, Thielemans felt as though Grannick was sitting right next to him. Glancing at Michelle and seeing the mixture of fear and hatred in her eyes, he realized the sound of her former abductor's voice was leaving Michelle with the same sensation.

"Yes, Bishop Grannick," Thielemans replied, signaling Michelle to remain silent. "What can I do for you?"

"I'm sure you remember Father Gordon Kittrick from Saint Declan's Church in San Diego," Grannick continued.

"I remember him very well," Thielemans answered.

"Well, I don't know if you've heard, but Father Kittrick died unexpectedly a few weeks ago," Grannick said with a slathering of manufactured sorrow.

"Bishop, I was actually talking with him on the phone when he died," Thielemans admitted. "He called and asked me to come to San Diego to give him Last Rites. Unfortunately, I was stuck in Los Angeles traffic four hours away when he called. As I was explaining to him why

I wouldn't be able to drive to San Diego, his heart stopped and he dropped the phone to the floor, terminating our connection. A nurse was nice enough to call me back an hour later and apprise me of Father's sudden death."

"I didn't know this," Grannick. responded. "I was at the Vatican on official Church business when Gordon died, and not notified of his death for several days. I was unable to make it back for his funeral, and I only returned to L.A. yesterday. I still have important meetings at the Vatican to attend. So, I'll only be in town for another few days before I have to fly back to Rome. Let me ask you, did you and Gordon strike up a friendship when you met? The reason I ask is he must have considered you a good friend to request you be the one to give him Last Rites."

"I wouldn't say we became close friends," Thielemans replied. "Father Kittrick did invite me back to Saint Declan's after I returned from the bishop's conference in Honolulu, and I did accept his invitation. At our meeting, we talked for a while and had a few beers, but when I left, I didn't know if I would ever see him again."

"Gordon must have respected you to invite you back to his rectory," Grannick suggested. "You know, he was very particular who he spent time with. Not everyone understood Gordon. In fact, very few priests ever got to know him well enough to develop close relationships with him. Gordon must have seen something in you that put him at ease. It wouldn't surprise me if he even asked you to hear his confession during your meeting."

"Why would he have asked me to hear his confession?" Thielemans inquired. "After all, I hardly knew him."

"Gordon set high standards for his confessors," Grannick explained. "He never felt comfortable discussing his shortcomings with just any priest. He needed to be inspired by a confessor which is why I thought he might have asked you to hear his confession."

"Bishop, how did you get to know Father Kittrick so well?" Thielemans asked, not expecting Grannick to admit he was Kittrick's uncle.

"Father, I answer directly to the spiritual leader of an entire Ecclesiastical Province," Grannick revealed, sounding like a true politician. "The Province includes the Archdiocese of Los Angeles, which serves the counties of Los Angeles, Santa Barbara, and Ventura, as well as the Dioceses of Fresno, Monterey, Orange, San Bernardino, and San Diego. As an auxiliary bishop, I am called upon to perform many tasks within the Province. I'm a canon lawyer and also serve as a clerical advocate. I get directly involved with priests in matters that could potentially require the intervention of the archbishop. So, I have to know all the priests within the entire Ecclesiastical Province, even those who may never require my advocacy. I got to know Gordon early in his priesthood, and we've stayed in touch ever since."

"It sounds like you're a busy man," Thielemans replied.

"I certainly am," Grannick chuckled. "As they say, 'there's no rest for the wicked.'"

Hearing Grannick's comment, Michelle silently scowled and flipped the middle finger of her right hand toward the dashboard speaker.

"I appreciate you calling me to let me know about Father Kittrick's death," Thielemans said diplomatically. "Is there anything else you wanted to discuss?"

"There is," Grannick answered cautiously. "Does the name, Bobby Kucera, mean anything to you?"

317

"Yes, it does" Thielemans admitted, as he removed Bobby's photo from the car's sun visor and stared at it. "I met Bobby the night I arrived at Saint Declan's, and then again, the following morning when he served Mass."

"I thought so," Grannick mumbled. "Are you aware the boy committed suicide a few days after you met him?"

"Yes, I am," Thielemans sighed, as he continued staring at Bobby's photo.

"Did you and Gordon discuss Bobby Kucera during your return visit to Saint Declan's?" Grannick inquired.

"Yes, we did," Thielemans confirmed. "Father Kittrick and I had a long talk about Bobby."

"I see," Grannick said. "Well, let me get right to the point. The San Diego Police Department is investigating Bobby Kucera's suicide. In fact, the police recently called my office and want to talk with me about the matter in person. Before I schedule a meeting with them, I was hoping to meet with you and get a better understanding of Gordon's interaction with Bobby. You, of course, saw the two of them together, and I'm sure you could provide a credible account of how much Gordon tried to help the boy. I never met Bobby Kucera. So, there's nothing I can tell the police that would aid in their investigation."

"Bishop, I'm afraid I'm no longer in California," Thielemans explained. "I'm currently driving through the Gulf Coast states and have a very busy lecture schedule and meetings for the next several weeks. I'd be happy to meet with you, but I'm not sure when I can."

"Couldn't you find an airport tomorrow morning and fly out here for a quick meeting?" Grannick suggested.

"I'm afraid that's out of the question," Thielemans revealed. "I'll be happy to meet with you at a future time, but I have long-standing professional commitments and can't meet with you anytime soon."

"But you will meet with me," Grannick emphasized.

"Of course," Thielemans replied reassuringly.

"To be very honest with you, I've followed your career for quite some time and have been very impressed with your theological writing," Grannick stated with a generous application of soft-soap. "I know the Holy Father and many of the cardinals personally, and I consider your religious acumen to be unsurpassed by anyone in the Catholic Church. So, for selfish reasons, I'd like to get to know you better and be able to quote you when I speak to other members of the clergy. I'd also like to develop a meaningful personal relationship with you and have you to call when I need a friend to talk to."

"I'm honored," Thielemans said facetiously.

"Paul, I must confess I envied Gordon when I heard the two of you shared a conversation over a glass of beer," Grannick revealed. "That's the kind of meeting I'd like to have with you - one in which two friends can relax, share a drink, and speak openly."

"I'll bring the beer," Thielemans offered.

"That would be wonderful," Grannick exclaimed. "I can hardly wait to see you. I'll be in touch in the coming weeks. In the meantime, I may just cut short my stay here and fly back to Rome tomorrow. God bless you, my son."

"And you," Thielemans responded, as he closed the connection, took a final look at Bobby Kucera's photo, and returned the photo to its shrine in the mirror compartment of the car's sun visor.

"That's one meeting I plan to attend," Thielemans promised, as he looked at Michelle.

"Me, too," Michelle added. "I think it's time I paid my old lover another visit."

"We may need extra beer," Thielemans replied with a faint smile, as the two continued their trip through Cajun country.

CHAPTER SEVENTEEN

In the days that followed, Reenie reviewed medical records, interviewed physicians, and talked with a poison control expert. When her research was complete, she returned to the office of Sheriff Hector Aguilar.

"So, how are the zebras running this year, Reenie?" Aguilar chuckled, as the homicide detective entered his office.

"I haven't lassoed any zebras yet, Sheriff," Reenie answered. "But I may have a few in my sights."

"So, what gives?" the sheriff inquired.

"As instructed, I reviewed the hospital records of the three deceased priests from Los Angeles County," Reenie began. "Then, I personally interviewed the doctors and hospital personnel at the hospital where each priest was being treated at the time of his death. Finally, I made a call to a supervisor at the state forensics lab and asked him questions relative to deaths from poisoning."

"Go on," Aguilar said.

"Case 1 is Reverend John Iagi, a 47-year-old from El Segundo," Reenie read from her extensive notes. "He reported first feeling ill three days before hospitalization when he started experiencing fulminant diarrhea which was clear at first but later bloody. He self-medicated with Pepto-Bismol, canceled his daily Masses, and went to bed. The priest lived alone, and when he failed to answer his telephone on the morning of his hospitalization, the church caretaker went to the rectory and found him in his bed, stuporous and lying in a pool of bloody diarrhea. The caretaker called the ambulance, and the priest was taken to the hospital. Reverend Iagi's past medical history included hypertension which he reportedly managed himself by monitoring his own blood pressures with an electronic machine and self-medicating with the diuretic, furosemide. He also reported controlling his hypertension by eating a diet rich in seafood and fresh vegetables. On admission to the hospital, his blood tests were compatible with anemia, a non-specific infection, dehydration, and very low potassium. His E.K.G. showed atrial fibrillation with a rapid heart rate, and C.T. scan showed gastric and colonic inflammation. After he was given I.V. fluids in the E.R., he became lucid enough to give a medical history, but shortly after being admitted, his blood pressure bottomed out and his heart rate became dangerously high. During attempted cardioversion, his heart stopped and he could not be resuscitated. The admitting physician felt Reverend Iagi initially developed colitis and later became dehydrated and hypokalemic after experiencing prolonged diarrhea. The physician theorized Reverend Iagi could have eaten some bad seafood which caused the diarrhea, and because he self-medicated with furosemide, his potassium could have been low before the diarrhea started and dangerously low after the diarrhea continued. The doctor didn't know if Reverend Iagi was in atrial fibrillation before the colitis began or if he developed the arrhythmia as his condition worsened. The priest's stool, urine, and blood cultures were negative, as was his toxicology report."

"Nice job," Sheriff Aguilar said. "Next case."

"Case 2 is Reverend Ryan Poser, a 37-year-old from Torrance," the detective continued reading. "Reverend

Poser was found having a prolonged seizure in his rectory by paramedics who were sent there by a 9-1-1 dispatcher after she received a hysterical call from an unidentified female. The caller, whose voice sounded like that of a Hispanic teenager to the dispatcher, was not present in the rectory when the paramedics arrived. Reverend Poser was taken to the hospital by the paramedics, and he died later that evening in the hospital's I.C.U. after continuing to experience uncontrollable seizures. C.T. scan of the brain was unremarkable, although movement artifact made interpretation difficult. Renal ultrasound was compatible with acute renal failure, showing increased kidney length and cortical thickness. A lumbar puncture was attempted but could not be safely completed because of the patient's violent seizures. Blood and urine cultures were negative. Blood tests showed an elevated white blood cell count, very high urea nitrogen and creatinine levels, elevated sodium, potassium, and phosphate levels, and decreased total protein and calcium levels. Urinalysis showed large amounts of protein and blood. Occult blood was present in the stool. The toxicology screen showed the presence of marijuana and cocaine, but no anticonvulsant drugs. Reverend Poser's final diagnosis was status epilepticus, secondary to acute renal failure. He died before hemodialysis could be performed. The attending physician didn't know if Reverend Poser had any previous history of epilepsy or kidney disease."

"Yoiks," Aguilar exclaimed. "Next case."

"Case 3 is Reverend Timothy Elliot, a 39-year-old from Santa Clarita," Reenie began.

"Is that the survivalist who worked with juvenile delinquents?" the sheriff asked curiously.

"Yes, it is," Reenie revealed.

"*Ay, Chihuahua,*" Sheriff Aguilar exclaimed. "Please proceed."

"Reverend Elliot was found unresponsive by his housekeeper the day after he returned to the rectory from a long hiking expedition with a group of teenagers," Reenie continued reading. "The housekeeper told paramedics she was already asleep when he returned to the rectory at night and shopping while he was still sleeping the next morning. She found him in the afternoon when she returned to the rectory. Reverend Elliot was hospitalized, but he never regained consciousness. He sustained a cardiopulmonary arrest on his second day in the hospital and could not be successfully resuscitated. C.T. scan of the brain showed encephalopathy but no aneurysms or focal lesions. C.T. scan of the abdomen showed an enlarged liver with multiple cysts but no other hepatic abnormalities. Lumbar puncture showed non-diagnostic abnormalities but no bacteria. Blood, urine, stool, and cerebrospinal fluid cultures were negative. Laboratory analysis of his stool showed occult blood but no ova or parasites. Blood tests showed extremely high ammonia levels, highly elevated liver enzyme levels, and low sodium, potassium, and hemoglobin levels. The toxicology screen showed marijuana but was otherwise negative. The attending physician felt Reverend Elliot died of hepatic encephalopathy. Although the physician felt the liver failure that led to the encephalopathy was acute, he couldn't say what caused it and could not rule out poisoning. The physician knew of Reverend Elliot's reputation as an avid outdoorsman and theorized the priest could have eaten poisonous berries, leaves, grasses, roots, or mushrooms he thought were safe. He also wondered if the priest drank creek water that may have been contaminated by some kind of hepatotoxic chemical. After I spoke with the physician, I called the youth services office near Santa Clarita and apprised its director of Reverend Elliot's death. She had a list of everyone who accompanied the priest on the hiking expedition, and after she talked with each of the teenagers who were on the trip, she called me back to tell me no one else became ill or remembered seeing Reverend Elliot eating or drinking anything unusual."

"Anything else?" Aguilar inquired.

"I called Itchy Stepanski at the state forensics lab and talked with him about undetectable poisons," Reenie revealed.

"Itchy Stepanski," the sheriff chuckled. "How is Itchy? I haven't talked to him in ages."

"He's fine, and he sends his regards," Reenie replied. "His wife is pregnant again – Number 7."

"Good old Itchy Stepanski," Aguilar chuckled. "Please continue."

"So, Itchy proceeded to lecture me on poisons that were undetectable by conventional means, those that could only be detected by elaborate technology, those that could only be detected by elaborate technology under highly specific conditions, poisons that were principally used in bioterrorism, and poisons that have yet to be officially named," Reenie stated.

"Did Itchy leave you with any practical take-home points during his lecture?" the sheriff asked facetiously.

"As a matter of fact, he did," Reenie remarked. "He told me the secret to identifying poisons was to understand what poison you were looking for ahead of time. It's his belief, if you don't know what poison you're looking for, it's unlikely you'll find it with conventional screening. He also told me the elaborate technology capable of identifying uncommon toxins is better suited for identifying them in fluids rather than dead bodies. To wit, today's sophisticated technology may be able to identify an uncommon poison in milk or the body fluid of a human or animal but unable to detect it in a corpse. Even when the technology is capable of identifying a toxin in human blood or urine, there has to be an ample quantity of the fluid available to test and the fluid has to be fresh. Although antibody testing to specific toxins and the identification of specific toxins through sophisticated biochemical assays has come a long way in recent years, such testing still has many limitations and may render only incomplete or non-specific results. What's more, such testing may only be available at a limited number of laboratories and may come with a prohibitive cost. Evidently, the chemical reagents used in these tests are extremely expensive. Finally, I talked with Itchy about the three cases, and it was his professional opinion that poisoning could have played a role in any or all of the three cases. He also stressed there was a much greater statistical probability that the cases did not involve poisoning."

"If you can, please sum up everything you learned from Itchy in one sentence," the sheriff requested.

"If you suspect someone has been poisoned with ricin, you may be able to identify ricin in the body fluids of that person if you obtain sufficient quantities of fresh body fluids from the person and can safely and expeditiously transport the fluids to a sophisticated laboratory that has the technology capable of identifying such toxins," Reenie replied succinctly.

"Okay, Reenie," Aguilar chuckled. "For $64,000, I'd like you to come up to the whiteboard and diagram that sentence, just like you used to do in grade school."

"Show me the money first," Reenie answered straight-faced.

"Good job, Reenie," the sheriff laughed. "So, what do you plan to do with all this information?"

"I need to know more before I turn this into a real investigation," Reenie admitted. "I want to get search warrants and take a closer look inside the rectories where each of these priests lived. I also want to interview anyone who knew these priests or worked for them."

"I taught you well, Reenie," Sheriff Aguilar boasted. "So, go, get it done. While you're at it, two other relatively young priests died outside the county during the same period of time. One was from San Diego and the other was from Redlands. Contact the police in those two cities and see if they know anything about the recent deaths of any priests. Come back after you've done your homework, and we'll talk some more."

"Thanks, Sheriff," Reenie said, as she exited his office.

"Itchy Stepanski," Aguilar chuckled, as he walked into the utility room and poured himself a cup of coffee.

As Reenie scurried off to search for clues, another peace officer was making an unexpected house call.

Manu Salopo, a 37-year-old native of American Samoa, showed his badge to the young female receptionist at the Saints of the Desert Assisted Living Villa in Twentynine Palms. As he was being escorted to Mother Murray's room, a dozen residents who were congregated in the lobby of the villa stared at the 6'2", 240-pound, former San Diego State linebacker who was impeccably dressed in a tan suit, white shirt, and maroon tie.

"Margaret, there's someone here to see you," the thin, copper-haired receptionist mumbled nervously, as she knocked on Mother's door.

"I hope it's the Publishers Clearing House Prize Patrol and they've got a big check for me," Mother shouted, as she slowly made her way to the door.

Opening the door, Mother's neck audibly cracked as she raised her head to see her visitor's face.

"Heaven help us," Mother exclaimed, taking one look at Salopo. "You're not Ed McMahon. Who are you?"

"Detective Manu Salopo," the investigator announced through a mouthful of perfect ivory teeth, as he presented his credentials.

"San Diego Police Department," Mother read from his badge. "I think there's been some mistake, Detective Darling. I haven't ordered tickets for the Policeman's Ball since my dear husband passed away, may he rest in peace."

"I'm not delivering tickets for the Policeman's Ball," Salopo chuckled. "If I may, I'd like to come in to ask you a few questions."

"And you're sure you're not with the Prize Patrol or anyone else who has money for me," Mother reiterated.

"No, I'm not with the Prize Patrol, Mrs. Murray," the detective laughed.

"Then, come in and take a load off," Mother said, as she welcomed the detective into her room and pointed to a chair. "And call me, Mother, if you'd be so kind. "

Not outwardly showing the nervousness she felt inside, Mother sat down in her recliner.

"Mother, I understand you worked at Saint Declan's Rectory in San Diego as a live-in housekeeper before you came to the villa," Salopo politely stated.

"That I did," Mother admitted. "Why, I was taking care of priests at Saint Declan's before the Catholic Church discovered wax and started making candles."

"I see," the soft-spoken detective chuckled. "I also understand the last pastor you worked for at Saint Declan's was the late Reverend Gordon Kittrick."

"Late?" Mother questioned. "What was the pastor late for this time?"

"Father Kittrick died recently which is why I referred to him as 'the late pastor,'" Detective Salopo explained. "He had a heart attack and died. Didn't you know?"

"Heaven help us," Mother whispered. "I had no idea the pastor died. No one told me. To answer your question, Father Kittrick was the last pastor I worked for at Saint Declan's."

"Mother, why did you leave Saint Declan's?" the detective inquired.

"To be honest with you, Detective Darling, I didn't leave Saint Declan's," Mother revealed. "I was fired. My son unexpectedly showed up at the rectory one morning and told me to pack my things because I was being retired by the parish and sent to a beautiful retirement community. If you ask me, my son took a wrong turn somewhere because, instead of taking me to a beautiful retirement community, he brought me here to the Bates Motel. Can you imagine the nerve of anyone telling me I was being retired? Why I worked from dawn to dusk at that rectory for more years than Methuselah could remember, and I was just as chipper my last day there as I was my first. And can you imagine anyone telling me my reward for all those years of faithful service was a room at this place? I tell you true, Detective Darling, for how hard I worked, I earned a lot more than whatever this dump is being paid to keep me dry and serve me T.V. dinners thrice daily."

"Mother, I've got to hand it to you, these are the kind of interviews I enjoy," Detective Salopo admitted. "I really like it when someone answers five questions at a time when they're only asked one."

"And what part of the Emerald Isle did you say you came from?" Mother joked. "County Cork would be my guess since it appears you've kissed the Blarney Stone."

"I come from an island, but not the one you're thinking," the investigator answered with a smile. "I come from American Samoa which is in the South Pacific."

"Oh, I loved that movie," Mother swooned. "Rossano Brazzi could sing me to sleep any night of the week."

"I'm afraid that movie was before my time," Salopo chuckled. "So, Mother, why do you think you were fired from your housekeeping job at Saint Declan's?"

"Detective Darling, the answer is as plain as the nose on your handsome face," Mother replied. "The pastor fired me because I saw and heard too many things at Saint Declan's over the years. He gave me the boot because I knew too much. In fact, he exiled me to the desert in hopes this day would never come, and you wouldn't be here right now, waiting to ask me the real questions you came here to ask."

Listening to her insights and candor, Salopo looked at Mother in disbelief.

"So, Mother, what are the real questions I came here to ask?" he inquired.

"The ones about Bobby Kucera, of course," Mother sighed. "You came here to ask me what I know about the dear boy's death."

"What do you know?" the detective asked.

"What I know, Detective Darling, is Bobby Kucera should still be alive," Mother said, as tears slowly filled her aging eyes. "After his father was killed in a tragic motor vehicle accident, neither his family, teachers, nor friends helped him with his depression. He dearly loved his father and greatly depended on the man. Without his father, Bobby had no one to turn to for the kind of help a boy needs when he's about to become a teenager. Father Kittrick saw what was happening to Bobby and seized the opportunity to take advantage of the poor boy."

"How did Father Kittrick take advantage of Bobby?" Salopo questioned.

"For several months, he took Bobby down into the rectory cellar where there was a small gym," Mother continued. "Father wrestled in college, and he promised Bobby he would teach him the sport. I hate to tell you what he taught Bobby down in that dungeon. At first, Bobby trusted the pastor because he desperately needed a father figure and wanted to become a priest. When wrestling turned into sexual abuse, the pastor tried convincing Bobby that seminarians were required to become sexually submissive to their superiors as a secret rite of passage into the priesthood. After months of being sexually abused, Bobby no longer trusted the pastor or anyone else for that matter. Any hope Bobby had of becoming a priest died. Bobby believed the lies Kittrick told him and thought years of being sexually submissive to older men was too great a price to become a priest. He became despondent, and with no hope for any kind of future, the poor boy killed himself."

"Mother, if you knew Father Kittrick was sexually abusing Bobby, why didn't you report it to the police?" the detective asked.

"In all honesty, I had no way of contacting anyone," Mother stated defensively. "I was abandoned here immediately after Bobby's death without so much as a cheap cell phone or the money to have a phone installed in my room. I didn't even have enough spare change to make a long-distance call from the payphone in the lobby."

"Why didn't you call the police before Bobby died?" the investigator inquired.

"I didn't think anyone would believe an old woman like me or take my word over that of a priest," Mother explained. "You see, I had no proof Father Kittrick was sexually abusing young boys, only Mother's intuition. I never witnessed the pastor abusing Bobby or any of the other youngsters he lured into the rectory cellar. I just saw what Bobby and the other boys looked like before and after they spent time with the pastor. I hid a tape recorder in the cellar and recorded what was going on down there. Unfortunately, listening to the recordings confirmed my suspicions. When Bobby committed suicide, I panicked and destroyed the tape. Had I known Bobby was capable of taking his own life, I would have contacted the police. But I swear to you, I had no idea he found life so unbearable. The rectory was my home, and I had nowhere else to go, but I would have gladly traded the roof over my head for the chance to save Bobby's life. I just didn't know how desperate he had become. I didn't know."

As Mother started crying, Salopo patiently waited.

"Shortly after Bobby died, my son came to the rectory, and a few hours later, I wound up here," Mother continued, as she dried her eyes with a handkerchief. "I was told the diocese would be paying all my bills in gratitude for my years of faithful service. Since my own children couldn't take me in, I agreed to stay here, but I've been stewing in my own juices ever since I arrived. All the while, I've been thinking about Bobby and realizing I was moved far out in the desert so no one would ever find me or be able to ask me what I knew about Bobby or that monster who caused the dear boy to take his own life."

"I have to say, you weren't easy to find, but we have our ways," Detective Salopo admitted. "Mother, do you know who specifically in the diocese is responsible for paying your room and board here?"

"Oh, no one in the diocese is paying my bills," Mother stated unequivocally. "They just told me that to get me out of the rectory. It's the archdiocese that's paying my bills but not realizing it. More specifically, it's Bishop Joseph Grannick who has been diverting funds from the archdiocese to pay for the sins of many priests, including those of his nephew, Father Gordon Kittrick."

"Are you saying Bishop Joseph Grannick, the canon lawyer from Los Angeles, is Reverend Gordon Kittrick's uncle?" Salopo asked incredulously.

"Father Kittrick's mother is Bishop Grannick's sister," Mother explained emphatically. "That makes Bishop Grannick the uncle of Father Kittrick."

"Mother, you just said Bishop Grannick has been diverting funds from the archdiocese to pay for the sins of many priests," Salopo reiterated. "Could you explain how he's been doing that?"

"Bishop Grannick has been working for the archdiocese for many years," Mother began. "The archdiocese is a part of the Ecclesiastical Province of Los Angeles. So are several smaller dioceses, like the one that governs the Catholic parishes in San Diego. The archbishop oversees the operations of the Ecclesiastical Province. Needless to say, he relies on many auxiliary bishops to help him manage things. Are you with me?"

"Yes, I am," Detective Salopo confirmed.

"Managing the operations of an Ecclesiastical Province is very complicated, and many auxiliary bishops play many different roles in dispersing funds," Mother continued. "Someone like Bishop Grannick who has been around for a long time understands the complexities of management and ways to profit financially from those complexities. By channeling money into various funds, a bishop could draw on those funds and arrange payments that appear to be on the up-and-up. One example would be financial payments or scholarships to the families of children who were sexually abused by priests. Another would be retirement benefits to a retired rectory housekeeper who knew too much. The financial records of the diocese or archdiocese would only reflect what appeared to be reasonable employment perks or retirement benefits. There would never be any mention of families being paid money or given scholarships to remain quiet about their children being sexually abused by a priest. In my case, I'm sure there's no mention of money being spent to keep me exiled and far away from curious investigators like yourself."

"So, what you're saying is Bishop Grannick has dispersed hush money to the families of Father Kittrick's victims," the detective suggested.

"He has indeed," Mother exclaimed. "He's been doing it for years, and not only for Father Kittrick. He's also been doling out hush money on behalf of many other perverted priests. What has made Bishop Grannick so effective is his ability to divert funds within the archdiocese and cover his tracks without raising any suspicion. The archdiocese has no idea what Bishop Grannick has been doing."

"Mother, can you prove this?" Salopo asked.

"No, I can't," Mother conceded. "It's pure speculation on my part, based on decades of listening to hearsay, snooping around, and eavesdropping. However, you should be able to prove my allegations very easily. I understand Bobby Kucera's mother and sisters moved out of town a few days after Bobby's funeral. That would be fine and dandy if the woman wasn't as poor as a church mouse and couldn't afford to take her children for a cab ride around the block. So, locate the Kucera family and find out who is helping them pay for their new lifestyle. In my case, find out who is sending checks to this place to pay for my lavish retirement. Then, be careful not to trip over the paper trail you'll be following."

"Mother, this seems a little thin," the detective suggested. "It's hard to believe someone approached a grieving mother and offered her a payoff to remain silent about her son being sexually abused by a priest before he committed suicide."

"Would it be easier to believe someone approached a grieving mother and offered her money from a diocesan memorial fund in gratitude for her son's inspirational work as an altar boy before he died?" Mother countered. "That someone would never have to mention anything about sexual abuse, especially to a mother who wasn't smart enough to realize something was seriously wrong with her child before he committed suicide."

"Point taken," the investigator said. "Mother, have you ever heard of Reverend Paul Thielemans?"

"Heard of him?" Mother chuckled. "Why he and I had a date a few months ago. My heart still races whenever I think of him."

"I don't understand," Salopo admitted.

"Father Thielemans visited Saint Declan's back in late April," Mother explained. "He was invited to say Mass because Father Kittrick was going out of town to a conference for the weekend."

"Who invited him to say Mass?" the detective asked.

"Bishop Grannick," Mother revealed.

"How did the bishop know Father Thielemans?" Salopo questioned.

"The two met at one of Father Thielemans' lectures," Mother answered. "Father is a famous author, you know, and he lectures at Catholic colleges all over the country. I forget exactly where they met, but it was definitely at a college lecture. Father told the bishop he was coming to San Diego to take a cruise to Hawaii. That's when the bishop asked him to cover for his nephew and say Mass."

"Was Bishop Grannick present at Saint Declan's at any time during Father Thielemans visit?" Detective Salopo inquired.

"No, he wasn't," Mother replied. "The bishop only visited Saint Declan's when he thought the pastor would be alone. Father Thielemans came to the rectory on a Saturday afternoon. He arrived two hours earlier than expected which aggravated the pastor. You see, the pastor was down in the cellar with Bobby Kucera when Father

Thielemans arrived ahead of time. Father's early arrival forced the pastor to curtail his activities with Bobby. When the pastor finally came upstairs to the kitchen, he was perspiring profusely and his face was beet red. Bobby appeared frightened and physically distressed. I had my special pot roast and peach pie in the oven and planned to serve it to the pastor and Father Thielemans for dinner. For some reason, the pastor and Father Thielemans didn't hit it off when they met. So, the pastor invented the excuse that he couldn't stay for dinner because he had to drive Bobby home and catch a flight to San Francisco. He lied because his flight was two hours later than he stated. The pastor probably wasn't finished with Bobby when Father Thielemans arrived. That would explain why he decided to skip dinner and take Bobby somewhere private where he could finish what he started in the cellar. I was actually glad the pastor left Father Thielemans and me alone for the rest of the night. We had a wonderful dinner, drank the special beer Father brought as a gift to the pastor, and watched Bing Crosby movies until the wee hours of the morning."

"Did you say Father Thielemans brought Father Kittrick beer as a gift?" the investigator asked.

"Father Thielemans always brings a six-pack of Belgian beer and a special beer glass to priests when he visits them," Mother answered. "You see, his father was an exporter who helped make Belgian beer popular in the United States. In fact, over there on my hutch is the very glass Father Thielemans brought the pastor. He also brought that book which is right next to the glass. The pastor acted very rudely when he met Father Thielemans. He acted as though he didn't want any part of the gifts. So, I kept the glass and book. In fact, Father even autographed the book for me. I probably don't have to tell you Father Thielemans and I drank the entire six-pack of beer while we watched our movies. The next morning, Father said two Masses at Saint Declan's before boarding his ship and cruising to Hawaii. I didn't see Father in the morning because my son picked me up while Father was still asleep. My son took me to Mexico for the day."

"How would you describe Father Thielemans," Salopo inquired, as he walked over to the hutch and picked up the beer glass.

"Detective Darling, I've met many fine priests and many wonderful men in my life, but I've never met anyone as special as Father Thielemans," Mother revealed. "He's strong, handsome, successful, charming, and by far, the most intelligent human being I've ever met. I tell you true, I dearly loved my husband and was faithful to the man for all the years of our marriage, but if I met Father Thielemans back in the day, I'd still be doing penance for all the times I tried talking him into breaking the sixth commandment with me."

Salopo shook his head and laughed.

"Does Father Thielemans work alone?" he questioned.

"His sister used to travel with him, but she recently moved back to Belgium," Mother revealed. "He travels alone now, but I believe his sister still does his scheduling and handles his business affairs from abroad."

"Mother, why do you think Fathers Thielemans and Kittrick didn't hit it off when they met," the detective asked, as he continued to laugh while taking photos of the beer glass with his iPhone.

"I'd say it was a pure and simple personality clash," Mother explained. "Father Thielemans was everything the pastor wasn't, and the pastor realized it. Most importantly, Father Thielemans was a highly moral man and a champion of his faith. On the other hand, the pastor was an immoral pedophile who used his position in the Church to satisfy his sex habit."

"Did Father Thielemans detect a pedophilic relationship between Father Kittrick and Bobby Kucera when he saw the two of them together at the rectory?" Salopo inquired, still standing.

"I don't believe so," Mother answered. "Of course, he was only in their presence for a matter of minutes. After the pastor met Father Thielemans, he rushed Bobby out of the rectory quicker than Arkle through the steeplechase."

"If Father Thielemans had detected any pedophilic relationship, do you think he would have confronted Father Kittrick on the spot?" the investigator questioned.

"I have no doubt," Mother replied. "I think Father Thielemans would have considered it his religious duty. You see, Detective Darling, a true priest like Father Paul Thielemans lives his religion. He practices what he preaches and is willing to fight to the death for his beliefs."

"Mother, you told me you weren't aware of Father Kittrick's death," Salopo reiterated. "You also told me he wrestled in college and lured the boys down into his cellar gym where he engaged in physical activity with them. This would imply he was still in reasonably good shape and health before he died. Was he?"

"Yes, I'd say so," Mother responded. "The pastor spent a lot of time exercising in his gym, even when he was alone."

"Considering his apparent health, were you surprised to hear he died of a heart attack?" the detective inquired.

"I was surprised to hear he had a heart," Mother quipped.

"I hear you," the investigator laughed. "Do you think Father Kittrick was capable of taking his own life?"

"A priest who knows he's going to hell does everything he can to prolong his life," Mother replied. "The pastor knew he was responsible for Bobby's death, but he didn't have the courage or good sense to end his own miserable existence."

"Mother, that's all the questions I have for now," Salopo said. "I may need to speak with you again. I want to thank you for all the information you provided and assure you your cooperation will not be forgotten. Before I leave, do you have any questions you'd like to ask me?"

"As a matter of fact, I do," Mother answered. "Now that I've said too much and will probably be forfeiting my retirement benefits from the archdiocese, do you know anyone who needs a good housekeeper?" Mother asked with a twinkle in her eye.

"I'll give Norman Bates a call," the detective chuckled, as he walked toward the door.

"May the road rise up to meet you, Detective Darling," Mother Murray sighed, as she watched her visitor leave. "Heaven help us."

CHAPTER EIGHTEEN

As Salopo was driving out of the villa's parking lot, he received a phone call from San Diego Chief of Police, Ronald Lipfert.

"Manu, am I interrupting anything important?" the chief asked courteously.

"Not at all, Chief," the detective answered. "I'm leaving the Saints of the Desert Assisted Living Villa in Twentynine Palms as we speak. I just finished questioning Margaret Murray, the former housekeeper at Saint Declan's Rectory, about the Bobby Kucera suicide."

"So, what did you find out?" the chief inquired.

"A lot," Salopo exclaimed. "Mrs. Murray is a pleasant, cooperative, and credible 77-year-old with time on her hands and no one to tell all her secrets to. She also has a chip on her shoulder because she was fired from her housekeeping job after decades of what she described as 'seeing and hearing too much at the church rectory.' She alleged Bobby Kucera's suicide was caused by the late Reverend Gordon Kittrick who sexually abused Kucera and other young boys while he was the church's pastor. She stated Kucera became despondent after his father died in a motor vehicle accident, and hopeless after he turned to Father Kittrick for help, only to find out the hard way the priest was a pedophile. A month after Kucera's suicide, the 49-year-old Kittrick died of a heart attack."

"That is a lot," Chief Lipfert agreed. "It's also timely because I just received a call from Sheriff Aguilar in L.A.

That's why I'm calling you. He wanted to talk with me about Father Kittrick who was one of five relatively-young Catholic priests to recently die in Southern California. It seems one of the sheriff's homicide detectives put a bug in his ear about some or all of these priests possibly being murdered instead of dying from what appeared to be natural causes. Three of the priests died within the sheriff's jurisdiction, another died in Redlands, and Kittrick died in San Diego. At first, I didn't think there was too much to the theory these priests were murdered because they were pedophiles, but what you just told me about Kittrick changes things. Do you know Detective Reenie Behan from the L.A. Sheriff's Department?"

"No, I don't," Detective Salopo answered.

"I want you to give her a call and set up a time when the two of you can compare notes about these cases," Lipfert requested. "I'll text you her cell phone number. I don't know if there's anything to this pedophile murder theory, but I guess it's worth a look. Learning more about Kittrick may help us wrap up the Kucera case. By the way, have you reviewed Kittrick's hospital records yet?"

"I've looked through them briefly but not really studied them," the detective admitted. "I have the Kucera case file with me. So, I'll give Kittrick's hospital records a look and discuss them with his doctors if necessary."

"When you talk to the docs, make sure to ask them about the possibility of Kittrick being poisoned," the chief advised. "It's not uncommon for heart attacks to be secondary events that follow primary events like poisonings. Also, have you been able to get in touch with Bishop Grannick from the archdiocese yet? He officiated at the Kucera boy's funeral Mass which makes me think he may know something about Kucera, as well as Kittrick. The last time we talked, you said he was at the Vatican on Church business."

"Bishop Grannick is still at the Vatican, and no one at the archdiocese seems to know when he'll be returning," Salopo replied. "However, the housekeeper I just interviewed told me a lot about the bishop. For starters, she told me Bishop Grannick is Father Kittrick's uncle. She also alleged Grannick has been responsible for paying hush money to the families of children Kittrick and other local priests have sexually abused."

"Wowzers," Lipfert exclaimed.

"I've finally been able to track down Bobby Kucera's family," the detective revealed. "As we previously discussed, they unexpectedly moved from San Diego a few days after Bobby's funeral without leaving a forwarding address. I plan to drive to Anaheim in the next few days to interview the mother."

"Nice work, Manu," the chief said proudly. "Keep your eye on the ball and stay as inconspicuous as possible. Remember that we're dealing with a lot of conjecture here and not really sure how credible the housekeeper is. The last thing we need to do is tackle a church dignitary and get penalized for unnecessary roughness. Do you hear me?"

"Loud and clear, Coach," Salopo chuckled. "Let me get back to the game, and I'll call you when we score."

"See you around campus, Manu," Lipfert closed.

"Around campus, Chief," the detective answered, as he ended the call.

Several minutes later, Salopo received a text message with Reenie's cell phone number. As he continued driving, he dialed the number.

"This is Detective Behan," the young woman confidently answered.

"Detective Behan, this is Detective Manu Salopo of the San Diego P.D.," the investigator began. "How are you?"

"Fine, thank you," Reenie replied. "And you?"

"Fine, thanks," Salopo said. "I'm calling because my chief recently spoke with Sheriff Aguilar about the recent deaths of the five Catholic priests in Southern California. I'm working on a suicide case involving a young boy who has been linked to Reverend Gordon Kittrick, a priest from San Diego who was among those who recently died. I understand you are currently investigating the deaths of three priests from the Los Angeles area, and I'd like to get together with you sometime to compare notes."

"Sure," Reenie responded. "I'm on my way to Redlands right now to discuss the death of Reverend Peter Pauley with a detective I know. So far, the Redlands P.D. hasn't begun any formal investigation into the priest's death, but the detective I'm meeting is interested in talking about it. It's too bad I didn't speak with you before I set up the meeting. Perhaps the three of us could have gotten together to discuss our cases."

"You won't believe this, but I'm currently driving back to San Diego from Twentynine Palms," Salopo revealed. "I'm on Route-62 now, but I'm not far from the junction of Interstate-10. I could hop on the interstate and be in Redlands within an hour."

"Great," Reenie exclaimed. "I'll meet you in an hour at Saint Daniel's Roman Catholic Church in Redlands."

"I'm on my way," Salopo closed.

Before he continued driving, Salopo pulled over on the side of the road and spent a few minutes reviewing

Kittrick's hospital reports. Retrieving the name of Kittrick's attending physician, he called Scripps Mercy Hospital, and while waiting for the physician to come to the phone, got back on the road and continued driving.

Arriving at Redlands an hour later, Salopo got out of his unmarked Ford Police Interceptor and approached Saint Daniel's Rectory where Detectives Reenie Behan and Lawrence Hanrahan were waiting. As the two detectives watched Salopo approaching, Reenie could feel Cupid's arrow penetrating her lonely heart, and Lawrence could feel the arrow's breeze swirling around his perfect hair.

"Manu Salopo," the detective announced, as he extended his enormous right hand.

"Reenie Behan," the young woman reciprocated, as she watched her hand disappear in Salopo's.

"Lawrence Hanrahan," the 39-year-old Redlands detective said, as he cautiously shook Salopo's hand.

As Cupid flew away and an uncomfortable silence fell over Saint Daniel's Rectory, Hanrahan removed the rectory keys from the pocket of his suit jacket.

"Shall we go inside?" he suggested. "I got the keys from the church janitor. He said no one has been inside the rectory since Father Pauley died."

Entering the rectory through the kitchen, Reenie turned on the lights and sat down at the table. Following her lead, the other detectives took their seats.

"So, let's talk about our cases," Reenie advised, as she adjusted the jacket of her brown polyester pantsuit.

"Of course," Salopo agreed, unbuttoning his suit jacket and leaning back in his chair.

"Sure," Hanrahan echoed, as he moved his chair closer to the table and placed his clasped hands on his lap.

Opening her case files, Reenie proceeded to read the notes from her interviews with the physicians who took care of Reverends Iagi, Poser, and Elliot. Then, she shared the details of her lengthy discussion with the state forensics lab supervisor, including his opinion that any or all of the cases could have been caused by poisoning, although none of the cases were diagnosed as such.

Salopo followed with an overview of his involvement in the Kucera suicide case and brief synopsis of his recent talk with Mother Murray. As he showed the other detectives the photo of the Saint Bavo beer glass he took with his iPhone while interviewing Mother, he mentioned Father Thielemans' name and the priest's ritual of bringing a six-pack of Belgian beer and signature beer glass to the priests he visited.

Revealing the reasons there was alleged animosity between Reverends Thielemans and Kittrick, Detective Salopo informed his colleagues Thielemans' cell phone number had been called from Kittrick's rectory phone on numerous occasions prior to Kittrick's unexpected death. Salopo finished his presentation with a summary of Kittrick's hospitalization.

Using hospital records as a guide, Salopo explained how Kittrick presented to the hospital with symptoms of peptic ulcer disease, only to be diagnosed with the acute myocardial infarction that ultimately claimed his life. As Salopo concluded his remarks and referenced his recent phone call with Kittrick's attending physician, Hanrahan sat attentive and motionless.

Resembling a television anchorman much more than a detective, Hanrahan was of average height and weight, extremely well-groomed, and stylishly dressed in a gray

Glen Plaid suit, crisp white shirt, and gold-barred, powder-blue tie. From his salon-styled, silver hair to his veneered teeth, and his deeply-tanned skin to his manicured fingernails, Hanrahan gave the appearance of someone who was self-indulgent and highly invested in himself.

When it was his turn to talk, Hanrahan revealed he discussed the death of Reverend Peter Pauley with the priest's attending physician only after he was called by Detective Behan. He admitted the Redlands P.D. had not planned to investigate the priest's death because he appeared to die of natural causes.

Reading from his notes, Hanrahan reviewed the salient points of Father Pauley's hospitalization:

"Reverend Peter Pauley called 9-1-1 from this rectory at 3 a.m. on the morning of his hospitalization. The 42-year-old reported vomiting blood, having chest pain, and being unable to breathe. Paramedics responded and transported Father Pauley to Redlands Community Hospital where he was evaluated in the emergency department and admitted to the intensive care unit. Father Pauley lived alone, and there was no one available to give his attending physicians a medical history or any pertinent information. The priest was intubated and placed on a ventilator, and intravenous fluids were given to combat his very low blood pressure. A gastroenterologist performed emergency endoscopy on Father Pauley and discovered fulminant esophagitis and gastritis with copious bleeding. Then, he performed esophagogastric tamponade by introducing a balloon catheter into the esophagus and inflating it to put pressure against the bleeding esophageal walls. Multiple drugs were given intravenously in an attempt to stop the disease progression, bleeding, and shock. Because of significant blood loss, Father Pauley was transfused with multiple units of packed red blood cells, platelets, and fresh frozen plasma. His hemoglobin on admission was 6.9, and one hour later, it was 5.1. White blood cell count was elevated at 22,000. Most of his blood chemistries were abnormal. In particular, his renal studies and liver function tests were elevated. Urinalysis showed protein and blood. Blood, throat, stool, and urine cultures were negative. Toxicology was positive for alcohol, but no prescription or over-the-counter drugs. E.K.G. was unremarkable and troponin-I and cardiac enzymes were normal, ruling out a myocardial infarction. Chest x-ray showed aspiration pneumonia. Father Pauley died after a twelve-hour hospitalization. The gastroenterologist felt Father Pauley had chronic, untreated esophagitis and gastritis for a prolonged period of time, and presented to the hospital with an acute exacerbation of his underlying condition. The physician didn't know what caused the exacerbation. He also felt Father Pauley aspirated gastric contents into his lungs, and with time, the developing pneumonia would have probably killed him."

"Is it my imagination or do we have a common thread running through each of these cases?" Reenie asked rhetorically, as she straightened her eyeglasses. "We have five relatively young priests who died unexpectedly within days of each other after experiencing illnesses that, at least in part, involved the digestive system. Manu's guy had an ulcer flare-up that strained his heart. Lawrence's fella had hemorrhagic esophagitis and gastritis. My three guys all died of different causes but had blood in their G.I. tracts. My point is each of these priests could have been poisoned to death."

"But, why?" Lawrence inquired skeptically.

"Manu's priest was accused of being a pedophile by an eye witness," Reenie replied aggressively. "Two of my three fellas were rumored to be sex offenders. How about your guy? Was he a child molester?"

"I'm not sure," Lawrence answered with hesitation. "Before Father Pauley came to Saint Daniel's, he was the director of an upstate orphanage. He was never formally charged, but there were some rumors he was relieved of his position at the orphanage because he made a habit of taking sexual liberties with young boys."

"Lawrence, did you ever meet Father Pauley?" Manu questioned.

"I attend Mass at Saint Daniel's and have spoken to him on several occasions over the past few years," Lawrence revealed.

"Did Father Pauley impress you as being the kind of priest who was capable of sexually abusing children?" Manu queried.

"I honestly don't know," Lawrence admitted. "I will say, I never felt comfortable around him. I never thought of him as someone who raped children, but I'm not sure I would have recommended him as a babysitter."

As Manu and Reenie laughed, Lawrence cordially smiled and adjusted his tie.

"For argument sake, let's just say all five of these priests were sex offenders," Reenie continued. "All five could have been poisoned by someone who hated pedophilic clergymen. That someone could have been a victim of previous sexual abuse by a priest, a person who has gotten caught up in all the recent media frenzy about pedophiles in the Catholic Church, or an individual who has taken it upon themself to rid the Church of dirty priests. For all we know, that someone could be a devout Catholic by day and a psychopathic serial killer by night."

As the other detectives nodded their heads in silent agreement, Reenie looked around the kitchen and wiggled her toes in her tight tactical utility shoes. Seeing something through a cabinet's glass door, she got up from her chair and walked toward the cabinet.

"What do we have here?" Reenie asked, as she carefully examined an unusual beer glass.

"It looks like the same glass I found at Margaret Murray's," Manu observed, as he quickly pulled up a photo of the beer glass on his iPhone.

"It is the same glass," Reenie exclaimed, as she compared the beer glass in the photo to the one in her hand. "Look at the colored crest, man's caricature, and inscription."

"The glasses are the same," Lawrence concurred. "They're both inscribed, 'Saint Bavo Witbier.'"

"Didn't you say the priest who visited Father Kittrick brought a six-pack of beer and signature beer glass to every priest he visited?" Reenie inquired, as she stared expectantly at Detective Salopo.

"Yes, I did," Manu confirmed. "Maybe we should check the refrigerator and trash can for beer bottles."

"Good idea," Lawrence said, walking over to the refrigerator.

As Lawrence searched inside the refrigerator, Manu dumped the contents of the trash can into the kitchen sink and started sifting through the mess.

"Bingo," Lawrence exclaimed, as he removed an unopened bottle of Saint Bavo Witbier from the fridge.

"Hellllo," Manu swooned, as he removed five empty bottles of Saint Bavo from the sink and carefully checked the bottles for residual beer.

"It looks like we hit the jackpot in Redlands," Reenie stated enthusiastically. "Forensics, here we come. Lawrence, what forensics lab do you use up here?"

"We have our own," Lawrence answered, as he continued to inspect each bottle of beer. "We send everything to our own lab, and if they need extra help, they consult the state forensics lab or the F.B.I. lab."

"There's actually some beer and sediment left in three of these bottles," Manu interjected. "The caps are still here in the sink. So, I'll recap all five bottles, and you can add them to your collection."

"Sounds like a plan," Lawrence replied, as he appeared mesmerized by the contents of the unopened beer bottle. "I must confess, I've never given any thought to how easy it would be to slip poison into a bottle of cloudy beer, especially cloudy beer with a visible layer of sediment on the bottom of the bottle."

"But if you gave someone a six-pack of beer knowing you would be invited to sit down and have a bottle with them, you wouldn't be able to poison every bottle," Manu suggested. "And even if you poisoned only one of the bottles in the six-pack, you'd have to be able to make sure the other person got the poisoned bottle and you got a bottle without any poison. If the other person was the one serving the beer, you might not be able to control who got the poisoned bottle. It could turn into a game of Russian Roulette."

"Not if you gave the other person an unadulterated six-pack of beer, as well as a beer glass that was treated with poison ahead of time," Reenie argued, as she placed the beer glass on the kitchen table. "Look at the inside of this glass. The glass is etched and the thick bottom of the glass is opaque. There's also a shadow behind the colored crest. A glass constructed like this could be soaked in a clear solution that contained poison or a paste could be made from powdered poison and applied to certain areas inside the glass. Once the poison dried, no one would be able to detect it. That's why you have to also take this glass to the forensics lab."

"It looks like the glass has already been cleaned," Lawrence observed.

"Take it anyway," Reenie insisted.

For the next fifteen minutes, the three detectives discussed what each of them had to do to further their own investigations. Manu had to return to Saint Declan's Rectory to search for beer bottles and additional glasses, something he never thought of doing when he was only investigating Bobby Kucera's suicide and not the death of Father Kittrick.

Reenie had to thoroughly search the rectories where Fathers Iagi, Poser, and Elliot lived, and also interview Elliot's housekeeper. Similarly, Lawrence had to continue searching Saint Daniel's Rectory for other clues.

Concluding their meeting and exchanging business cards, Lawrence stayed behind to continue searching Saint Daniel's Rectory while the two other detectives left. As they walked to their cars, Manu and Reenie both wanted to say things they typically had difficulty saying to members of the opposite sex.

"So, what do you think about Dirty Larry?" Reenie eventually asked, ending an uncomfortable silence.

"Dirty Larry?" Manu repeated.

"Lawrence - the guy you just spent the past hour with," Reenie stated emphatically.

"Oh, Lawrence," Manu exclaimed.

"Yeah, Lawrence," Reenie reiterated with affected annoyance. "I call him Dirty Larry - Dirty Larry Hanrahan. He's the only detective I know who never musses his hair, wears the same outfit twice, or soils his hands at a crime scene."

"Dirty Larry," Manu chuckled. "Now, I get it."

"I'm glad," Reenie said with a smile. "For a minute, I thought I might have to draw you a map."

"You know, Reenie, I really like you," Manu proclaimed with a shy smile. "You're smart, professional, and even funny when you want to be."

"Thank you, I think," Reenie replied, overwhelmed by Manu's unexpected compliment.

"You're probably married, engaged, or otherwise spoken for," Manu suggested.

"Not really," Reenie responded. "How about you?"

"To be truthful, I've been engaged to three girls in Samoa and another three at San Diego State for a long time," Manu confessed. "The thing is, one of the three girls in Samoa joined the convent, and the other two left the islands and became professional wrestlers. As far as the three at San Diego State, two of the girls got tired of waiting for me and married each other, and the third ran away with the team's mascot and joined the circus. So, I guess you could say I'm still available theoretically."

"It must be nice being so popular," Reenie quipped.

"There's nothing wrong with being popular," Manu countered. "You never know when you might want to run for congress, dog catcher, or some other important public office."

"You got me there," Reenie conceded.

"You know, you're very easy to talk to," Manu observed. "I'd like to take you out to dinner sometime. I could come to L.A., you could come to San Diego, or we could just meet somewhere in the middle."

"Dinner?" Reenie questioned. "Well, yeah, sure. But why would you drive all the way to L.A. to have dinner with someone like me when you could have dinner with thousands of beautiful women who live closer to you in San Diego?"

"Why would I drive all the way to L.A. to have dinner with someone like you?" Manu repeated. "Because you're someone like you."

"Oh, my," Reenie thought to herself, resisting the temptation to verbalize the only words she could think of at the moment.

"So, I'll call you," Manu promised, as he leaned over and kissed Reenie on the cheek.

"Well, yeah, sure," Reenie sighed, as she watched him cross the street and get into his S.U.V.

"It was nice meeting you," Manu yelled from his vehicle, as he slowly drove away.

"Call me," Reenie shouted, as she waved at Manu until his S.U.V. was no longer in sight.

CHAPTER NINETEEN

As thoughts of citations, promotions, and interviews on television crime shows danced in their heads, the three detectives went searching for clues. While they did, Thielemans and Michelle drove into Florida.

During the next two weeks, Thielemans and Michelle would explore the Sunshine State from its panhandle to its keys, from its swamps to its beaches, and from its historical cities to its entertainment meccas. They would eat Conch Fritters and Cuban Sandwiches, boat through the Everglades and along the coastlines, and learn about Soaring at Walt Disney World and the Fountain of Youth in Saint Augustine.

Although they were busy exploring, vacationing, and falling deeper in love as they traveled through Florida, Thielemans still found time to lecture in the Miami area at Ave Maria University, Barry University, Saint John Vianney College Seminary, and Saint Thomas University, and in the Tampa area at Saint Leo University. He also managed to discuss his program and drink Saint Bavo Witbier with a dozen priests, including three suspected sexual predators.

The first alleged sex offender Thielemans met in Florida was Reverend Sean Citrocelli of Tampa. The 37-year-old was a parish priest and successful softball coach at a local parochial high school.

Because it was unusual for a senior starter on one of Citrocelli's softball teams not to graduate without a college athletic scholarship, many parents sent their daughters to Angels and Saints High School for no other reason than to play softball. Disregarding the formidable expense of attending the private school and considerable commuting time and distance to the school from many of Tampa's outlying areas, these parents spared no personal expense in giving their daughters the opportunity to win the coveted prize of a college softball scholarship.

Insofar as Angels and Saints High School attracted many of the best softball players in the Tampa area, Citrocelli usually had many players on the bench who were talented enough to be starters and play softball at the college level. Having so much available talent, Citrocelli was able to play any combination of players and still win high school championships on a regular basis.

Being a virile man who appreciated the curves of a teenage girl as much as the curves she could throw with a softball, Citrocelli welcomed the opportunity to show a curvaceous benchwarmer how she could break into the starting lineup. From past experience, he realized many benchwarmers knew what they had to do to become a starter, and a select few were actually willing to do it.

Following a few personal workouts with Coach Citrocelli in the training room of the high school gymnasium, a member of the select few would usually break into the starting lineup. When this happened, another talented player would return to the bench where she would immediately start pondering how long she would have to work at Burger King to afford college without an athletic scholarship.

Such a demotion would invariably force the new benchwarmer to consider meeting with Citrocelli to discuss how she could regain her starting position. Such activity would keep the priest's carousel in perpetual motion and allow him to develop an intimate relationship with several new players each season.

Citrocelli was so skilled at getting into the minds of his players that most of the young girls who accompanied him into the training room left with the distinct impression they were the ones who initiated sexual activity. The priest was smart enough to surround himself with loyal assistant coaches who swore by his lies and quickly squelched any rumors of his romantic involvement with players.

His assistant coaches invariably claimed they were with Citrocelli whenever he held special training sessions with a player. They also went out of their way to caution players about saying the kind of things that could ruin the fine reputation of a Catholic priest, as well as their own futures.

On a single occasion during Citrocelli's decade of coaching at Angels and Saints High School, an accusation of sexual impropriety was made by the parents of a graduating softball player who failed to receive a college scholarship. In response, the parents of many current and former softball players rushed to Citrocelli's defense.

From every corner of Florida, eminent doctors, lawyers, sports dignitaries, politicians, and Indian chefs vocalized their support for the man who won so many championships for Angels and Saints High School and helped so many of its students obtain college scholarships. The parental support for Citrocelli was so vigorous no one ever dared question the way he ran his softball program or controlled the lives of his players again.

Several days after having a cordial discussion and few beers with Citrocelli, Thielemans met with Reverend

Michael Bluholic in Miami. Cut from the same cloth as Citrocelli, the 34-year-old priest used his position as one of Florida's top junior high school basketball coaches to feed a rampant case of pedophilia.

A former Florida All-State basketball player, Bluholic took the advice of his parish priest and turned down basketball scholarships from major universities to attend a small Catholic college and prepare for the priesthood. From the day he started college to the day he was ordained, Bluholic deeply regretted his chosen path in life.

While in college, Bluholic easily outplayed the stars of the varsity basketball team in pickup games, but was expected to attend religious services or engage in charitable community projects while the college basketball team was playing its games. While in the seminary, Bluholic joined his fellow seminarians as they knelt in prayer, but was unable to meditate on anything but basketball.

In college, Bluholic never explored the opportunity to date young women, choosing to socialize with other future seminarians instead. In the seminary, he discovered how dangerous social awkwardness and sexual naiveté could be when he was unwittingly led into homosexual relationships by several older seminarians and one of his professors.

As a young priest assigned to an inner-city parish, Bluholic struggled with his identity and lingering questions about his true sexual orientation. When given the opportunity to return to the game of basketball as the coach of a parochial junior high school team, he thought his problems were over, but quickly discovered his problems were just beginning.

Bluholic inherited an unsuccessful junior high school basketball team, largely comprised of troubled teens from broken homes, unruly foster children, and displaced immigrants. The players were generally tall, strong, and athletic, but undisciplined and without parental support.

In short order, Bluholic won the respect and confidence of his players and constructed a winning team that quickly caught the attention of the varsity basketball programs throughout the entire Miami region. With time, Bluholic's personal endorsement was all one of his players needed to get accepted at a high school with a successful basketball program and experienced coach capable of obtaining college athletic scholarships for his players.

Coaching junior high school basketball brought out the best in Bluholic - and the worst. It allowed him to return to the game he loved but also forced him to deal with his inner demons.

From the very first weeks of his coaching career, Bluholic realized he was sexually aroused by the young, naked bodies he watched showering after basketball practices. It didn't take long for Bluholic to figure out ways to get an unsuspecting player alone in the shower room.

Telling a player to stay on the court after practice to work on his foul shots or run extra laps, Bluholic would wait for the other players to shower and leave the gym before returning to the court and instructing the lone remaining player to shower and go home. As the player was starting to shower, Bluholic would enter the shower room naked, and after some playful shower antics, turn the fun and games into sexual molestation.

Bluholic always told his sexual conquests they were good players who he could help get into a high school where they would be able to play varsity basketball and win a college athletic scholarship. He also told his victims priests were not allowed to marry which is why the Church allowed them to have sex with other males.

Realizing the potential consequences of his actions, Bluholic carefully chose young boys who came from unstable families with poor parental support, were highly motivated to play high school and college basketball, and could be reasonably expected to keep their mouths shut between showers with their new best friend. As an insurance policy, Bluholic hired an assistant coach who had a poor memory and firm recollection he was always the last one to shower and shut off the lights in the gym every night after practice.

At the end of the day, Bluholic felt comfortable trading basketball lessons for sexual gratification. He realized he was the closest thing to family most of his players had, and if anything went wrong, he knew no one was going to take the word of an incorrigible teenager over that of a respected clergyman and sports legend.

After Thielemans met with Bluholic, he and Michelle headed north to Kissimmee where they spent three nights at Disney's Polynesian Village Resort. Over a four-day period, they explored each of the Disney parks, SeaWorld, and several other smaller attractions in the area.

Thielemans didn't meet with any priests while he and Michelle vacationed in the Kissimmee area, but he started meeting priests again in the stretch between Orlando and Sanford. He met many interesting clergymen in that region but none more interesting than Father Fyodor Krasnov, a 39-year-old priest whose parish was in Sanford but whose real interests were in Daytona.

The Daytona area, including its famous beach, has long been one of the most popular tourist destinations in

America. Visited annually by millions of auto racing fans, bikers, college students on spring break, sun worshipers, and vacationers of all ages, the area has also attracted many vagrants.

Over the years, various entities established homeless shelters in the Daytona area to provide for the large vagrant population. Unfortunately, the multiple shelters have frequently been unable to keep up with demand and forced to turn away vagrants.

When Krasnov first became aware of the situation in Daytona, he inquired to see how he might be able to help. He was told shelters were always looking for volunteers to transport vagrants to, from, and between Daytona's various shelters.

Acquiring a commercial van, Krasnov began transporting vagrants between homeless shelters one night a week. Over several months, he became highly regarded as a reliable, personable, and considerate volunteer.

On many occasions, Father Krasnov would be asked to pick up a vagrant who called a shelter from an interstate rest area or highway gas station. Frequently, the vagrant who called the shelter would be a young woman who was hitchhiking alone.

Krasnov was frequently asked to drive to various locations to pick up a young woman who was in dire need of food and shelter. Favoring the conventional apparel, persona, and identity of a paramedic rather than priest, Krasnov would drive to his designated pick-up locations in a van that had been converted into a mini-camper, and equipped with a refrigerator, microwave, and mattress.

Young women instinctively trusted Krasnov when he promptly arrived at their location, politely introduced himself, and kindly apprised them of their destination. They were grateful when he told them fresh pizza and soft drinks awaited them inside the van.

Helping a young woman into the passenger seat of his van, Krasnov would quickly bring her two warm slices of pizza and a bottle of soda. Giving a hungry woman the chance to finish her first slice of pizza and have a few swallows of her beverage, Krasnov would make small talk before starting to drive to the appropriate shelter.

Within a few minutes, the potent drugs Krasnov added to the pizza and soda would take effect and the young woman would quickly fall into a deep sleep. Taking a few back roads to an isolated location, Krasnov would move the unconscious woman from the passenger seat to the mattress, remove her clothing, and have sex with her.

Krasnov always used a condom and powderless exam gloves, and was able to quickly complete a sex act in a way that made it difficult for the woman to realize she had been sexually violated while asleep. Redressing the woman and returning her to the passenger seat, Krasnov would proceed to the shelter as though nothing ever happened.

When he finally arrived at the shelter, Krasnov would gently coax the woman out of her slumber and cheerfully announce a warm bed was waiting for her inside. Typically feeling drowsy but unaware she had been raped by a priest, the woman would thank Krasnov for the ride, get out of the van, and proceed to claim her free night in the shelter.

While the young woman was still staggering through the shelter in search of her bed and forgetting how she got where she was, Krasnov would be driving back to his parish in Sanford, prepared to resume his life as a trusted and respected priest. As he drove away from the scene of the crime, he would relive the events of the preceding hour, and then, fantasize about his next sexual conquest.

After Thielemans finished meeting with Krasnov and other priests in Sanford, he and Michelle drove to Daytona Beach where they enjoyed dinner and a moonlight stroll before retiring for the night. The following day, Thielemans met with two priests before he and Michelle drove to Saint Augustine to visit the Fountain of Youth.

While Thielemans was meeting with priests in Saint Augustine, Michelle received a phone call, requesting her to return to the convent because of a pressing legal matter. The convent was being sued by a former nun, and Michelle's deposition was required to aid the convent in defense of the lawsuit.

Reviewing Thielemans' itinerary, Michelle realized he had lectures and meetings scheduled throughout Georgia and the Carolinas for an additional two weeks, followed by a one-month respite in Virginia and Maryland. When Michelle offered to return to the convent in two weeks and provide the necessary deposition, she was told the convent required her deposition immediately.

When Thielemans returned to the hotel following his meetings, Michelle informed him of her call from the convent. Having unexpected news of his own to share, Thielemans smiled and shook his head in disbelief.

"It looks like we're both in great demand," Thielemans joked. "I received a phone call from a San Diego detective this morning. He politely asked if I could meet with him in his office in the next few days. I asked him what he wanted to talk about, and he told me he was unable to discuss the matter over the phone. I told him I was in Florida and might not be able to get to San Diego for another week.

He was nice about things and scheduled a meeting a week from today. I may be wrong, but I think he probably wants to talk to me about my hit-and-run accident. Maybe they finally found the guys who were responsible."

"This whole thing is giving me a headache," Michelle complained. "So, what do we do now?"

"The first thing to do is postpone my lectures and meetings for the next two weeks," Thielemans replied. "The next thing to do is book a flight for you to Baltimore. You can fly out of Jacksonville which is just up the road. I'm sure you'll be able to find a flight that leaves tomorrow. I should probably fly from Jacksonville to San Diego, but they're talking about severe storms, possibly even a hurricane, hitting Florida and the Carolinas in the next week or two. I wouldn't want to leave my car parked here during a hurricane, and if I fly to San Diego, I'll have to take all my luggage on the flight and rent a car when I get there. So, I may be better off just driving cross-country from Jacksonville to San Diego. If I drive six-hundred miles a day, I should be able to get there in four days."

"Do you have any idea how long you'll be in San Diego?" Michelle asked.

"I don't," Thielemans answered. "However, the detective said something curious. He told me I should be prepared to stay in San Diego for a few weeks. The only thing I can figure out is I may be needed to testify in court against the guys who hit my car. I guess I'll just have to wait until I get to San Diego to see what this is all about."

"If that's the case, I should probably take all my luggage to Baltimore," Michelle suggested.

"That's probably a good idea," Thielemans agreed. "While you're at it, why don't you take the bag of rosary peas and accessories with you, and see if someone at the convent can make several rosaries for me. I'd like to have three or four to use as special Christmas gifts this year."

"No problem," Michelle replied. "I know a few of the older nuns who enjoy making rosaries."

"Make sure you warn them about the contents of the peas," Thielemans cautioned. "I wouldn't want to see anyone meet Saint Peter sooner than necessary."

"Will do," Michelle said.

"And while you're at it, take my spare iPad and iPhone with you, just in case you need them," Thielemans added.

"Good idea," Michelle responded. "There's some credit card information I have to get off the old iPad. I still haven't added my Mastercard information to your laptop. I'll put everything together and plan to update your laptop when we hook up again."

"Sounds like a plan," Thielemans replied.

The next morning, Thielemans and Michelle drove to Jacksonville. After he watched Michelle's plane take off for Baltimore, Thielemans drove his car to Interstate-10 and headed to San Diego.

As the casually-dressed priest was beginning his long trip west, Detective Manu Salopo was meeting with San Diego Police Chief Ronald Lipfert.

"So, where are we at with the Kucera case?" Lipfert, a thin, 55-year-old with straight brown hair asked, as the two sat down with cups of hot green tea.

"Quite a lot has happened since we last spoke, Chief," Manu began. "A few weeks ago, I attended a meeting with Detectives Reenie Behan of the L.A. Sheriff's Office and Lawrence Hanrahan of the Redlands P.D. They're both investigating the unexpected deaths of priests."

"So, you got to meet the famous Reenie Behan and the infamous Dirty Larry Hanrahan," Lipfert interrupted.

"Yes, I did," Salopo acknowledged.

"I hear Reenie's really something," the chief added.

"She is," the detective agreed, not mentioning he had already taken Reenie out on two dates and had sex with her four times. "At our meeting, we concluded the deaths of Father Kittrick in San Diego, three priests in L.A. County, and one priest in Redlands were suspicious because five apparently healthy priests died within days of each other. We also concluded the deaths could have been caused by poisoned glasses from which the priests drank beer."

"How did you come to that conclusion?" Lipfert inquired.

"Even though poisoning was not felt to be the cause of death in any of the five cases, the oral ingestion of a poison could have led to the secondary organ damage seen in each case and believed to be responsible for each death," Salopo stated. "What's more, an unopened bottle of Saint Bavo Witbier, five empty bottles, and a signature beer glass were found in the rectory of the deceased priest from Redlands. They were sent to the Redlands Forensics Lab where preliminary testing for poisons was negative. Also, two unopened bottles of Saint Bavo Witbier, four empty bottles, and an identical beer glass were found in one of the rectories in L.A. County. The glass and bottles were sent to the state forensics lab where preliminary testing for poisons was also negative."

"What did you find in the San Diego rectory?" Chief Lipfert asked.

"I found boxes of condoms and a bottle of Viagra in the cellar, but I was unable to find a beer glass or any unopened or empty beer bottles," Detective Salopo answered. "I did find a Saint Bavo Witbier glass in Margaret Murray's apartment. She was Father Kittrick's housekeeper at Saint Declan's. She admitted taking the beer glass from the rectory after Kittrick told her he didn't want it. She also alleged the beer glass and a six-pack of Saint Bavo Witbier were given to Kittrick by Reverend Paul Thielemans who visited Saint Declan's in late April. Thielemans is a renowned author who always brings a beer glass and six-pack of Saint Bavo Witbier to priests he visits. I found records of multiple calls to Thielemans on Kittrick's telephone. Many of the calls were made in the days immediately preceding Kittrick's death."

"Did Father Thielemans visit any of the other deceased priests?" the chief questioned.

"As a matter of fact, Thielemans' name was found in the appointment book of the Redlands priest, and his visit to one of the priests from L.A. County was confirmed by the priest's housekeeper," the detective responded. "I just spoke with Thielemans who is in Jacksonville, Florida at the moment. He agreed to drive back to San Diego for questioning."

"So, do you think Thielemans poisoned the five priests?" Lipfert inquired.

"Possibly," Salopo replied.

"What was his motive?" the chief asked.

"In addition to Kittrick, several of the other deceased priests were rumored to be pedophiles," the detective answered.

"So, what you're saying is a famous author – a priest no less, murdered five fellow priests because they were rumored to be pedophiles," Chief Lipfert stated succinctly.

"And what you're also saying is there is absolutely no proof any of the priests were poisoned or reason to suspect Thielemans is a serial killer."

"I see your point, Chief," Salopo conceded.

"So, what else do you have for me?" the chief requested, as he prepared to take a sip of hot tea.

"I tracked down Bobby Kucera's mother who is now living with her two daughters in a home outside Anaheim," the detective began. "I asked her why she moved from San Diego a few days after her son's funeral. She told me she was having a tough time paying her bills before Bobby died, and after the funeral, she spoke with Bishop Grannick who offered to help her financially because her son was an altar boy. The bishop arranged for her to move her family into a nicer home and get a better paying job at a large hotel near Disneyland. He also arranged for her two daughters to receive full-tuition scholarships to a parochial school close to their new home. Seemingly overnight, the bishop arranged for her old house to be bought by a new bank with the net proceeds to be used as the down-payment on her new house. Said house is a federally-subsidized unit with a long-term mortgage and low monthly mortgage payments. Because of the size of the down-payment, Mrs. Kucera won't have to start making mortgage payments until she's lived in the house for two years. As far as her new job, I was informed by the hotel manager that Mrs. Kucera was hired to fill an immediate opening in the hotel's hospitality department. She evidently carries out food for the hotel's free breakfast buffet, cleans the area after the buffet closes, and then, maintains the coffee machines, water dispensers, and snack baskets throughout the hotel for the rest of her shift. As far as her daughters' scholarships, I was told by the parochial school principal the scholarships were granted on the basis of financial need. So, on the surface, everything appears copacetic, but if you give me some more time, I'll get to the bottom of things. There's something going on here."

"Where are we at with Bishop Grannick?" Lipfert inquired. "Have you talked with him yet?"

"According to his staff, he's still on official business at the Vatican and no one knows when he will be returning to L.A.," Salopo revealed. "From what they told me, because he's a canon lawyer, he could be tied up in litigation, and no one knows how long the litigation will take. His secretary told me no one would expect a lawyer handling a case before the U.S. Supreme Court to leave the proceedings before they were completed. So, no one can expect a canon lawyer who is handling a case at the Vatican to leave Rome before his work is finished. I tried to get an estimated date when he would be returning to L.A., but his staff said they didn't have one."

"You may have to start calling the Vatican and trying to speak to him directly," the chief advised.

"Gotcha," the detective said.

"So, here's how I see things," Chief Lipfert began. "First of all, I'm not buying into this whole poisoning theory, at least not the part that pertains to Father Kittrick. You have absolutely no proof he was murdered and only conjecture as a motive. It's not a crime to give someone a beer glass or six-pack. So, we won't pursue the murder of Father Kittrick any further, but we will cooperate in anyone else's investigation of the deaths of local priests."

"Do you think there will be a statewide or federal investigation?" Salopo inquired.

"If Reenie pushes Hector Aguilar hard enough, he won't cave in and pursue a homicide case that has no proof murder was ever committed, but he may call in the F.B.I. just to keep Reenie quiet," the chief replied.

"How do you think she will react if the sheriff hands the case over to the F.B.I.?" the detective asked.

"I've never met the girl, but I understand Reenie is gung-ho and fond of chasing zebras," Lipfert responded. "I understand she's also a good cop who follows her intuition no matter what anyone else thinks. She's solved some nice cases in L.A. and Hector thinks the world of her, but that won't force him to pursue a case that doesn't exist. Reenie won't want to give up the case, but she's been around long enough to know the difference between the cards you hold and the ones you fold. At the end of the day, there's no one better at taking one look at a potential homicide case and seeing right through it than Joanne Faraday, who works out of the F.B.I.'s L.A. field office. Everyone in L.A. calls her, 'Jo Friday.' If push comes to shove with Reenie, Hector will give Jo Friday a call."

"Okay," Detective Salopo sighed. "So, if we won't be pursuing any murder case, where does that leave us?"

"Bring in the Murray woman and get a statement from her," the chief ordered. "Make sure she comments on Kittrick's pedophilia as a contributing factor to the Kucera kid's suicide, the relationship between Kittrick and Bishop Grannick, and Grannick's history of paying off the families of kids who were sexually abused by local priests. If you dig deep enough, you may find sufficient reason to initiate a racketeering investigation which will give the F.B.I. more reason to get involved. Also, bring in Father Thielemans and check under his fingernails. Just for kicks, try to assess his personal feelings about his pedophilic brethren. When you're taking a statement from him, make sure he includes his observations about Kittrick and Bobby Kucera. Finally, find Grannick and tell him we need to talk. Get this done, and we may be able to close the file on Kucera and open up a can of worms for our esteemed bishop."

"Gotcha, Chief," Salopo said, as he got up from his chair, retrieved his cold green tea, and left the room.

The next day, Reenie, who dramatically changed her appearance since meeting Detective Salopo, decided to pay Sheriff Aguilar a visit. Forewarned by her new boyfriend of the doubts their bosses had about their potential murder cases, Reenie walked into Aguilar's office loaded for bear.

The last time Aguilar met with Reenie, her pantsuit was haggard, tactical utility shoes cumbersome, and oversized eyeglasses distracting. Her auburn hair was mousey, skin pale, and overall appearance lackluster.

As the new Reenie Behan entered Aguilar's office, the sheriff's eyes bulged and his jaw dropped. From Reenie's vibrant auburn hair to her tan skin, from her white designer blouse and tight gray skirt to her sheer nylons and black high heels, and from the way her new contact lenses highlighted her big blue eyes to the way her new lipstick painted "kiss me" all over her lips, Reenie Behan had undergone an unexpected metamorphosis and suddenly become a beautiful, sensual, and desirable woman.

"If this is your way of telling me you want to start working undercover, the job is yours," Sheriff Aguilar joked, as he sat down and motioned for Reenie to do the same. "You look great. Why the sudden change?"

"Walmart had a sale," Reenie joked, not mentioning she had fallen in love since her last visit to Aguilar's office.

"So, tell me what you've been able to learn about the deaths of those three priests in the county," the sheriff requested, not mentioning he already spoke with Chief Lipfert over the phone and discussed the cases at length.

As Reenie shared most of the same information Detective Salopo had provided Chief Lipfert a day earlier, Sheriff Aguilar sat and patiently listened to every word she had to say.

"Nice work, Reenie," the sheriff said enthusiastically. "I really don't know what I'm going to do when some Hollywood talent scout takes you away from me and puts you in the movies. But before that happens, what do you want to do to prove your theory about the deaths of these priests?"

"I spoke to Detective Manu Salopo of the San Diego P.D. who informed me Father Thielemans will be returning to California sometime next week," Reenie replied. "He's currently driving to San Diego from Jacksonville. I'd like to bring him to L.A. for questioning. I also want to review his 2018 itinerary to see which priests he's previously met with in our county and throughout the rest of the state."

"Reenie, you realize, of course, Father Thielemans has not been charged with any crime in San Diego or here in Los Angeles County," Aguilar cautioned. "So, he doesn't have to answer any of your questions or any of the questions they plan to ask him in San Diego. He can hide behind the Fifth Amendment and walk out of here or San Diego anytime he pleases. I'm saying this because I want you to acknowledge you have no evidence of any wrongdoing in the deaths of those three priests. Any theories you have about their deaths are purely speculative.

So, I don't mind you having a sit-down with Father Thielemans as long as you completely understand I will not charge a man with a crime unless I have a lot more evidence than you currently have. I won't do it today, tomorrow, or ever."

"I understand, Sheriff," Reenie acknowledged with disappointment evident in her voice. "It's just that I have a gut feeling about this guy. Down deep, I have a feeling Thielemans is an ultraconservative Catholic who despises pedophiles and considers it his sacred duty to stop them from abusing children. I think he knows more about poisons than we do and uses beer or treated beer glasses to poison his victims."

"Point taken," the sheriff said. "However, Father Thielemans is also one of the most respected theologians in the entire world and not the kind of man you casually accuse of committing heinous crimes unless you have very good reason. So, tell me you understand I will not charge a man with a crime unless I have sufficient evidence that a crime was actually committed and the man who I am about to charge with the crime is the one who actually committed it."

"Point taken," Reenie repeated, as she got up and started walking out of the office. "Thanks, Sheriff."

"Thank you, Reenie," Aguilar replied, staring at the detective's tight backside and shapely legs as she walked away. "*Ay, Chihuahua.*"

Aguilar sat at his desk, lost in deep thought for several minutes, before he retrieved a phone number from his Rolodex. After staring at the number and giving the matter further thought, he finally picked up the phone and dialed the L.A. field office of the F.B.I.

"I'd like to speak to Special Agent, Joanne Faraday," he informed the operator. "Please tell her Sheriff Aguilar is calling."

CHAPTER TWENTY

Following his third day driving on Interstate-10, Thielemans decided to get some rest at a Holiday Inn near Tucson. After he checked in, one of the two clerks at the front desk told him she would show him to his room.

When Thielemans asked why he was being given such solicitous service, the clerk informed him the Tucson area had a serious problem with insects over the summer, and she wanted to quickly inspect his room to make sure he wouldn't be bothered by any insects during his stay.

"Many hotels run into problems with cockroaches every so often, and in this part of the country, hotels occasionally get moths inside their rooms," the clerk revealed. "But the summer of 2018 has been different. The Tucson area has been infested with bed bugs, mosquitos, and false chinch bugs. It's been like something out of the Bible. All we need now is a flood and a plague."

After the clerk checked his room and left, Thielemans thought about Kittrick's threat to send pestilence, floods, and a plague to the world if he went to hell. Reassuring himself Kittrick probably had nothing to do with Tucson's bug problem and was probably in hell anyway, Thielemans settled in for a few hours' sleep before continuing his journey.

The next morning, Thielemans got back on the road, left Interstate-10 west of Tucson, and picked up Interstate-8 which would take him into San Diego. As he drove, he had a difficult time keeping insects off his windshield.

Shortly after he crossed the Arizona state line and entered California, he came upon the California Border Protection Station. Seeing vehicles quickly entering and exiting the checkpoint after inspectors looked inside each vehicle to see if any fruits, plants, or other items that might harbor disease-transmitting insects or pests were being brought into California, Thielemans considered the temporary stop a mere formality.

As Thielemans moved to the head of the line, a state inspector approached his Cadillac, took a look inside the vehicle, and asked the requisite questions. Then, he asked to see Thielemans' driver's license, car registration, and an additional form of identification, such as a credit card.

After he ran a handheld scanner over Thielemans' cards, the inspector returned them to the priest and asked him to open the trunk of his car. Taking one look inside the trunk, the inspector closed it and asked Thielemans to drive his car to a special inspection area that was adjacent to the border station's administration building.

When Thielemans asked why he was being detained, the inspector told him the border station was required to make several complete vehicle inspections each day. The inspections were randomly selected by a computer.

Estimating the inspection time to be an hour, the inspector told Thielemans complete inspections could take longer if there were a lot of heavy items inside the car or trunk. The inspector reassured Thielemans he would do everything possible to quickly complete the inspection.

Hot, tired, and thirsty, Thielemans complied with the inspector's request and drove his car to the inspection area. When he arrived there and parked his car, the inspector instructed him to leave his keys in the ignition and go inside the air-conditioned administration building until the inspection of his car was finished.

As he was sitting down inside the small building, Thielemans could see his car being driven into a metal shed which was located two-hundred feet away. Seeing the shed's door being closed behind his car, Thielemans started feeling anxious.

All kinds of thoughts ran through Thielemans' mind as he kept his eyes fixed on the shed door. Feeling more anxious by the minute, he sat down in a corner of the empty waiting room and prayed the rosary.

Two hours later, Thielemans saw the shed door open. After his car was driven back to the administration building, the inspector entered the building, apologized for any inconvenience the inspection might have caused, and handed the priest his car keys.

Thielemans drove to San Diego with no further interruptions and checked into the Wyndham San Diego Bayside. As he unpacked his clothing, the location of certain items inside his luggage made him suspicious his bags had been opened and searched at the border station.

Bothered by this unsettling discovery, Thielemans realized there was nothing he could do about it. Trying to forget his entire border station experience, Thielemans continued unpacking before calling Detective Salopo to inform him he was in town.

Agreeing to have their previously scheduled meeting moved up to the following day, Thielemans showered and took a walk outside. Arriving at the Coronado Bridge, he sat down and prayed to and for Bobby Kucera.

The next morning, Thielemans, dressed in his finest priestly garb, reported to the headquarters of the San

Diego Police Department where he was taken into an interrogation room. After taking a seat and waiting several minutes, he was joined by a detective.

"Father Thielemans, I'm Detective Manu Salopo," his interrogator said, smiling and shaking the priest's hand. "Thank you for coming today. I'm sure you wondering why I asked you here."

"I hope it's to tell me you found the individuals responsible for the hit-and-run accident I had in April when I was in San Diego," Thielemans replied.

"To be honest with you, I wasn't aware of that event, but I can certainly check the status of the investigation if you'd like," the detective offered. "Actually, the reason I requested this meeting was to ask you a few questions about the time you spent last April at Saint Declan's Rectory. For the record, you have not been charged with any crime. Coming in today is completely voluntary on your part, and you are under no obligation to answer any questions. However, everything you say here today will be recorded and could be used in future legal proceedings."

"Detective, I was under the impression I was being asked to come here today to answer questions related to my hit-and-run accident in San Diego," the priest revealed. "I'll be happy to talk with you about my visit to Saint Declan's, but should I be saying anything to you without having a lawyer here to advise me?"

"Father, you have the right to have a lawyer here with you, and if you'd like to retain one before we speak, we can reschedule this meeting," Salopo confirmed. "However, as I previously stated, you are not being charged with any crime. If you were being formally charged with a crime, I would have to read you your Miranda rights before continuing. Your presence has been requested to answer questions that might help us in our investigation of the death of Robert Kucera."

"I see," Thielemans said. "If that's the case, I'll be happy to answer any questions I can. I don't think I need a lawyer to just tell you the truth."

"That's the spirit," the detective chuckled.

For the next two hours, Thielemans answered Salopo's questions about the time he spent at Saint Declan's Rectory with Father Kittrick, Bobby Kucera, and Mother Murray. When the detective started asking him questions about Mother, Thielemans immediately knew Salopo had not only located and interrogated the loquacious woman but probably learned a great deal more than he expected.

Realizing he was not only being recorded but probably watched as well, Thielemans tried to stay relaxed and put to use the interrogation skills he learned while studying criminal justice at Harvard. While he was learning how to beat a lie detector test in his criminal justice course, he also learned how to testify as a credible witness, a skill he put to good use while answering Salopo's questions.

Another skill he put to use during the interrogation was the ability to control his voice and breathing, a skill he carefully honed years earlier while taking professional speech classes. During those classes, he learned law enforcement agencies were beginning to use Computer Voice Stress Analysis (C.V.S.A.) as an alternative to polygraphs to help determine when someone was lying.

By interpreting microtremors in the voice, the software used in C.V.S.A. purportedly detects the kind of stress that occurs in the voice when someone is being deceptive. Although neither polygraphs nor C.V.S.A. are admissible in court, they are still used by law enforcement to monitor the credibility of statements made during interrogations.

Just as Thielemans learned how to control his breathing while singing, lecturing, or delivering a homily, he also learned how to breathe slowly and deeply between questions in an interview to decrease stress in his voice. Realizing C.V.S.A. was probably being used during his interrogation by Salopo, Thielemans tried to control his voice and breathing as inconspicuously as possible.

Among the more difficult questions Thielemans was asked were those concerning his understanding and tolerance of pedophilia in the priesthood, why he was not able to identify Kittrick as a pedophile when he first watched him interact with Bobby Kucera, and the reasons for Kittrick's repeated phone calls to Thielemans just prior to his death.

Among the questions he was asked for no apparent reason were those concerning his ritual of bringing beer and souvenir glasses to the priests he visited, the reason he visited so many priests, and how he planned his itinerary.

Because Salopo asked questions politely, joked about some of the answers, and conducted the interview more like a friendly conversation than a police interrogation, Thielemans felt at ease and was able to answer each of the questions to the detective's complete satisfaction. Because the priest answered each question spontaneously and wore his morality like a new suit of expensive clothes, Salopo felt he was honest, cooperative, and the last person on earth capable of poisoning anyone to death.

Following their meeting, Salopo thanked Thielemans for his help and told him to expect a call from Detective Reenie Behan of the L.A. Sheriff's Department later in the day. Salopo explained Detective Behan was involved in a related matter and wanted to speak to him while he was still in California.

Promising to call the priest about the status of his hit-and-run investigation, Salopo showed Thielemans to the door. As the clergyman left police headquarters, he got a strange feeling he would be spending more time with California investigators than he originally anticipated.

Several hours later, Thielemans received his call from Reenie who asked him to bring a copy of his 2018 California itinerary to a meeting she scheduled at the L.A. County Sheriff's Department the following afternoon. For the rest of the day, Thielemans walked around San Diego, thinking about Bobby Kucera and realizing how all the time he was spending in California was keeping him from his work.

That evening, Thielemans made his nightly call to Michelle and discovered she took a bus from Baltimore to Bethesda where she planned to stay with Fathers Prosky and Conyngham for several days. She reported her legal proceedings were finally over, but the entire ordeal took a lot out of her.

She also reported having a dull headache since the legal proceeding started, as well as the onset of several new neurological symptoms that began when she resumed taking the medications intended to control her manic-depressive illness. Because of her new symptoms, Prosky made an appointment for Michelle to see her psychiatrist who he felt would adjust her medications to eliminate the untoward side-effects.

When asked when she would be rejoining Thielemans, Michelle told the priest Hurricane Florence, which was causing widespread flooding and property destruction along the east coast, forced many airlines to cancel flights to and from the Carolinas, Virginia, and Maryland. Because of this, she wasn't sure when she would be able to get a flight from Baltimore to San Diego.

After Michelle reminded Thielemans about Kittrick's final words, the priest told her about the pestilence he recently experienced while driving through Arizona. Laughing about Thielemans' inability to keep insects off his windshield, the two joked about the kind of plague Kittrick was planning and when it would occur.

While Thielemans was talking with Michelle, Manu Salopo was telling Reenie about his recent interrogation.

"Reenie, I know how strongly you feel about your cases, but if any of the priests were poisoned, I don't think Father Thielemans did it," Manu stated unequivocally. "The man comes across as a highly moral, credible, and exemplary human being, and not some nefarious serial killer. My chief watched and listened to my entire interrogation from behind the glass this morning, and he wholeheartedly agreed. What's more, we used C.V.S.A. which confirmed Thielemans' credibility. I'm not saying Thielemans couldn't get shaken by the right kind of questioning, but I've got to tell you, the man seems to be in total control of everything he says and does, and by all measures, seems imperturbable."

"We'll see how imperturbable the Reverend Jame Gumb is tomorrow afternoon when I get my hooks into him," Reenie promised.

While telephone conversations were continuing across the nation and Southern California, Steve and Jo Faraday were beginning a quiet evening at home. Having just finished a dinner of third-generation leftovers, the couple sat on their living room couch, drinking hot tea and trading sections of the Los Angeles Times.

"I may be home late tomorrow," Jo revealed, as she spoke while trying to simultaneously read a newspaper crime story. "Hector Aguilar asked me to come to his office to observe an interrogation. You'll never guess who is being interrogated tomorrow afternoon."

"Keyser Soze," her disinterested husband quickly answered, as he continued reading a sports story.

"Steve, seriously," Jo exclaimed, as she continued reading. "You'll never guess who is being interrogated tomorrow afternoon."

"Would you like me to start naming every other person who may be getting interrogated tomorrow afternoon until I pick the right one?" Steve asked facetiously, as he continued reading. "I could do it alphabetically, by their date of birth, social security number, street address, astrological sign…"

"Do you remember the celebrity priest my father told us about on the cruise – the one who Dad had dinner with in that expensive suite on the Eurodam?" Jo inquired.

"Sure, I remember," Steve acknowledged, as he put his newspaper down and looked at his wife. "Your dad told us he had dinner with Father Paul Thielemans, the Belgian theologian. You can't be serious. What is the Sheriff's Department interrogating Father Thielemans for – making too much money from his book sales?"

"Would you believe, murder?" Jo asked.

"Who did he murder?" Steve exclaimed.

"The correct question is, who didn't he murder?" Jo responded.

"I think the sauerkraut you served with the leftover pork roast must have fermented and is starting to pickle your brain," the perturbed husband observed.

"Okay," Jo said, as she put down the paper and turned toward her husband. "Let me give you an update on that internet story you read while we were on the cruise – the one about priests dying in California. During a one-month trip through California, Thielemans visited fifty priests to promote some kind of new Church program. During each visit, he brought the priest a six-pack of beer and a souvenir glass. In the period of time Thielemans was in the state, fifteen California priests died. Of those fifteen, one middle-aged priest died in a motor vehicle accident, nine elderly priests died in nursing homes, and five healthy priests, between the ages of 37 and 49, died within three to five days of drinking beer with Thielemans. He hasn't been charged with anything, but he is being treated as a person of interest by the L.A. Sheriff's Department and interrogated tomorrow. Hector asked me to come in as a silent observer and referee the proceedings. It seems Reenie Behan is in charge of the investigation, and she already has Thielemans convicted, drawn, and quartered before the guy has even been read his Miranda rights."

"If he's suspected of murdering the priests, why hasn't Father Thielemans been charged yet?" Steve inquired.

"The priests who died were from San Diego, Redlands, El Segundo, Torrance, and Santa Clarita," Jo explained. "The last three towns fall under the jurisdiction of the L.A. Sheriff's Department. The death certificates of all five priests listed natural causes of death. So, Thielemans hasn't been charged with murder yet because murder has not been determined to be the cause of death in any of the cases. However, Reenie came up with the theory Thielemans poisoned each of the five priests because they were sex offenders. So, Hector is letting her run with the ball until her legs get tired. He wants me to referee the game because he's concerned Reenie may talk him into doing something that could lead to political suicide. Under other circumstances, I might have told Hector I was too busy to help him, but these cases actually intrigue me. There may be just enough meat on the bones of these cases to make them worthy of being pursued as homicides and Father Paul Thielemans pursued as one of the most dangerous serial killers the United States has ever seen."

"How is that even remotely possible?" Steve asked incredulously.

"Thielemans began his current tour in California, but since he left the state over two months ago, he has visited, Nevada, Arizona, New Mexico, Texas, Louisiana, Mississippi, Alabama, and Florida," Jo replied. "Hector and Reenie are only aware of what he may have done to three priests in their jurisdiction and an additional two priests in San Diego and Redlands. However, I know every place Thielemans has been for the past three months and every priest he has met. For obvious reasons, I haven't shared what I know with anyone."

"So, exactly what do you know?" Steve inquired.

"In the past three months, Thielemans had meetings with more than one-hundred priests, and to my knowledge, drank beer with each of them," Jo answered. "Of that number, sixteen have died of what were believed to be natural causes, and three are still alive but not expected to survive. In fact, the three remaining priests are all brain dead and waiting to be taken off life support."

"How did you find all this out?" Steve questioned.

"Hector called me last week, and after he explained his predicament, he asked for my help," Jo revealed. "He told me Thielemans was driving from Jacksonville to San Diego. So, I located Thielemans on I-10, using his car's built-in tracking system. After I calculated his daily mileage and estimated time of arrival at the California-Arizona border on I-8, I assigned an agent to the California Border Protection Station and had him pose as an inspector. When Thielemans arrived at the station, my agent told him his vehicle had been randomly selected to undergo a complete inspection. The agent also asked to see Thielemans' driver's license, car registration, and credit card – which the agent reviewed and scanned. Thielemans' car was driven into an inspection shed where swab samples were taken from inside his luggage. While my agent was taking the samples to be tested for different poisons, he downloaded information from Thielemans' laptop and iPad, and call history from his iPhone. After the agent took swab samples of the trunk and glove compartment, he began his most difficult task – testing the beer and beer glasses in Thielemans' trunk. Fortunately, the beer bottles were held in open six-pack containers which permitted their easy removal and return. Also, the beer bottles had twist-off caps which permitted a half-ounce of beer to be taken from each bottle and the bottle to be easily recapped. The beer samples taken from each bottle were added to a single container which was sent to our lab for analysis. There were only a few cases of glasses in the trunk. So, the agent had enough time to open each case, take a swab sample of each glass, and after returning the glasses to their cases, reseal the cases with a fast-drying adhesive."

"Did your agent have a search warrant," Steve asked.

"He didn't need one," Jo explained. "The F.B.I. can legally search a vehicle without a warrant as long as internal policies and minimization procedures are followed."

"What about probable cause?" Steve inquired.

"What if the F.B.I. received an anonymous tip about a Cadillac driving on I-8, carrying poison from state to state?" Jo hypothesized. "There's your probable cause."

"What about acquiring info from his laptop, iPad, iPhone, and credit card?" Steve questioned. "Don't tell me that's legal without a warrant."

"It's not," Jo conceded. "The F.B.I. hasn't been officially brought into this case. I'm just doing Hector a favor. For now, I'm in this by myself and just trying to catch a break. My agent was simply following orders. He owes me big time and doesn't ask questions. If I need to, I'll get warrants and legally search everything again at a later time. Until then, what nobody knows won't hurt them."

"You know, this could get you fired," Steve warned.

"Hey, I'm on a mission from God," Jo insisted.

"Whatever," Steve scowled. "Tell me more."

"So, the agent phoned me as soon as he got Thielemans' credit card information, and I immediately ran a transaction history," Jo continued. "I was able to determine that Thielemans travels, stays in hotels, and dines alone. This was confirmed by a review of his hotel records. He uses one credit card to pay all his bills, and all his transactions appear to business-related expenses."

"So, how did you learn about the priests dying in the other states?" Steve asked.

"When I got my hands on the information from Thielemans' laptop, I reviewed his 2018 itinerary," Jo explained. "Then, I used our data bank to find every Catholic priest who died in every state Thielemans visited since leaving California. After I determined the deceased priests Thielemans visited in each of the states, I contacted agents in the cities where the deceased priests lived and requested any available information on the priests, especially any suspicions of pedophilia, other forms of sexual abuse, or federal law violations. So far, I have gotten responses on two-thirds of the deceased priests. Significantly, the F.B.I. was aware of suspected pedophilia or other sexual abuse in one-half of the deceased priests but unable to substantiate any of the allegations. Additionally, an agent in New Mexico informed me about unsubstantiated rumors of one of the deceased priests being involved in human trafficking. So, the bottom line is Thielemans has visited more than one-hundred priests in three months, and of that number, sixteen priests who Thielemans visited have died and three more are about to die. More than one-half of the deceased priests Thielemans visited were suspected of engaging in pedophilic activity or other forms of sexual abuse, and it is not totally inconceivable that all of the deceased priests Thielemans visited were sex offenders who were able to escape detection or pay off the families of their victims. Herein lies Father Paul Thielemans' motive for murdering priests. In short, he wanted to rid the priesthood of sex offenders."

"You're not really buying into any of this, are you?" Steve inquired.

"Yes, I am," Jo admitted with a hint of arrogance. "Unless I'm proven wrong tomorrow, I plan to go after Father Thielemans and become the F.B.I. special agent who put the collar on one of America's most dangerous serial killers. It's hard to believe you and I have been struggling with the decision to move to Quantico and take the promotion I've been offered. After tomorrow, we may be able to forget all about the F.B.I., promotions, and moving to Quantico, and start thinking about book deals, movie consulting fees, and a new home in the hills."

"You're dreaming," Steve exclaimed.

"In a way, I probably am," Jo admitted.

"You're probably also dreaming of having sex with all those movie stars in Hollywood who have pretty faces and big dicks that still work," Steve said sarcastically.

As he got up from the couch and started walking away, Jo grabbed him by the arm.

"So, before you crawl back into your shell, tell me one thing," Jo requested. "How do you explain the deaths of all those priests Thielemans visited?"

"I don't know," Steve replied angrily. "Maybe it was a coincidence they met Thielemans and died in the same lifetime. Maybe it was natural causes that killed them all, and not poisoning by Thielemans or anyone else. You know what? Maybe they all died because God was watching and He got tired of them raping altar boys, and then, touching the host – the Body of Christ, with their filthy hands."

As Steve left the room, Jo followed him into the bedroom.

"Steve, I don't dream of having sex with movie stars," Jo insisted, as she threw her arms around her husband. "I only dream of making love to you."

"I wish I could show you how much I love you right now," the impotent husband revealed, as he embraced his wife. "Unfortunately, a priest took that away from me years ago. If you want my advice, I'd let Thielemans keep drinking beer with pedophilic priests until every last one of them was dead. Then, I'd send him a thank you card."

"Steve, don't give up on us," Jo whispered, as she tenderly kissed her husband on the cheek.

"I'll never give up on us," Steve replied, as he held Jo tighter. "Just don't give up on me. I'll keep searching for an answer, and maybe someday soon, I'll find one. When I do, I'll put a smile back on your face."

"I'll be here," Jo promised.

CHAPTER TWENTY-ONE

Early the next morning, Thielemans drove to Los Angeles. As he did, he began to understand what his predecessors must have felt like when they were invited to the Holy Inquisition.

When he arrived at the L.A. Sheriff's Department, Thielemans was immediately shown to an interrogation room. As he patiently sat in the room, fully aware many sets of eyes were watching him from behind the mirrored walls, he tried to relax and appear confident.

After waiting thirty minutes, his interrogator finally made her grand entrance. Dressed in a blue, pinstripe pantsuit, blue shirt with a pointed collar worn outside her suitcoat, and black high heels, Reenie walked confidently into the room.

"Father Thielemans, I'm Detective Behan," she said, as she shook his hand, more in a display of grip strength than friendship. "Thank you for coming today. Please understand you have not been charged with any crime, but have been asked to shed some light on a case currently under investigation by the Sheriff's Department. Did you bring your itinerary with you?"

"Yes, I did," Thielemans replied, as he handed a copy of his 2018 California itinerary to the detective.

As Reenie perused his itinerary, Sheriff Aguilar, Jo Faraday, and forensic psychologist, Dr. Vin Lee, carefully observed Thielemans as he calmly waited for his interrogation to begin.

"Are you ready to begin the interview?" Reenie asked.

"Yes, I am," Thielemans confidently replied.

"Very good," Reenie said. "The interview begins now:"

Detective Irene Behan: "Please state your name."

Reverend Paul Thielemans: "Paul Thielemans."

Behan: "And you're an Episcopalian minister. Is that correct?"

Thielemans: "No, that is not correct. I am a Roman Catholic priest."

Behan: "I see. So, Father Thielemans, what are your duties as a Roman Catholic priest?"

Thielemans: "I am currently on a special leave of absence from the Archdiocese of Mechelen-Brussels in Belgium. I conduct theological research and publish my findings in books which I publish and promote by lectures at Catholic venues in the United States, as well as private meetings. While I am conducting my research, I live in Alexandria, Virginia, and lecture at the Catholic University of America in Washington, D.C."

Behan: "Are you a citizen of Belgium?"

Thielemans: "I was born in the United States to Belgian parents. Therefore, I have dual citizenship. I was ordained in Belgium which explains my affiliation with the Mechelen-Brussels Archdiocese."

Behan: "You stated that you have private meetings. Are these meetings with Catholic priests?"

Thielemans: "Usually."

Behan: "Father, do you remember meeting with Reverend John Iagi, a Catholic priest who was stationed at Our Lady of the Sea Roman Catholic Church in El Segundo, California?"

Thielemans: "Yes, I do."

Behan: "And what was the purpose of your meeting with Reverend Iagi?"

Thielemans: "I met with Father Iagi to promote my latest book, *Catholicism Astray*, and to request his participation in a program that uses principles from my book to help restore membership in the Catholic Church."

Behan: "Father, did you bring a gift of any sort to Reverend Iagi when you visited him?"

Thielemans: "I brought Father Iagi a six-pack of Saint Bavo Witbier and a souvenir beer glass. This is the same gift I bring every priest I visit."

Behan: "Isn't beer a strange gift to bring to a Catholic priest?"

Thielemans: "Not at all. Priests enjoy beer as much as everyone else, and I am very proud of Saint Bavo Witbier because my father was the exporter who introduced the beer in the United States."

Behan: "Did you drink beer from the same six-pack with Reverend Iagi?"

Thielemans: "Yes, I did."

Behan: "Father, were you educated in the United States?"

Thielemans: "I attended several different elementary and secondary schools in the United States before going to Harvard University. Following my graduation from Harvard, I studied for the priesthood at the North American Pontifical College in Rome."

Behan: "What did you major in at Harvard?"

Thielemans: "International business and theology."

Behan: "While you were at Harvard, did you take many science courses?"

Thielemans: "Not really. I took an entry-level general science course but no advanced courses."

Behan: "What about in high school?"

Thielemans: "I took courses in general science, biology, chemistry, and physics in high school."

Behan: "Were you ever interested in any kind of science as a hobby?"

Thielemans: "Not really."

Behan: "Do you follow news reports about chemical warfare and bioterrorism?"

Thielemans: "Not as closely as I should."

Behan: "What are some of the chemical agents you've read about?"

Thielemans: "I've read a few articles about chemicals like mustard gas, arsenic, and sarin. I've also read articles about anthrax and how terrorists are supposed to be developing weapons containing deadly bacteria."

Behan: "Have you ever read about ricin?"

Thielemans: "I've heard the name but I don't know much about it."

Behan: "Father Thielemans, do you remember meeting with Reverend Ryan Poser, a Catholic priest who was stationed at Saint Conrad's Roman Catholic Church in Torrance, California?"

Thielemans: "Yes, I do."

Behan: "And what was the purpose of your meeting with Reverend Poser?"

Thielemans: "I met with Father Poser for the same reason I met with Father Iagi – to promote my book and solicit his participation in my program."

Behan: "Did you bring Reverend Poser beer and a beer glass when you visited him?"

Thielemans: "Yes, I did."

Behan: "And did you drink beer from the same six-pack with Reverend Poser?"

Thielemans: "Yes, I did."

Behan: "Father, were you ever in the military?"

Thielemans: "No, I wasn't."

Behan: "Are you a hunter or a marksman?"

Thielemans: "I went hunting with my father on several occasions as a boy, but I never killed anything. I don't own a gun or a rifle, and I don't fire weapons competitively."

Behan: "Have you spent a lot of time in Belgium?"

Thielemans: "Yes, I have."

Behan: "How about other countries?"

Thielemans: "I've traveled the entire world, but spent the most time in the United States, Belgium, and Italy."

Behan: "How many languages do you speak?"

Thielemans: "I speak English, Dutch, Italian, French, German, Polish, Russian, and Spanish."

Behan: "Did you ever visit the Belgian brewery where Saint Bavo Witbier is brewed?"

Thielemans: "Of course."

Behan: "Did you ever study the science of brewing?"

Thielemans: "No, I didn't"

Behan: "Weren't you interested in how beer was made?"

Thielemans: "I was very interested, but the science of brewing beer is very sophisticated, and not the kind of thing you can learn just by taking a few brewery tours."

Behan: "Father, do you remember meeting with Reverend Timothy Elliot, a Catholic priest who was stationed at Sacred Martyrs Roman Catholic Church in Santa Clarita, California?"

Thielemans: "Yes, I do."

Behan: "And what was the purpose of your meeting with Reverend Elliot?"

Thielemans: "I met with Father Elliot for the same reason I met with Father Iagi and Father Poser."

Behan: "Did you bring Reverend Elliot beer and a beer glass when you visited him?"

Thielemans: "Yes, I did."

Behan: "And did you drink beer from the same six-pack with Reverend Elliot?"

Thielemans: "Yes, I did."

Behan: "Father, was Reverend Iagi in good health when you met him in El Segundo?"

Thielemans: "To my knowledge, he was. I don't recall him complaining of any ailments during our visit."

Behan: "And were you aware Reverend Iagi died a few days after you visited him?"

Thielemans: "No, I wasn't…I'm sorry to hear that."

Behan: "Did you remain in contact with Reverend Iagi after your meeting?"

Thielemans: "No, I didn't."

Behan: "Was Reverend Poser in good health at the time of your visit?"

Thielemans: "As I remember, Father Poser appeared to be in good health and spirits."

Behan: "Were you aware Reverend Poser died a few days after you met with him?"

Thielemans: "No, I wasn't."

Behan: "How about Reverend Elliot? Did he appear to be well at the time of your visit?"

Thielemans: "He appeared to be in very good health. As I recall, he was a very robust individual."

Behan: "And were you aware he died a few days after you visited and drank beer with him?"

Thielemans: "No, I wasn't."

Behan: "Father Thielemans, are pedophilia and other sexual offenses perpetrated by Catholic priests a reality, or are they just media hype?"

Thielemans: "I'm afraid they're very real."

Behan: "Have you ever met any Catholic priests who were sex offenders?"

Thielemans: "I have met several priests who were pedophiles and others who raped young women. Only one of the priests ever admitted he was a sex offender."

Behan: "What was your opinion of that priest?"

Thielemans: "I despised him."

Behan: "Did he ever ask for help with his problem?"

Thielemans: "Not really."

Behan: "Father, what would you do if you were absolutely certain a priest was a pedophile?"

Thielemans: "If I thought my intervention would do any good, I'd advise the pedophile to leave the priesthood immediately and try to make restitution for his sins."

Behan: "What if you didn't think your intervention would help?"

Thielemans: "I'd arrange a private meeting with someone I was certain would immediately remove the pedophile from his priestly duties."

Behan: "Someone like a bishop?"

Thielemans: "In most cases that someone would be a bishop. In certain cases, however, if I wasn't sure a bishop would immediately act on the matter, I'd go over his head."

Behan: "And do you have that ability?"

Thielemans: "Fortunately, I do."

Behan: "Father, do you think most pedophiles can be rehabilitated and trusted to return to parish life?"

Thielemans: "No, I don't."

Behan: "Why not?"

Thielemans: "In my opinion, anyone who would sexually abuse a child is beyond redemption."

Behan: "Father, in all honesty, that's not the kind of response I'd expect from a Catholic priest."

Thielemans: "I've seen what pedophilia does to children and their families, and I have very little sympathy for pedophiles. I know you want me to be as truthful as possible here today, and I truthfully believe pedophiles are beyond redemption."

Behan: "How would you judge an angry father who murdered a pedophilic priest after he sexually abused one of the man's children?"

Thielemans: "Such a parent wouldn't be mine to judge. Let me just say I'd understand the feelings and emotions that would make a parent want to retaliate and kill someone who hurt one of their children, but I don't condone murder."

Behan: "Do you believe murder is a sin?"

Thielemans: "Of course."

Behan: "Do you believe murder is a sin that can be forgiven?"

Thielemans: "All sins can be forgiven."

Behan: "Even pedophilia?"

Thielemans: "Pedophilia could be forgiven if the pedophile was truly repentant, planned to amend his ways, and sin no more. Unfortunately, from what I've been seen and been told by at least one psychologist who has studied pedophilia for more than forty years, pedophiles seem to be consumed by their illness. They seem to be obsessed with sexually molesting children, and because of their obsession, repentance is the farthest thing from their minds. If they can't repent, their sins can't be forgiven."

Behan: "Father, have you ever had the urge to kill someone? You know, the urge to grab someone by the neck and strangle them to death?"

Thielemans: "No, I haven't."

Behan: "Never?"

Thielemans: "Never."

Behan: "Could you imagine any circumstance in which you could kill someone?"

Thielemans: "Possibly in self-defense, especially if the life of someone I loved was being threatened."

Behan: "Do you believe in the death penalty?"

Thielemans: "Not really. The death penalty has never been shown to be a deterrent to murder. I think a lifetime of solitary confinement would be a greater deterrent and would protect against executing an innocent person."

Behan: "Father Thielemans, as I previously mentioned, three different priests died just a few days after you visited them. Do you have any explanation for this?"

Thielemans: "This is the first I'm hearing about their deaths. I have no explanation because I don't know what illnesses took their lives. As I'm sure you know from your police work, death can occur unexpectedly, even in apparently healthy people, and priests do not have any kind of dispensation from unexpected death. I'm sure you also realize the timing of people's deaths can be coincidental."

Behan: "Were you aware Reverend Gordon Kittrick from San Diego also died just a few days after you visited him, as did Reverend Peter Pauley from Redlands?"

Thielemans: "I knew about Father Kittrick because I was on the phone with him when he died. As for Father Pauley, I didn't know he died, and I have no explanation for his death."

Behan: "Father Thielemans, what would you say if I told you all five of the deceased priests that I've mentioned today were suspected of being sex offenders?"

Thielemans: "I'd say we should postpone this discussion until you were able to prove they were sex offenders. Even then, I'm not sure what else I'd be able to tell you other than there are too many sex offenders in the Catholic Church."

Behan: "So, what's your solution to the problem?"

Thielemans: "The solution is to identify sex offenders in the priesthood as soon as possible and immediately relieve them of their priestly duties. That includes sex offenders in the seminary, in the parishes, and in the hierarchy of the Church. At the same time, the Church has to do a much better job screening candidates for the priesthood."

Behan: "Father Thielemans, that's all the questions I have for you today. Thank you for your cooperation. I'd ask you not to leave Southern California for the next few days while our department continues its investigation. I'll call you with a status report in a day or two. Thank you again. The interview is now over."

As soon as Thielemans left the room, Reenie met with Sheriff Aguilar, Jo Faraday, and Dr. Lee, a 65-year-old forensic psychologist whose erudite countenance, curious eyes, and prominent gray ponytail, eyebrows, and beard gave him the appearance of an astute mind reader.

"Nice job, Detective," Aguilar said.

"So, what do you think?" Reenie asked those who observed Thielemans' interrogation.

"The question is, what do you think?" Aguilar queried.

"Guilty as sin," Reenie replied. "There were a few times during the interrogation when I wanted to stop asking questions and just throw the cuffs on him."

"Dr. Lee, what do you think?" Aguilar inquired.

"The man appears rock solid," Lee observed. "The way he answered Reenie's questions – even the trick ones, his body language, and his self-control all supported high emotional intelligence. He answered your questions confidently, logically, and consistently. What's more, he was cooperative and didn't need a lawyer to hold his hand."

"What about his comments about pedophiles being beyond redemption?" Reenie questioned.

"As he told you during the interview, he was expected to tell the truth - which is exactly what he did," Lee emphasized. "He told you what he believed. He gave you his honest opinion. You may have been surprised to hear some of his answers, but that may be because of your preconceived notions rather than his beliefs."

"Didn't you get the feeling he was lying through his teeth?" Reenie insisted.

"If he was lying, which is a possibility, he's very good at it," Lee opined. "The results of C.V.S.A. and a closer look at his facial expressions and pupillary reactions on the video recording should give us a better idea."

"Jo, what do you think?" Aguilar asked.

"To be honest, I really don't know," Jo answered without providing any of the information she independently obtained on Thielemans. "I want to review the C.V.S.A., video recording, and hospital records of the priests, and then, talk with someone before I give you my opinion. That being said, I'd like everyone to remember there is no evidence any of the priests were murdered or Father Thielemans committed any crime. The priests died from the same conditions many other people die from every day of the week, and the fact they died within days of meeting Father Thielemans could be coincidental. The state forensics lab and the Redlands lab have not been able to detect any unusual substances in the evidence they were provided. So, the next step in searching for clues would be to exhume the bodies, and I don't have to tell you how disappointing the results might be. First of all, recovering poisons like ricin from corpses can be difficult, if not impossible. Secondly, exhuming the bodies of dead priests can be unpopular. Finally, not finding what you're looking for can have serious political consequences. So, give me a day to review everything, and then, we can sit down and talk some more."

For the rest of the workday and greatest part of the next, Jo closely reviewed Thielemans' C.V.S.A., carefully watched and rewatched the video of his interrogation, and painstakingly scrutinized the hospital records of the three deceased priests from Los Angeles County. She also reviewed the F.B.I. lab's negative toxicology reports on the samples that were taken from Thielemans' car and made a few phone calls to clear up some questions she had about his itinerary.

Phoning the event planner at Mount Saint Mary's University, she discovered Thielemans lectured at the university on multiple occasions over the years. She also learned his lectures were always scheduled by his sister who, during their last call, told the event planner she was returning to Belgium and would be working from home.

Jo also called three different priests who were visited by Thielemans. Each priest told her their meetings were scheduled over the phone by a woman whose name they couldn't remember and were enjoyable visits in which they drank beer and learned about Thielemans' program to restore Church membership.

During the calls, the university event planner and three priests all spoke very highly of Thielemans. They were also able to confirm he traveled and worked alone.

Before she left work for the day, Jo called the "someone" she told everyone at Thielemans' interrogation she wanted to talk with before she made up her mind about the case.

"Hi, Dad," she said enthusiastically over the phone.

"Why, Joanne, what a nice surprise," Father Frost replied warmly. "I was just thinking about you."

"Now, remember, Dad, it's a sin to tell a lie," Jo chuckled. "Hey, if you have a minute, I want to talk with you about something – well, actually, someone."

"There's nothing more important to me than hearing your sweet voice," Frost crooned. "How can I help you?"

"Dad, what was the name of that famous priest whose expensive suite on the Eurodam you showed me?" Jo asked, fully aware of the name.

"Father Paul Thielemans," Frost answered. "Why do you ask?"

"Someone at work mentioned his name, and I just wanted to check to make sure we were talking about the same guy," Jo claimed. "As I recall, you spoke very highly of him."

"I'm sure I did," Frost acknowledged. "I've never met a nicer person or a more impressive priest than Father Thielemans. We spoke at length on several occasions when he was on the ship, and I absolutely marveled at his knowledge of the Church and command of theology. I don't remember if I told you this during your cruise, but he identified me as a former Episcopalian minister who transferred to the Catholic Church in the first few minutes of our very first meeting. In our discussions, he was knowledgeable without being condescending, friendly without being phony, and more interested in hearing my opinions and beliefs than expecting me to listen to his. We talked morality at length, and I must confess he spoke from a moral high ground I have yet to visit."

"Didn't you tell me he talked you into having a beer with him in his suite?" Jo asked.

"Yes, he did," Frost laughed. "I've never been much of a drinker, but just to be social, I agreed to have one of his Saint Bavo beers when we had dinner in his suite. I enjoyed it so much, I drank a second bottle that night, and have since bought a six-pack and stashed it away in the refrigerator in my cabin. In fact, I have to pick up some more because I only have one bottle left."

"So, Thielemans turned you into a lush," Jo joked.

"I don't know if I've turned into a lush quite yet, but I have to tell you, I've enjoyed working at it," Frost revealed.

"Hey, doctors say a glass of beer or wine every so often is good for you," Jo suggested.

"I don't doubt it," Frost agreed. "You know, I didn't want to drink any beer that night in his suite, but the man was so friendly, generous, and charismatic, I just couldn't refuse to join him in drinking a few beers."

"The way you talk, it sounds like Father Thielemans is too good to be true," Jo implied.

"I'd say he's too good because he is true," Frost opined. "There's not a phony or insincere bone in his entire body. I know the old saying about things that sound too good to be true usually are, but Father Thielemans is the real deal. I only wish I'd met him much sooner in life and had many other opportunities to spend time with him, learn from him, and share his friendship."

"Wow," Jo exclaimed. "I don't think I've ever heard you speak so enthusiastically about another person. Do you think even Father Thielemans may have a darker side to him, just like all the rest of us do?"

"I suppose," Frost concurred. "However, if he does have a darker side, it's probably just as genuine as the side I saw. I'm sure he has his own flaws and shortcomings, but I have to honestly say he is the most complete human being I've ever met. Even as a priest, he is in total control of his life. I'm sure God put him on earth to improve the world."

"Double-Wow," Jo proclaimed. "Coming from you that's saying an awful lot. You know, Dad, we're sitting here praising a guy we hardly know, and his ears are probably ringing by now. Wouldn't it be funny if we picked up the newspaper tomorrow and found out the guy was a serial killer or something like that?"

"It wouldn't be funny," Frost laughed. "It would probably mean aliens transported us to a different planet where everything was the complete opposite of ours. You don't have to worry about ever reading anything negative about Father Paul Thielemans. He's a good man who is incapable of hurting other people. God must have used a special mold to create him. Trust me on this one."

"So, now that we've all but canonized Father Thielemans, what's new with you?" Jo inquired.

"Not much," Frost answered. "We're on the last legs of the Alaska run and will be heading south again in a few weeks. I've already been notified I won't be needed after the Eurodam is finished in Alaska. So, maybe I'll have the chance to visit you for several days before I head home. Charles has already asked me to return to Honolulu and Michael has asked me to visit him in Key West. So, I'll have to see if I feel more like eating pineapples or oranges before I decide who to visit next."

"So, come visit Steve and me before you go anywhere else," Jo proposed. "I'll get you all the pineapples and oranges you want."

"Sounds like a plan," Frost said warmly. "I love you, Sweetheart."

"I love you, Dad," Jo answered with tears in her eyes. "Let me know when we can expect you."

"God bless you," Frost prayed.

"He already has," Jo replied. "He gave me you for a father."

After she completed her call, Jo put her head down and cried. Drying her eyes, she looked at Steve's photo on her desk and started crying all over again.

CHAPTER TWENTY-TWO

The next morning, Jo called Aguilar and scheduled a meeting for that afternoon. Later in the day, as the sheriff and Reenie walked into her office and sat down, Jo took one last look at Steve's desk photo before proceeding with the difficult task at hand.

"So, here's the deal," Jo began, as she rolled up the sleeves of her cardigan sweater a few inches. "I've done nothing but think about this case since I left you, and I don't believe there is any evidence to support the theory Father Thielemans murdered three priests in L.A. County and two priests elsewhere in California because they were sex offenders. He indeed visited each of these priests several days before they died and gifted each of them a six-pack of beer and a souvenir glass from which they drank. But it's also true, during his one-month stay in California, he visited forty-five other priests and gifted them the same brand of beer and glass without any of the priests dying or becoming ill. I called three of the priests, and each one raved about Thielemans - and the beer."

Jo paused and adjusted her retro-style eyeglasses.

"As you well know, the state forensics lab and one in Redlands examined recovered glasses and bottles, both unopened and empty, and were unable to detect any toxins," she continued. What's more, teams of licensed and board-certified physicians ran toxicology screens on the deceased priests while they were still alive without discovering any toxins capable of causing death. These same teams of experienced physicians were able to confidently diagnose the causes of death in each priest."

Jo paused and readjusted her eyeglasses.

"Now, although it's true there were rumors about several of the priests being sex offenders, the lack of proof makes a theoretical hatred of pedophiles inconsequential as a motive," she suggested. "So, the fact five priests were visited by Thielemans just days before they died is certainly a curiosity. However, without evidence to prove the priests were sex offenders who were poisoned by Thielemans because he hated clergymen who committed sex crimes, the close proximity of their deaths can only be regarded as coincidental."

"But poisoning could have caused the organ damage that ultimately killed each of the priests," Reenie loudly objected. "The hospital records clearly stated blood was found in the gastrointestinal tracts of each patient, and primary disease in their gastrointestinal tracts from poisoning could have led to secondary damage to other organs which ultimately caused their deaths."

"You're absolutely right," Jo calmly agreed. "However, poison of any kind was not detected in any of the deceased priests, and blood in the gastrointestinal tract is not an uncommon finding in deceased patients. It's caused by stress ulceration which is how the gastrointestinal tract frequently reacts to serious illness elsewhere in the body."

As Reenie was about to turn the meeting into a debate, Aguilar put his hand on her arm to calm her. At the same time, Jo sensed the building tension and walked over to a table that supported a Keurig coffee machine.

"Can I get anyone a cup of coffee or tea?" Jo asked.

"I could go for a cup of coffee," Aguilar replied.

"Green tea for me, please," Reenie requested.

After Jo prepared two cups of green tea and one cup of coffee, she served the drinks and returned to her desk.

"So, without actual evidence to prove any or all of the priests were murdered by Thielemans, what we are left with is his interrogation," Jo stated. "As you will recall, Dr. Lee told us he thought Thielemans was mentally sound and his answers to Reenie's questions were logical and consistent. Of course, a lot more would have to be done to fully determine Thielemans' psychological profile, but I think it's safe to say, he doesn't come across as being out of touch with reality. As far as the results of his C.V.S.A., let me remind you the test is not admissible in court but it is the closest thing to a lie detector we currently have. That being said, the computerized analysis of Thielemans' voice was quite remarkable in that it failed to detect any kind of vocal microtremors that are typically seen when a person is trying to be deceptive. Even when Reenie tried to corner Thielemans or throw him off balance, there was nothing in his vocal analysis to suggest he was lying or trying to be evasive."

"The C.V.S.A. can be tricked by someone who understands what the test tries to measure and knows how to control their voice," Reenie protested. "There are special breathing exercises, called the Papworth Method, which a person can do to relax their voice. These exercises cause oxytocin to be released into the blood. Oxytocin relaxes the entire body."

"Oxytocin is also released into the bloodstream during labor," Jo commented. "It helps the mother bond with her new baby and aids in milk production. If you'll agree Thielemans wasn't going into labor at any time during the interrogation, I'll agree the C.V.S.A. can be beaten by someone who knows what the test measures and how to control their voice. By the way, did you detect Thielemans breathing by the Papworth Method during your interrogation?"

Instead of answering the question, Reenie just stared at the F.B.I. special agent and felt Aguilar's calming hand touch her arm again.

"I didn't think so," Jo said sarcastically. "Now, because the C.V.S.A. can be beaten, we also study the facial expressions and pupillary changes of the person being interrogated. Without getting into a lot of specifics, let me just say, after multiple reviews of the video recording, Thielemans' facial expressions and pupillary changes were appropriate throughout the entire interrogation, even during periods when Reenie surprised him with unexpected questions or comments. Significantly, they were appropriate when he was told five of the priests died shortly after he visited them. His responses suggested he was unaware the priests had died and truly surprised to learn of their deaths. So, by all accounts, Thielemans was truthful and appropriate during his interrogation."

"Interpreting facial expressions can be very subjective," Reenie opined.

"You're right again," Jo conceded. "But the eyes don't lie. A person can't will their pupils to dilate or constrict. So, in conclusion, I don't believe you have a case against Thielemans. First of all, you have no proof any or all of the priests were poisoned by him. Secondly, you have reasonable causes of death that were determined by competent physicians who found no signs of poisoning in any of the priests. And finally, Thielemans passed his interrogation with flying colors, and his C.V.S.A. and video recording analysis both strongly suggest he was telling the truth throughout the entire interrogation. What's more, your forensic psychologist felt Thielemans was credible, cooperative, and honest. So, my best advice is for you to either come up with some compelling evidence Thielemans poisoned the priests or file the case under 'C' for curious, confounding, and coincidental. I'd seriously advise you to let this one go. You've done some nice police work, brought up some important questions, and conducted a solid interrogation. Unfortunately, sixteen tons of hard work and good intentions don't count as much as a single ounce of evidence in a court of law. To take the next step legally, you'd have to formally charge Thielemans with the deaths of the priests. Unfortunately, you have no proof they were actually murdered or Thielemans killed them. So, I'd advise you to let him walk. You can always bring him back if you come up with some real evidence."

"Well, you heard the lady," Aguilar said, as got up from his chair, smiled, and shook Jo's hand. "Time to move on to another crime. Thank you, Jo."

"Call me if you come up with anything new," Jo replied, as she watched a satisfied sheriff and angry detective leave her office.

Sitting back down and picking up her cup of tea, Jo looked at Steve's photo and raised her cup as if to propose a toast to her husband.

"This one's for you," she thought to herself, as she took a long sip of tea.

Realizing eleven other priests who Thielemans visited consecutively in a direct path from Nevada to Florida were dead and three more were about to be taken off life

411

support, Jo realized Thielemans could be the serial killer Reenie insisted he was. She also realized she couldn't prove he was a mass murderer at the present time but might be able to in the future if he continued poisoning priests.

Having studied Thielemans' entire itinerary for 2018, something Aguilar and Reenie were unable to do, Jo knew the universities and priests Thielemans planned to visit for the rest of the year. She planned to keep a close eye on the deaths of priests in the states he was scheduled to visit in the coming months and quickly intercede if any of the priests listed on his itinerary started dying.

With a copy of his itinerary to guide her, Jo knew there were many ways she could trap Thielemans if he really was a serial killer. She also knew she would have to be at the top of her game to catch a criminal who was capable of murdering so many priests in so little time without leaving any incriminating evidence.

Jo realized the sheriff's office and San Diego P.D. had access to much of the information the F.B.I. did and would eventually become aware of the deaths of the priests Thielemans visited outside California. She also realized there were fewer deaths in the other states and longer periods of time between them which would most likely obviate any suspicion of foul play by law enforcement agencies in the other states.

Looking at Steve's photo again, Jo could understand why decent people were capable of hating priests who abused children and even wishing the priests were dead. Realizing how much the sexual abuse by just one priest was ruining the life of her husband and her marriage, Jo was content to patiently watch Thielemans until the time came when she couldn't afford to watch any longer.

As Aguilar and Reenie got into the sheriff's SUV, Aguilar gave his detective a tap on the arm.

"In one sentence, tell me what you're thinking," Aguilar said, as he watched Reenie pout.

"The F.B.I.'s not what it used to be," she replied.

As Aguilar drove away, Reenie phoned Thielemans and told him he was free to leave California, although he could be asked to return for further questioning. After he spoke with Reenie, Thielemans decided to call Michelle.

When Thielemans told Michelle that he was finished answering questions for the San Diego P.D. and L.A. Sheriff's Department and preparing to return to the east coast, Michelle asked him for a huge favor. She asked if he would be willing to cancel his lectures and meetings for a few additional weeks and take her on a dream vacation.

Not understanding the reason for her unusual request but feeling fatigued from the events of the past few weeks, Thielemans granted Michelle her wish and gave her permission to book the entire vacation. The more he thought about the specifics of the trip, the easier it was for him to understand why she came up with the idea.

As Michelle explained, cruise ships stopped visiting the Big Island of Hawaii after Kilauea unexpectedly erupted in May. With its Alaska season near completion, the Eurodam was preparing to return to Hawaii as part of an 18-day, roundtrip cruise from Seattle.

During its cruise, the Eurodam would be stopping at San Diego before proceeding to Nawiliwili (Kauai), Honolulu (Oahu), Lahaina (Maui), Hilo (Hawaii), and Ensenada, Mexico, and then, returning to San Diego and Seattle. Michelle saw a second cruise on the Eurodam as an opportunity to experience everything she missed on her first cruise while she was tending to the needs of Sister Regina and Fathers Ed Prosky and Bill Conyngham.

Thielemans wanted to get back to lecturing and meeting with priests throughout the Mid-Atlantic and New England states more than he wanted to go on another cruise, but he sensed urgency in Michelle's voice and knew he would be able to adjust his schedule and make up for lost time when they returned. Hearing Michelle enthusiastically talking about going on a cruise together as a couple helped Thielemans understand why this cruise was so important to her.

As Michelle enthusiastically explained her dream cruise, she talked about being able to dress up every night, have dinner in the ship's restaurants, and attend theater and lounge shows. She also talked about being able to visit the church in Kauai where Thielemans found his special rosary, all the beaches Thielemans visited the night he was stranded in Honolulu, and their favorite resort in Maui where they could leisurely dine, drink Asti Spumante, and make mad, passionate love.

The cruise was scheduled to leave Seattle on September 29th and stop at San Diego two days later. That gave Thielemans several days to prepare.

Michelle had already contacted a travel agent who told her the Pinnacle Suite was still available for the cruise and agreed to hold it for twenty-four hours until Michelle was able to confirm the reservation. Telling Thielemans that she would use his Visa card to pay for his cruise and her Mastercard to pay for hers, she also informed him she planned to fly to Seattle and board the Eurodam there.

At first, Thielemans didn't understand why Michelle would be flying to Seattle rather than San Diego, but she explained how she wanted to spend a day sightseeing in Seattle before beginning the cruise, and have a few days to herself on the Eurodam before being joined by the man of her dreams. Without trying to fully comprehend the mind of a woman in love, Thielemans agreed to board the Eurodam in San Diego and immediately go to the Pinnacle Suite where he would find Michelle waiting for him.

During the next few days, Thielemans went shopping for a tuxedo and took long walks through downtown San Diego. Most walks included a stop at the Coronado Bridge where Thielemans could still envision Bobby Kucera in angel wings, hovering over San Diego Bay.

While he walked, Thielemans frequently allowed his imagination to run wild. Wondering if Michelle wanted to go with him on another cruise because she wanted to get married or get pregnant were just a few of the ideas that ran through his head.

As Thielemans was wandering around San Diego and Michelle was flying to Seattle, Reenie was still bending Aguilar's ear about L.A. County's dead priests and what the Sheriff's Department could do to prove they were murdered. Trying to sell the idea of exhuming the body of just one priest in hopes of identifying the poison that killed him, Reenie got no satisfaction from a boss who was beginning to get tired of her persistence.

When Reenie finally realized she was getting on Aguilar's nerves, she started pitching her latest ideas to her boyfriend. In response, Detective Manu Salopo commiserated with his girlfriend as much as he could, but when he could no longer tolerate listening to her theories and proposals, he began using her as a sounding board for all the problems he was having at his own workplace.

In San Diego, Chief Lipfert was trying to close the case on Bobby Kucera but couldn't until Bishop Grannick was brought in for questioning. Despite repeated attempts at getting Grannick's office to tell him when the bishop would be returning to L.A., Salopo had no answer and Lipfert was getting tired of waiting for one.

When Salopo was unable to contact Grannick at the Vatican, Lipfert became impatient and contacted INTERPOL. Realizing the international police agency would now be looking for Grannick, Salopo decided to spend less time on crime and more time on Reenie.

Although Thielemans crossed Manu's mind occasionally and Reenie's frequently, the priest was constantly on the mind of Jo Faraday. Reviewing the priest's itinerary daily, she continued monitoring his activity and waiting for a new pattern of deaths to develop.

While Thielemans was thinking about returning to the Hawaiian Islands, a full spread of law enforcement officers continued thinking about him. A cruise was about to take him out of their sight, but until someone could start explaining why priests were unexpectedly dying, Thielemans would remain not so gentle on their minds.

On the night before Thielemans was scheduled to board the Eurodam, he received a phone call from Archbishop Palmieri's assistant, Monsignor Janulis. The monsignor called Thielemans to see if he was still interested in providing a status report on his program at the November meeting of the U.S. Conference of Catholic Bishops.

Reporting only five priests agreed to participate in his program to date, Thielemans advised Janulis he was not interested in speaking at the next conference. Accepting

Thielemans' decision with regret, Janulis proceeded to engage in some small talk.

Recalling Thielemans had asked him about Bishop Grannick at the last bishop's conference in Honolulu, Janulis inquired if Thielemans was able to eventually find him. Thielemans told the monsignor he had spoken to Grannick on the phone in August but didn't know where the bishop was at the present time.

Thielemans also informed Janulis the bishop's secretaries were telling callers Grannick was at the Vatican on Church business and his estimated return to L.A. was uncertain. Hearing this, the monsignor offered to make a call to the Vatican to see exactly where the bishop was and how long he might be expected to be there.

A few hours later, Janulis called Thielemans back to inform him he spoke with a Vatican official who had access to a list of everyone who was currently authorized to be working inside the Vatican. According to the official, Grannick left the Vatican several weeks ago.

Janulis also informed Thielemans he called a friend who worked at the Archdiocese of Los Angeles and was told Grannick was still listed as being at the Vatican with an uncertain estimated date of return. The friend also told Janulis several law enforcement officials were trying to get in touch with Grannick, but for unknown reasons, the bishop was not answering his cell phone.

After Thielemans spoke with Janulis, he reviewed the call history on his own cell phone and found the phone number Grannick called him from in August. Surmising the phone number was that of Grannick's cell phone, Thielemans briefly entertained the notion of calling the bishop before deciding not to make the call.

Writing down the phone number on a business card and placing the card inside his wallet, Thielemans remembered Michelle still wanted to make a surprise visit to the bishop. Realizing the visit would have to wait until Grannick decided to come out of hiding, Thielemans closed his wallet and walked over to the window of his oceanfront hotel room.

Looking across the street from the hotel, Thielemans could see the beautiful San Diego harbor by night and the empty berth where the Eurodam would be docking in a few hours. Feeling fortunate to be able to leave his car parked in the Wyndham's garage and walk across the street to the cruise terminal the next day, Thielemans felt even more fortunate to be sailing back to the Hawaiian Islands.

As Thielemans gazed at the dark ocean, he imagined Michelle sitting on the balcony of the Pinnacle Suite and waiting for San Diego to appear. As Michelle gazed at the sea from the balcony of the Pinnacle Suite, she imagined Thielemans waiting on the dock and preparing to hold her in his arms forever.

CHAPTER TWENTY-THREE

Boarding the Eurodam with much less difficulty than he experienced the first time he cruised to the Hawaiian Islands, Thielemans, dressed in casual attire, went directly to the Pinnacle Suite. Waiting for him in her silk pajamas and high heels was Michelle.

Setting the tone for the entire cruise in the first five minutes they were back together, Michelle pulled the man of her dreams into the bedroom and quickly reminded him of everything he had been missing since they parted company a month earlier.

Committed to giving Michelle a real dream vacation, Thielemans agreed to do everything she wanted to do on the cruise when she wanted to do it. From dress-up dinners in the ship's different restaurants to nights in the theaters, from pre-dinner serenades by the string trio to after-dinner music in the lounges, and from lazy days in each other's arms to busy days on each of the islands, Thielemans signed up for everything Michelle's heart desired.

From his very first moments on the ship, Thielemans began realizing many things had changed on the Eurodam since their last cruise. As he and Michelle would quickly discover, Father Frost and Winston were no longer on the ship, a different string trio was playing on the Lincoln Center Stage, and a different band was performing in the B.B. King Blues Club.

Thielemans and Michelle immediately found the different complexion of the Eurodam to their liking. No one on the ship knew Thielemans was a priest or Michelle was a nun, everyone smiled when they saw the handsome man and beautiful woman walking together, and the couple's Gala Night portrait seemed to capture the true happiness they were experiencing on the ship.

While the Eurodam was cruising to the Hawaiian Islands, Thielemans and Michelle spent a lot of their daytime hours leisurely exploring the ship and luxuriating in their suite. On each of the islands, they used every possible minute to make their visits memorable.

When they arrived in Kauai, Thielemans and Michelle took a complimentary shuttle to the car rental agency, picked up a blue Camaro convertible, and drove to the Hanapepe Lookout and Waimea Canyon State Park. After they spent ample time at both attractions, they drove to the small church where Thielemans found his special rosary.

Entering the vacant church, Michelle took Thielemans by the hand and walked with him to the altar. Standing there, she faced him and took hold of both his hands.

"I, Michelle, take you, Paul, as the man I will love for all eternity," she said with tears in her eyes.

"I, Paul, take you, Michelle, as the woman I will love for all eternity," he replied sincerely.

"You may kiss the one you will love for all eternity," Michelle announced with a smile.

Taking Michelle into his arms, Thielemans gave her the longest kiss ever recorded inside a Catholic Church. When he finally finished kissing her, he proudly walked with her, arm in arm, down the aisle.

As they were leaving the church, Michelle noticed five pairs of rosaries for sale on a small table in the room the church used for confessions. Informing Thielemans that she didn't have time to have rosaries made from the rosary peas she took back to Baltimore, Michelle asked him if he wanted to buy the church's rosaries.

Placing a $100 bill in the slotted, wooden lockbox that was used for donations, Thielemans removed the rosaries from the table. Turning around and taking one last look at the church's interior, Thielemans escorted Michelle back to the car and began their return trip to Nawiliwili where the Eurodam was preparing to sail to Honolulu.

As soon as the Eurodam arrived in port to begin its long day in Honolulu, Thielemans and Michelle took a cab to the airport car rental agency, rented a black Mercedes convertible, and made quick stops at Waikiki, Diamondhead, Maunalua Bay, and the beach parks at Wawamalu, Makapuu, Kaiona, and Waimanalo. Picking up a Hawaiian Pizza and bottle of Zinfandel from a local store, they proceeded to the Kailua Beach Park where they ate, drank, and stared at nearby Popoia Island.

From Kailua, they took a leisurely drive to the North Shore of Oahu where they picked up a container of takeout barbecue and six-pack of local microbrew before parking at a scenic overlook. Following their moonlight dinner, they returned their car to the rental agency and took a cab back to the Eurodam, arriving there just in time for the ship's overnight passage to Maui.

When the Eurodam arrived in Maui the next morning, Thielemans dressed in a burgundy golf shirt, khaki slacks, and brown boat shoes, and Michelle, dressed in the same white shirt, shorts, and baseball cap, strapped wedge sandals, and sunglasses she wore during her last trip to the island. After they took a tender to the pier in Lahaina, they called for a shuttle to take them to their resort.

Arriving at the resort, Michelle handled the room check-in while Thielemans went to the car rental office and picked up a red Corvette convertible. After Michelle dropped off a shopping bag in their room, she joined Thielemans for a tour of Maui.

Following lunch at a local fish shack, the two visited the Haleakala crater, and then, took a long walk along the beach. Before returning to the resort, they drove to another shore point and drank rum punch as they watched the sun begin to set over the ocean.

Arriving back at the resort, Thielemans drove Michelle back to their room before returning the Corvette to the rental agency. Michelle showered, dressed in the same floor-length, floral-patterned dress she bought on her first trip to Lahaina, and put a plumeria over her left ear.

After she draped a Hawaiian shirt over a bedroom chair, Michelle returned to the living room. As Thielemans entered the room, he stared at his beautiful companion the same way did the first time he saw her wearing her flattering dress and plumeria.

Thielemans left the room to shower, and while he was gone, a Hawaiian waitress delivered dinner and two bottles of Asti Spumante. Placing several covered dishes on the dinner table and both bottles of Asti into a large, ice-filled punch bowl, the young waitress smiled at Michelle, nodded her approval, and quietly left the room.

As Michelle started rearranging the various dishes on the dinner table, Thielemans returned, wearing the Hawaiian shirt Michelle gave him the last time they visited the resort. While Thielemans started wondering if he was experiencing *deja vu*, Michelle approached him and handed him a long-stem, pink lokelani.

Following a scrumptious seafood dinner, topped off by pineapple cheesecake and Kona coffee, Michelle filled their champagne glasses with Asti Spumante, handed one to Thielemans, and led him by the hand into the bedroom. Making love to Thielemans with greater passion than she had ever done before, Michelle pledged her eternal love and listened to Thielemans pledging his.

After they showered together and finished the last of the Asti Spumante, Thielemans and Michelle took a cab to the pier, caught the last tender, and returned to the Eurodam just as it was about to sail to the Big Island of Hawaii. Before they retired for the night, Michelle told Thielemans she planned to wear her religious habit when they visited Hilo and asked Thielemans if he would dress in his priestly attire.

The next morning, Thielemans and Michelle had breakfast in their suite before preparing to go ashore. As Thielemans stepped out on to his balcony to take a look at Hilo and finish his coffee, Michelle removed two suitcases from the hall closet and placed them by the door.

When Thielemans asked Michelle about the suitcases, she told him she brought clothes to donate to the people of Hawaii who were displaced by the Kilauea eruption. She went on to say more than four-hundred people died during the eruption and more than six-hundred houses were destroyed by the lava flow.

Hearing the statistics, Thielemans immediately asked where he could donate money for the relief effort. When Michelle asked him how he could be so generous, Thielemans laughed and reminded her of all the money he had earning interest in banks and brokerage houses all over the world.

Taking a shuttle to the car rental agency, the two picked up the black Chevy Suburban Michelle previously reserved. When Thielemans asked Michelle where she wanted to go, she asked him to drive to the Paauilo Cemetery where her Aunt Regina was buried.

Driving to the outskirts of Hilo, the couple arrived at the cemetery and parked near Sister Regina's grave. After she knelt and prayed at the gravesite, Michelle got back on her feet and asked Thielemans to accompany her to a nearby bench.

As they walked toward the bench, the uncommon serenity made them realize they were the only two visitors in the small cemetery. Arriving at the bench, Michelle paused for a moment to look at the beautiful surroundings and loudly sighed before sitting down with Thielemans.

Taking Thielemans' hands in hers, Michelle stared into his deep eyes. Kissing his hands, she started to cry.

"Paul, there are things I have to tell you," she said, as she wiped the tears from her eyes and tried to compose herself. "This won't be easy. So, please bear with me."

Reaching for his hands again, Michelle tried to smile.

"I have a brain tumor," she revealed with a quivering voice. "It's cancer, and it's inoperable. They call it a glioblastoma, and it's the worst kind of cancer imaginable. While I was in Baltimore, I went to visit Ed and Bill in Bethesda. I mentioned to Ed I was having dull headaches, and he made an appointment for me to see my psychiatrist. When I told the psychiatrist that I was also starting to see colored halos around certain objects and smell things that weren't there, he sent me for an M.R.I. When the M.R.I. showed the tumor, the psychiatrist sent me to see a neurosurgeon at Johns Hopkins. It didn't take long for the neurosurgeon to determine the tumor was an inoperable glioblastoma. He told me chemotherapy and radiation wouldn't cure the tumor but might slow down its progression. He gave me some literature to read and told me to contact him if I wanted to proceed with any treatment. When I asked him what he would do if he had a tumor in the same location, he just stared at me, and without answering my question, told me how fortunate people were that had faith in God and believed in an afterlife."

Looking at Thielemans, Michelle saw a level of fear in his eyes she had never previously seen.

"Did the neurosurgeon tell you how much time you have left?" Thielemans asked with a tremulous voice.

"He told me, he could tell my tumor had been there a while because of its size on the M.R.I.," Michelle answered. "Then, he reluctantly told me my life expectancy could be anywhere from six weeks to three months without treatment. That was a few weeks ago. So, it looks like it won't be long before I'm living on borrowed time."

"Why won't you consider chemotherapy or radiation?" Thielemans inquired expectantly.

"I knew a young nun in the convent who had the same kind of inoperable tumor," Michelle replied. "She did everything the doctors recommended – chemo, radiation, everything. To be honest, I wouldn't want to die like she did. I'm sure treatment might help some people, but I don't think it would help me. Fortunately, I don't feel too bad right now. I've found the headaches are manageable as long as I stay on my manic-depressive medications. As far as the halos and phantom smells, I've gotten used to them, and they haven't gotten any worse. Since I was still feeling pretty good, I contacted Aunt Regina's friend, Nellie Opunui, and discussed my situation. She invited me to come here and live with her. She offered to take care of me while I was still alive and after I was gone. She owns the entire row of cemetery plots next to Regina's, and she told me I could be buried right next to my aunt. She also remembered how kind you were to everyone here when Regina died, and she asked me to offer you the plot next to mine, as long as you agreed not to claim it anytime soon. So, if you look over there, next to Regina's grave, that's where you'll be able to find me in the not-too-distant future. And you know what? Knowing you may decide to be buried next to me in another hundred years makes the whole ordeal slightly more tolerable."

"Listen, this is crazy," Thielemans argued. "I'll stay here and take care of you. I'll go back to the ship right now, get my things, and be back before you know it. If you'd rather go somewhere else, I'll take you anywhere in the world and never leave your side."

"I knew you'd say something like that," Michelle said with a smile. "Unfortunately, I don't want you to remember me the way I'll look on my death bed. You still have your whole life ahead. I want you to remember me exactly the way I was at the top of Haleakala, on the beach, and at the resort in Maui. I plan to be buried in the dress I wore last night, and that's the way I want you to remember me – plumeria and all."

Thielemans reached for Michelle, embraced her, and started crying.

"Hey, Rock Star, no tears," Michelle whispered. "Let's not forget who's the one dying here."

"I love you so much," Thielemans cried.

"I love you, too," Michelle replied, as she kissed the distraught priest on the cheek. "My life began the moment you came to our table that first night on the ship. Before then, I had no idea how wonderful life could be."

Thielemans pulled away from Michelle and gently grabbed her arms with his hands.

"Listen to me carefully," Thielemans insisted. "If you won't let me stay with you, at least let me make sure you'll be comfortable. Keep the Visa card and Mastercard, and use them for anything you or Nellie might need. Also, keep your iPhone and call me whenever you can. If, at any time, you want to get out of here, just call. I'll fly right back and take you anywhere you want to go. Understand?"

"Paul, you're the most generous man God ever created," Michelle suggested. "When you die a hundred years from now, I'll be waiting in heaven and be the one to introduce you to God. When I introduce you, I'll remind God you were His finest work."

"I don't know about that," Thielemans replied.

"But I do, Darling," Michelle argued. "Now, there's still a lot I have to say, and Nellie will be coming here to pick me up in a half-hour. So, we don't have a lot of time left. But before we move on to more important things, I want you to know I left you a present in the hall closet. Make sure to open it as soon as you get back on the ship. Also, there's one more favor I need to ask of you. I want you to hear my confession."

Without waiting for a reply, Michelle knelt in front of Thielemans. Without objection, the priest reached for the stole in his coat pocket and put it around his neck.

"Bless me, Father, for I have sinned," the penitent nun began. "It has been five months since my last confession, and I have committed the following sins: I received Holy Communion when I wasn't in a state of grace. I was short-tempered with my dying aunt when I should have been more understanding. I lied and used vulgar and insulting language. I strayed from the life of poverty, chastity, and obedience I vowed to follow as a nun. I missed Mass. I loved a man with all my heart and freely gave myself to him sexually. Even though I do not believe I committed any sin by doing so, I forced him to break his own vow of priestly celibacy, and for this, I am sorry."

Michelle paused and dried the tears in her eyes.

"Father, confessing this next sin will be difficult for me," she continued with a broken voice. "You see, I murdered nineteen priests because they were sex offenders who continually injured innocent children and helpless adults. I was worried they would continue their evil ways if they weren't stopped. In killing them, I was sacrilegious because I extracted the poisonous pulp from seeds that are used to make rosaries. I used the pulp to create a paste that I applied to the insides of beer glasses I knew would be used by the priests I wanted to kill. While I was poisoning the priests, I continued developing a list of other priests who were sex offenders, and I eagerly awaited the opportunity to kill them as quickly as I could. I must also confess I have been unable to forgive the bishop who kidnapped and sexually abused me. I intended to kill him before I learned I was dying of cancer. Although I know thou shalt not kill, I am still obsessed with the idea of killing Bishop Joseph Grannick and would do so if I had the chance. For this, I am sorry."

Michelle paused again, dried her tears, and took a deep breath.

"Finally, Father, through my actions, I betrayed the person I love the most," she concluded. "I used you to deliver poison to the priests without telling you what I was doing. I also talked with you on the phone each night and listened to your stories about being interrogated by the police. Realizing they suspected you of being the one who killed the priests, I should have told you I was the real murderer and offered to take your place in front of the interrogators. I didn't because I was frightened, and for this, I am sorry. Saying I'm sorry seems inadequate after all the wrong I've done, but for these and all the sins I do not remember, I am truly sorry and ask you, Father, for penance and absolution."

As Michelle bowed her head, Thielemans looked at her in disbelief. Taking a minute to gather his thoughts, he finally reached down and put his hands on her head.

"There is no sin that cannot be forgiven if a sinner is truly repentant," Thielemans reminded Michelle. "So, for your penance, I want you to say a prayer for me each night and pray that God helps me deal with the many obstacles I still have to face in my lifetime. Now, make a good Act of Contrition."

As Michelle recited the Act of Contrition out loud, Thielemans quietly said a different prayer. When she finished, she raised her head and looked into her confessor's eyes.

In response, Thielemans caressed her face with his hands, smiled and prayed: "God the Father of mercies, through the death and resurrection of His Son, has reconciled the world to Himself and sent the Holy Spirit among us for the forgiveness of sins. Through the ministry of the Church, may God give you pardon and peace, and I absolve you from your sins in the name of the Father, and of the Son, and of the Holy Spirit, Amen."

"Thank you, Father," Michelle whispered, as she made the Sign of the Cross and got back on her feet. "Thank you for everything."

As the two held each other's hands and looked into each other's eyes, they could hear a vehicle starting to climb the hill that led to the cemetery.

"That must be Nellie coming up the road," Michelle surmised. "So, I guess this is so long - for now."

"Call me when you want me to come back for you," Thielemans answered with a forced smile. "I give you three days here before you're begging me to come back and rescue you."

"You've already rescued me," Michelle tenderly replied.

"I was just returning the favor," Thielemans said, as he took Michelle into his arms and passionately kissed her.

Hearing the vehicle getting closer, Thielemans slowly moved away from Michelle.

"I'll love you, forever, and ever, and always," Thielemans promised.

"You'd better," Michelle replied, as she dried her tears.

When the Ford Explorer that was carrying Nellie and her entourage pulled up next to Thielemans's S.U.V. and a group of nuns exited the vehicle, Thielemans and Michelle looked into each other's eyes and got up from the bench.

"I love you," Thielemans whispered, as he stepped away from Michelle.

"I love you," Michelle replied.

After she finally got out of the S.U.V., Nellie slowly walked up to Thielemans with a big smile on her face, and as the two renewed their acquaintance, the other nuns quickly transferred Michelle's suitcases from Thielemans's Suburban to their Explorer. Seeing the nuns flocking around their new sister and realizing he and Michelle had been effectively separated by the reality of the situation, Thielemans waved to Michelle and made the "call me" sign with his left hand.

Preparing to get into his S.U.V. and leave, Thielemans made eye contact with Michelle who pointed to her right eye, and then, made the letters, O and U, with her arms, while whispering, "I owe you."

Realizing there must have been a reason God gave elderly nuns cataracts and glaucoma, Thielemans ran toward Michelle and watched as the beautiful nun ran toward him. Seemingly unaware of the curious nuns who were closely watching, Thielemans and Michelle embraced and kissed as no priest and nun had ever done on a hillside in Hawaii or anywhere else in the wide, wide world of Catholicism.

With a final look into each other's eyes, a final squeeze of the hands, and a final momentary pause, Thielemans and Michelle separated without saying a word. As Michelle returned to the group of confused and speechless nuns, Thielemans got into his Suburban and quickly drove away without looking back.

At the beginning of the day, Thielemans planned to drive around Hawaii with Michelle to see how the volcanic eruption changed the Big Island's landscape. As he drove back to Hilo without Michelle, the thought of seeing Kilauea's destruction never occurred to him.

Arriving at the ship well in advance of its departure from the Hawaiian Islands and return voyage home,

Thielemans turned and took a final look at the hills on the outskirts of Hilo. Saying a silent prayer for Michelle, he boarded the Eurodam, truly anticipating a lonely evening, cruise, and lifetime.

CHAPTER TWENTY-FOUR

Going directly to his suite, Thielemans filled a glass with ice cubes and Old Grand-Dad 100-proof bourbon before sitting down on the balcony. Putting his feet up on a second chair, he sipped bourbon, stared at Hilo, and patiently waited for his body to start feeling as numb as his mind.

For the first time in his life, Thielemans was afraid to think because of all the pain the process might cause. Instead of thinking, he drank, merged with the surreal, and felt the anesthetic effects of bourbon starting to spread through his body.

Drifting off into a deep sleep, he dreamed of soaring through the heavens in search of Michelle. Unable to find her, he continued searching until his sleep was disrupted by the prolonged blaring of the ship's horn.

Violently exiting from sleep, Thielemans struggled to determine where he was. Eventually realizing he was on the balcony of his suite on the Eurodam, he watched as the ship pulled away from the Hilo pier and began the homeward leg of its cruise.

Feeling like someone who had been shot at and missed, Thielemans made a cup of coffee, completely undressed, and got into the hot tub on his balcony. As he watched the Big Island of Hawaii vanish from sight, he tried remembering what it felt like holding Michelle in his arms.

Making the mistake of allowing a first question to enter his mind, Thielemans quickly found himself deluged with questions that had no answers. Unable to definitively solve any of the riddles Michelle left behind, the frustrated priest resorted to the art of rationalization and quickly realized even his most cogent rationalizations failed to give him better insight into Michelle's mind.

As night began to fall on the Pacific Ocean, Thielemans started feeling chilly. Getting out of the hot tub, he showered and changed into casual attire.

Remembering Michelle told him she left a present in the hall closet, Thielemans retrieved a gift-wrapped box and carried it into the living room. Removing the bow and wrapping paper, he opened the box and discovered an envelope, a small vile of Rosary Peas, a cellophane-sealed Saint Bavo Witbier glass, and a large folder that contained their Gala Night portrait, a wallet-size photo of Michelle as a novice, and the spare Visa card he loaned Michelle.

Opening the envelope, Thielemans removed the enclosed letter and read:

"P,

"I wanted to leave you something to remember me by, although I couldn't blame you if you were already trying to forget me. I realize I caused you problems by many of the things I did, and for this, I am truly sorry.

"Unfortunately, it is what it is, and there are reasons for everything I did. I truly believe, like my namesake, Michael the Archangel, I was created to wage war against the forces of evil and protect those who couldn't protect themselves.

"I believe I was especially created to fight the sexual predators who wear the clothing of a priest for no other reason than to lure their unsuspecting victims. Everyone is put on this earth for a reason, and I truly believe my reason was to rid the world of those who would come in the name of God but do the work of the devil.

"Please be careful with the beer glass you see in front of you. It has been covered with protective cellophane wrap, but it is a loaded weapon.

"This was the last beer glass I treated with the poisonous core of the Rosary Pea. This was the glass I reserved for Bishop Joseph Grannick, the man who kidnapped and forced the young novice in the enclosed photo to be his sex slave.

"If you look very carefully at the opaque bottom on the inside of the glass, you won't be able to detect the thin layer of paste I applied there. The paste is virtually invisible but highly poisonous.

"The paste contains the poison, abrin. When a cloudy beer like Saint Bavo Witbier is added to the glass, the paste immediately dissolves and is undetectable.

"Part of the penance for my sins is the realization my impending death will not allow me to poison Bishop Grannick and later hear he died a slow, gruesome death. Fortunately, my efforts were not totally wasted.

"I would like you to keep this letter, sealed beer glass, and vile of Rosary Peas as proof I, Michelle Erzengel, was the one who murdered nineteen priests in the year 2018. I would also like anyone who reads this letter to know I alone planned the priests' deaths, and Father Paul Thielemans was completely unaware I poisoned the glasses before he gave the glasses to the deceased priests.

"I'm truly sorry I used you to do my dirty work. This letter will show you unwittingly participated in my plan, but in no way, anticipated or condoned my actions.

"Please also be careful with the portrait you see in front of you. It is for your eyes only, and will hopefully allow you to remember us in our happiest of times.

"You gave my life meaning and made my life worth living. You taught me about love, and in a few short months, helped me try to forget all the misery I experienced before you came into my life.

"Thank you, Paul, for so many things. Thank you for loving me, making me feel like my life mattered, and actually restoring my faith in God.

"If there is an eternity, and by some miracle, I earn a place there, I'll be waiting for you to join me. If a cemetery on a hill in Hawaii is where my existence ends, I'll cease to be, but die knowing my life was worth living because I was the woman a truly great man chose to love.

"Please know that your beautiful face will be the last thing I think about when I am about to take my final breath in this lifetime. I love you, my Darling, and will - forever, and ever, and always."

"M"

After he finished reading the letter, Thielemans dried the tears in his eyes, put everything, except the portrait, back into the gift box, and returned the box to the hall closet. Taking the portrait into his hands, he stared at Michelle's face until his eyes could no longer focus.

Moving the portrait to his bedside table, Thielemans called his steward, Albert, to inform him about Michelle's departure and order dinner. As he waited for his dinner to arrive, he got down on his knees and prayed the rosary.

For the next two days, Thielemans remained in his room, counting the days until the cruise would finally be over and fantasizing about Michelle phoning and asking him to fly back to Hawaii. With the homeward leg of the cruise approaching its midpoint, Thielemans continued spending most of his waking hours staring at the portrait, his watch, and a quiet cell phone.

Finding it difficult or impossible to sleep most nights, Thielemans found it necessary to catch up on lost sleep by taking afternoon naps. As he was napping and once again dreaming of soaring through the clouds and searching for Michelle, his cell phone rang.

Startled by the sound, Thielemans grabbed the phone and looked at the caller I.D. Seeing the call was coming from Michelle's cell phone, he quickly pushed the answer button.

"I knew you wouldn't last very long without me," Thielemans announced joyously into the phone.

"Hello, Father?" a frail, elderly voice interrupted. "Hello, Father Paul?"

"This is Father Paul," the priest confirmed.

"Father Paul, this is Nellie Opunui, phoning you from Hawaii," the caller stated.

"Nellie, how are you?" Thielemans inquired.

"Oh, I'm, fine, Father Paul," Nellie responded.

"And how is Sister Michelle?" Thielemans asked expectantly.

"Father Paul, this is why I'm calling," Nellie answered nervously. "Sister Michelle died this morning."

"No," the frantic priest shouted, dropping the cell phone to the floor. "Please, Dear God, No!"

As Thielemans started sobbing uncontrollably, he could hear Nellie's voice coming through the cell phone. Ignoring her voice, he continued crying.

Several minutes later, Thielemans was able to regain his composure. Picking up his cell phone and realizing the connection had been terminated, he returned Nellie's call.

"Hello?" Nellie answered cautiously.

"Nellie, this is Father Paul," the priest announced with a loud sigh. "I'm sorry we got cut off before."

"Oh, that's okay, Father Paul," Nellie said. "I know how hard this is for you."

"Nellie, what happened to Sister Michelle?" Thielemans asked with a tremulous voice.

"I went into Sister Michelle's bedroom this morning but couldn't wake her," Nellie replied. "She was completely unresponsive. So, I called my doctor. He immediately drove to my home and carefully examined Sister Michelle. He felt she had no neurological activity, and while he was still at her bedside, she stopped breathing. After the doctor determined Sister Michelle had passed on, he sat down with me and asked about her medical conditions. When he heard that Sister Michelle had an inoperable glioblastoma, he thought the enlarging tumor may have eroded through blood vessels in her brain, causing severe hemorrhaging and death. The doctor felt it was fortunate she died in her sleep. He told me about other patients with brain tumors who experienced uncontrollable seizures for hours or even days before they finally died. He said Sister Michelle didn't suffer at all."

"That's good to hear," Thielemans said, as he wiped tears from his eyes. "So, where do we go from here? I'm currently on a cruise ship in the middle of the Pacific Ocean. It will be another two days before I can get off the ship in Ensenada, Mexico and hopefully get a flight to Hawaii."

"Father Paul, you don't have to do that," Nellie kindly advised. "Sister Michelle told me she wanted to be buried as soon as possible after she died. She specifically requested no embalming and no delays. She didn't want you rushing back here. I've already spoken to our parish priest. We can have her funeral Mass and burial tomorrow."

"I understand," Thielemans agreed with a sigh. "You know what's best. Nellie, I can't thank you enough for all you did for Sister Michelle or for calling me so quickly."

"Oh, you're welcome, Father Paul," Nellie replied.

"Before you go, I'd like you to do a few things for me," Thielemans continued. "Sister Michelle had a Mastercard in her possession, and you're currently using her iPhone. I'd like you to use the credit card to pay all of Sister Michelle's living expenses before she died, today's bill from the doctor, and all her funeral expenses. I'll receive the bills from the credit card company and pay them. I also want you to have a florist make a full spray of flowers to cover her casket. I want the florist to use plumeria and whatever else is necessary to make the casket spray look beautiful. On the spray, I want the inscription, 'May the Good Lord bless and keep you, until we meet again.'"

"Okay, Father Paul," Nellie agreed. "I can do that."

"After you've paid all the bills, I want you to keep the credit card and iPhone for your personal use," Thielemans advised. "I want you to buy whatever you need and call whoever you like. I'll cover all your expenses, and if I ever have to talk with you about any bills, I already know how to get in touch with you."

"Father Paul, why are you being so kind?" Nellie asked.

"A hundred years from now, I plan to be buried at the Paauilo Cemetery, next to Sister Michelle, Sister Regina, and Sister Nellie," Thielemans answered. "If I'm going to be lying helpless in the ground and surrounded by so many nuns, I guess I'd better be kind to everyone now."

"I guess so," Nellie laughed.

"Aloha, Nellie Opunui," Thielemans closed. "Thanks again, and may God bless you."

"Aloha, Father Paul," Nellie responded. "God bless you, too."

After he finished speaking with Nellie, Thielemans picked up the portrait and stared at Michelle. Realizing she was gone, he put down the portrait and covered his face with his hands.

As he started crying again, he heard his front doorbell chime. Walking to the door and opening it, he was surprised to see Albert.

"Father Paul, I was just passing by and wondered if you needed anything," the tall, dark, and well-groomed Indonesian steward revealed, as he watched the priest drying his eyes with a handkerchief. "Are you all right?"

"I'm fine," Thielemans replied. "I was washing my face and got some soap in my eyes."

"Let me get you a moist towel," Albert offered.

As the middle-aged steward quickly retrieved a wet towel from the bathroom, he had Thielemans sit down before placing it over the priest's eyes.

"This cruise has passed by quickly," Albert said, trying to make small talk. "We'll already be stopping in Ensenada in just two days, San Diego in three, and Seattle in five. Where will you be disembarking the ship?"

"San Diego," Thielemans answered.

"Will you be getting off the ship in Ensenada?" the steward asked.

"I don't plan to," Thielemans responded, as he removed the towel from his eyes. "I've been there before and took a guided tour of the entire region."

"I understand," Albert said with a smile. "Is there anything else you'll be needing this evening, like something to eat, perhaps?"

"I don't believe so," Thielemans replied. "I think we're good to go. I'll call room service if I get hungry later."

After Albert left the suite, Thielemans poured a snifter of Courvoisier and went out onto the balcony. As he sipped cognac and stared at the sky, he thought about Michelle and how hard she worked to make his program a success.

Realizing only a handful of priests agreed to participate in his program, Thielemans wondered if the time had come to stop promoting it and start redirecting his energies toward a different project. Michelle was such a driving force behind the program, and with her gone, Thielemans could feel his enthusiasm for the program starting to wane.

The more Thielemans thought about Michelle and what a good assistant she had been, the more he started thinking about his first assistant. Looking at his watch and calculating the time in Brussels, he decided to call his sister.

After he spoke with his sister, Veronique, for more than an hour, Thielemans refreshed his drink, returned to the balcony, and tried to digest some of the things she advised. Although he never seriously considered returning to Belgium before, Veronique's advice for her brother to get off the lecture circuit, return to Belgium, and write his next book in different surroundings seemed intriguing.

The introspective priest felt *Catholicism Astray* had been a noble effort but not the literary equal of any of his previous books. Although the book became a best-seller, Thielemans realized it lacked the personal conviction of his earlier literary endeavors.

After Thielemans gave Veronique's valued input some consideration, he recalled her talking about his close friend, Bishop Davet Pender of the Belgian Archdiocese of Mechelen-Brussels. Looking up his friend's cell phone number, he decided to surprise the bishop with a call.

"Bishop Pender," his friend announced, as he answered the phone.

"So, did you hear the one about the priest, the minister, and the rabbi?" Thielemans joked.

"Paul, is that you?" Pender asked incredulously, immediately recognizing his friend's unmistakable voice.

"Who else do you know that speaks English without sounding Dutch?" Thielemans responded.

"How are you?" the bishop inquired enthusiastically. "I can't tell you how good it is to hear your voice."

"I'm fine, Dave," Thielemans said in a tired voice. "How are you?"

"I'm okay," Pender revealed. "I'd be better if I had you to talk with more often, but I'm okay."

"Dave, I'm calling to let you know I've been thinking about coming back to Belgium and teaching at the seminary again?" Thielemans clearly stated.

The surprised bishop paused before replying.

"Paul, I suddenly feel like an unanswered prayer is finally being answered," Bishop Pender enthusiastically responded. "When were you planning on returning?"

"Sooner than you think," Thielemans revealed. "*Catholicism Astray* hasn't gained much traction in the United States. The book has been commercially successful, but my program to restore Church membership has fallen on deaf ears."

"You know, of course, you couldn't have picked a lousier time to publish that book," Pender opined. "The Church seems to be having some pressing issues in the United States right now, and your program calls for more manpower than the Church can currently spare in the good old U.S. of A."

"I hear you," Thielemans lamented. "Dave, a lot has happened in my life in the past few months, and I just started feeling the need for a change of scenery about five minutes ago. That's why I'm calling you before I start making any plans."

"Paul, you'll always have a home here," the bishop said reassuringly. "The seminary hasn't been the same since you left, and the Church in Belgium is struggling with a lot of problems. We've spawned a new race of pedophiles here, and most of the Belgian clergy are demanding major changes in the Church. We need the kind of phlegmatic leadership only an internationally recognized authority like you can bring. Reverend Paul Thielemans coming back to Belgium would be a Godsend. Even if you only came back here to teach and inspire us until your next book was published, you'd put the Belgian Church lightyears ahead of where we are now. By the way, what's the subject of your next book?"

"I want to write a book that analyzes the roots of Church law," Thielemans explained. "I want to analyze laws that come from Church dogma and are immutable, and laws that are man-made and able to be changed. Then, I want to theorize what the Church could look like, absent some of the man-made laws. I personally would like to see priests having the option to marry, nuns treated differently, divorce laws revamped, certain forms of contraception allowed, and general absolution instituted. I want to see the Church start growing again, and my book would draw a blueprint for change that respected Church dogma and challenged outdated man-made doctrine."

"Paul, I hope you realize such a book, however popular with Catholic clergymen and laity, could conceivably force certain Italian cardinals to stop quoting you and inviting you out to dinner when you were in Rome," Bishop Pender joked.

"That's a chance I'll have to take," Thielemans acknowledged.

"I would," the bishop chuckled. "It's about time the Catholic Church woke up and joined the 21st century. The book you're describing might allow the Church to do just that."

"Thanks, Dave, but before we get too carried away, we need to sit down and talk about some things," Thielemans suggested. "I'm afraid I've strayed from the straight and narrow, Old Friend, and I've sinned – really sinned."

"Paul, we've all sinned," Pender observed. "And never forget, there is no sin that cannot be forgiven if a sinner is truly repentant."

"I hear you," Thielemans sighed. "Well, look, I'll be in touch. I'm on a cruise ship heading toward San Diego right now. I'll be there in three days. When I get there, I have to pick up my car, drive cross-country from California to Virginia, and along the way, give this entire matter some more thought. Assuming I want to start drinking beer with you again on a regular basis, I'll probably need a month or so to close up my townhouse, put my car in storage, and cancel the commitments I have for the remainder of the year. Theoretically, I could move back to Belgium and start teaching at the seminary again by the beginning of the first semester in 2019."

"I can't believe this is actually happening," the bishop stated enthusiastically. "But tell me one thing. This sin of yours isn't a grievous mortal sin like a priest might commit if he started drinking American beer and lost his taste for Saint Bavo Witbier. Is it?"

"My sins are serious, Dave, but nothing's that serious," Thielemans answered reassuringly. "I'm a Saint Bavo man through this life and the next."

"Oh, that's a relief," Bishop Pender exclaimed. "For a minute, you had me worried."

"I'll call you soon," Thielemans promised. "Thanks, and may God continue to bless you, Your Excellency."

"Godspeed, Paul," the bishop closed.

Starting to feel hungry, Thielemans called room service and ordered a bowl of chicken noodle soup, a cold roast beef sandwich, and some fruit. After he pondered the rest of his life over a late-night snack, he retired for the evening and quickly fell asleep.

The following morning, Thielemans was startled out of a deep sleep by the ringing of his cell phone. Looking at the caller I.D., he was surprised to see a call coming from Saint Declan's Rectory.

At first, the bewildered priest considered ignoring the call. As the phone continued ringing, he finally decided to answer it.

"This is Father Paul Thielemans," he announced.

"Well, I should certainly hope so," Mother Murray said with a thick Irish brogue. "How are you, Father Darling?"

"Mother, is that you?" Thielemans asked incredulously.

"Well, of course, it's me," Mother emphatically replied. "Who in heaven's name were you expecting, the ghost of Gordon Kittrick?"

"What are you doing at Saint Declan's?" Thielemans inquired.

"Well, let's just say a funny thing happened to me on my way to jail," Mother chuckled. "You see, Father Darling, when my son heard they were calling me into the San Diego P.D. headquarters for an old-fashioned brow beating, he told me I needed a lawyer. So, knowing I didn't have any money to afford one, he made a call to some legal aid office and hooked me up with an attorney who is paid by the state to help paupers like me. Sonny Davis is what my lawyer calls himself. He claims to be Irish, but I'm not sure he knows his Gaelic from his garlic. Nevertheless, with the aid of my newly-acquired legal counselor, I met the San Diego P.D. head-on and prevailed. At my inquisition, Detective Salopo and two other Dick Tracy's asked me the same things I was asked when Detective Salopo visited me at that assisted living dump in the desert. Unfortunately, they also asked me a lot of questions about your relationship with Kittrick, and even though I spoke very highly of you, I'm afraid my big mouth got you pulled into their investigation of Bobby Kucera's suicide. So, I'm calling to tell you how sorry I am I ever mentioned your name."

"Mother, it's not your fault I got pulled into their investigation," Thielemans argued. "The San Diego P.D. had me on their radar from the moment Kittrick died. They searched through his phone records, and since Kittrick called me on multiple occasions before his death, police realized they had to bring me in for questioning. I met Detective Salopo and think he is a fine young man and a good detective who was only doing his job. So, I hereby absolve you of dragging me into the San Diego P.D.'s investigation. For your penance, you owe me a pot roast dinner with peach pie for dessert."

"Consider it done, Father Darling," Mother answered.

"You still haven't told me what you're doing at Saint Declan's," the curious priest insisted.

"Well, while my attorney was providing me legal counsel during my interrogation, he was also carefully listening to my testimony and taking notes," Mother explained. "Now, I'm still not sure the lad knows the difference between the Fifth Amendment and the Fifth Commandment, but to his credit, he was bothered by the way I was unfairly dismissed from my housekeeping job at Saint Declan's. So, as soon as the San Diego P.D. signed off on me, my lawyer called the diocese and threatened them with a shopping basket full of lawsuits. He reminded the diocese I was at Saint Declan's before the *New Testament* first appeared on any Bestseller List, and then, threatened them with lawsuits for unfair labor practices, unlawful dismissal, elderly discrimination, *Ex Post Toasties*, and a few other statutes that are so old they're still written in Latin. Well, lo and behold, the diocese was so impressed with my lawyer's arguments that they reinstated me as the housekeeper at Saint Declan's – forthwith and forsooth. I've been here a few days now, and I'm still busy getting the place ready for the new pastor's arrival next week. When I sat down in the living room to watch my shows a few minutes ago, I remembered the wonderful night we drank beer and watched Bing Crosby movies. Since I still have your cell phone number, I thought I'd give you a ring and apologize for any inconvenience I may have caused you."

"It was just a minor annoyance," Thielemans said reassuringly.

"To be honest with you, Father Darling, I wasn't too impressed with all the goings-on during the investigation," Mother suggested. "All through my interrogation, the detectives kept asking me the same irrelevant questions over and over again, but they never asked any pertinent questions."

"What kind of pertinent questions?" Thielemans inquired.

"Well, for example, the detectives asked a lot of questions about Bishop Grannick," Mother answered. "In between questions, the detectives kept talking amongst themselves and mentioning how the bishop was still missing in action. Evidently, no one at the archdiocese knew where he was, no one at the Vatican knew where he was, and no one at INTERPOL knew where he was. They also mentioned how Bobby Kucera's suicide case couldn't be closed until Bishop Grannick was questioned and curtained matters were resolved. I couldn't believe these professional crime solvers asked me so many meaningless questions but failed to ask me the one question I could have easily answered to help their investigation. They never asked me if I knew where Bishop Grannick was. Now, even though I knew where the bishop was hiding all along, I wasn't about to volunteer any more information to the police than I had to. I may not be the brightest lightbulb in the hardware store, but I'm smart enough to know what things are better left unsaid."

"Mother, are you telling me you know where Bishop Grannick is hiding at the present time?" Thielemans asked incredulously.

"Of course, I do," Mother boasted. "The bishop is hiding right now where he always hides when he gets in trouble. He owns a big house, overlooking the ocean in Ensenada, Mexico. I understand it's a grand place. I've actually seen pictures of it and heard Grannick and the pastor talking about it on many occasions. Of course, neither the bishop nor the pastor ever suspected I was eavesdropping on their conversations. The bishop has owned the house for as many years as he's been visiting the pastor at Saint Declan's. When the bishop isn't using his house to hide or rape young girls, he has a realtor in Ensenada rent it out by the week. The pastor visited Grannick in Ensenada on several occasions, but to my knowledge, no one else knows about the bishop's secret hideaway."

"Mother, you never cease to amaze me," Thielemans admitted. "I'm not in San Diego at the moment, but I may be passing through town in a few days. If I do, I'll call ahead of time and possibly take you up on that pot roast dinner you owe me."

"Well, it's off to the market with me, then," Mother said enthusiastically. "It'll be nothing but a prime roast, hand-cut to my very own specifications, and the finest hand-picked peaches money can buy for someone the likes of Father Paul Thielemans."

"You've got my mouth watering already," Thielemans exclaimed. "Since you'll be preparing a feast, I'll bring enough Saint Bavo Witbier to get us through dinner and a double feature."

449

"I'd expect no less of you," Mother swooned. "May the road rise up to meet you, Father Darling."

"And until we meet again, may God hold you in the palm of His hand," Thielemans replied.

CHAPTER TWENTY-FIVE

For the rest of the day, Thielemans kept thinking about Mother's phone call. Although it was hard for him to believe Grannick was hiding out in Ensenada, it was harder for him to deny the possibility.

Searching for inspiration, Thielemans retrieved Michelle's gift box from the hall closet, emptied the contents, and carefully studied each item. As he read and reread her letter, gazed at her novice photo, and stared at the poisoned beer glass, he found himself trapped in a moral dilemma.

Deciding to take a walk around the ship to stretch his legs and clear his mind, Thielemans entered one of the shops and bought a few items which he had gift-wrapped. After the items were placed in a gift bag, he returned to his cabin.

Entering his suite, he removed the wrapping paper from his recently purchased items and used it to wrap the poisoned beer glass and his personal glass. Placing the wrapped glasses and sales receipt into his new gift bag, he returned everything else to the hall closet and called Albert to order dinner.

As soon as the Eurodam docked for its four-hour stay in Ensenada the following afternoon, Thielemans, dressed in priestly attire, exited the ship with his gift bag and sales receipt. Explaining to a customs agent he bought the gift-wrapped items on the Eurodam as presents for a friend he was about to visit in Ensenada, the agent reviewed the sales receipt and allowed the priest to enter Mexico with his gifts.

Hailing a taxi, Thielemans asked the driver to be taken to a local beer outlet that sold foreign beer. Arriving at a large beer distributorship near the Ensenada seaside resorts, Thielemans instructed the driver to wait while he went inside to buy a six-pack of Saint Bavo Witbier.

As he was paying for his purchase inside the beer outlet, Thielemans asked the clerk at the cash register if he could borrow a cell phone to make a local call. After the offer of a $20 tip finally persuaded the reluctant clerk to loan the priest his cell phone, Thielemans retrieved Grannick's cell phone number from his wallet and sent the bishop a text message:

"Just arrived in Ensenada…Flying out in three hours…Have important info about SDPD investigation… Gordon game me your address before he died…Be there momentarily with beer…Hope you are home and thirsty…Message sent from a borrowed phone."

Leaving the beer outlet, Thielemans returned to the taxi and gave the driver directions to Grannick's house. Arriving there in fifteen minutes, Thielemans paid the cab fare, gave the driver a big tip, and asked him to return in one hour.

Approaching the front door of the house, Thielemans kept thinking about Michelle's novice photo and how the young girl in that photo must have suffered inside the large dwelling. Ringing the doorbell, Thielemans patiently waited for Grannick to answer the door, but realized the bishop might not be in the mood for company.

Becoming impatient and ringing the doorbell again, Thielemans stepped off the porch and beheld the magnificent ocean. As he continued studying the seascape, the front door opened and Grannick, dressed in priestly attire and elevator shoes, appeared.

"Father Thielemans, I can't believe it's you," the bishop exclaimed, as he held the door for his guest. "Please, come in. I can't tell you how long I've waited to see you."

"I'm glad you're home," Thielemans said, as he handed the six-pack of beer to the bishop. "I knew I was taking a chance catching you on the fly, but I did promise both you and Father Kittrick I'd pay you a visit as soon as I could. So, here I am. I'm flying from San Diego to Australia, and as luck would have it, the plane's first stop was Ensenada. I only have an hour before I have to get back to the airport, but that should give us plenty of time to have a beer and talk about things."

"Now, you say Father Kittrick gave you my address," Grannick reiterated suspiciously, as he sat down at the living room table and motioned for his guest to do the same. "Could you explain how that happened?"

"As you may or may not know, I had a long visit with Father Kittrick just a few days before he died," Thielemans revealed, as he removed the poisoned beer glass from the gift bag and handed it to Grannick. "He tried calling you several times, but you were away, and he wasn't able to reach you on the phone."

"What do we have here?" the bishop asked, as he removed the wrapping paper from the glass.

"To really appreciate good beer, you have to drink it from a proper glass," Thielemans clearly stated.

"And it is a beautiful glass," Grannick admitted. "Thank you very much, Father. I'll cherish it for the rest of my life."

"That's the general idea," Thielemans answered, tongue-in-cheek, as he removed the protective cellophane wrap from the top of the glass. "I sterilized and sealed your glass and mine before I packed them in my carry-on bag. I've heard so many bad things about the water in Mexico, I didn't want to take any chances."

"You're always thinking," the bishop chuckled. "That's what I like about you."

"Now, with your permission, I'd like to teach you how to drink Belgian beer so you can enjoy every sip," Thielemans said with a nervous smile. "So, grab us two bottles from the container."

Removing two bottles of beer from the six-pack, the bishop handed one to Thielemans.

"First, I'd like you to pour beer into your glass, leaving an inch or two of beer in the bottle," Thielemans instructed, as he demonstrated the technique with his own bottle of beer.

Fully aware of Thielemans' beer spiel, Grannick played along and followed his guest's directions.

"Now, take a healthy swig of beer," Thielemans advised while preparing to do the same.

"This is good beer," Grannick exclaimed after taking his first sip.

"Finally, swirl the remaining beer in your bottle to free up the filtrate, add it to your glass, and then, take another swig," Thielemans requested.

Following the instructions and tasting the filtrate-rich beer, the bishop looked at Thielemans and smiled.

"Father, just when you think you know everything, you discover you're never too old to learn something new," Grannick stated in an obvious attempt to steal Thielemans' thunder. "The second sip was much better than the first."

"I couldn't have said it better myself," Thielemans acknowledged with a smile, as he raised his glass to propose a toast. "To Father Gordon Kittrick."

"To Father Kittrick," the bishop replied, raising his glass and taking a healthy swallow of beer.

Reaching over to the six-pack, Thielemans removed another bottle and topped off both their glasses.

"Now, what were we talking about before you taught me how to drink Belgian beer?" Grannick asked.

"You were asking why Father Kittrick would have given me your address," Thielemans responded. "To answer your question, he wanted me to discuss his illness with you in person. You see, he confided in me and told me many things about you, including the fact you were his uncle. He tried calling you and discussing his illness, but as I previously mentioned, you were away, and he couldn't reach you by phone."

"I was at the Vatican, handling important Church business," Grannick insisted, taking another healthy drink of beer. "You know, it's almost impossible to receive private phone calls there. The place is like a machine that never quits running. So, tell me about Father Kittrick's illness. This will be the first I'm hearing about it."

"Well, for years, Father Kittrick thought he was suffering from peptic ulcer disease," Thielemans began. "But when his heartburn and nausea got too severe, he made an appointment to see a doctor. After diagnostic tests were performed, he was told he had almost total blockages of three of his coronary arteries. He was scheduled for heart surgery, but before the surgery could be performed, he had a massive myocardial infarction and died."

"This is all news to me," the bishop stated. "However, none of this surprises me. Gordon was a very hyper individual. He had a Type A personality, and they're the ones who are prone to heart attacks."

"To Gordon," Thielemans toasted again, raising his glass and finishing the contents.

"To Gordon," Grannick slurred, doing the same.

Removing two more bottles of beer from the six-pack, Thielemans filled both glasses, making sure to include the filtrates.

"Now, what's been happening back in California?" the bishop inquired, taking another liberal sip of beer. "What's all this nonsense about investigations and the police looking all over creation for me?"

"If I may be frank, Gordon talked with me at length about his pedophilic tendencies just before he died," Thielemans revealed, as he looked directly into Grannick's beady eyes. "He told me he was inappropriate with Bobby Kucera on several occasions, and he also admitted Bobby's suicide was his fault."

"That's nonsense," Grannick shouted. "Gordon told you that?"

"Yes, he did," Thielemans confirmed.

"So, what does all this have to do with me?" the irate bishop questioned.

"Gordon also explained how you arranged payoffs to families whose children he sexually abused," Thielemans answered. "In fact, he told me you have been arranging similar payoffs for other pedophilic priests for many years. So, if you're wondering why the San Diego P.D. and other law enforcement agencies have been looking for you, that's the reason."

"I'm sure you're aware Gordon had profound psychological issues," Grannick suggested.

"Every pedophile does," Thielemans laughed.

"So, it's obvious you believed Gordon when he told you he was a pedophile," the bishop observed. "Do you believe the things he said about me?"

"Which ones?" Thielemans inquired.

"Which ones?" Grannick shouted. "What else did that pathological liar say about me?"

Chugging the rest of his beer, Grannick angrily removed the final bottle from its container and poured it into his glass, sans filtrate.

"Well, in addition to telling me about your role in protecting the pedophilic priests of Southern California, he also told me you wear three-inch lifts in your shoes," Thielemans quipped. "He also assured me you were not a pedophile."

"How thoughtful of him," the bishop scowled.

"However, he did say you were fond of drugging young girls, bringing them here, and using them as sex slaves," Thielemans clearly stated.

"And you believed him?" Grannick screamed.

"In all honesty, I didn't believe a lot of what Gordon Kittrick had to say," Thielemans admitted, as he reached into his coat pocket, removed Michelle's novice photo, and handed it to the bishop. "However, I believed everything the young girl in that photo had to say. Do you remember her, Your Excellency?"

Staring at the photo, Grannick's eyes bulged.

"Why, I've never seen that girl before in my life," the frightened bishop insisted.

"You may not remember her face," Thielemans conceded. "It's hard remembering the face of someone you spent so much time screwing from behind. But you have seen that girl. You've seen her, drugged her, kidnapped her, raped her, and abandoned what was left of her in the Arizona desert. And you know what? In doing so, you took away her innocence, her joy of living, and her soul. You gave her a guided tour of hell, right here in this house, and after you were through, you left her alone to search for meaning in what was left of the miserable existence you condemned her to. The girl in that photo told me many different things about you, Your Excellency, and I believe every word she told me."

As Thielemans was finishing his scathing diatribe, Grannick started hyperventilating. A minute later, he started clutching his chest and experiencing a full-blown panic attack.

While the bishop was staggering toward the back of the house, lightheaded and panting, Thielemans got up from his chair and carried both beer glasses to the kitchen sink where he quickly rinsed and dried them. Returning the glasses to the gift bag and empty beer bottles to their container, Thielemans picked up the wrapping paper, bottle caps, and Michelle's photo from the table and added them to the bag.

Taking a final look at Grannick's infamous den of iniquity, Thielemans grabbed his belongings and quietly left the house. As he walked toward the road, he could see his taxi approaching.

With Grannick still on his mind, Thielemans took the taxi to the cruise terminal. Before he entered the terminal, he threw the empty beer bottles and caps into a trash can, rewrapped both beer glasses, and returned the glasses to his gift bag.

Seemingly unaware of the noisome and barking sea lions that occupied an embankment next to the docked ship, Thielemans boarded the Eurodam without difficulty and went straight to his cabin. Filling a glass with ice cubes and bourbon, he removed his suit coat and Roman collar and walked out onto his balcony.

Taking a seat, Thielemans sipped bourbon and stared at downtown Ensenada. Hearing the siren of an ambulance echoing through the nearby streets, he thought about Grannick and wondered if the bishop would die in a hospital-bound ambulance in the next few days or be found lying face down in his bathroom weeks from now.

Either way, Thielemans knew Grannick's one-way ticket to hell had been punched and no innocent girl would ever be his sex slave again. Either way, Thielemans knew the world was about to become a better place.

As soon as the Eurodam sailed away from Ensenada, Thielemans fell asleep on his balcony. A few hours later, he awoke and decided to have dinner in the ship's dining room.

Wearing casual attire, he dined alone before visiting one of the lounges where he nursed a cognac and listened to music without hearing it. Sensing profound loneliness, he returned to his cabin, filled a glass with Macallan scotch, and ventured out onto his balcony.

For the next few hours, the lonely priest stared at the ocean, confident his cerebellar gyroscope was accurately guiding his eyes in the direction of Hawaii. Looking at his watch and realizing it was 3 a.m., he walked back into his suite and removed the previously poisoned beer glass from the gift bag.

Returning to the balcony, Thielemans stood at the railing, firmly grasping the beer glass. Looking at it a final time, he threw the glass into the ocean.

As he watched the glass reflecting the moonlight as it bobbed up and down in the water, Thielemans imagined it being carried by the waves of the Pacific Ocean to the foot of a Hawaiian hillside. Atop the hillside rested a timeless cemetery, the spirit of someone he loved, and the place his heart would remain for the rest of time.

After the Eurodam docked in San Diego the next morning, Thielemans walked across the street and checked into the Wyndham. Calling Mother Murray, he made a date to visit the housekeeper at Saint Declan's Rectory, feast on pot roast and peach pie, and watch old movies.

The following morning, Thielemans checked out of the Wyndham and began his cross-country trip from San Diego to his townhouse in Virginia. Hoping drives through Kansas City, Saint Louis, and Memphis would help take his mind off his loneliness and the uncertainty of his future, Thielemans drove toward Interstate-40 and a clear shot to the east coast.

Shortly after he picked up I-40 in Arizona the next day, Thielemans received a phone call from Father Ed Prosky, informing him Father Bill Conyngham died. For more than an hour, the two priests talked about Father Bill, Michelle, and Father Ed's future plans.

For the past few years, Prosky's main occupation was taking care of Conyngham in their Bethesda apartment.

Although he was arthritic and had prostate cancer, Prosky was still in reasonably good health for a 71-year-old and interested in traveling.

When Prosky told Thielemans that the only thing standing between him and the open road was his need for a dependable vehicle and inability to afford one, Thielemans thought for a few seconds before offering Prosky the dependable 2018 ebony Cadillac CT6 sedan he was currently driving. Explaining his planned return to Belgium and need to do something with his car before he left the United States, Thielemans was able to convince Prosky to accept his car as yet another gift.

Returning home after his long cross-country drive, Thielemans started settling all his affairs, including the transfer of his car to Father Prosky. After he drove to Bethesda and helped Prosky get the car retitled, registered, and fitted with a Maryland state license plate, Thielemans agreed to go to Prosky's apartment and have a drink.

"My life seems empty without Michelle," Prosky sighed, as he took a healthy swig of J&B scotch.

"Mine, too," Thielemans sadly agreed, as he lifted his glass toward heaven before taking a sip.

"I hope I'm not being too personal, but Michelle told me the two of you were in love," Prosky said.

"Michelle and I fell in love shortly after we met," Thielemans admitted.

"So, your love affair was real," Prosky surmised.

"It certainly was," Thielemans confirmed.

"I wasn't sure," Prosky admitted. "Michelle told me so many different things before she died, I didn't know what was real and what was imaginary. The last time she came to see me, her bipolar disorder was completely out of whack and her brain tumor was starting to affect her. When she told me the two of you were lovers, I took it with the same grain of salt I almost swallowed when she told me she poisoned all those priests who recently died. I must say, I'm relieved something she told me was actually true."

"Did Michelle tell you how she poisoned the priests?" Thielemans carefully asked, unwilling to divulge anything Michelle told him during her confession.

"She told me she made a paste from the pulp of the Rosary Peas you bought in Kauai," Prosky answered. "Then, she applied the paste to the insides of the beer glasses you gave to the sex offenders you visited. She believed drinking beer from the glasses poisoned them."

"Why didn't you believe her?" Thielemans inquired.

"Michelle never poisoned anybody," Prosky chuckled. "With her bipolar disorder out of control, she probably imagined poisoning the priests. This would have allowed her subconscious to right the imaginary wrongs she claimed to have suffered when that imaginary bishop kidnapped her, drove her from Arizona to Mexico at warp speed, and raped her in that rental house in Ensenada."

"What would you say if I told you Michelle identified the man who raped her as Bishop Joseph Grannick from L.A.?" Thielemans questioned. "And what would you say if I told you there was proof Grannick actually owned the house Michelle showed us in Ensenada?"

"I'd say you must have truly loved Michelle to believe everything she wanted you to believe," Prosky replied.

"I did believe her," Thielemans insisted. "I still do."

"Paul, even if Michelle did try to poison those priests, there's no way she could have," Prosky revealed. "Bill tested your Rosary Peas, and none of them had poison inside. Why, Bill even tried poisoning the mice in our apartment with them, and the mice ate them like candy with no ill effects. Seeds dry up over time, and when they do, the chemicals inside can become inactivated. So, the Rosary Peas you bought couldn't have poisoned anybody."

"Michelle told me your clergy sex offender surveillance group knew all about Gordon Kittrick," Thielemans said. "Did you know Bishop Grannick was Kittrick's uncle? And did you know Grannick was a rapist? And did you know Grannick was the one paying the hush money to the families of kids who were sexually abused?"

"Of course, I knew," Prosky calmly replied. "That still doesn't prove Grannick raped Michelle, and it doesn't prove Michelle wasn't bipolar."

"Ed, I'm sure you heard what I went through in San Diego and Los Angeles," Thielemans stated. "There were detectives in those cities who actually thought I was the one who killed all the priests."

"I heard all about it from Michelle," Prosky admitted.

"Then, consider this," Thielemans requested. "I unwittingly gave a large number of priests beer glasses Michelle told you she poisoned with the Rosary Peas. What are the odds of so many priests dying after drinking beer from the glasses if Michelle didn't poison them?

"The odds are astronomical," Prosky exclaimed. "So, what?"

"Ed, if Michelle didn't poison the priests, how do you explain their deaths?" Thielemans asked.

"Natural causes," Prosky chuckled. "There's also the possibility God was watching. Who knows?"

After the two finished their drinks and tried to part company amicably, Thielemans returned to Alexandria by train. While he was traveling home, he called his friend, Monsignor Janulis, and inquired about Grannick.

"Oh, I thought you would have heard by now," Janulis said. "They found Bishop Grannick in Mexico. He died of a massive heart attack on October 13th. The word is, he died in an ambulance on his way to the hospital."

"Are you sure of the date he died?" Thielemans asked.

"I'm looking at his obituary on my laptop as we speak," Janulis answered.

Turning on his iPad, Thielemans quickly reviewed the itinerary from his most recent cruise and confirmed the Eurodam was in Ensenada on October 13th. Seeing this, it became apparent Grannick died from a heart attack after Thielemans' visit and before any poison had the chance to affect him.

Although closing all his accounts took a month longer than anticipated, Thielemans was finally able to leave the United States and return to Belgium by the third week of January 2019. From the moment he returned, he was respected and revered by everyone.

For the rest of his life, Thielemans would wonder if Prosky told him the truth in Bethesda or if Michelle did in Hawaii. He would be haunted by his inability to ever know.

One year after Thielemans returned to Belgium, Jo Faraday called Sheriff Aguilar.

"So, how's 2020 been treating you so far?" Jo asked.

"Oh, you know, same ole, same ole," Aguilar replied. "So, to what do I owe the honor of this call?"

"I just wanted to pass some information on to you and ask you to share it with Reenie," Jo said. "It seems we were all wrong about Father Paul Thielemans. At one time or another, we all suspected he was a serial killer who hated pedophilic priests, but it looks like we were all barking up the wrong tree."

"What makes you say that?" the sheriff asked.

"I've been monitoring the unexpected deaths of Catholic priests in the United States ever since you guys let Thielemans walk," the F.B.I. special agent revealed. "After he left California, Thielemans returned to Virginia for a few months, and then, flew to Belgium where he has been for the past year. A few months after Thielemans left the United States, I started seeing the unexpected deaths of priests, ages 30 to 50, cropping up throughout the southeastern and mid-Atlantic states. The deaths were all spaced a few months apart and attributed to natural causes, but following closer investigation, several of the priests who died were suspected of being sex offenders."

"Yoiks," Aguilar exclaimed.

"Recently, the unexpected death rate of priests has picked up," Jo continued. "I'm now starting to see such deaths every two to three weeks. What's more, a new pattern seems to be emerging. Reverend Richard Implantur, a 49-year-old, died in Washington, D.C. four months ago. Reverend Thomas Heeley, a 31-year-old, died in Richmond, Virginia three months ago. Reverend Kim Waterloo, a 39-year-old, died in Virginia Beach, Virginia ten weeks ago. Reverend Harlan Pubar, a 46-year-old, died in Wilmington, Delaware two months ago. Reverend Aldo Selueces, a 43-year-old, died in Atlantic City, New Jersey six weeks ago. Reverend Marcel D'Aille, a 37-year-old, died in Philadelphia, Pennsylvania two weeks ago. Interestingly, three of these guys were rumored to be sexual predators."

"Is there any possibility Father Thielemans could be sneaking in and out of the country?" the sheriff asked.

"No way, José," Jo responded. "I have a friend who covers Belgium for the C.I.A., and he's been keeping an eye on Thielemans for me. He said, with the exception of several trips to the Vatican, Thielemans has not stepped outside Belgium. So, if someone is murdering priests again in the United States, it's not him."

"It's a good thing we followed your advice and decided not to charge Thielemans," Aguilar admitted. "Not to change the subject, but what are you guys hearing about this virus that people are catching from infected bats in China? They say there's no cure for the virus, and it could lead to a pandemic."

"My office has been detailed on COVID-19 by the Bureau, but the World Health Organization just came out with a bulletin stating human-to-human transmission of the virus is unlikely," Jo answered. "So, it probably won't be coming here. Nevertheless, plagues can and do occur. The last one was in 1918. So, who knows what might happen? Considering how easy international travel has become, anything is possible. Personally, I wouldn't worry about things until we start seeing floods and pestilence."

"Plagues, floods, and pestilence," the sheriff laughed. "As if we didn't have enough problems in L.A. already."

"Hector, if you have any specific questions about COVID-19, call Itchy Stepanski at the state forensics lab. He's a real fund of knowledge when it comes to viruses."

"I'll keep that in mind," the sheriff promised. "Thanks for calling, Jo, and good luck finding your serial killer. If anyone can collar this guy, it's you."

"Keep in touch, Hector," Jo requested. "And be kind when you break the news to Reenie."

"I'll try," Aguilar promised. "*Adios*, Jo Friday."

Hanging up the phone, the sheriff got up from his desk and walked into his utility room to fetch a cup of coffee.

"Itchy Stepanksi," he chuckled. "*Ay, Chihuahua.*"

At the same time Jo and Aguilar were finishing their phone conversation, a business meeting was ending at Saint Wilfrid's Rectory in Allentown, Pennsylvania. During the session, Reverend Raymond Stork, a tall 45-year-old with blonde crewcut hair, agreed to earn money for his parish and support a foundation that provided financial support to retired priests and nuns by selling Belgian chocolates.

As the representative of the foundation gave Father Stork a chocolate-covered cherry to sample and explained how the chocolates were incomparable in taste and quality, reasonably priced, and handcrafted by Belgian monks, Stork began to see dollar signs. Realizing Saint Wilfrid's would be keeping one-half of the sales price of every box of chocolates sold, Stork saw participation in the fund-raising program as a way for his parish to make some easy money, while also helping retired priests and nuns.

Unbeknownst to most of his parishioners, Stork had a weakness for chocolate, loose cash, and altar boys. To the corruptible priest, participation in a program that had the potential to get him all three seemed like a no-brainer.

As the meeting ended, Father Stork watched the foundation representative, a 71-year-old, white-haired priest, leave the rectory and slowly walk to his car with the aid of a wooden cane. With the taste of Belgian chocolate still lingering in his mouth, Stork waved as the elderly priest quietly drove away in his ebony Cadillac sedan.

ABOUT THE AUTHOR

BERNARD LEO REMAKUS, M.D. is a native of Wilkes-Barre, Pa. He received his B.S. degree from King's College, M.Ed. degree from East Stroudsburg State College, and M.D. degree from the Temple University School of Medicine. He completed a three-year residency in internal medicine at Abington Memorial Hospital which led to his certification as a Diplomate of the American Board of Internal Medicine.

Dr. Remakus has practiced Internal Medicine in a rural, physician-shortage area of Northeastern Pennsylvania for 40 years. During that time, he has published five novels, *The Paraclete, Keystone, The Lame Duck, Mia,* and *Cassidy's Solution*; three works of non-fiction, *The Malpractice Epidemic, Medicine from the Heart,* and *Medicine between the Lines*; and one screenplay, *Mia*. His novel, *The Lame Duck,* won the bronze medal for medical thrillers at the 2019 *Readers' Favorite* International Book Awards. He has also authored more than 200 scientific articles that have been published in: *The New England Journal of Medicine, The Journal of the American Medical Association, Newsweek, Medical Economics, The Archives of Internal Medicine, Internal Medicine News, Consultant, Geriatrics, Modern Medicine, Medical World News, Hospital News, The American Magazine, Pride, KevinMD,* and *Internal Medicine World Report*. From 1991 to 2002, Dr. Remakus was the featured columnist and a member of the Editorial Advisory Board of the medical publication, *Internal Medicine World Report*. His column in that publication had the distinction of being one of the longest-running and most widely-read physician-written columns in America.

When not practicing medicine or writing, Dr. Remakus serves as a professional speaker. In previous years, he has served as an Assistant Professor at the Health Science Center of the State University of New York and Temple University School of Medicine. He has also performed clinical drug research, worked as a medical examiner and consultant, and coached his local high school baseball team to a league championship and four post-season district playoff appearances in six seasons.

The recipient of numerous awards and citations, Dr. Remakus received the *Albert Nelson Marquis Lifetime Achievement Award* in 2020. He is listed in multiple "Who's Who" publications, including *Who's Who in the World, Who's Who in America, Who's Who in the East, Who's Who in Medicine and Healthcare, Who's Who in Science and Engineering,* and *Who's Who in American Education.*

Dr. Remakus and his wife, Charlotte, who is a school psychologist and educator, have been married for 46 years. Their three children, Chris, Ali, and Matt, are all physicians. Their son-in-law, Mark, is also a physician, and their daughter-in-law, Sanda, is a Ph.D. in medical microbiology. Dr. and Mrs. Remakus have four grandchildren, Jake, Betsy, Anabelle, and Charlie.